S0-BCA-883

WHEN FAITH JONES IS AROUND, EVERYTHING'S AN ADVENTURE . . .

"So, what did you buy?"

"Everything but the counters and racks," she answered, grinning up at him. "Want to see?" She grabbed the closest bag. Bottles and jars collided. "You'll like this."

Curiosity drew him closer, inch by inch, until he sat beside her. "What?"

"Passion."

He unscrewed the top of the purple flask and inhaled. "This makes a man want to beat his chest and howl at the moon."

"Really?" He was teasing her, she thought, but had to check to make certain. She put her wrist close to his nose. He sniffed, then began nibbling at her arm.

"Stop that," Faith laughed.

"Can't." His lips touched the ticklish place on her inner arm, then her bare shoulder. "Smells ravishing up here."

"There's no perfume there!" she gasped. The slide of his whiskers against her skin drew goosebumps in their wake. "It's just plain old soap."

"You must have been a good girl and washed behind your ears," he said. Her curls swept against the strong line of his jaw as he nuzzled her ear. Jason smiled. A genuine smile. One that not only reached his eyes, but his heart, too.

Her hand moved to the side of his jaw and her finger defined the line where his lips pressed together. He nipped her finger. Her eyes rounded when his tongue traced the edge of her oval fingernail.

"Jason?"

"Hmmmm?" His lips vibrated against her fingers, humming a song of passion that the perfume had promised.

"Why don't you kiss me?"

He did.

**PUT SOME FANTASY IN YOUR LIFE—
FANTASTIC ROMANCES FROM PINNACLE**

TIME STORM   (728, $4.99)
by Rosalyn Alsobrook
Modern-day Pennsylvanian physician JoAnn Griffin only believed
what she could feel with her five senses. But when, during a freak
storm, a blinding flash of lightning sent her back in time to 1889,
JoAnn realized she had somehow crossed the threshold into another century and was now gazing into the smoldering eyes of a
startlingly handsome stranger. JoAnn had stumbled through a rip
in time . . . and into a love affair so intense, it carried her to a point
of no return!

SEA TREASURE   (790, $4.50)
by Johanna Hailey
When Michael, a dashing sea captain, is rescued from drowning by
a beautiful sea siren—he does not know yet that she's actually a
mermaid. But her breathtaking beauty stirred irresistible yearnings
in Michael. And soon fate would drive them across the treacherous
Caribbean, tossing them on surging tides of passion that tran-
scended two worlds!

ONCE UPON FOREVER   (883, $4.99)
by Becky Lee Weyrich
A moonstone necklace and a mysterious diary written over a century ago were Clair Summerland's only clues to her true identity.
Two men loved her—one, a dashing civil war hero . . . the other, a
daring jet pilot. Now Clair must risk her past and future for a passion that spans two worlds—and a love that is stronger than time
itself.

SHADOWS IN TIME   (892, $4.50)
by Cherlyn Jac
Driving through the sultry New Orleans night, one moment Tori's
car spins out of control; the next she is in a horse-drawn carriage
with the handsomest man she has ever seen—who calls her wife—-
but whose eyes blaze with fury. Sent back in time one hundred
years, Tori is falling in love with the man she is apparently trying to
kill. Now she must race against time to change the tragic past and
claim her future with the man she will love through all eternity!

*Available wherever paperbacks are sold, or order direct from the
Publisher. Send cover price plus 50¢ per copy for mailing and handling to Penguin USA, P.O. Box 999, c/o Dept. 17109, Bergen-
field, NJ 07621. Residents of New York and Tennessee must
include sales tax. DO NOT SEND CASH.*

ANNA HUDSON

GLORY

PINNACLE BOOKS
WINDSOR PUBLISHING CORP.

PINNACLE BOOKS are published by

Windsor Publishing Corp.
850 Third Avenue
New York, NY 10022

Copyright © 1994 by Jo Ann Algermissen

All rights reserved. No part of this book may be reproduced in any form or by any means without the prior written consent of the Publisher, excepting brief quotes used in reviews.

If you purchased this book without a cover, you should be aware that this book is stolen property. It was reported as "unsold and destroyed" to the Publisher and neither the Author nor the Publisher has received any payment for this "stripped book."

The P logo Reg U.S. Pat. & TM off. Pinnacle is a trademark of Windsor Publishing Corp.

First Printing: July, 1994

Printed in the United States of America

The steadfast, unconditional love from my family is one of life's greatest gifts. As a small token of my love for them, Glory *is dedicated to Henry, Hank, Jane and Scott.*

Prologue

June, 1994
Backwater, Missouri

"Let me carry you to the hospital in Springfield," Faith Jones pleaded as she placed the rim of the jelly-jar glass to Jonathan Seaton's dry lips. "Please, Papa Jon?"

Too scared to voice her entreaty, she silently chanted, *Please don't die. Please don't die. God, please don't let him die! Help me!*

As though the powers above granted her fervent prayer, Jonathan's eyelids fluttered and parted. He sipped the cool spring water she offered. His piercing blue eyes darted around his beloved home, then rested on his adopted daughter's face. He winced; his callused hand reflexively massaged his chest. "No hospital."

"You're sick, Papa." Faith leaned closer to him, wanting to absorb his pain, to breathe precious life back into him. "Real sick. You've been delirious all night."

"No," Jonathan forbade sternly.

He seemed to gather strength from the sun's rays as dawn crept through the window, spilling sun light across the bed like a spring bouquet of wild flowers. He loved the Ozark Mountains. God's hands had sculpted rolling, tree-covered hills, with soaring stark granite cliffs, and deep crevasses filled to the brim with spring-fed streams. Heaven couldn't be a much better place to live. He'd often thought God should sell heaven and buy back the Ozarks.

"Please," Faith begged.

"You know I don't want some quack hooking me up to one of their infernal electric machines. I'll be damned if I'm waiting for a lightning storm to disconnect me from life!"

Faith smiled, but hot, salty tears slid down the back of her raw throat. She swallowed, hard, and set the glass on the bedside table. Papa Jon hated to see her cry. She wouldn't distress him with her tears.

"That's better. You keep smiling, child. Me passing over to the gloryland isn't any cause for the wailing and gnashing of teeth."

He allowed Faith to fluff his goose-down pillow as he summoned his meager strength. God knew he'd been tempted to let loose of his tenuous hold on life when His hand had reached down and squeezed his aging heart. The impact had caused him to drop the posthole digger, and fall to his knees.

Jonathan believed in messages sent from above. As he'd watched Faith racing toward him, he'd heard the Lord's voice loud and clear: *Open the breech in the barbed-wire fence and set Faith free, only then will you find the peace you seek.*

"Be a good girl and fetch me the family Bible."

Glad to hear the familiar tone of command return in his voice, Faith crossed the width of the bedroom to the mahogany stand which held Papa Jon's prize possession, the Seaton family Bible. Out of reverence her palms swiped down the seams of her faded jeans before she picked up the weighty, leather-bound volume. The pages, yellowed with age, were open to Corinthians, chapter 13.

Faith knew the verses by heart. They defined love.

"Love does not delight in evil but rejoices with the truth," Jonathan quoted, his eyes intensely watching the graceful movement of his adopted child's hands as they fluttered down the page. "It always protects, always trusts, always hopes, always perseveres."

"Love never fails," Faith said, joining her treble voice to his melodious bass tones.

As her brown eyes met his and she saw a single tear form in the corner of her beloved father's eyes, her heart thudded heavily against her chest. Love communicated the truth: Jonathan Seaton would never see another sunrise.

She wanted to scream in protest. She wanted to wrap her arms around his frail shoulders and hug him so tightly his spirit wouldn't be able to depart. She wanted to clamp her hands over her ears, instinctively knowing she did not want to hear what he was about to say.

Jonathan Seaton had been her savior, literally. She'd been three when he'd fought the blazes that had destroyed her home and taken her family. Alone, hunkered under the bed, coughing in fits from the fingers of black smoke sagging downward in the fierce heat, she'd heard glass break. She'd squealed as flames sucked through the open door. Through shimmering tears she saw a wild man, his face painted with black swipes, his grayish-white beard and hair going every whichaway, with reddish-orange flames forming a garish halo behind him.

The bogeyman had come to cart her off to hell.

Then, as now, she'd wanted to kick and scream in protest. Jonathan had pulled her from under the bed, cradled her in his arms, and promised to take care of her. Over the loud protests of the good citizens in Backwater, Jonathan had bucked the system and filed adoption papers. In court, he'd been described as a "middle-aged flower-child," "a hermit," "a reject from the sixties." But the judge had put credence to her description: Papa Jon was her new father. She wanted him to replace the family she'd lost.

And now, as sure as fragrance from the lilacs blooming outside the window scented the air, she was going to lose him.

"Turn the pages to the entries of the Seaton family," Jonathan bade her, not trusting his feeble hands to complete the task. "There, sweetheart. See your name? You're one of us."

"I don't belong with the *real* Seatons," she answered, feeling her heart sink. Whenever she'd asked about the other handwritten names on the page, Jonathan had clamped his mouth closed and refused to speak of them.

Thoughtfully, Jonathan rubbed his coarse beard. "They are a mite peculiar," he admitted drily. A sharp pain shot down his left arm, reminding him not to waste time explaining old feuds. "You'll find an envelope pasted behind the inside cover. It contains a letter of introduction. Get it."

Every bone in Faith's twenty-three-year-old body wanted to defy Jonathan. She'd never been rebellious, not when she'd been scolded for playing too close to the creek's edge, not when she'd seen the yellow school bus pass by their lane, not even when she'd heard the town's church bells echoing through the Ozark hillsides. Defiance was alien to her nature.

She carefully turned the pages back to the front cover, hesitating only when faced with the necessity of damaging the family treasure by peeling back the glued binding.

"Do it." Jonathan gulped for air as his fingers curled into a knot.

His labored breathing gave Faith the courage to extract the envelope from its hiding place. She unfolded the page of parchment and read, "The last will and testament of Jonathan C. Seaton. Being of sound mind . . ."

"They'll say I'm a crazy ole coot." His grin began to fade as her eyes warily skimmed the legal document. "Everything I own is yours. It'll cause a family ruckus. Hell, that's an understatement . . . their faces will pucker up tighter than a bull's ass in fly season." Jonathan chuckled, then coughed.

Confused and heartsick, Faith dropped the legal document as though it burned. She curled her fingers around his gnarled hand. Time stood still as he slowly, patiently, unfurled her fingers and brought her palm to his lips. She felt his warm breath gently cross her lifeline. He kissed her hand, then closed her fingers around it for protection.

"Love never fails, Faith. You've meant more to me than all my worldly possessions. Promise me you'll take what I bequeath you and be happy."

A knot of emotion lodged in her throat prevented her from saying anything. She nodded, which dislodged the tears clinging to her dark eyelashes.

"Don't cry. If I wasn't such a selfish old fool I'd have sent you to St. Louis years ago."

"I wouldn't have gone," she murmured hoarsely. She felt his strength ebbing, flowing away from her. Her grip tightened.

"You have to let go of me, Faith."

She couldn't. Deep in her heart she knew for certain Papa Jon would die if she did. She'd be an orphan, again. Alone, with no family that loved her. "I love you too much to let go, Papa."

"Open your eyes and look at me." Jonathan whispered his final command.

She did. Through a hazy mist she witnessed something so beautiful she felt as though her heart would burst. Gone were the fine lines of pain etched around the corners of his mouth. His ruddy skin had taken on a translucent color. His blue eyes shone with love, clear and bright. He looked like a younger man about to embark on a wonderful adventure.

"You be my eyes, my ears, my heart. We're family. My spirit will always be with you."

A gentle breeze soughed through the screened window, ruffling the pages of the Seaton family Bible. Jonathan took one last breath of the sweet fragrant air, held it, then passed in peace from the world he'd left behind.

One

"Glory!" Faith declared, awestruck. She shifted Papa Jon's 1957 Studebaker into park and turned off the ignition. Wide-eyed, she gazed at the impressive three-story, brick mansion with wide stately pillars that overlooked Forest Park. Flowering shrubs and flower beds hugged the foundation while the limbs of century-old oaks reached toward the sky.

The Seatons much be richer than the United States government, she thought, comparing the dilapidated county court house in her home town to the meticulously maintained building she stared at.

Faith grinned, delighted with the Seatons' prosperity. She'd imagined her new "kinfolk" to be from the same cut of cloth as Jonathan. Worldly things meant little to him, or to her either. They'd bartered for most everything they needed. Her grin spread into a full-fledged smile when she thought of the people who lived here trading chicken eggs for laundry detergent.

"Mountains out of molehills," she murmured, shaking her head as she quoted Papa Jon. During the four-hour drive to St. Louis, she had fretted needlessly about taking advantage of Jon's real family by accepting her legacy. Assuming Walter and his family were as unworldly as her adopted father had been, she'd felt a moral obligation to sign over her legal claim to the farm. Now, gauging from the splendor of their home, giving up her legacy would not be necessary.

Happy for the Seatons and for her own good fortune, Faith scooted across the seat and opened the passenger door. Soon, she promised herself silently, she'd talk the mechanic at Mac's garage into fixing the driver's door so she wouldn't have to muss up her Sunday-go-to-meeting dress by crawling out of the car.

From the backseat she retrieved her hat and a bulging brown grocery sack; it contained the Seaton Bible, Jonathan's will, a couple of pairs of blue jeans, tops, and two sets of unmentionables. She placed the sack on the hood of the car, closed the door, and positioned the flower-bedecked straw hat on her curly blond hair.

Some farmers' wives wore hats to keep the sun from turning the backs of their necks red. Church-going women wore hats to be stylish. But Faith donned this hat for the same reason an ancient warrior wore a helmet, for protection. She could pull the wide brim down over her eyes to conceal her thoughts. She could push it back on the crown of her head to keep from being pelted by spitballs shot by mischievous schoolboys during lengthy church services. Most often though, she wore it with the brim military straight, to give her courage.

She might not need her courage hat to confront Papa Jon's relatives, but she wasn't taking any chances. After all, there had been a family feud that had kept Jon from living in harmony with his brother. With a bold flourish, Faith tied the hat's wide pink ribbons that matched the rosebuds on her dress in a bowknot beside her cheek.

Shoulders back, head held high, her arms filled with her belongings, Faith marched up the granite steps with her eyes focused on the large brass door knocker. It would have been more friendly to just open the door, poke her head in and give a yoo-hoo, to get Uncle Walter's attention, but she decided against it. Maybe next time, when she was really part of the family.

Faith settled the sack on one hip, which freed one hand to lift the knocker and let it drop. Her stomach did a nervous flip-flop as brass struck brass, timidly. She waited, shifting from one foot to the other.

And waited.

When the carved oak door remained closed after several patience-straining minutes, she grabbed the brass ring and slammed it down hard enough to be heard at the Pearly Gates.

"Yes."

She leaped like a bullfrog being goosed by a fuzzy cattail. Nobody had opened the door, and yet a voice seemed to be coming from out of nowhere.

"Yeeessss?" the ominous voice repeated, louder.

Faith sighed with relief when she realized the voice came from a small, black box set inside the bricks next to the doorframe, with a white button below it. She peered into the box, but couldn't see anyone. Uncertain of what to say and feeling a bit foolish talking to an empty box, she cleared her throat and tried to adapt to the peculiar situation by mimicking the voice she'd heard. "Yeeessss?"

"Is someone there?"

"Yeeesss!" Faith shouted. She could hear him. Couldn't he hear her? Maybe he was a tad hard of hearing. She cupped her hand beside her mouth and bellowed, "Open the door!"

The door swung open abruptly. What Faith saw had her grasping the crown of her courage hat and wishing she'd brought a slingshot. The man in the black mortician's suit was the height and breadth of Goliath!

Glen Morrison studied the petite woman through his wire-framed spectacles, noted the grocery sack, and announced, "Deliveries in the rear. See Mrs. Cavendish."

"Uncle . . ."

The heavy door slammed shut.

"Of all the rude, disagreeable men I've ever met, Uncle Walter takes the cake! No wonder Papa Jon ran away from home!"

While Faith stomped down the steps, Glen strolled into the kitchen. "Delivery woman."

"Couldn't be." Gertrude Cavendish finished flattening the pastry dough with a marble rolling pin and glared up at her arch enemy. "I didn't order anything."

"Must be. She had a bag of groceries in her arms."

"Have you gone deaf as well as blind?" the cook snapped. "I told you that I didn't place any orders."

Glen slid the nosepads to his glasses to the flare of his nostrils and glowered over his thick lenses. "I don't need these Nordon bombslights to see that you have enough makeup on for an Indian war party. Do you get a discount by ordering it by the gallon?"

Offended, but thick-skinned from years of working with this pompous ass, Gertrude's hot coral lips smiled as she replied with saccharine sweetness, "When a house begins to show its age, paint restores the natural beauty."

"You should have sandblasted first."

Her lips drooped; his raised at the corners.

"Is that what you did to your hair, Chrome-dome? Why don't you have the gardener sprinkle Cow Power on your head, stick you in the cellar, and see what sprouts?"

"Is that what José uses to make your mud packs?"

"No, but it's what I used for the thickener in the beef pot pie you gobbled down last night. Yummy, huh?" she gloated when her tormentor's face paled to the shade of the flour on her hands.

The sound of knuckles rapping sharply against the glass panes of the back door distracted Glen from returning a spiteful reply. Just proving the quarrelsome woman wrong would soothe his wounded male ego. "The groceries you did not order have arrived. I'll get them." He opened the door, grabbed the girl's sack, and then slammed the door shut.

"Here!" Glen crowed. He placed the sack on the center cutting board and gave the cook's rosy plump cheek a pinch. "Your groceries, Mrs. Cavendish."

Gertrude swatted his fingers aside. She extracted several faded garments and gloated, "Would you like these sauteed, broiled or fried?"

Realizing he'd made an error, but refusing to admit it, Glen pivoted on one foot and retraced his steps. Only bag ladies carried their belongings around in a sack. He had to stop that girl.

"Oh, Miss!" he called to Faith's retreating form. "Miss! Don't leave without taking your things!"

Faith stopped. She'd pulled her hat down so far her

head made a bulge in the crown. She had to tilt her head way back to see as high as his bow tie.

"Don't bother apologizing to me. You are precisely what Jonathan told me to expect."

"I am?" he asked, motioning for her to come into the house.

Her head bobbed. "Exactly. Papa Jon warned me your face would pucker up like a bull's . . ." She paused, reluctant to repeat one of Jon's earthy metaphors. "Never mind."

Bull's ass in fly season, Glen silently completed. His eyesight had dimmed in twenty years, but his memory was as sharp as a tack. He could trace his sour disposition back to the day Jon-boy had departed for parts unknown, never to be heard from or seen again.

"Jonathan Seaton?" he dared to ask.

"Of course. Why else would I be here?"

"Why else, indeed." Glen's broad smile revealed a gold eye tooth replacing the one that Jon-boy had accidentally knocked out while Glen had been attempting to wash Jon's mouth with soap. "I'm Mr. Morrison, the butler. And you're Miss Seaton, I presume?"

"Jones," Faith corrected, not wanting to be invited through the sacred portals of the Seaton residence under a false flag. "Jonathan saved my life when I was three, then adopted me."

Glen nodded. Foolhardy and brave. A champion for the weak and defenseless. Jon's finest trait had been the root cause of the volatile disagreement between the two brothers. "Where is he?"

Tears shimmered in Faith's eyes. She thought she'd shed more fluid than a human body was allowed. Blinking to maintain her composure, a single drop escaped, trickling from the outside corner of her eye.

"Memorial Park Cemetery in Backwater, two weeks ago," she answered, her voice a notch above a whisper. "He made me promise to come here, to be with family."

Uncertain of what to say or do, Glen awkwardly patted her shoulder. Tears totally unmanned him. When her arms wrapped around his waist, giving him a mighty hug for such a small thing, he felt protective instincts, that had lain dormant since Jonathan left, surge through him.

"You just come right on in the house and Mrs. Cavendish will fix you a pot of tea." What *he* needed was a stiff shot of brandy! All hell would break loose when Walter and his son, Jason, found Jonathan's heir waiting for them. He herded Faith toward the kitchen. "Mrs. Cavendish!"

Faith peeked from under the brim of her hat at the formidable woman scowling at her unmentionables. Gertrude held them high, between her thumb and forefinger, at arm's length from her massive breasts.

"Country girl," Gertrude deduced, dropping the panties and bra back into the sack.

"How'd you know?"

"I haven't seen plain white cotton underwear since I moved here from Sikeston, forty years ago."

Faith nodded, uncertain what to make of the middle-aged woman with lilac-colored eye shadow and orangish-red lips. She watched Gertrude's brown eyes move from the silk daisies on her hat to the patent-leather shoes on her feet.

"She's Jonathan's daughter," Glen announced with pride.

Taking a second look, Gertrude arched one eyebrow and waved a dismissive hand. "A blond-haired, blue-eyed Seaton? Not likely, you addled-brained old fool. She's an impostor—just like the ones who showed up when Walter filed that missing-persons report after Jonathan left here."

"Don't you call Miss Faith an impostor," Glen ordered with indignation, shielding Faith under his arm. "She's not like those . . . floozies."

"I can prove who I am," Faith said, blushing so hard at Gertrude's accusation that she felt certain the heat would cause her freckles to pop off her cheekbones. "My name is in the Bible."

"Yours and several dozen other female names," Gertrude scoffed. A pang of discomfort knifed through her heart as she watched Glen's hold tighten around the young woman's shoulders. The old fool was smitten!

"I meant the family bible." She broke loose from Glen's protective clutch to dump the entire contents of the paper sack on the counter. For protection, she'd wrapped the volume in a towel. Slowly, she began to unwind it. "Jonathan wrote my name in here, below his name . . . and right next to Walter and Jason's name. And, he wrote a will, too."

"Oh, m' God," Glen gasped, his knees buckling under him. There was no mistaking the handsome, gold-scrolled, black leather volume. "Don't you remember, Gertie? Along with the missing-persons report Walter filed, he'd also threatened to file criminal charges against Jonathan for stealing a family treasure!"

"I don't claim to be Jonathan's flesh-and-blood daughter," Faith continued, holding her proof close to her chest. "Though I'll admit to wishing I were."

Brushing past Faith, Gertrude hustled to Glen's side. She masked the shock of hearing him calling her by her nickname by giving his arm a sharp pinch as she hissed, "She could have bought it at a yard sale and written her name in it. These girls nowadays are clever!"

"I can show you the will." Faith lifted the front cover. She began unfolding the piece of paper for their inspection. "It's in Jonathan's own handwriting."

Gertrude sliced her hand through the air as though she wielded a butcher knife. "Just stop right there, young woman. We don't believe a word you've said, and we don't want to be implicated in your scheme."

"Speak for yourself, Miss Cavendish," Glen contradicted, rubbing the sore spot she'd left on his arm. "I think Faith is who she says she is."

"Five minutes ago, you thought she was delivering groceries, *that I didn't order.* You let me take care of this." She grabbed Faith by the sleeve of her dress and marched her out of her kitchen domain, down the hallway that led to the study. "You mark my words, missy, Mr. Seaton won't be easily convinced."

Faith glanced over her shoulder at Mr. Morrison. The giant-sized man shrugged his shoulders, unable to help her.

"I am who I say I am," Faith insisted.

"And I'm Anastasia, the long-lost princess of Russia," the housekeeper replied sarcastically. Once she'd deposited Faith inside the study, Gertrude released Faith's arm. "You sit down and stay put. And keep your sticky little fingers off things that don't belong to you. Got it?"

The implication that she might be a thief as well as an impostor hurt. Faith ducked her head, hiding behind her straw hat. She wanted to staunchly defend her honor, but sensed it would be futile to argue. Better for her to follow Mr. Morrison's example and simply acquiesce, for the time being.

"Yes, ma'am."

She heard the latch click before she raised her chin off her chest. Enthralled by what she saw, her eyes darted from the floor-to-ceiling bookcases, to the highly polished desk, which was larger than her kitchen table back at the farm, to the chairs covered in forest green leather. Rich brocade swags draped over the windows, allowing the trees to filter the sun through their leaves and cast shadows on the thick cream-colored carpet.

This one room was larger than her entire house! And it held more books than Backwater's public library!

When she saw a hand-carved book stand, much like the one Jon had kept the Seaton Bible on in his bedroom, Faith quickly unloaded her arms of her "proof." She took a step backward, realizing that it looked as though it belonged there, safe and secure, and yet easily accessible.

What a glorious place, she thought, wondering how Jonathan could have borne the pain it must have cost him to leave home, such a handsome home.

Although she'd intended to take a seat and wait patiently for her uncle's arrival, she simply could not. She yanked the ribbons that held her hat in place, removed it, and tossed it on the cushions of the curved window seat that lined the bay window. Then she took a deep breath, closed her eyes, and inhaled the fragrances of lemon oil, and leather.

Another familiar scent tingled her nose and tantalized her memory, but she couldn't place it.

Curiosity compelled her to move to the bookshelves. She swiped her hands down the side of her dress, just in case her hands actually were sticky, before she allowed her fingers to walk along the bindings of the classic tales she'd read. They skipped over the many titles she had yet to read. Smiling, she knew she could spend hours, days, *weeks* in this one room and be perfectly content.

She crossed to the walnut-stained desk. She circled it once, avoiding the temptation to test out the cushion in the plush swivel chair.

Miss Cavendish had ordered her to be seated; she hadn't said where. She probably meant the footstool, something lower than low, she mused. Grinning, she glanced at the door. But, then again, the cook had not specifically pointed her painted red fingertip at the desk chair and said, "Do not sit there!"

Faith shook her head. Her naturally blond curls lightly whipped her cheeks. That kind of logic could get her in trouble. She remembered the time Papa Jon had warned her not to plant her backside on the hollow log that spanned the creek. She had. It had taken an hour for him to pluck the bee stingers out of her hide.

Of course, she didn't have to worry about bees swarming out of the seat cushion, did she?

She took a second glance at the door and listened for footsteps. Deciding no one would care where she sat, she quietly slipped around the desk and eased herself onto the chair. Slowly she revolved around on its pedestal, then just a tiny bit faster. Whirling around as fast as she could, the subdued colors of the room had a kaleidoscope effect, blurring together, changing into bright streaks of color.

When she stopped, the room kept spinning. Dizzy as a bear being circled by coon hounds, she put her head down on the cool surface of the polished wood to restore her equilibrium. That's when she noticed the pipe rack and recognized the elusive smell pervading the air: cherry-flavored pipe tobacco.

The two brothers smoked the same tobacco? A good omen? Papa Jon had always appreciated the way she'd fixed his pipe for him. She could do the same for Uncle Walter. It pleased her to know she'd be able to do something useful, something that might make her uncle happy.

Her gaze moved to a small snapshot of a glamorous woman, whose long dark hair and ankle-length dress had been caught by the wind as she smiled and waved at the camera. A neatly penned signature in the corner of the photo identified the woman as Caroline.

"Caroline," she mouthed, instantly liking the name as she wondered who Caroline could be. "Did Uncle Walter remarry?"

Unless this was an old photo, Caroline was too young for a middle-aged man. But she wasn't too young for Jason.

"Maybe you're Jason's wife," she said, speculating on the identity of the mystery woman. It seemed logical that Walter would put a picture of his daughter-in-law on his desk. "Caroline Seaton . . . Mrs. Jason Seaton."

Wouldn't it be wonderful, she mused, if her new family did include Caroline? Once they got to know each other, they could be like cousins, or maybe as close as sisters.

She hugged her midsection at the prospect of having a woman near her age living in the same house.

Were there more pictures inside the desk? Maybe a letter or two?

Faith touched the brass knobs on the drawers while furtively glancing toward the door. Sourpuss Cavendish would have a conniption fit if she caught her rummaging through Uncle Walter's desk. With good reason, she added with a deep sigh. It wouldn't be right to snoop.

To avoid temptation, she bolted upright. Unexpectedly, the seat tilted backward, which banged her knees into the bottom of the center drawer. Her feet flew up. Reflexively, Faith clutched the padded arms of the chair in anticipation of it toppling over.

"Whoa!"

It tilted to a forty-five degree angle, then stopped.

Faith giggled nervously. This chair was a mite tricky!

Shifting her weight to the front of the seat, Faith was restored to an upright position. Somehow, between her knees' knocking the drawer's bottom and her toes pulling against it, the center drawer had opened a few inches.

Clumsiness or God's will? she ruminated. She believed in miracles, but wanting to poke through the drawers to satisfy her curiosity wasn't exactly on the same pious level as Moses' parting of the Red Sea to save his followers.

Resolved to do the right thing, she placed her fingers on the desk and her thumbs against the drawer. Slowly, she began to ease the drawer shut.

A lazy farmer plows rows in the ground faster, Faith admonished silently, feeling guilty as sin as her eyes quickly scanned the contents.

She would have been able to complete her pharisaic

task, if she hadn't noticed that the top sheet of paper had a column of numbers improperly tallied. She paused, mentally retabulating the row and came up with the same answer. Someone had made an error.

"Providence must have guided my knees," she whispered, feeling a little less guilty.

Automatically, she picked up a writing utensil from the pencil tray, uncapped it and drew a line through the sum. She wrote the correct total in the margin. Whoever made the mistake would notice her correction because the pen contained bright red ink.

Faith held the felt-tipped pen up closer to examine it. The housekeeper's lips were almost the same color. She touched her mouth, gliding her forefinger over her lips. Caroline's lips were red. Why not? Papa Jon had told her she would have to adapt. This was as good a time as any to begin. Using the polished desk like a hazy mirror, she penned the rosy-red color on her lips.

Practice makes perfect, she thought, when she saw the curve on one side fatter than the other.

She wiped the fat lip where she'd gone above her lip line, but the ink was indelible. So, she switched to the other side and fattened it up. Fascinated by how vivacious her mouth looked, she smiled, pouted, grimaced, and laughed aloud. Her lips no longer looked pale and plain; they were beautiful!

She put the red cap back on the pen and returned it to the tray. There were other pens in assorted colors. Purple would look good on my eyelids, too, she decided impulsively.

Minutes later, Faith had given herself a complete make-over—lips, eyelids and fingernails.

* * *

Jason Seaton shot a baleful glare at the classic Silver
Hawk Studebaker as he unlocked the front door of his
father's home. Obviously Walter had squandered another
fistful of dollars on a spending spree. For the hundredth
time in the same amount of days, Jason wondered what
had changed the man who'd raised him, the man who'd
sternly taught him that fiscal responsibility meant
squeezing a nickel until the buffalo squealed—then required a detailed cost analysis before he'd buy a used
Ford Pinto.

"It's me," Jason shouted, as he strode into the foyer,
"Walter left some papers in his desk that I need at the
bank. I'll let myself out when I've collected them."

Not waiting for a reply or expecting one since he lived
here, Jason entered his father's study. He shook his head
when he noticed Walter had moved the furniture, again.
The two wing chairs were supposed to be in front of the
desk. One had been moved over to the corner of the
room, facing the bookshelves.

"The old man would have blown a gasket if I'd dared
to move a piece of furniture so much as an inch."

Although his dictatorial father had recently abdicated
his throne by taking leave of his senses, a cold shiver
prickled Jason's spine each time he entered his father's
private domain. Every harsh lecture he'd received had
taken place within the confines of these four walls. It
wasn't a place to dally. He advanced to the desk, looking
to neither the right nor left.

"He knew I needed that quarterly summary," he muttered, jerking open the center drawer. "Well, at least he remembered where he put it. That's new and different!"

Jason swung his briefcase on the desk, dialed the combinations on the locks, flipped them open, and tossed the report inside. He slammed the drawer shut, hard enough to jar Caroline's picture. In his present frame of mind the last thing he needed was to be tormented by a photograph of his father's latest bizarre folly.

What particularly perturbed Jason was the knowledge that he had introduced Walter to Caroline. Never in his wildest dreams could he have imagined the same cold-hearted, hard-nosed man who'd raised him transforming into a middle-aged lecher, horny as a ten-balled tomcat! This was not the same man who chewed his ass out royally for the slightest infringement of the Seatons' strict code of morals and ethics.

Automatically, Jason's dark eyes glanced at the book stand where, as a child, Walter had often made him place his hand on the family Bible and swear he was telling the whole truth and nothing but the truth.

His narrowed eyes widened. The stand wasn't empty. Forgetting his anger, he swiftly crossed the room. Where in the world had Walter found such a close replica? His callused fingers reverently skimmed gold-leafed *S* embossed on the Bible's cover.

"This isn't a reproduction," he said in hushed tones as he opened it to the center where the family names had been entered. "It's the original, the one Uncle Jonathan stole."

Jason spun around, fully expecting to see his uncle standing behind him, with a wide smile, and his arms flung wide open in expectation of getting a bear hug. A stab of disappointment jabbed him when he found himself alone.

Then, he noticed a bundle of floral printed fabric, with a basket of daisies perched on top of it, draped over the arm of the wing chair that had been moved.

Warily, he moved closer. From the far reaches of his memory, he recalled that Uncle Jonathan had dressed like a sixties flower-child reject—wearing grungy overalls, with flowers stuck in the buttonholes, and sporting a chest-long beard. Unless his uncle had switched to dresses, shaved his beard, and had a sex change, the person napping in the chair couldn't be his long-lost relative.

Definitely a woman, he decided, noting the gentle swell of her breasts. From beneath her hat a wild tangle of honey-colored curls dangled against her nape, others curled against her cheeks. He hunkered down beside the chair, intent on getting a closer look before he awakened her.

There had to be a correlation between the family Bible being returned and the arrival of this . . . urchin.

Clown, Jason corrected silently, as he lifted the straw hat. Splotches of purple dotted the mystery woman's closed eyelids, and she'd painted a big red smile on her mouth. His fingers curved across his lips to keep a boisterous peal of laughter contained.

Faith shifted restlessly, straightening her legs. The pleasant dream of being enthusiastically welcomed into the Seaton family began to fade into oblivion. Through a thick fringe of parted eyelashes she detected only a few rays of sunlight. She could catch a few more winks of shut-eye before the roosters began to crow.

"Wake up," Jason ordered, impatient to find out who the hell she was.

Disoriented by the sound of an unfamiliar voice, Faith cautiously opened one eye. She studied the face only inches away from her own. His dark eyes danced with merriment as she stretched her arms to relieve the kink in her back. "Who are you?"

"Jason Seaton. Who are you?"

"Faith Jones."

"Care to explain what you're doing in my father's study?"

Rather than chase her tail, like she had with Miss Cavendish and Mr. Morrison, she reached inside her scooped neckline and pulled out Jonathan's will.

"This explains everything."

"Hmmmm." He took the single page of paper, but he seriously doubted such a limited amount of information would even begin to explain Faith Jones. He read the first line, skipped to the signature, then glanced back at the rainbow-colored face. This had to be bad news, but Jason continued to have difficulty maintaining a straight face. He pointed to the door situated behind the desk and suggested, "Maybe you'd like to go into the restroom and freshen up?"

"I slept like a bump on a log, right here in this room."

"Maybe wash your face and hands?" he hinted delicately.

Faith nodded, glad to know they had running water in these fancy city houses. "My mouth does taste like the bottom of a birdcage."

Chuckling as he assisted Faith to her feet, he realized that the women employees at the bank would have to be balanced on a wobbly chair, with a hangman's noose around their necks, before they'd make such an honest confession.

No longer in the shadows of the high-back chair, Faith stared at Jason. Only a few brave men had dared to cross Jonathan's barbed-wire fence to make her acquaintance. Those who had were encouraged to backtrack with a double-barreled shotgun loaded with rock salt. Deep in her heart, Faith felt certain none of them were as handsome as Jonathan's nephew.

Lordy, it almost made her eyes ache just looking at him.

Faith blushed. It was rude to openly stare at a grown man. Her eyes dropped to her crimson fingernails. "I'll be right back."

Quick as lightning, she streaked across the study and into the restroom. When she closed the door, she leaned against it, eyes shut so she could catch her breath. It hadn't been too long ago that she'd asked Papa Jon about love. He'd said she'd know when the right man came along. She'd feel all twittery on the inside. Her heart would feel like it was going to explode. And she'd feel light-headed and woozy. Faith touched her stomach, her heart, then her forehead. There was no doubt. She had all the classic symptoms of a woman who'd fallen in love.

On the other side of the same door, Jason gritted his teeth as he finished reading his uncle's will. He seldom lost control and never cursed, but as he heard Faith's startled high-pitched wail, he cut loose with several choice words that should have charred the pages of the holy book she'd returned.

Two

Faith clamped her hand over her mouth to quiet her scream. The closer she came to the mirror, the more she looked like a raccoon who'd devoured wild raspberries.

"What must Jason think of me!" she wailed.

Mortified, she splashed water on her face before thoroughly lathering it with soap. She scrubbed hard. See what vanity gets you? It would serve you right, she scolded, if those hideous colors stayed there, forever. When she rinsed with clear water and discovered the purple and red had faded, but not vanished, her fear of being permanently disfigured grew.

She applied soap again, and lathered longer, harder, faster.

This stuff has to come off. It just *has* to! What if it didn't? What if Miss Cavendish was my age when she painted her face and it never came off!

As she washed and rinsed, again and again, she came to realize that Jason had to be the nicest, kindest man walking God's green earth not to have taken one look at her and busted his britches with laughter.

Faith blotted her face with a soft, monogrammed hand towel and gave a huge sigh of relief. Other than being pinker than usual and feeling tight, her skin was back to normal. She pushed her fingers through the damp locks of hair curling around her face to restore her hair to some semblance of neatness.

Walking back into the study, she looked for Jason and found him standing by the window, with Jonathan's will in his hand. Rays of sunshine lit one side of his face and cast the side closest to her in shadows. His high cheekbones, straight nose and square jaw looked as though a master craftsman had carved them from hard rock maple.

Jason sensed he was no longer alone. According to the document in his hand, Southern Bank's largest stockholder had just returned, like a bad penny.

Without the slightest residue of the laughter his eyes had held when he first saw her, Jason scrutinized the woman who could upset the balance of power between him and his father. This pint-sized beauty, with her claim to half of everything he'd rebuilt after the banking scandals of the last decade, was no laughing matter.

He crossed to the desk chair and gestured for her to be seated in front of him. "Congratulations, Miss Jones."

The cold tone of his voice and his choice of words had the same shock treatment effect as throwing a pail of icy spring water on Faith. Her back stiffened; her hands clenched. Her mind sputtered. She couldn't believe she'd just been congratulated on the death of her adopted father!

"Sit down," Jason ordered briskly, choosing to ignore the sharp blink of her eyelashes. "State your intentions."

"My intentions?" Her knees caved beneath her the instant their backs touched the leather. "What do you mean?"

"You made plans, didn't you?"

"Of course I did." Beginning to feel slightly peeved, Faith had to reminded herself that she was a guest, an uninvited guest.

"Well?" Jason demanded. "What are they?"

"I aimed to get acquainted with you and your father."

"And?"

Faith shrugged, wondering if she'd caused this inter-rogation by not asking permission to use the pens in his desk. Contrite, wanting to make amends, she said, "And I'm sorry I colored my face with your pens. I won't do it again. I promise."

"They're your pens as much as they are mine," Jason replied, disgruntled with the thought of dividing up ev-erything the Seatons owned. Her female tactic of switch-ing the subject to avoid giving a straightforward reply wouldn't work. "What do you plan on doing with your inheritance?"

She glanced around the richly appointed study. "I thought about giving everything to you all, you being Jonathan's only blood relatives, but I've decided against that."

"Do you expect us to buy you out?"

"Is that why you think I came here? To get money?"

"Why else?"

"Why else, indeed!" Faith jumped to her feet. She shook her finger in his face and scolded, "You know, when I saw you by the window, you reminded me of one of Jonathan's figurines. You and a block of hard rock maple have only one thing in common . . . a wooden heart!"

"Now just a damned minute . . ."

"Don't you cuss at me."

"Then get your finger out of my face."

"Why? So you can shake my hand to *congratulate* me on the death of Papa Jon?"

"I congratulated you on your windfall! You're an heiress!"

"Compared to you, I'm poor as a church mouse!"

Jason pushed back his chair and rose to his full six-foot-plus height. "Don't play innocent with me. Jonathan must have told you he owns half interest in Southern Bank." His arms swung wide. "Hell, he inherited half this house from my grandfather!"

With Jason towering over her like a mythological dragon breathing fire, Faith had no choice other than to plop back in her chair. Disbelieving every word Jason Seaton had spoken, she stuttered, "P-p-papa Jon said a rich man had as much chance of entering the gates of heaven as a camel passing through a needle's eye."

"That depends on the man, the camel and the size of the needle's eye," Jason refuted.

"He said a man's worth couldn't be measured in gold coin. The best things in life . . ."

"Are free? Not in St. Louis." Jason gave a mirthless laugh. "Where have you been living? Outer space?"

"In Backwater . . . on Jonathan's farm." Her head jerked up until her blue eyes clashed with his dark eyes. She raised one hand and said solemnly, "I swear to you, I thought the farm and the house was everything he bequeathed to me."

"Which brings us back where we started. What are your intentions?"

Faith dropped her eyes to her lap. Her fingers nervously twisted knots into the rosebud print fabric. Jason would never believe being part of the Seaton family was more important to her than their wealth. She felt as though she'd been born on the morning side of the Ozark mountains, and he'd been raised on the twilight side of the hills. What each of them held dear was as far apart as . . . Backwater and St. Louis.

Jason realized he was holding his breath while he waited for her reply and quietly exhaled. He continued to stare at Faith, but his mind returned to the day his Uncle Jon stormed out of the house, never to return. He'd been what? Five? Maybe, six? As far back as he could remember, Walter and Jonathan had been like two wild animals tethered together on a short rope, each straining to go in their own direction.

The power struggle continues, Jason mused as he picked up the red pen, turning it end over end while he waited for Faith to say what he wanted to hear: Nothing will change.

The room had fallen into an uneasy silence.

Finally Faith spoke. "Well, I can't dance and it's too wet to plow. I guess I'll just have to tend to this problem later."

"And what am I supposed to do while you learn how to dance and the fields dry out?" Jason snapped.

"Pray for high winds and that I have a sense of rhythm?"

Jason wasn't amused. "Southern Bank is *mine*," he stated unequivocally. "Let's get that clear from the start."

"What about Uncle Walter?"

"He's a figurehead, president of the bank in name only. For the last six months, I've made all the major decisions. He takes his salary and his share of the profits and keeps his nose out of the daily operations. You'd be well advised to do the same."

That didn't seem fair to Faith. "I wouldn't expect you to do all the work and give me the fruits of your labor. I'm fit and able. I can help."

"How?"

"I don't know. I guess you'd have to teach me." Faith liked the idea of working beside Jason, being there by him to do whatever it was that bankers do. "I could learn the family business."

Jason sucked in his breath. "Banking isn't like farming a crop, Faith. You don't drop a penny in the ground and expect a dollar tree to sprout."

"Would you hand me one of those pens and a pad of paper?"

"What for?"

"I want to write down every little word of wisdom that you teach me so I won't forget them."

"Are you being sarcastic?"

"Were you?" she asked brightly. When his lips clamped into a thin line, she added, "I may be ignorant of how to make money grow, but I'm not stupid."

Jason wheeled back from the desk, taking another long hard look at Faith. What little control he had of this situation was slipping away from him, fast. What he needed was a clear-cut strategy of his own, or before he knew what was happening he'd be unscrewing the Vice President name plate off his office door and screwing it into the door of her new office.

"No," he agreed with candor, "you aren't."

Rising from the chair and simultaneously opening his briefcase, Jason placed his uncle's will on top of the papers he'd collected earlier. Two witnesses had signed it and a notary had sealed it, but just in case there were any improprieties he'd have the legal department check out the document's authenticity.

Sensing he'd made a decision that did not include her, she asked, "Are you going somewhere?"

"I have a quarterly audit to check before I meet with a loan officer later today, so I need to get back to the bank. I'll inform my father of your arrival and the three of us will continue our conversation at dinner. Until then, I want you to make yourself at home."

Faith winced at what sounded to her like a prepared speech, delivered without any inflections or welcome in his voice.

"Mr. Morrison, would you come into the study, please?" Jason asked after he'd pressed the intercom system button. "And Mrs. Cavendish, would you prepare the Truman suite for our guest?"

"She's staying?" Faith heard, coming from beneath Jason's hand. She watched his finger depress the lever. What an amazing contraption!

"Yes."

"How long?"

Jason raised a dark eyebrow, silently passing the house-keeper's question to Faith.

Grinning, Faith reached across the desk and pushed the button and replied, saucily, "Until I learn how to grow money."

Jason watched the stacks of money growing taller as the head cashier, Luke Cassidy, counted the bundles and arranged them on a cart. Agitated, he paced the width of the vault. This was one of Walter's menial chores, only his father hadn't returned from lunch, therefore he'd taken responsibility for making certain that adequate funds were available for Friday's banking demands.

"Tens and fives," Luke said, making a notation. "We're long on twenties. Short on ones."

"Call the reserve bank and add what you need to the morning delivery," Jason instructed. "Make certain you include the denominations Lorna will use to load the automatic teller machines."

Jason waited until Luke had replaced the stacks inside the walk-in vault, then he pushed the stainless steel door closed and spun the latch wheel. For security reasons, no one was allowed in the back section of the vault alone.

As they passed through the front section where the deposit boxes resided, Luke withdrew a handkerchief from his back pocket and buffed fingerprint smudges off several compartments. Usually Luke's being as persnickety as an old-maid schoolteacher amused Jason; today it annoyed him.

Everything had irritated him since the bank's attorney had cautiously given an opinion on the validity of Jonathan Seaton's will, after he'd made a few phone calls to southwest Missouri. It appeared as though Faith Jones had hired an attorney to file her case in probate court. Although it would take a year for final action, the legal implications were enormous. For the next hour, Jason had had to control his temper while he listened to the ramifications of what a single sheet of paper would have on his future.

"It's almost four o'clock," Jason said, glancing at his

wristwatch, anxious to get his hands around his father's neck.

"Yes, sir." Luke neatly folded his handkerchief and stuck it back in his pocket. "The drive-up tellers should be balancing their windows."

"And I still have to speak to Walter." They passed through the gate and began climbing the steps to the main lobby. "Have you seen him this afternoon?"

"No, sir."

"If you do see him during your rounds, tell him it's imperative I speak to him."

"Yes, sir."

They parted company at the top of the steps where they entered the bank's spacious lobby. Luke turned right, heading toward the teller's stations; Jason turned left, striding toward the glass-enclosed offices. His direction altered when he noticed Walter spinning through the revolving door.

"It's about time," he muttered, scowling meaningfully at his watch. Six months ago Walter would have fired a bank employee who dared to take a three-hour lunch.

But, Jason reminded himself, that was before his father's dramatic personality change. This stranger with the bounce in his step and a wide smile on his face, who wore a dapper three-piece, pin-striped suit—and loafers—was not the business-before-pleasure-man who'd raised him. Jason's eyes were drawn to the loud, yellow deco-print tie that had replaced the circumspect red one he'd worn earlier in the day. This tie looked as though Walter had used it as a bib at an Italian restaurant.

"Like it?" Walter asked, beaming with pride. "It's a present from Caroline."

Tact glued Jason's lips closed. For an attorney who works for a staid, Mid-west corporation, the woman has garish taste, Jason mused silently. Or did she think selecting a tie appropriate for a teenager and looping it around a middle-aged man's neck would shrink the number of years that separated their ages?

Begrudgingly, Jason had to admit Walter did look younger than his fifty-plus years. Since he'd met Caroline, his father's stooped shoulders had straightened; he walked tall. His dull pewter hair color had brightened to sterling silver. Jason couldn't imagine what had been done to his father's teeth, but they actually gleamed with pearly whiteness.

Jason fell into step beside Walter, guiding him toward his own office. Not only did Walter look younger, he smelled like a cologne salesman! Definitely not like the Old Spice aftershave tyrant who'd raised him.

Inside Jason's office, Walter automatically circled behind the desk to seat himself in the place of authority. Once, that had bothered Jason, now it gratified him to know his father hadn't completely transformed into an addlepated fashion model.

The knife-edge-crease in Walter's pants had barely touched the leather chair when he popped up and hastily moved around the desk.

"Sorry," Walter said, a sheepish grin accompanying his apology. "Sometimes I forget who's running the bank."

Jason dismissed the excuse with a shake of his head. Rather than take the vacated chair, he sat on the corner of his desk. "We've got a problem we need to discuss."

"Whatever you decide is fine with me," Walter said,

abdicating responsibility for any and all business decisions. "I have a problem of my own that I'd like your advice on. It's about my relationship with Caroline."

The hand Jason had dropped on his kneecap tightened as he watched Walter sinking to the depths of the chair. "Let's deal with the important matters first."

"Caroline is important."

"Not in comparison with Faith Jones," Jason averred.

Walter repeated the name several times, then shrugged. "I don't even know a Faith Jones. Who is she?"

"She's Uncle Jonathan's adopted daughter. She's at the house." Jason picked up the will from his desk and handed it to his father. "She's inherited your brother's half of . . . everything."

"Jonathan is dead?" His hand trembled as he took the sheet of paper. It dropped to his lap. Walter's head bowed. "He can't be dead."

"Can and is. He's buried on a farm outside some podunk town in southeast Missouri. I had the lawyer verify the death certification and the will."

All the changes in his father's appearance and behavior did not prepare Jason for what he saw when Walter raised his head. Tears ran down his cheeks. Unabashed. Unchecked. He'd never seen his father cry. His father wasn't supposed to shed tears—especially over the death of the brother he'd vowed to hate through eternity! A Seaton, no matter how great the pain or anguish, showed no emotions!

"J-j-jonathan's daughter?" Walter asked hoarsely.

"*Adopted* daughter."

"At Seaton Place? You left her there alone?"

The recrimination in his father's voice galled Jason.

"A year ago you'd have packed her off to the Park Plaza Hotel."

Walter flinched as though he'd been struck. Silently, but with great dignity, he rose from the chair and strode toward the door. Jonathan's will fell unnoticed to the carpet.

"Just where do you think you're going?" Jason demanded, appalled by his father's reaction.

"Home."

"Not before we come up with a strategy to deal with this crisis. I suspect one of our employees is embezzling money." He wanted to physically block his father from leaving the room, but stopped short of throwing a body block. He sensed the futility of trying to stop him with words.

"You have your priorities and I have mine. Right now, I'm going to welcome my niece into our home . . . such as it is."

"What the hell do you mean by *such as it is?*"

Walter turned. He took a long look at the young man standing belligerently in front of the desk, with his fists on his hips, his wing-tipped shoes arrogantly spread apart. He looked at Jason and saw a younger version of himself.

Like father, like son, he mused, ashamed of himself and the child he'd reared. If there was an embezzler, he or she would be at work tomorrow. To leave a young woman alone, in a strange house, with strangers, was rude.

"I could talk from now until doomsday and you wouldn't understand a word I said," Walter lamented.

"We used to speak the same language."

Walter agreed with a small nod, before he exited.

Hurrying from the bank, Walter regretted never giving Jason a lecture on love and compassion. Jason the Stoic—a title his son had earned at a young age—would have been totally perplexed by such incomprehensible sentimentality. And Walter would have felt like an incompetent fool delivering the lecture.

"Jonathan could have explained," Walter mumbled, dashing the trace of salty tears from his cheeks.

From the day Jason had been born and his mother died of complications, Jonathan had gently pointed out the multitude of mistakes Walter made with his son.

Commercially produced diapers were environmentally dangerous; cloth diapers were reusable.

The baby wasn't a calf; Jason needed a wet nurse.

While other children chose their friends willy-nilly, suitable playmates were chosen for Jason, based on their parents' financial statements.

None of Jonathan's silly fairy-tales for the son of Walter Seaton. Bedtime stories were recounts of his day at the bank—the exciting adventures of high finance.

Smugly, Walter pointed out Jason's ability to recognize coins before Jonathan could teach him his ABC's.

The animosity between Walter and his brother festered beneath the surface, at the bank and at Seaton Place. Jonathan's obstreperous affection was countered by Walter goading Jason to do better, reach higher, obtain more.

After five years and a thousand arguments, Jonathan admitted defeat by vanishing into thin air. Walter remembered their final quarrel with crystal clarity, as he slid in behind the steering column of his Mercedes.

It happened on Jason's first day of kindergarten. Walter

should have known his brother was up to something when he appeared at the breakfast table, unshaven, wearing a disreputable pair of boxer shorts and muscle shirt, with holes.

"This isn't a locker room," he'd said, his voice as cold and tart as the freshly squeezed orange juice that he sipped. He raised the morning copy of the *Globe Democrat* to block the disgusting view of hairy, bare flesh from his sight. "Go shave and get dressed or you'll be late for work."

The next thing he knew, Jonathan had lunged across the table and ripped the morning paper from his hands.

"I'm taking a mental health day," Jonathan growled, wadding the newsprint into a tight ball and throwing it across the room.

"Not today. The loan committee . . ."

"Screw you and your committee of pantywaist, suckups!"

For several seconds, Walter believed Jonathan was going to smash his fist into his face. He wanted to. Desperately. Walter could see it in his eyes, smell it on his breath.

"Get dressed," he ordered coldly, not intimidated by a show of brawny strength.

Jonathan catapulted backward, then began pacing the dining room like a ferocious caged animal. His fierce blue eyes remained riveted on Walter's bland expression. "You're driving me crazy!"

"Hardly a drive," he retorted with a sneer. "More like a short putt."

Surprised by Walter's weak attempt at humor, Jonathan paused, towering over his arch enemy. He reached toward

Walter's starched shirt front, but stopped himself before his fingers coiled around his silk tie.

"I'm taking Jason to school."

"Glen is perfectly capable of driving Jason to the academy." Walter smiled, goading him to do his worst by adding, "Unless, of course, your rag-picker attire indicates a burning desire to be a bum, . . . permanently."

Jonathan's restraint broke. He grabbed Walter's shirt front, shaking him hard, endeavoring to knock some sense into his brother's head by bouncing it off the back of the chair.

"I'll pick shit with the chickens without a steel craw before I let the butler take my nephew to school. You heartless bastard, don't you remember how scared you were the first day of school?"

"My son isn't afraid." Completely unruffled by his brother's temper tantrum, Walter stood. He glanced down at the creased fabric clamped between Jonathan's fingers, then straight into his brother's defiant face. He edged forward, forcing Jonathan to take a step back. He brushed the flat of his hand down his crumpled shirt, which dislodged Jonathan's hand. "He's more of a man at five than you are at thirty-five."

"Jason is not your clone. He's creative . . . sensitive. He has a heart. Don't break it."

Walter raised one dark eyebrow. "Hearts don't break. Men do. Why don't you stop preaching goodness and light and start teaching him survival skills?"

"He's a kid! That's why!" Jonathan plowed both hands through his hair, tugging on the ends in frustration. "Do you realize you've never do anything *fun* with him? Forest Park is at the doorstep, but you've never taken him fishing. Or canoeing. Or taught him how to fly a kite. He wouldn't own a tricycle or be able to ride one if it weren't for me!"

"I've taken him to the bank."

"Whooppee! I'll bet that was a barrel full of chuckles for a kid. Did you at least give him a penny for the gum machine?"

"He earned a penny doing errands, but unlike you, he didn't squander it on sweets. It's in his piggy bank."

"How noble," Jonathan retorted sarcastically. "Why don't you pay him in plugged nickels? That's almost what a penny is worth today!"

"That would be better than frittering his money away on toys."

"Playhouse Toys isn't located on the road that leads to bankruptcy! Let him be a child, for heaven's sake!"

"For his own sake, I'm teaching him . . ."

"You're making a nervous wreck out of him." When Walter resumed his seat and began cracking the shell of his three-minute egg with a spoon, Jonathan knew he'd lost the final battle. "Why won't you listen to me?"

"You haven't said anything worth hearing."

"I can't stand watching you mentally abusing your own flesh-and-blood. I'm out of here," Jonathan said, pivoting on one bare foot and striding to the door. "For good."

"Good riddance," Walter remembered calling after him.

Jason rode to school with Glen; Jonathan walked out of Seaton Place taking the family Bible with him. Walter went to work and vetoed loan approval on the only application Jonathan had submitted to the committee.

If Jason missed his uncle, he didn't dare question his father. His solemn dark eyes rounded when the police arrived to take the information necessary to file charges against Jonathan for theft. As far as Walter was concerned, Jonathan Seaton no longer existed.

Unhampered by Jonathan's gentle influence, Jason began to follow his father's example. Like a miser, he hoarded the allowance he earned. While other children struggled to comprehend percentages, Jason could not only calculate them, he could compound them. His savings compounded, too.

Walter had been proud the day the junior high principal had called and accused Jason of being a "pint-sized loan shark" for lending kids lunch money and expecting to be repaid, with interest. No one interfered with Walter's master plan to make Jason a financial wizard. Within thirty days, the principal was transferred to another building.

While less-gifted boys dribbled basketballs and chased after skirts, Jason not only organized the Stockbroker's Club in high school, he'd been the only member to qualify for the millionaire's pin. He'd graduated at the top of his class, but the honors bestowed on him meant little compared to the joy Jason derived from being treated with respect by the employees at the bank. He knew the names and responsibilities of every officer. Before he went to college he understood the intricacies behind financing everything from cars to shopping centers.

That wasn't to say there weren't any debits entered on Jason's morality statement. Against his father's advice, he had joined a fraternity, mistakenly believing he'd raise hell and sow wild oats with the other young men. It hadn't taken a semester for that misconception to be corrected. When the treasurer misappropriated dues to pay a gambling debt, it was Jason who threatened prosecution if the money wasn't returned in a timely manner. Perhaps a smidgen of compassion motivated Jason to use part of his savings to cover the debt, but when the young man reneged on the financial arrangement, Jason contacted the national organization and had him ousted from the fraternity. After several beer-drinking buddies of the embezzler expressed sympathy, Jason chose to be placed on inactive status.

Birds of a feather flock together . . . eaglets don't fly with dodo birds.

As a banker, Walter admired Jason's impeccable decisions when it came to deciding who qualified for a loan from Southern Bank. He took bold risks on people who'd been turned down by every loan officer in St. Louis. But it wasn't love for his fellow man or compassion that swayed his decisions. Jason had an uncanny sixth sense when it came to the integrity of the borrower. Seldom was he disappointed.

And yet, for all his son's admirable accomplishments, Walter never praised him. If Jason wasn't figuratively stumbling, falling down every day, then he wasn't reaching beyond the goals set for him. There were no quick ways to achieve success. He had to put in before he could take out. Deposit before he could withdraw. Pay the price for success, in advance.

Walter took a shaky breath and glanced at his reflection in the rear view mirror. "You were a know-it-all, pompous ass. You should have listened to Jonathan. Your son is what you made him."

Jason had learned his lessons well. So well that he'd mercilessly edged his father out of power at the first opportunity. Walter had no one to blame but himself, and admitted it.

A small smile twisted his lips as he wondered if Jonathan had made any mistakes raising the child he'd adopted. He extracted his car keys from his pocket. Automatically his thumb lightly caressed the bright red heart Caroline had painted in fingernail polish on the key to her condo.

Because he did love his son, he'd wanted to prepare Jason for the bombshell she planned on dropping during dinner. In comparison, Faith Jones's arriving at Seaton Place would be a firecracker.

He shrugged as he inserted the key in the ignition. The earth could shake beneath Jason's feet, the world could threaten to topple, and his son wouldn't so much as raise an eyebrow or bat an eye. For the sake of the woman he loved and Faith Jones, Walter prayed Jason would maintain his composure.

Three

Faith waited patiently for Mrs. Cavendish to back out of the gas oven. Peering at the woman's enormous backside reminded Faith of two watermelons fighting for space in a tight gunny sack. The cook had been inside the oven so long, she was beginning to think the woman was trying to do away with herself.

"Excuse me?"

"Dinner is served at six," Gertrude huffed. "If you want a snack, there's ice cream in the freezer."

Although the offer of an icy treat appealed to Faith, what she hungered for was companionship. After she'd unpacked her treasures, neatly put away her clothes, and scrubbed her face again to remove the last traces of her "makeup," there was nothing upstairs for her to do. When she'd found herself gawking at the monstrous bed and considered finding out how high she could bounce on it, she'd reminded herself that idle hands were the devil's workshop. Or in this case, not her hands but her haunches.

She'd been in enough trouble for one day. Immediately, she'd changed clothes, from her dress into a pair of faded cut-off jeans and a yellow, checkered blouse and set out for the kitchen.

Now, she sidled closer to the stove. The strong smell of ammonia assaulting her nostrils explained why Mrs. Cavendish was so unsociable. Oven cleaning was a nasty chore.

"I thought maybe I could help you."

She heard what sounded like a pig snort.

Not one to be easily dissuaded from giving a helping hand, Faith knelt down beside the cook. She picked up a clean rag from the stack piled on the oven door. "Could you use some extra elbow grease?"

Gertrude glared at the intruder. This kitchen was her domain. She stuck her blackened rag under Faith's nose. "Grease I don't need."

"Glory!" Faith gasped, getting a snoot full of fumes. "That stuff will melt the hair in your nose."

"And peel the skin off your hands and the polish off your nails," Gertrude added grimly.

"That would be a cryin' shame, being as you have such pretty fingernails." She held her hands out for Mrs. Cavendish to inspect. "It won't hurt mine."

"Neither would an emery board or some cuticle remover," Gertrude observed drily.

Faith bent her fingers, feeling as though they'd been chopped off at the knuckles. She thought she saw a twinge of guilt flash across the other woman's face, but she must have been mistaken. Mrs. Cavendish resumed cleaning the oven as though she weren't there.

"If you don't trust me to clean the oven, is there something else I can do to help you?"

"Nope."

"I'm a good cook."

"So am I."

"I could set the table."

"It's set."

"Make iced tea?"

"It's made."

"Dessert?"

"The pies are cooling on the counter."

"There must be something I can do." Faith poked her head into the oven. "Clean the refrigerator? Mop the floor? Wash windows? Take out the trash?"

"Are you implying my kitchen is filthy?"

"Heavens to Betsy! No! It's clean as a whistle."

"You're darned tootin' it is." Gertrude plopped her haunches back on her heels and began to strip the soiled rubber gloves off her hands. Once they were bare, she braced her hands against her waist to ease the stiffness in her lower back. Both her knees popped loudly as she lumbered to her feet.

She shot Faith a nasty look as she watched the younger woman gracefully get up.

"I know it must be hard for you to find something for me to do, but I need to be useful," Faith pleaded. "I can't sit up in that elegant room picking my nose just to have something to do!"

Gertrude almost choked on her own saliva. A few unrefined remarks like that and Walter would be rid of her for sure.

"Well," Gertrude drawled, appearing to relent while she was actually thinking up a disagreeable job, "If you must do something, I need some onions and celery chopped to put in the chicken à la king. The onions are in the pantry, the celery is in the fridge, the knives are in the drawer beside the sink. Use the cutting board on that counter."

Beaming a smile of gratitude, Faith followed the direction of the cook's polished nail and crossed to the pantry. She realized Mrs. Cavendish had relegated her to the far corner of the kitchen to do her chore.

As she chopped and diced, tears dripping from her chin, she had to keep telling herself she'd won a small victory in what she was beginning to believe would be a major war to gain acceptance in this house. The growing mound of vegetables was an indication of her determination to be liked. Whatever sort of exotic concoction chicken à la king was, it would be chock full of fresh vegetables, thanks to her diligence.

She nearly sliced her thumb when she heard what seemed like Papa Jon's voice calling her name.

"Faith! Where are you?" Walter bellowed.

"In the kitchen!"

Gertrude waddled faster than a duck chasing a June bug to her counter, swooshed the vegetables into a bowl, and ordered, "Go wash your hands and face. You look a mess."

She didn't have time. A man who could have been Jonathan's twin stepped through the swinging doors into the kitchen. There were subtle differences, she noted quickly. No beard or moustache, more weight, and an undertaker's suit, but the broad smile that lit his blue eyes was the same. Or it was until he saw her.

"What did you do to make her cry, Gertrude?" he commanded, his voice suddenly unrecognizable. He folded Faith into his arms in a protective bear hug.

"Nothing," Faith replied, but her mouth was pressed against Walter's yellow tie.

"She chopped onions," Gertrude explained.

Faith felt his wiry arms tighten; her face smashed so hard against his front that she could feel the buttons through the layers of silk. "You commandeered my *niece* to do your scut work?"

"No!" Faith protested.

"She insisted," Gertrude replied. "I didn't want her in my kitchen. She doesn't know the difference between mince and pulverize!"

"Your kitchen?" Walter inquired in a voice that could have flash-frozen fresh meat. "Half this house belongs to me and the other half my brother left to Faith Jones. Where does that leave you?"

Gertrude untied her apron strings. "Working for the Sanders family next door where I'll be appreciated. I quit!"

"Wait! That's not fair!" Faith squirmed, but her uncle only patted the back of her head to silence her. She couldn't let Mrs. Cavendish quit. It would be her fault! And yet, held in a death grip, she realized that anything she said sounded as though her mouth was stuffed with oatmeal.

Knowing that the consequences of what she was about to do would be exigent, Faith squeezed her eyes shut, raised one foot and stomped her heel against Walter's instep.

"Don't quit, Mrs. Cavendish! *Please!*" Faith begged, when Walter freed her and grabbed his wounded foot. She darted to the cook's side and hugged the back of her expansive waist. The older woman scowled, her lips pursed, and her purple eyelids closed as she folded her arms across her enormous chest. "Uncle Walter, you can't let her leave. I pestered her into letting me help fix chicken ergo queen!"

"À la king," Gertrude corrected snidely.

"À la king," Faith repeated, hoping to placate Mrs. Cavendish. "I swear on the family Bible, this wasn't her fault. Tell her you're sorry, please."

Walter straightened, gingerly placing his foot back on the floor. The sight of his niece defending a woman twice her own size and squashing his foot for the honor fascinated him. Didn't Faith realize he could turn his wrath on her? Competent servants were in short supply in St. Louis. He noticed her chin wobble and deduced that she was afraid, but also surmised that Jonathan's country girl would defend Gertrude until the cows came home.

"I apologize, Mrs. Cavendish," he said sincerely. As a peace offering, he added, "Tomorrow I'll have the microwave oven installed that you requested."

Gertrude's arms unfolded, but her nose still stuck in the air.

"And he won't fuss if you let me help you," Faith promised.

That brought her nose down. "I don't need your help, *Miss* Faith."

"But I need yours," Faith assured her, giving the cook a friendly pat on the arm. "I'd consider it a favor if you teach me how to mince vegetables properly."

Walter grinned; Gertrude gaped.

The formal address Gertrude had stressed was intended to put Faith in the parlor, at the opposite end of the house from Gertrude's lowly kitchen. Her reverse snobbery had hopscotched right over the golden curls on Faith's head.

Chuckling, Walter limped over to Faith and fondly draped his arm across her shoulders. "You do remind me of Jonathan."

"I do?" Faith sagged against him as he led her out of the kitchen. Consternation always left her feeling weak as a newborn kitten. She still felt terribly guiltly for causing a stink. "He never caused problems."

Walter could have strenuously argued the point, but sensing that she would be devoutly loyal, he said, "He ferociously championed the underdog, even at great personal risk."

"I'm sorry I smashed your toe, Uncle Walter."

"I'm lucky there weren't any two-by-fours available. Caroline says sometimes I'm like a Missouri mule. I have to be slammed up side of the head to get my attention."

Grinning because she liked the way he could make light of himself, she asked, "Caroline? The pretty woman in the picture on your desk?"

"Yes. She's my . . . fiancée." Walter chuckled. "Caroline would knock me for a loop if she heard me call her that. She's an extremely independent young woman who insists on being called my significant other. Don't ask me exactly what that means. I'll let her explain." He checked his wristwatch. The two hands overlapped on the five. "She'll be here shortly. I hope you'll like her."

"I'm sure I will." What an understatement! Knowing Caroline belonged with Walter and not his son was enough to make her heart sing. Attracted though Faith was to Jason, she'd never allow temptation to lead her into the evil of trespassing on another woman's territory. "In the picture, she doesn't look much older than Jason."

Walter watched those expressive blue eyes of hers to see if they narrowed with criticism. The only thing he saw was mild curiosity. They were as guileless as those of the trusting blond cocker spaniel puppy he'd had as a child.

"Actually, he introduced us."

"Wasn't that nice of him?" A delicate smile curved her lips. "He must have known after all the years you've lived without a woman's love how lonely you must have been."

Chuckling, Walter shook his head. "I doubt it crossed his mind."

"Why?"

"Because he sees Caroline as a competent lawyer. I'm not certain he has noticed that she is a woman."

Good! Faith crowed silently. She sifted the excitement out of her voice and asked, "Does he have—what did you call it? A significant other?"

"Jason? Hardly. His mistress is Southern Bank. He loves it. The bank is all he lives, breathes and thinks about."

Faith frowned. "I find that hard to believe."

"Why? You met him. Did Jason charm you? Did he tell you that you're pretty as a black-eyed Susan? Or that when you laugh it reminds him of wind chimes blown by a summery breeze? Or that you smell as fresh as a sprig of freshly picked mint?"

"Uncle Walter, stop!" Faith clapped her hands together then covered her face to hide her blush. Jason hadn't

flattered her, but he hadn't laughed, either. "Jason was
. . . kind."

"Are you certain you met my son? He's six-two, dark
hair, blue eyes. Blue suit, white shirt and plain red tie."

"Don't josh me," Faith laughed. "Jason is your son.
How could he be anything other than as kind and generous as you are?"

Walter tossed the remains of his double scotch to the
back of his throat. The icy liquid burned until he swallowed. Until he'd started medical treatment, he and his
son had been like two peas in a pod: twin tyrants.

"Good question." He rolled his tongue in his cheek.
"I can't imagine why women your age who work at the
bank find Jason difficult."

"He's the boss," Faith answered simply.

"I can't picture you being aloof if you held his position."

Faith laughed. "I wouldn't have to carry a hanky to
wipe the drool off their chins. In case you haven't noticed, Jason is very handsome. He probably has to be
stand-offish. I wouldn't have that problem."

Walter wanted to delve further into how Faith thought
a boss should treat an employee, but he heard the front
door open.

"Caroline, sweetheart, we're in the parlor," he called,
jumping to his feet as though he was closer to sixteen
than sixty.

"Sweetheart isn't here," Jason mocked. He strode into
the parlor and headed straight for the bar. "The two of
you appear to be having a jolly reunion. Did I miss anything important?"

Faith didn't know whether to stand up, remain seated,
or hiccup. Jason Seaton had the strangest effect on her

nervous system. Her heart and lungs ceased to function. And if the heat in her face reached her hands, she'd have to drink boiling white wine.

"Actually, your ears should have been buzzing," Walter replied, joining his son and liberally pouring another double scotch. "We were discussing how nice and generous you are."

"How many of those have you had?" Jason inquired drily of his father.

His gaze drifted to the camelback sofa where Faith sat on the edge of the cushion. He watched as she set her wineglass in a coaster, wiped her palms on her jeans, and then primly folded them on her lap.

She was nervous as hell, and that's exactly how he wanted her.

The cold gleam Walter saw in his son's eyes as Jason studied Faith warned him that his son had worked out a strategy for dealing with Jonathan's daughter. He'd have to choose sides in the power struggle that would ensue. He dreaded the thought of battling with his son, again, as he had so often with Jonathan.

Walter capped his drink off with a splash of seltzer water. "Don't scowl at me. I haven't had enough drinks to embarrass you."

"Faith?" Jason asked coolly.

"No!" Remembering her manners, she flashed him a pert smile. "No, thank you. I'm not used to drinking anything stronger than hard cider. On my eighteenth birthday I celebrated too much and spent the night on my knees, praying to the porcelain goddess."

She realized her tongue was running wild, but hadn't

been able to stop. Walter stared at her, thoroughly puzzled, but the amused light had returned to Jason's eyes.

"I wasn't being blasphemous, Uncle Walter," she explained. "That's what Papa Jon used to call puking up his guts."

"Quaint," Walter said, taking another slug of scotch.

"Indeed," Jason agreed, grinning at his father, waiting for him to trot this young lady upstairs and wash her mouth out with soap. Seatons never over-imbibed. And if they did, they certainly did not mention it in polite company. "Tell us more about Uncle Jonathan."

Walter raised one hand to stop her and shot his son a nasty look. "Spare me the details."

Aware she transgressed, but unsure of how, Faith jumped to her feet and crossed the room to Walter's side. "I wasn't speaking poorly of the deceased, was I?"

"No, little one, you weren't." He took her hand and gave it an affectionate pat. He hated to chastise Faith, especially when Jason had encouraged her outburst. "It isn't polite to elaborate on one's illnesses."

Jason groaned.

"Don't be sticking up for me when I do something wrong, Jason. Papa Jon warned me that things would seem a mite peculiar around here." She hugged Walter. "I appreciate being told when I say something wrong."

Walter burst out laughing. "You don't worry your pretty little head about Jason being too nice to you."

"I won't." She could feel the hostile vibes electrifying the air between Walter and Jason. The last thing she wanted to do was cause another problem. "I just don't want there to be any misunderstandings, you know, like there was between you and Mrs. Cavendish. I wouldn't want Jason to threaten to quit because of me."

"I won't quit," Jason assured her glibly.

Walter nodded. "Now that, you can bank on. And speaking of the bank . . ."

"I've decided to teach Faith the family business."

Jason smiled politely at Faith while Walter's jaw dropped.

"Wonderful!" Exhilarated to know Jason accepted her as part of the family, she wanted to clap her hands and slap her thighs!

"Y-y-you're going to mentor her?" Walter stammered in disbelief.

"I'll start her from the ground floor up—exactly the way you mentored me. Is that agreeable with you, Faith?"

"Now wait a minute, son. You were ten. You began in the business by printing checkbooks. The printing press is long gone. Deluxe prints them."

"Lucky for you, Faith. The old-fashioned way of printing checks was a nasty job. I went to school with black ink staining my hands like a garage mechanic who has grease under his nails. You should have heard the snickers when I raised my hand in class."

Faith could feel the undercurrent of hostility between father and son growing stronger.

"You could have told me the boys were making fun of you."

"And have you say, 'toughen up' or 'don't be so sensitive?' "

She watched Walter turn a guilty beet red.

Jason flip-flopped his immaculate fingernails beneath his father's nose. "Another favorite of yours was 'don't get mad, get even.' Those same boys are men who come to the bank for financial backing. Believe me, they aren't snickering now."

To change the subject, Faith asked, "What did you do next?"

"I filed checks. Mountains of checks. Daily. But you can't do that, either." His eyes narrowed as Walter began slowly rotating his finger on the rim of this crystal glass, making an annoying low humming sound. "We don't do things the old way anymore. Checks are sent to a clearing house where computers sort and file them."

"The bank is a shell of what it was when I ran things my way," Walter grumbled, circling his finger faster and faster. "No proof-machines. No bookkeeping department. Just tellers, loan officers and customer-service people. Half the people who worked at Southern Bank are gone."

"On to better jobs," Jason appended.

The peal of the doorbell ended another round of countercharges. Faith had the distinct impression as Walter bounded off the high stool and charged toward the door, that he'd been saved by the bell.

Left alone with Jason, she smiled and said, "It's very kind of you to find a job for me to do at the bank."

"We'll see how *kind* you think I am after you've been there a while." Jason hoped he could drive Faith off by overwhelming her. He figured it would take less than a week for her to pack her Studebaker and head for the hills. Being fair-minded, he'd send her a quarterly dividend. "I'll arrange for Luke Cassidy to show you the ropes."

Faith's heart sank with disappointment. "I hoped you'd be my mentor."

"I'll keep an eye on you."

"I'll work hard," she promised sincerely. "I want to make my new family proud of me."

Her pledge pulled at something deep within Jason, something obscured by printer's ink, piles of paper and harsh criticism from a heartless, driven father. An image of her curled up in an overstuffed chair, with a daisy hat on her head and ink on her face still evoked a smile he had to hide. She was sweet and innocent, different from any woman he'd known.

Certainly different from Caroline, he thought, as Walter escorted her into the parlor. Clothed in a classy, red, power suit, with her dark hair freshly coiffed by a hairdresser, and three-inch stiletto heels on her feet, from head to toe she was the complete opposite of Faith.

"Caroline, this is Faith," Walter introduced, "my brother's adopted daughter who has come to live with us."

"You're much prettier than your picture," Faith said, in awe. She took the hand held toward her and pumped it vigorously. "Walter sure knows how to pick 'em."

"I picked *him*," Caroline said, returning Faith's grin as she flexed her fingers to restart the circulation pumping through her fingers. Laughing, she confided, "Flirting with Walter didn't catch his attention. I had to invite him for a moonlit walk under the Arch beside the Mississippi River."

"It's where I think we should get married," Walter said pointedly.

Caroline shrugged her slender shoulders and winked

at Faith. "He's old-fashioned. I keep telling him we don't need a legal document to improve our relationship."

"Lawyers," Walter groaned, affectionately nipping her waist with his fingers. "You'd think she'd want everything legalized, in triplicate, with no loopholes!"

Perplexed, Faith listened to the good-natured squabbling, not fully understanding why Caroline would refuse to marry Walter. It was plain as the nose on Walter's face that he loved her and equally apparent that Caroline loved him. She glanced at Jason. Was he the problem? His face was stark, unreadable. He appeared neither to approve nor disapprove.

When in doubt, ask. "Do you think they should get married, Jason?"

The room became so quiet Faith thought she could hear the electricity in the light fixture over Jason's head.

"She's a divorce lawyer," Jason said matter-of-factly. "She shreds marriage contracts for a living."

Caroline bristled. "I defend women who'd be left penniless if their husbands were allowed to determine what maintenance and child support they paid."

The rebuke bounced off Jason, but hit Walter. "I offered to sign a prenuptial agreement."

"What's a prenuptial agreement?" Faith inquired when she saw a mulish glint in Walter's eyes that Caroline's gaze met with equal obstinacy. Only Jason remained detached and uninterested, sipping his drink as though he could care less.

"Written promises made under duress, is how one lawyer defined his client's prenuptial agreement." Caroline bit her lip, but Faith knew she couldn't stop herself. "Any legal document a person is forced to sign is invalid in a court of law, not worth the paper it's written on."

Faith coughed and swallowed while Jason saved her from innocently asking another provocative question by saying, "Caroline, can I fix you a martini?"

"No, thanks." Her hostility vanished as she looked up at Walter shyly. "I'm on the wagon."

"Yes, well, uh," Walter stammered, "why don't we all go into the dining room? Caroline and Faith must be starving."

Picking up on Walter's cue, Faith rubbed her stomach and said, "My belly feels like my throat has been slit."

That earned her three frowns.

Her hand flew to her wayward mouth. "Did I say something wrong?"

Walter opened his mouth, but before he could chastise Faith, Jason stepped from behind the bar and held his arm out for Faith to take. "Shall we?"

Nodding, noticing the flickers of amusement in his eyes, Faith placed her hand on his arm and promptly forgot about Walter's being displeased with her. Jason could have been inviting her to walk beside him into hell's fires and she'd have gladly gone.

"We'll be in directly," Caroline said. "I need to have a word in private with Walter before dinner."

She waited until Jason and Faith were across the hall before she whispered, "You didn't tell him, did you?"

"I tried. He wouldn't listen. Faith arrived unexpectedly and . . ."

"Dammit Walter, all you had to do was take him into your office and simply tell him."

"Nothing is simple when it comes to Jason," Walter

lamented. "In one breath he told me about Jonathan's death and in the next, he wanted to devise a strategy for getting Faith out of town, before I'd even met her. I swear, I couldn't get a word in edgewise."

Caroline blinked back tears. "Oh, Walter, I am sorry about your loss. You must think I'm a heartless, selfish shrew."

"Not at all, my dear." Walter embraced Caroline and dusted a line of kisses along her cheek. "You're all heart. The most unselfish woman I've ever met. Otherwise, you wouldn't put up with me."

For several seconds Caroline held on tightly to the man she loved with all her heart and soul. "You aren't afraid to tell Jason, are you?"

"Are you?" Walter tucked a tendril of hair that had fallen loose behind her ear.

"Jason is formidable," she sighed, less distraught with Walter. "I know he respects me as a professional, but I don't think he likes me."

Walter chuckled. "You're one up on me. He doesn't like, or respect me."

"He does, too."

"He just doesn't show it," they chorused quietly.

Caroline gazed at Walter with complete adoration. "What are you going to do about Faith?"

"Jason decided to put her to work at the bank. My guess is that he'll work her until she drops."

"In hopes that she'll quit?"

"Or that she'll do something outrageous." Walter grinned. "The young woman does have a propensity for getting into trouble."

"I imagine she feels like a battered wife testifying in

front of an all-male jury and judge." Her eyes sparkled as though a light had just clicked on. "I could help her."

"Would you?"

She brushed her lips across his mouth. "I'd do almost anything for you."

"Anything, but marry me?" Walter groaned in frustration.

"You'll have to convince me," she teased, lightly swishing her hips against the fly of his trousers. "Do you think you could come over to my place, later?"

Walter took advantage of Caroline's parted lips and kissed her with all the pent-up frustration of a man desperately in love with an independent woman who'd declined his offer to make an honest woman of her. Life was too short for a man in his fifties to conduct a clandestine affair with savoir-faire. He wanted to be her husband.

"Is that a yes?" Caroline whispered against his mouth.

"Wild horses couldn't stop me," Walter vowed.

"Me, either."

His arms crossed her back and hers rested on his waist as they entered the formal dining room. Walter took a deep breath and without preamble, looked his son square in the eyes and stated baldly, "Caroline is pregnant."

Four

Unperturbed, Jason draped his napkin across his lap.

Perturbed, Faith dropped hers in the center of her plate. Her middle-aged uncle was about to become a father? An unwed father? And his significant other wouldn't marry him? She shook her head in disbelief. Things weren't a mite peculiar in St. Louis, they were complete chaos.

She nudged Jason's shoe with the toe of her sneaker. Say something, her dark eyes pleaded.

"Artificial insemination?" Jason droned.

Walter pulled Caroline closer to his side. "It's my child."

Jason nonchalantly straightened the perfectly aligned forks beside his gold-rimmed plate. His hands were steady, but his insides burned with rage. Faith's arrival threatened to upset the balance of power; Walter's overactive libido jeopardized the entire organization. In less than twenty-four hours, his fifty-percent control of the family stock, that included all the important decision-making powers, had dropped to less than thirteen percent!

While Walter seated Caroline across from her and took the chair at the end of the table, Faith kicked Jason's ankle, twice. The muscles in his face rearranged his bland expression into what Faith couldn't decipher as a grin or a grimace.

"I helped Papa Jon inseminate a cow," she chirped inanely to fill the lengthening silence. When Walter shook his head at her, she argued, "I did. Honest."

"Faith," Walter chastised, stretching the vowels until they sounded like an airplane dive-bombing its target.

She smiled, knowing Walter did not want explicit details regarding insemination, but she was bound and determined to take the spotlight off Caroline.

"You don't believe me? Just because we were isolated in a rural community didn't mean we weren't up on the latest technology. We do have electricity. All Papa had to do was download a list of sperm banks on the computer, type in the necessary information on the application form, then mail off a cashier's check. *Voilà!* Within days old Daisy-bell was all fixed up."

That drew Jason's attention away from Caroline to her beaming face. "You had access to a computer?"

Uh-oh! In her haste to dominate the conversation, she'd forgotten Jason believed her to be ignorant of modern conveniences.

"Uh-huh," she mumbled, waiting for him to start kicking her foot while she daintily spread her napkin on her lap the way Caroline had. She moved her feet beneath the chair. Through her long lashes she peeked at Jason. He hadn't attempted to kick her, but he looked as though he could cheerfully throttle her.

"I'm a computer illiterate," Caroline confessed, casting Faith a grateful smile as she placed her hand over Walter's fingers to quiet him. "The instructor I had in college excused me from class the first day when he said, 'Boot up,' and I raised my foot."

Walter and Faith laughed loudly at Caroline's small joke; Jason gave her a pseudo-smile, but his piercing glare quickly returned to Faith.

"Did your professor find you an apt pupil?" Jason inquired suavely of Faith.

"I wasn't allowed to attend schools."

"The state requires school attendance."

Faith shrugged. "I don't know how Papa kept me from going to school. He just did."

"Jonathan signed up for night classes right up until the day he left St. Louis," Walter said, thoroughly confounded. "Why would he stop you from attending school?"

"He didn't want me . . . quote, 'under the influence,' unquote."

"The influence of what?" Jason asked quietly.

The longer he was around Faith, the more she intrigued him. She was like the gift Jonathan had given him the last Christmas he'd been at Seaton house. Jason recalled ripping off the ribbon and paper, opening the box, only to find another gaily wrapped package. Nine boxes later—Walter had made him count them—he unwrapped a miniature carving of a boy on a tricycle, with his hands flung wide out. Although the block of wood couldn't speak, he could almost hear himself yelling, "Look, Uncle Jon! No hands!"

"What influences?" Faith repeated. "The list went on forever and ever."

Jason propped one elbow on the table and his hand cupped his chin as he listened intently. "Name one."

"Misinformation. He said he wanted me to learn only pure truths, not the bastardized version that has its roots in cynicism instead of love. He said I'd begin to want things that would be bad for me if I was allowed to associate with other children at school."

Just talking about him made her heart ache with homesickness. But she knew home didn't have the same meaning without him. She needed all of his relatives seated around the table to be her family, to fill the emptiness in her heart that his passing on had caused. She also knew they'd never accept her unless they knew what she'd been raised to believe. Her values were the emotional foundation Jonathan had instilled deep inside her for her to build upon when he was gone.

"What things?" Caroline probed. "Alcohol? Drugs?"

"Something equally addicting . . . television." Faith made a perfect imitation of what Jonathan called his TV face: jaw dropped, eyes drooped, chin declined. She broke her catatonic state with a pert grin. None of them were thinking about Caroline's pregnancy. "It also stops children from reading books and brainwashes them with lies or half-truths every ten minutes. He said the devil must have invented it."

"So you've never watched television?" Walter asked.

"No, when I wasn't working in the garden or taking care of the animals, I read."

"Don't forget the computer," Jason reiterated. Feeling as though he was about to pop another box open, he asked, "Did you take correspondence courses?"

"Yes." Jason had the most indescribably beautiful blue eyes, bluer than spring water on a hot summer's day. She could hardly think, when he was focusing his attention solely on her.

"High-school courses?"

"Yes."

"College?"

"Yes."

"Do you have a sheepskin?"

Mesmerized, her head tilted when she heard his strange question. He'd jumped from her schooling to the farm so quickly, he'd left her a mile down the road. "No sheep at the farm, but I do have an angora skin that one of Papa's friends in Peru sent him. It's softer than the down on a baby goose."

"I meant, did you earn a college degree . . . they used to be lettered on sheepskins."

"Oh!" Pleased she had what he wanted, she replied, "In that case, I do have one."

"What is your major?"

"Mathematics."

"That should be helpful," Jason said. "Any advanced degrees?"

Walter rapped his knuckles on the white linen tablecloth. "This is beginning to sound like a police interrogation, Jason. Whatever job you have in mind for her doesn't require a doctoral program, does it?"

"Quite the opposite."

Intrigued by Faith's answers, Jason resented his father's interference. A few more layers of fancy paper stripped off the gift box, he mused silently, would have revealed all her secrets. This afternoon, he'd vastly underestimated Faith. He'd assumed he'd be training a country bumpkin with no practical skills. It wasn't that she'd lied to him.

He simply hadn't asked the right questions. Temporarily thwarted, he reached for the silver bell beside his plate and gave it a shake. "She's probably overqualified for what I had in mind. This will take some rethinking on my part."

"Dinner?" Glen boomed, magically appearing at the door to the butler's pantry.

"Oh, my goodness, Mr. Morrison," Faith said, giggling as she bounced to her feet and danced around him. Dressed in a dark, three-piece suit with a starched white shirt and a black bow tie, he looked as though he should be seated at the head of the table in Jason's chair. "You look magnificent! Is Mrs. Cavendish joining us, too?"

Glen retained his composure, but it almost made his eyes cross. "I'll be serving you, Miss Faith."

It didn't take three sets of eyes boring into her back like a three-pronged pitchfork for Faith to know she'd made another social blunder. Adopting a false air of sophistication she had difficulty carrying off, she smiled up at Glen and said, "Of course. I knew that. What I meant is, will Mrs. Cavendish be helping you?"

For Faith's ears only, he muttered under his breath, "She'd rather die." He winked, and said louder, "She's too busy in the kitchen."

Faith did an abrupt about-face and proudly marched back to her seat as though every guest should be inquiring about the cook. She was learning, slowly but surely. Jason standing, attending to her chair made the error not so horrible.

"Well done," Caroline mouthed to Faith from behind her napkin. "Walter, I think the annual Fourth of July company picnic should be more elaborate this year. Instead of restricting the guest list to the employees, why don't you and Jason invite several of your friends and business acquaintances? Everyone should meet Faith."

"Splendid idea, darling." Walter turned to his niece. "Maybe in the next thirty days you can convince Caroline to make this a *real* celebration."

"A baby shower?" Jason quipped bitterly.

"Thank you, but no thanks," Caroline replied. To counter Jason's smart remark, she smiled at Walter and suggested he come to her office first thing Monday morning to sign the legal papers they'd discussed.

"What papers?" Jason demanded in a voice that could have frozen milk to ice cream.

"Walter wants to make arrangements for his child's future," Caroline replied sweetly. "Initially, I refused to let him sign over stock in the bank, but I'm having second thoughts."

Faith drew a long breath, trying to think of another diversionary tactic. Her opportunity arrived when she saw Glen place a bowl of steaming soup in front of Caroline.

"Is that true?" Jason held a tight restraint on his self-control. Did his father think so little of him that he'd give away the shares he'd earned without consulting him? When Walter nodded, he wanted to throw down his towel and leave.

"Let's see now," Caroline crooned, silently counting to nine on her fingers. "I don't have a sheepskin in mathematics, Faith, but I do believe within nine months, you will be the majority stockholder."

Faith expected scathing recriminations to erupt from Jason, directed at everyone at the table. Seated closest to him, only she could see the red tide of anger slowly creeping up his neck. To the others, he appeared to be reacting with quiet, unemotional calm. She wasn't fooled. One more comment from either Caroline or Walter, and Jason would explode.

She had to say or do something to stop her first evening at the Seaton house from turning into a family brawl! In Faith's peripheral vision she saw Glen remove her soup from the silver tray.

"I can't . . ." Her hands flailed. She intended to knock Glen's wrist, spilling the soup on the table, but his reflexes were quick. Her fingers flicked the lip of the bowl. Her brown eyes widened in horror as hot contents of the bowl poured into Jason's plate, splashing down the front of his shirt and tie.

Jason jackknifed backwards as Glen stabilized the dish and Faith began dabbing at noodles that slithered down his front, sliding below his belt.

"I'm sorry," Faith cried, trying to catch the squirmy noodles. Her fingers smashed more than they caught. "How could I have been so clumsy?"

"My fault," Glen contradicted, willing to take the blame.

"Absolutely not." She wasn't about to get Glen fired! "Papa Jon always said I wouldn't be able to speak if my hands were tied behind me!"

Jason grabbed her wrist. Her hand rubbed frantically up and down against his zipper, causing an involuntary response that no man could control. Hell, the scalding soup should have taken care of that, he raged silently. He had to get her out of his lap or be thoroughly humiliated.

"Faith, stop!" he roared.

Both Walter and Caroline, who'd jumped to their feet,

glanced at each other. Jason Seaton never, ever, *ever,* raised his voice.

"Did it burn you?"

"No!" He clamped his hand on her wrist and held it away from him.

"Your beautiful suit is ruined," Faith wailed dramatically.

Through clenched teeth, Jason berated her, "The cleaners will take care of it if you will just stop mashing the noodles through my zipper as though it's a strainer!"

The three adults hovering nearby knew Jason was not joking, but Walter had to cough to cover his laughter, Caroline pinched her lips closed with her hand, and Glen strode quickly from the room.

Only Faith remained stoically solemn. She slipped her hand into Jason's and tugged on it. "Come on, Jason. The sooner you get out of those soggy britches, the better you'll feel."

"Where do you think you're going?" he asked, quelling the note of hysteria in his voice.

"Up to your bedroom, of course." She glanced from his flustered face to Walter and Caroline. "You don't want to shuck off those pants down here, do you?"

He shook his hand free, then placed his fingers on her shoulders and pushed her back in her chair. "You . . . aren't needed," he said slowly, bluntly, for emphasis. "I can take care of myself."

By the time Jason had left the dining room, Walter and Caroline had regained their composure.

"Don't worry about it, Faith," Walter consoled. "Jason has dozens of suits."

Slumping down, Faith was inconsolable. Nothing

worked the way she'd planned. She'd only meant to temporarily distract everyone. The hateful look in his eyes when he'd told her that he didn't need her was worse than if he'd slapped her wayward hands and sent her to bed without supper.

"He hates me," she said ruefully.

Walter opened his mouth to repudiate her statement and Caroline started to shake her head. Both stopped. Jason had good reasons for disliking her, and each of them.

In sync with each other's thoughts, Walter and Caroline raised wineglasses and clicked them together. To make light of Faith's ominous remark, he said, "The dictatorial king is dead. Instead of his faithful shield, he has chicken noodle soup on his chest."

"Long live the queen."

Five

The next morning, Faith awoke before dawn. For a minute she felt disoriented in the unfamiliar room. And then she remembered where she was and how dismally she was failing her mission. Mentally, she tallied up her allies in one column and the enemies she made in another, then weighted the numbers by who meant the most to her. The list of enemies was the lengthiest.

Faith groaned and pulled the pillow over her snarled curls. She should have plaited her hair last night, but she'd been too disheartened to worry about her tender scalp.

Her tender heart had ached when Jason had not returned to the table. Later, after Caroline had volunteered to help her get acclimated, whatever that meant, and the two of them had departed, Faith had noticed Glen taking a tray into the study. To make amends for putting him on the spot, she'd offered to take it in. He told her that Jason had given him strict orders that no one was to enter the room.

She'd paced outside the door, from one end of the foyer to the other, whistling merrily, trying to get Jason to open the door. She might as well have whistled into the wind.

Jason remained cloistered inside the room.

After she'd exhausted her entire repertoire of hymns and couldn't bear to whistle another chorus of "Onward Christian Soldiers," she dared to knock. The least he could do was let her apologize, face to face. Determined not to go to bed with a bone of contention gouging her with feelings of guilt, her timid knock grew assertive. She pressed her ear to the door.

Any farfetched hopes she'd had of reconciliation were drowned in silence.

Faith pulled the pillow off her face, curled her arm around it, and stared at the ceiling. Her mind leapt from yesterday's debacles to the immediate future. Too restless to remain prone, she surged to her feet and continued where she'd left off the night before——pacing the room doggedly.

Faith picked up a silver-handled brush off the triple dresser and began unsnarling her hair.

With each tug she realized that the soup incident wasn't the root cause of Jason's silent treatment. Caroline had put her finger on the site where Jason's nose was out of joint: Faith Jones, a nobody from nowhere, owned controlling interest of the Seaton stock.

The simple solution to that problem would be for her to sign over Jonathan's shares to Jason. Simple*minded* solution, Faith corrected silently. The lawyer in Backwater had told her it would take a year for the estate to go through probate court. She could promise Jason the stock, but he'd have to trust her to deliver it.

"Jason isn't long on trust," she said aloud to see if hearing what she'd observed rang true.

It did.

The brush began to glide through her curly hair.

And, to be scrupulously honest with herself, she still liked the idea of working at the bank. With Jason her mentor, she tacked on. But just until she acquired the knowledge and experience for them to make joint decisions.

She wanted to be his equal.

"Well, slap your mouth and call yourself Brutus," Faith chided, as her betrayal began to gnaw at her innate sensitivity. "Jason does not want to share decision-making with his own father. Why would you think he'd be remotely interested in sharing with you? Didn't you hear the man? He does not need you!"

She sat gazing in the full-length mirror, waiting for an answer to the ultimate question: Why would Jason want you?

Because he's adorable? Because he was kind enough not to laugh when you made a clown of yourself? Or because he heroically saved you from falling on your face when you stuck your foot in your mouth and tried to walk?

"Yes! Yes! Yes!" she mouthed at her reflection.

Jason could do no wrong; she was the one who needed to straighten up and fly right.

And she would, she promised silently, if Jason would relent and give her another chance. That's all she needed. For now.

A light rap at her door startled her. "Who's there?" she called softly.

"Me. Caroline."

Faith hurried to the door and opened it. "Come in. Goodness, you're up before the rooster crows."

"I thought I'd drop by for a few minutes before I went to the office," Caroline said as she breezed into the room.

"I know it's presumptuous, but I made a list of places you should go and appointments you should make."

Scanning the long list, Faith asked miserably, "Are my shortcomings as long as your list?"

"No!" Caroline laughed and gave her a quick hug. "Walter wants you to go shopping and enjoy yourself today." She dug in her purse until she found the packet of charge cards Walter had given her. "You won't need money. Use these."

"That's very kind of him, but . . ."

"Kindness has nothing to do with it. He wants you to walk, talk, and look like an heir to the Seaton fortune."

"In that case, you'd better write down some more places for me to go," Faith groaned.

"Don't be ridiculous."

"That I can't help, either."

Caroline grinned, took Faith by the arm and marched her to the chaise longue. "I'm going to help. I can't tell much with you in a granny gown, but let's get started. First, I want you to walk across the room."

"Walk?" She strode across the width of the room. "Easy."

"Mmmmm," was the noncommittal comment she earned.

"Maybe we should start at the beginning. I'll crawl back to you."

"Did anyone ever tell that you have a delightful sense of humor?" Caroline asked, chuckling as she spoke. "There's nothing wrong with your walk. You have natural grace and excellent posture."

"But?"

"You aren't qualifying for the Olympics."

"I can walk slower."

"Let's see you."

Faith sauntered back, shortening her gait to please Caroline. "How's that?"

"Better. Much better. Would you mind if I take a look in your closet?" Without waiting for a reply, she opened the door nearest her. A single cotton dress hung from a coat hanger. For a woman who had more clothes than she'd need in a lifetime, there was something profoundly sad about discovering anyone this deprived. She schooled the pitiful look from her face before she whirled around and said brightly, "Good. There's plenty of room."

Abruptly, she picked up the telephone on the night-stand. As she punched in several digits, she said thought-fully, "I don't have any court appearances today. If you don't mind my tagging along, I'd love to shop for maternity clothes. The elastics at the waist of my suits are getting snug."

"How far along are you?"

"Almost eight months."

From Caroline's size, Faith would not have guessed the baby would be due so quickly. Her untrained eye would have guessed five, maybe six months. "I can't let you exhaust yourself on my account. Isn't there a K-Mart near Seaton Place?"

Before Faith could completely nix the idea, Caroline raised her hand to obtain silence. "This is Caroline. Please take my calls, Martha. I won't be in the office today or available on the cellular phone. See you Monday. Have a good weekend. Bye." Her hand dropped. She noted Faith's puzzled expression and explained, "It's an answering machine. You dial the number, wait for a beep and leave a message. They save everyone a great deal of time and trouble."

Another knock at the door brought Mrs. Cavendish into the room with a breakfast tray. She smiled at Caroline and scowled at Faith.

"Thank you, Gertrude," Caroline said as the cook placed the tray on the bed. "Don't plan on Faith being here for lunch. She'll be out for the day with me."

Before waddling through the door, Gertrude grouched, "You have my condolences."

Without a moment's hesitation, Caroline twisted the knob and reopened the door. "Excuse me, Gertrude? Did you offer condolences? Is someone ailing?"

"Not yet." Gertrude smiled apologetically at Caroline while she shot a dirty look at Faith.

"Let her go, Caroline," Faith implored, willing to turn the other cheek.

Caroline complied by slamming the door and whirling around. "You definitely are in dire need of a crash course in assertiveness training. You can't let anyone, male or female, insult you and get away with it."

"Mrs. Cavendish has good reason not to like me," Faith reasoned logically.

"I'm aware there was a misunderstanding. Walter told me. I've heard all the stories about Gertrude, from her banning Jason from the kitchen for sneaking a cookie, to serving hot dogs at a formal dinner because Walter asked her not to suffocate everything in cream sauces."

"Mrs. Cavendish must have a sheepskin in assertiveness training," Faith said drily as she pulled the handles on the bottom dresser drawer. "Cross her and she's on you like swarm of flies on ripe watermelon."

"Bend at the knees, please."

"Pardon?"

"Ladies don't bend at the waist and wave their fannies in the air." Caroline demonstrated what she meant by gracefully bending down beside Faith. "Like this. Your turn."

Faith complied, but had to try again because her knees spread apart. And again, because her elbows stuck out like chicken wings.

"That's right. Knees together. Arms tucked to your sides," Caroline praised.

While Faith rummaged through the drawer and picked out her cotton panties with *Friday* stitched on the hip, and a bra, she wondered how many things she'd done wrong yesterday without knowing it. "Are there any books on this sort of stuff that I could study?"

"I'm certain there are."

"Any downstairs?" Faith crossed to the bathroom, stopping to collect her dress off the coat hanger. Modesty prohibited her from getting undressed in front of anyone. "In the study?"

Caroline grinned. "I doubt it. Deportment is usually passed down from mother to daughter, Father to son."

"Jason has excellent deportment, doesn't he?"

"He should. Walter is a stickler for good manners."

Faith poked her head into the room. "Maybe Mrs. Cavendish should have given you her condolences."

"Why?"

"Because Papa Jon, bless his heart, didn't teach me girl things. Walter gave you a tough job." She smiled impishly. "You're going to mother me before you have his child." When she noticed Caroline practically worshipping the tray of food with her eyes, she said, "Go ahead and dig in while I get ready."

Fortunately for Caroline, she did not suffer from morning sickness, but unfortunately for her slender figure, her appetite had soared. She wanted to dig in, literally.

Later, fortified by three slices of buttered toast, Caroline sat on the edge of the bed and watched as Faith bent at the waist to tie her sneakers. She thanked her lucky stars that Walter's niece was a quick study and eager to please. She'd need the stamina of Mother Teresa for this shopping expedition!

"I'll be over first thing tomorrow morning," Caroline called through her car window, giving Faith a jaunty wave.

Faith smiled. Lord have mercy, even her cheeks hurt. She glanced down at her new skimmers, with their pointy toes and no arch support, then stared at the black wrought-iron benches decorating the front porch. A flash of homesickness came over her as she longed for the swing back at the farmhouse.

For two cents, she thought, I'd park my behind on the steps, kick off the torture chambers squeezing my toes, and rub my arches until my dogs stopped howling.

Deciding that wasn't such a bad idea, she sluggishly lowered her achy bones to the fourth step. Knees apart, she tucked the voluminous folds of her skirt between her legs. The sixth step was a perfect resting place for her elbows. Not as comfy as the swing, she mused, but tolerable.

"Need help carrying your plunder in the house?" she heard from behind her.

Recognizing Jason's voice, she let her head droop backward on her neck. Her eyes progressed from the polished tips of his shoes, up the sharp crease of his trousers, over the buttons of his shirt to his face. The only concession he'd made to being casual was his rolled-up shirtsleeves and the top button of his shirt being undone.

He looks as handsome upside down as he does right-side up, she thought, smiling at his kind offer to help her.

"I'll have Glen take them upstairs," Jason added. "Why don't you come inside where it's cool?"

"Why don't you come out here and grab some fresh air? If you listen closely you can hear the katydids and crickets."

Jason cocked his head to one side, but he only heard the sound of traffic moving on the four-lane street. "Have you eaten dinner?"

"Um-hmm."

And had my lesson in table manners, she reflected. Soup spoon goes to the back of the bowl. Finger foods aren't meant to be eaten with fingers. Straws are really stirrers, not meant to drink through. And she had to dab her mouth between bites, so she wouldn't leave lip prints on the water glass.

As she spoke, Jason watched her blond curls seductively bobbing and brushing against her shoulders, enticing him to sit beside her. He wondered if those curls were as soft to the touch as they appeared. Would they coil around his fingers like silken rings of gold? His mind's unruly thoughts caught him off guard.

"Come inside," he ordered gruffly, to regain control. Back inside the study he'd be able to keep his thoughts strictly on business. "It's supposed to rain."

"Rain?" Faith pointed at the moon that seemed to be hanging in the trees, then gave a pat to the curved step. "No ring around the moon. It won't rain."

Jason gave in to impulse, something he rarely did, and strolled down the steps. When Faith swept aside her full skirt to make room for him close to her, he defied the compelling urges his body signaled by leaning against the wrought-iron handrail. His arms folded against his chest.

"So, what did you and Caroline buy?"

Disappointed that he'd chosen to keep a safe distance, she wondered if she should take this opportunity to apologize for dumping soup in his lap. She decided it would be better not to mention it.

"Everything but the counters and racks," she answered, grinning up at him. "Too much to carry without a train of pack mules. I just brought the small stuff. Caroline told the clerks to have the rest delivered tomorrow."

"I'll have Glen leave room in the driveway for the eighteen-wheelers."

A joke or cynicism? Her heart began to thump irregularly when she saw his eyes light with amusement.

"Want to see?" She grabbed the closest bag, eager to please him. The bottles and jars collided. "You'll like this."

Curiosity drew him closer, inch by inch, until he sat beside her. "What?"

"Cosmetics." She emptied the contents into her lap. "Moisturizer. Mascara. Lipstick. *Passion*. Ooops, never mind that," she said, dropping a plastic tube back into the sack.

As she held up each feminine toiletry for his inspection, her leg and hip innocently pressed against his thigh. He took the box of perfume she handed him and wondered about the *ooops*.

"Passion." He unscrewed the top of the purple flask and inhaled. "This makes a man want to beat his chest and howl at the moon."

"Really?" He was teasing her, she thought, but had to check to make certain. She put her wrist close to his nose. "Sniff that. It's a combination of Opium, Spellbound, and Eternity. Guaranteed to drive a man wild," she teased.

He sniffed, then began nibbling at her wrist.

"Stop that," Faith laughed.

"Can't."

His lips touched the ticklish place on her inner arm, then her bare shoulder. "Smells ravishing up here."

"There's no perfume there!" she gasped. The slide of his whiskers against her skin drew her knees together and spread goose-bumps in their wake. "Just plain old Ivory soap."

"You must have been a good girl and washed behind your ears," he said. Her curls swept against the strong line of his jaw as he nuzzled her ear.

Something had come over him. Maybe it was the perfume, or maybe the moonlight, or maybe the sound of katydids and crickets. Whatever it was, cozying up to Faith on the front steps of Seaton Place seemed the most natural thing in the world for him to do.

Faith seemed like an unexpected, surprise gift sent to him from his favorite uncle.

"That tickles," Faith said, leaning back as her shoulder raised to her ear to stop him. His arm pillowed her head and she felt his hand cup the side of her face.

For a long moment, Jason stared at her as though it was the first time he'd really looked at her.

"You don't need cosmetics, Faith."

"I don't?"

His finger trailed down her flushed cheek. Moisturizer couldn't help her skin. Her dark eyelashes couldn't be enhanced with mascara. Her lips were the color of pale roses, without embellishment.

"No, you don't." Jason wanted to tell her why, but compliments were as unfamiliar on his tongue as apologies. His voice was strangely hoarse when he said, "You're a natural beauty . . . the way you are."

Instinctively, Faith closed her eyes and pursed her lips. He was going to kiss her. Her heart slammed against her ribs. She just knew he was going to kiss her and she wanted to be ready for her first kiss.

Jason smiled. A genuine smile. One that not only reached his eyes, but his heart, too.

Her rose-colored lips had puckered into an inviting rosebud that enticed his lips to taste hers. He wanted to brush his lips against hers, but to do so would sharply veer him from the straight and narrow path he'd charted for himself. The pad of his thumb lightly touched her mouth until it relaxed its pucker.

Faith sighed; her lips parted. She tasted the salt of his flesh on her tongue. Slowly, her eyelids lifted. "Is something wrong?"

"Not wrong exactly," Jason whispered. Her soulful eyes were darker than the sky above them. "More like unexpected."

"Do you have a significant other?"

Hearing her choice of words deepened the curve of his smile. "No. No one special."

Faith found that hard to imagine. In her mind, Jason was a man every woman would want to be significant. "Ever?"

"A gentleman doesn't kiss and tell."

"That leaves a lot to my imagination." Her hand moved to the side of his face as she felt his thumb wrap a fat curl around his finger. "I have a vivid imagination."

Jason chuckled. Not doubting her claim, but inquisitive about what she thought, he said, "Dozens of women?"

"More." His lips thinned; her hand moved to the side of his strong jaw and her finger defined the line where his lips pressed together. "Beautiful, sophisticated women."

Flattered, but knowing her calculations were pure fabrication on her part, he nipped her finger between his lips. Her eyes rounded when his tongue traced the edge of her oval fingernail.

For an instant, she retracted her finger from the heat of his mouth, feeling as though what was taking place between them was more intimate than the chaste kiss she'd yearned for. Timid, and yet excited, she rested three fingers across his lips.

"Jason?"

"Hmmmm?"

His lips vibrated against her fingers, humming a song of passion the perfume had promised.

"Why don't you kiss me?"

He did. He kissed her fingertips, one at a time.

"No. I mean a real kiss," she protested, removing her fingers and curling his kisses against her palm for safe-keeping. They might be the only ones she would get. She sent a swift prayer heavenward that they wouldn't be. She promised she wouldn't ask for anything for a month if Jason would kiss her. "Why won't you give me a real kiss?"

Jason formed his reply carefully as his thumb savored the texture of her hair. Believing honesty was the policy, he said, "There's too much between us. The bank. Jonathan and Walter's feud. The power struggle. Your inheritance."

Heaven isn't susceptible to bribes, she thought when she heard the multitude of reasons for him not wanting to kiss her. Damning her fate, she added, "And I'm backward and clumsy and say and do the wrong th- . . ."

Jason ended her castigation by swiftly blanketing her utterances by slanting his lips across them. He devoured their rose-petal sweetness with a hunger that stunned him. He was far from being the Romeo she believed him to be. There had been relatively few women in his life. None had the impact Faith had on him. She was a novice, inexperienced, and yet her lips parted beneath his, giving him access to the sweet, minty taste of her mouth.

He would have kissed her long, deep and often, if the sound of gravel spitting from car wheels at the end of the drive hadn't disrupted him.

His arms lifted Faith upright as he whispered, "Some-one is coming."

Bright headlights bathed the porch in glaring light. Dazed by Jason's kisses and the startling beams of light, she shielded her eyes with her forearm.

Jason resumed his nonchalant pose, with his back against the rail, although he felt like going non-linear! A Southern magnolia tree concealed his presence. Dammit! If the car held snoopy trespassers driving up to get a closer look at the mansion, he'd have them arrested!

Through the foliage he recognized Walter's car. He wasn't any less displeased. He could have followed the drive back behind the house.

"Why didn't you park in the garage?" he asked when his father exited his Mercedes. He stepped down, giving Faith time to completely recover by putting himself in front of Walter.

"I saw Faith and the packages, but I didn't see you. I thought she could use a little help carrying them inside."

"Thanks, Uncle Walter. That was very considerate of you," Faith said. She started to rise, heard the bottles clank in the well of her skirt, and began dumping them into the sack. "I was showing Jason my treasures."

Strrrreeeetch that truth, she thought, widening her smile to Cheshire-cat width. Perhaps it wasn't such a stretch. Her first kiss was something she'd treasure.

"I've been at Caroline's house." Walter laughed. "You two ladies certainly were a boon to the St. Louis economy. Did you leave anything on the shelves?" he teased.

"She bought out the maternity department. I bought out the petite shops. Every store closed after we'd departed," she bragged, one white lie giving birth to a whopper. She rattled the sack and lifted one sore foot. "No cosmetics or shoes left, either."

Walter poked Jason in the ribs. "Guess they emptied the bank's vault, huh?"

"No we didn't!" Faith denied before Jason could reply.

"Caroline handed those little plastic cards to the sales-clerks and said, 'Charge it, please and have it delivered.' " Her arms spread apart, encompassing her purchases. "Charge cards are better than having a fairy godmother. None of this is going to change into mice, pumpkins, and rags when the clock strikes midnight, will it?"

Jason glanced at his diamond-studded Rolex, frowned, then picked up an armload of packages. "These won't, but I will. I still have several hours of work ahead of me or the vault will be empty."

"All work and no play makes . . ."

"Money," Jason said, interrupting the rhyme and taking the steps two at a time.

Walter tucked his thumbs under his belt buckle and shook his head. "That's not how it goes, son."

Feeling the bad vibes begin to generate between the two men, Faith picked up several packages and darted up behind Jason. "You have until Monday, don't you? Isn't the bank closed until then?"

"We're open until noon on Saturdays."

"It's just another work day for him," Walter tacked on. "But not for me. Unless you mind, Caroline invited me to go along with the two of you tomorrow."

Jason crossed the threshold when he heard Faith's enthusiastic affirmative reply. He told himself that he didn't care if the three of them went carousing around St. Louis, spending money as though it was water. He told himself he liked the quiet solitude the bank afforded, after the morning rush.

He reached the landing at the top of the stairs and looked down on Walter and Faith. They laughed and chatted like two conspirators who'd successfully pulled off a bank heist.

He didn't care.

Really, he didn't.

Bullshit, he did!

And that bothered him.

Six

Work, work, work, Faith droned, staring spitefully at the closed study door as she mounted the steps to her room. Over the entire weekend, despite Faith's making every opportunity available for Jason to be included in the family activities, he avidly fulfilled his role as the family dullard.

Someone needed to stamp PLAY on his forehead so that when he looked in the mirror he might remember that the Seaton banking empire would not collapse in complete chaos if he missed one day of tending to it.

She slowed to a halt on the fifth step. Sunday was supposed to be a day of rest; she felt restless. Too restless to spend the evening reading magazines or a book, she decided.

Be assertive, she chided, quoting Caroline's favorite remark as she retraced her steps.

She strode to his study, raised her hand, then hesitated. Nervous, she worried her bottom lip. Knocking timidly and begging admittance into Jason's lair could hardly be classified as assertive. What would Caroline do? Barge in. Grab Jason by the nape. Then demand to know why he'd thoroughly kissed then completely dismissed her.

Her hand lowered to the brass knob. She felt it turn, but her reflexes weren't quick enough. The door jerked open and she was propelled forward, forcefully, straight into Jason's chest. Caught off balance, he staggered backward until his knees hit a cushion, buckled and caved him into the wing chair.

Faith, who'd wrapped her arms around his waist to keep them from falling, was sprawled between his legs with her nose practically buried in his bellybutton. When she squirmed, trying to escape the embarrassing position, Jason clamped his legs at her waist and his hands on her shoulders.

"Want something?" he asked drily. "Or were you peeking through the keyhole?"

"Why do these things always happen to me?" she groaned miserably.

"Because you're an accident looking for a place to happen?" Jason teased.

Faith grinned. "That's what Jonathan called me."

"Me, too," Jason confided, drawing her up and settling her on his lap. "After I borrowed his wood-carving knives and broke half the blades."

She leaned against his broad shoulder and looked up at him. "Did you hide from him, too?"

"I wasn't hiding . . ." He shook his head. Breaking off the blatant lie, he swapped it for a half-truth by gesturing toward the computer print-out sheets on the desk. "I have problems to solve."

Like why I run to the window when I hear a car door slam, he mused. Why I can't concentrate on a report when I hear soft footsteps padding up the steps. Why every blank page of paper miraculously forms a picture of a curly blonde with heart-touching brown eyes. Why . . .

"I'm good at solving math problems. Can I help?"

"Seatons solve their own problems."

Slightly wounded that he didn't consider her a Seaton worthy of helping him, she said, "Walter is a Seaton. Can't he help you?"

"He has his own problem. Caroline."

"And her baby. Walter teases Caroline about how he wants to marry her because she banks at Southwest, and because he wants free legal consultation, but she told me the only reason he's beseeching her hand in marriage is because of the baby."

"A man Walter's age should be worried about his son providing him with grandchildren," Jason said.

"He is."

"Oh, yeah?"

Faith nodded, constantly surprised by the lack of communication between the two men. "Caroline mentioned that one reason Walter is ecstatic about her being with child is because he thinks you'll never marry."

She clamped her lips closed to keep the rest of the conversation from spilling out of her mouth. Caroline had winked, given her a nudge in the ribs, then coyly asked Faith if Walter had been hallucinating or had he seen her kissing Jason on the front porch the previous night? Walter thought he must have been a victim of wishful thinking when he continued up the drive and found the two of them on opposite ends of the steps. To answer Caroline's question, she'd borrowed a page out of Jason's book on good manners by refusing to kiss and tell.

"Walter formed that opinion after he tried to badger me into a marriage of convenience," Jason replied bluntly.

"Who'd he want you to marry?"

"He had a long list of socially and financially acceptable females. Since then, I haven't made him privy to my personal affairs," he replied evasively, not wanting to offend Faith by revealing his shamefully materialistic thoughts regarding marrying her. "Would you marry for convenience's sake?"

"I want a family of my own more than anything," she answered truthfully. She ducked her head to conceal her flaming cheeks.

Last night, lying in bed with Jason's kisses fresh on her lips, listening to the water run in his shower, the thought of how convenient it would be for her to marry Jason had crossed her mind. But desire and passion mingled with plain, old-fashioned logic. She wanted him to love her.

"You've been around Caroline too much." He raised her chin, noting her heightened color, he teased, "Next thing I know, you'll be burning your bras."

"She did tell me to get rid of my farmer's underwear," Faith admitted.

Jason chuckled. He found her honesty refreshing, but felt obligated to explain what he'd meant, to prevent her from burning the house down. "In the sixties women burned their bras as a symbolic act of defiance against men who wanted to restrict them from equal opportunities in the work force."

"They didn't have much to burn," she confided. "The wisps of lace I bought barely cover the subject, if you know what I mean."

He barred his mind from picturing her latest purchases. His blue eyes remained in contact with hers,
when he wanted to let them drop of their own accord to
the scooped neck of her blouse. It proved to be a stringent
test of his self-control.

"Now, equal jobs for equal pay is required by law,"
he said, frowning as he finished his explanation.

"You don't have to worry about me starting a bonfire
or getting pregnant." She soothed the wrinkles that
pleated his brow. Fires still frightened her, a carry-over
from the disaster in her past. She was too cautious to
play with fire. Little did she realize that her pacifying
strokes kindled flames within him, ones that could
quickly get out of control and consume him if he'd let
them. "Sometimes Caroline says things that I don't know
whether I should take literally or figuratively."

"Like what?"

"Like her reasons for not marrying Uncle Walter. Do
you think she meant it when she said Walter fathering
her child is better than taking a chance with a sperm
bank?" Her fingers moved of their own volition from his
forehead to the small button constricting his neck when
he made a small strangling noise. "I figured she was
kidding when she laughed and said those banks weren't
backed by FDIC."

The thought of Caroline using his father for stud service infuriated Jason. His fingers clenched the arms of
the chair, but he kept a poker face.

"She wasn't kidding. Sperm banks aren't regulated by
the government."

Faith unbuttoned his collar. Familiar with animal hus-
bandry, she understood how sperm was collected from

bulls. Absentmindedly her fingers unbuttoned the second button and played with the tuft of dark springy hair at the V. How'd they get it from men? She didn't have the nerve to ask Jason.

Skipping to the next thing they'd discussed during their shopping excursion, Faith asked, "Do one out of two marriages end in divorce?"

Jason nodded.

"Caroline said they'd save a tree by not wasting the paper a marriage license is printed on."

"Her statistics are correct, but I think she stretched her logic to include saving the environment as a reason for not marrying Walter."

"I think the real reason has something to do with why she became a lawyer."

"How so?"

"She said her parents 'split the sheet' when she was a little girl. At first, they fought over her. Then her father disappeared. She missed him dreadfully. Her mother raised her without any financial help until she remarried. She didn't say so, but I think when her mother had her stepfather's children, she felt displaced. Caroline said her mission in life is to see that deadbeat dads don't desert their families. Maybe she's afraid Walter will desert her and the baby?"

"My mother died in childbirth. Walter stuck by me." Faith saw a flash of long-forgotten pain in Jason's dark eyes. She hadn't meant to hurt him by digging up old memories. "I'm sorry. I didn't mean . . ."

"You lost both of your parents. Don't waste your pity on me."

"Jonathan took good care of me."

"And I had Walter," he countered, defending his father.

Faith nodded, but she recalled Caroline's reaction when she'd pointed that out to her. No one had raised Jason; Jason had raised himself. Walter had admitted to Caroline that he'd been a poor role model for his son. Caroline explained that Jason was a prime example of Walter's money not being able to buy a child happiness.

Unwilling to argue the point, not knowing all the facts, she said, "Maybe single-parent families are better, like Caroline says."

"Children need two parents," Jason corrected unequivocally.

"Then you agree with me? You do think Caroline should marry Walter." Pleased that they were on the same side of the fence, she smiled widely. "I'm glad I have you as a mentor, to explain the peculiarities of city living to me."

Jason paused. She'd twisted his thinking until his logic was wrapped around her little finger as surely as she'd distracted him by twisting the hairs on his chest.

He was opposed to Walter's marrying anyone. Period!

"Ouch." He closed his hand around her busy fingers. He studied her face, wondering cynically what she'd do if her first lesson included him teaching her about the inevitable results of an innocent young virgin scrunching around on a horny man's lap. It would be strictly show and tell unless he took immediate action.

He spanned her waist with his hands and stood up, taking her with him. "All this talk of love and marriage and babies is unsettling for a confirmed bachelor," he joked wanly. "Where did you say Walter and Caroline went?"

"I didn't." Frustrated by being abruptly dumped from his lap, she wanted to thump his chest to get his heart pumping. Hers was racing at a full gallop. "They went to her place."

Jason raked one hand through his hair and crossed to the front window. He needed space. "How many suits did he take with him?"

"Three or four." Faith sat in the chair he'd vacated. The leather held the warmth of his body. She snuggled deeper into the cushion, tucking her legs beneath her. "He said they needed to be dropped off at the cleaners."

"With a short detour inside Caroline's closet," Jason commented drily as he meandered toward the desk. "He'll be back at dawn. I'm not supposed to know he lives with her. I wonder how Walter thinks I'm going to reconcile Caroline being pregnant with them not having sex."

"By using the same rationale his brother used." She watched him settle on the corner of the desk. "Papa Jon said he believed in free love, but he kept a double-barreled shotgun loaded with buckshot handy to keep me pure as new-driven snow."

"A do-as-I-say-and-not-as-I-do philosophy?"

"Precisely," Faith agreed, smiling sympathetically at Jason. "And hopelessly antiquated. According to the magazines I've been reading, sex comes shortly after a handshake."

"Where did you buy these magazines? Off the magazine rack or from behind the counter?"

Faith shrugged. "Caroline bought them. She said I'd get inspired by looking at the pictures."

"And did you?"

"Why are you scowling at me like a dog with his tail caught in the screen door?"

"Because there are some things you don't need to learn from a magazine."

"Like what?"

"Like when to shake hands and when to show off your . . . *farmer's underwear!*"

Faith captured her laughter behind her hands, but it filtered through her fingers. The way his dark eyebrows had risen in keeping with the volume of his voice tickled her funny bone.

Jason did not share her sense of humor. He reached down and pried her hands from her face.

"What is so damned funny?"

"You! Everyone says you're cold." She mimicked Walter's deep voice, "He's aloof . . . stand-offish." Then Caroline's treble voice, "Jason never raises his voice. His facial expression only changes from grim to glum. The employees all chipped in at Christmas to buy him a smile."

In her own melodic voice, she asked sweetly, "I shake you up, don't I?"

"It's nothing to gloat over," he rebuked in an effort to wipe the cheeky grin off her face. "Smart women pay heed to my reputation."

She bounced to her feet and playfully poked her finger against his chest before he could grit his teeth. "Never go where angels fear to tread?" Poke. "Never tease a dinosaur?" Poke.

"Never tease a man with a hard-on," he warned quietly, with deliberate crudeness. Shock tactics. Her inexperience could get her in big trouble with a man who had less control. He confiscated her ornery fingers by drawing her arms around his waist until she was flattened against him. Anticipating that she might try to escape, his hands slid from her slender waist, locking on the feminine flair of her hips. "That's lesson number one from your mentor."

"Country girls know the fundamentals of sex," she said provocatively, leaning back in his arms. Audaciously, her fingers climbed up the taut muscles of his back. Feminine instincts guided her as she rocked in the cradle of his hips. "It's an everyday part of nature."

Reluctantly, Jason smiled. "You're as green as a freshly printed dollar bill . . . with about as much sense as a copper penny," he countered without malice.

"I'm a fast learner. I liked the way you kissed me. It made my insides feel all hot and tingly." Faith's curly lashes flickered down, casting shadows on her flushed cheeks. She stared at him from under her lashes, half afraid she'd see his face turn stone hard. "I'd like for you to kiss me again."

His attempt to shock her had backfired. He'd expected her to take flight to preserve her innocence; she'd cuddled closer. Jason could understand why Jonathan had erected a barbed-wire fence around the farm. There wasn't a coy bone in her body! And it was damned exciting to a man who'd only heard insincere flattery from women.

Everyone had told her that he was a mean-tempered son-of-a-bitch, and yet, here she was snuggled up against him. It made him want to find out exactly how much this particular farm girl did know about sex.

"If I'd had any sense, I wouldn't have kissed you." Making a supreme effort to regain his normal sense of detachment, he dropped his hands to his sides. "Things are complicated enough with emotional entanglements between us."

Faith tipped her head back. His lips had formed a thin line, but the dark pupils of his eyes had expanded until they appeared as dark as her own. As they began to contract, she felt as though he was shutting her out. She couldn't bear to let that happen. She locked her arms around his neck and pulled his head down to hers.

"I won't let you shut me out, Jason Seaton. My middle name isn't Persistence for nothing!"

She felt his lips turn up at the corners when she slanted her mouth across them, bumping his nose in the process. She gave a low groan of delight when the disparaging difference in their height was diminished by Jason lifting her in his arms until her toes barely touched the laces of his shoes. She could feel the long, hard muscles of his upper thighs and arms as he held her suspended from the floor.

He took control, parting her lips with effortless ease. She was no longer doing the kissing; she became the one being kissed.

Although completely pinned against him, she felt as though she was flying. Sensation upon sensation assaulted her, clouding her mind of everything but him. She could breathe him, smell the tangy scent of his expensive cologne, taste the strong, smoky flavor of his after-dinner liquor.

All too soon, she felt herself being lowered. Don't stop, she pleaded silently, afraid he'd step away from her and revert back to being cold and distant. She gasped when she felt herself settled astride Jason's leg. Slowly, he raised his knee so she was riding his muscular thigh. After each swirl of his tongue, the muscle in his leg rhythmically contracted. The intimacy of his being inside her while he touched her there, in her most private place, made her hot, wet.

Unlike any sound she'd heard him make, she heard a deep, guttural groan sigh through his lips as he peppered a trail of kisses over her high cheekbones, along her arched neck. His teeth worried her small earlobe as his hand crept from her waist up her ribs until it cupped her breast; his thumb circled her nipple, matching the circular motion the tip of his tongue made on the shell of her ear.

In her mind she visualized his mouth and hand trading places. The exquisite ache between her thighs intensified until she could barely catch her breath. She clutched his broad shoulders as though holding on for dear life.

"Faith," he murmured, again and again.

A passionate incantation? A plea? Inexperienced, Faith knew not what he wanted or what she was supposed to do.

It was over as quickly as it had begun——a firestorm of passion instantly dowsed by the icy waters of Jason's immense self-control.

She opened her eyes and found herself in the same wing chair where he'd held her on his lap, only alone and shaken to her inner core. Jason stood at the window, one hand on his hip and the other plowing through his hair.

"Jason?" Her lips quivered as they formed his name. No sound passed between her lips. Her throat worked hard; her mouth felt parched. She looked down at her lap. Her new skirt was tucked between her legs where his leg had been. The cotton fabric felt warm, limp, and slightly damp. Embarrassed, her cheeks flamed as she pulled it loose, curled her legs underneath her to ease the pulsating ache, and covered her knees. She'd done something wrong. She must have. She always did. But, Lord have mercy, she didn't know what. "Jason?"

"Be quiet for a minute," he hissed softly through clenched teeth.

Jason despised his own weakness. He couldn't talk, not with his penis hard as a flagpole, or walk with what felt like boulders between his legs. She'd incapacitated him.

He'd meant to kiss her, to teach her a lesson she'd never forget so she wouldn't ask another man to kiss her, but that too had backfired. The honeyed sweetness of her mouth had been a strong aphrodisiac. One taste had stripped him of his original intentions. He'd wanted her, badly. Five minutes more and they'd have been on the floor, rutting like the animals on her farm.

She trusted him, called him her mentor, and he'd come damned close to violating her faith. Only when he'd spoken her name did a remote inkling of decency ravage through the passion coursing through his body.

He'd been able to stop, this time. He damned sure wasn't going to give his libido another opportunity.

Deciding it was better for her to hate him, than for him to hate himself, he said, "That's the end of lesson one. You'd better run along up to bed."

Faith's hands knotted. The harshness in his voice validated her theory that she'd done something bad. An assertive sophisticated woman, like Caroline, would make light of the awkward situation while demanding answers to the questions buzzing around in her mind.

"Care to tuck me in and read me a bedtime story?" she quipped, injecting a sassy note in her voice that cost a heaping tablespoon of courage.

It irked Jason. Minutes had withered his major problem, but his intestines still felt as though the big one was trying to devour the small one. He glanced at Faith. She missed her calling by majoring in math, he decided irritably. Sitting there, all wide-eyed and serene, with her hands folded demurely on her lap, she'd have made the perfect model for some demure feminine hygiene product. It was maddening.

Jason Seaton never got mad; he got even. He crossed to the bookshelves, dropped to his haunches, and thumbed through the stack of children's books. He passed over *Cinderella, Peter Pan,* and *Beauty and the Beast.* Finding a story suitable for their situation, he strode to the chair where Faith sat and handed it to her.

"You'd do well to set aside the magazines Caroline bought and start from the beginning."

Faith glimpsed at the cover. Unable to conceal her amusement, she grinned up at him. *"The Gingerbread Man?"*

"Uh-huh. It's the story of a sweet treat that wanted to cross the river on the back of a fox."

Faith knew the story well. "Am I the fox or the gingerbread boy?"

"I'd think that's obvious," he replied coldly. "I was the one nibbling on your ear."

Faith curled her arms around the book. She gracefully got up from the chair, the way Caroline had taught her, swished her skirt to get rid of the wrinkles, the way she always did at the farm, and taking small steps, minced toward the door.

Rhetorically, she asked, "Was it the sweet treat or the fox who chanted, 'Run, run, as fast as you can. You can't catch me. I'm the Gingerbread Man?' "

"Are you implying I ran from you?" His face paled as the distinct possibility of having hoisted himself up on his own petard dawned on him. He flatly rejected that idea. "You're going to gobble me up?"

She flashed him a double row of pearly whites. "I'll drive my car to the bank tomorrow. Want a ride?"

Not waiting for a comeback, she made a hasty exit, closing the door behind her with a sharp snap. Her knees trembled as she took the stairs two at a time, but she felt as though she'd grown several inches taller during the past hour.

Jason could run away by being aloof with everyone else, but not with her.

Once inside her room, she bounced flat on the bed and grinned at the wily fox on the book's cover. She wouldn't chase Jason. Other women must have tried and failed. What she'd have to do is be clever. Like the clever fox, she'd have to bide her time and wait for Jason to need her.

She gave the fox a kiss, then placed the fairy-tale on the nightstand and picked up an issue of *New Woman*. She was beyond primers. She held the magazine by the cover and let it open. Her eyes lit with amusement as she read the title of the article: Making Choices—My Way.

Next time, with careful preparation, she vowed that she'd be the one doing the nibbling!

Seven

Early the next morning Jason's thoughts were on Faith as he touched the remote control to lift the garage door. He'd reflected on little else while he'd showered, shaved and eaten breakfast. His first impression of her had changed drastically. Although disinclined to accept the facts, he had to admit she wasn't the backward Ozark hillbilly he'd believed her to be.

The double-wide garage door gradually rose. His eyes narrowed in disdain when he noted the empty space beside his Mercedes. His father could have kept up appearances for more than a few days. With Caroline confiding her innermost secrets to Faith, that was pointless. Faith had learned more about the intimacies between Walter and Caroline in two days than he'd been told during their entire courtship.

That exasperated Jason. Walter hadn't confided in him. He couldn't imagine why Caroline would blab nonstop to Faith. His lips cracked a small smile as he formed a hazy mental picture of Faith seated in Caroline's fancy sports car, with her mouth agape in horrified shock.

Much as he liked that image, it remained slightly blurred. Caroline was too smart a woman to share confidences with an unsympathetic listener.

Somehow he had to get the first impression he had of Faith out of his head!

Dammit, he relied on quick character assessments. On a daily basis he determined who got what loan for what amount using his instincts. He simply could not get his first impression of Faith out of his head. He'd vastly underestimated her.

Yes, his Uncle Jon had isolated her, but he'd remained true to his belief that education was important. She had earned a college degree. Truth be known, she was probably better read than any Seaton.

Yes, she'd arrived in out-dated clothes and smeared colored ink on her face as makeup. But, under Caroline's tutelage, Faith had quickly learned that when it came to cosmetics, less is better. Gertrude could use a few lessons from Faith, he mused, recalling the lime green eye-shadow and coral-colored lipstick he'd seen when she delivered his breakfast tray. It was enough to make a strong man lose his appetite.

He unlocked the car door, placed his briefcase behind the driver's seat, and slid in behind the steering column.

In contrast to any women he'd met, with or without makeup, Faith was the only one who had caused a gnawing, unappeased hunger deep inside him. She might look like the stereotype of a not-so-bright blonde, but those bouncy blond curls and doelike eyes were nature's disguise for a sharp-witted woman who could outfox him.

Although disinclined to change his first impression of her, he had no choice. Furthermore, he had to accept that once she completely adapted, both culturally and socially, she could be either a formidable foe or an awesome ally.

As her mentor, he could guide her footsteps in the direction he wanted her to go——if he could stifle his libido.

And hers. She was as innocent as a new-born babe, and yet, she'd responded to him like a sex kitten testing her claws.

Jason grimaced. He had to keep his wits about him whenever he was around her. Absolute, stringent control was essential. Last night he'd let her provoke him. In the future, he would not let her arouse his temper or his male hormones.

With that goal firmly implanted in his mind, Jason twisted the key in the ignition. No purr of the engine. No grinding of the starter. Nothing. Not mechanically inclined, he pumped the gas petal and tried again. Only the keys jangling broke the silence.

Irritated, Jason glanced at his watch as he jerked the key ring from the ignition. The bank wouldn't open for another fifty-seven minutes, he calculated silently. Luke Cassidy would have to unlock the bank for the employees. Since Luke had never missed a day of work in ten years, that wasn't a problem.

Damn, he hated having his routine broken.

As he climbed from the car and strode from the garage, he had the urge to kick the back tire in retribution for making him late. Being a person who weighed the consequences of his actions before making a move, and being an impeccable dresser who did not want a black tire mark on the toe of his polished shoes, he resisted the urge and chided, "Temper, temper."

Briskly, he stalked to the back door. He had two options: call a cab or hitch a ride with Faith. He'd have to wait for a cab. Jason scowled. The Studebaker was in the driveway. Why not take Faith up on her offer?

Unexpectedly, his scowl inverted into a grin. His Bible-packing guest probably loved tales with morals at the end. Earthy as the man who raised her, she'd be delighted to know that he was up Shit Creek—begging for a friendly vixen to paddle him up stream.

Faith sat at the small table in her room and suspiciously eyed the breakfast tray Mrs. Cavendish had delivered. She picked up the sizzled edge of the egg white with the tines of her fork. Cold grease sluggishly dripped off the hard, orange yolk. Rather than eating it, she considered substituting it for a Frisbee, one like she'd seen the teenagers throwing in the park. Her misgivings about the grits were confirmed when she dropped her fork, egg and all, and stuck her finger into the starchy mush. Withdrawing her finger she checked for frostbite. She glared at the large glass of fruit juice. By the color alone, she knew it had been squeezed from prunes. Drink it, and she'd spend the day in the solitude of her bathroom.

Mrs. Cavendish is still peeved, she deduced silently. Maybe that word belittled how the cook felt. Someone who was miffed would not take the time to remove the raisins from the toast, leaving disgusting brown pockmarks in the bread.

Pissed. That's the word Papa Jon would have chosen. It would have been far more accurate.

Faith sighed. Walter had told her to make herself at home, which she hoped gave her kitchen privileges. If not, the odds of getting caught while making midnight

forays into the kitchen in search of plain fruit and vegetables were against her. All hell would break loose if
Gertrude caught someone sneaking around in her domain, raiding the ice box and pilfering from the pantry.

She had to make amends or starve.

Stomach growling, she crossed the room to the dresser
where she removed a small package from the top drawer.
Caroline had laughed uproariously when she'd asked for
help choosing eye shadow for Mrs. Cavendish. After
she'd selected several hideous shades of pink, purple and
green, Caroline sobered up long enough to recommend
a pale blue-grey shadow guaranteed to soften the malicious gleam in Gertrude's eyes.

As she deposited the gift on the tray, Faith hoped and
prayed she wouldn't have to return it unopened. Her
sweet temperament became testy when her blood-sugar
count dropped. It just wouldn't do to have two crabby
women occupying the same house, fussing at each other.
Walter might want her to stay, but Jason would help Gertrude pack her sacks.

"Faith?"

She jumped at the sound of Jason's voice. So help me
Hannah, she derided silently, I'll never get used to that
squawk box.

"Yes, Jason?"

"Are you dressed?"

Faith shot a wary glance at the three-inch heels that
matched her suit. She'd nearly broken her ankles pacing
in them so she wouldn't get blisters. "All except for my
shoes."

"Can I get a ride with you to the bank?"

Had it taken him all night to think up a riposte to her

exit line? She doubted it. Checking to make certain, she said, "My Studebaker isn't amphibious. Will we be crossing any streams?"

"Streams of rush-hour traffic unless you get a move on it," he retorted glibly.

"I'll be right down."

Grabbing her shoes and purse and tucking them under her arm, she rushed from the bedroom, down the steps. Grim-faced, Jason stood in the foyer waiting for her.

"I'll drive," he volunteered. He held the front door open for her. "I know the shortcuts."

"You'll have to get in on the passenger's side," she warned.

Jason gave her a puzzled look. "Something's wrong . . ." Before she could explain the car's quirks, he'd pushed against the frame of the door while pressing his thumb firmly on the button beneath the handle. It opened as easily as it had the day it rolled off the assembly line. "You fixed it! Thanks! I don't know how I'd have crawled across the stick shift wearing this get-up."

Her hand drew his attention to the small slit at the back of her above-the-knee-length linen skirt. He avoided directly looking at her until now. Shapely legs, he thought, cursing himself for staring at her while she slipped her tiny feet into high heels that perfectly matched the burgundy color of her linen suit. The fabric molded against her backside to reveal the elastic of her garter belt.

There is no valid reason for a garter belt to excite a man, he scolded, feeling his blood rush to his loins. It's only a stretchy piece of lace that holds up her sheer nylons. Valid or invalid, reasonable or irrational, his mind could not convince his heart to stop beating like a freight train.

"Get in," he growled, moving his bench seat back to accommodate his long legs. "Before you shred your hose. I don't have time to wait for you to change."

Gingerly, just as Caroline had taught her, she sat on the cushion and swung her legs inside the car, knees together. It would have been perfectly executed, if her skirt hadn't bunched up around her thighs.

Jason groaned silently. A peek-a-boo sliver of her black lace garter exposed itself. She arched upward, shimmied her skirt down, and plopped back in the seat. Automatically her hand brushed a wisp of golden curls back from her face.

"Ready," she chirped, happy to start her new adventure with Jason beside her.

Air hissed between his teeth as he watched her wiggle and squirm. The freight train would jump its tracks if he didn't regain control soon.

"You look great. Are you going to continue to primp or can I have the car keys?"

Contrite, Faith scrambled to open her purse. "I'm a little excited."

"Me, too," he admitted drily.

"Have you decided what you want me to do?"

He had several things he wanted her to do. None of them related to banking. It had been a decade since he'd made out in a car, but he'd have liked to reverse that trend.

"Yes."

He took the key that dangled from a hand-carved wooden key chain. His thumb caressed the smooth surface for a second before he stuck the key into the ignition. The ancient engine started without a whimper. He adjusted the rear-view mirror, then reached for the lever to put the car in gear. When he couldn't spot a gear selector, he realized the car lacked an automatic transmission. Never having driven a stick shift, he was totally at a loss as to how to get the decrepit vehicle moving.

"You drive."

"Why? I thought you were in a big hurry to get there."

Jason momentarily considered lying to protect his male pride and rejected it as unworthy of him. "My cars have always had an automatic transmission."

"No problem. I'll teach you the same way Papa Jon taught me." She scooted across the bench seat, put her left arm across his shoulders, and her right hand on the gear shift. "Put your foot on the brake pedal and release the hand brake. When I say 'now,' push the clutch halfway to the floor and press on the gas."

He felt her thigh against his and the fullness of her breast teasing his jacket sleeve before the fragrance of white gardenias enveloped him. One or the other he could have managed—not all three—not and comprehend her instructions.

"Now!"

Brake pedal, clutch, goose the gas.

The car bucked forward, then stalled.

"You forgot the emergency brake." Faith released it. The car began to roll backward. "Stop! Brake it."

Valiantly trying to concentrate, his knuckles turned white from his hold on the wheel. "I can do this," he snapped.

"Now?"

"Now," he snarled, determined to vanquish the heady effect having her plastered against him caused. This reminded him of Uncle Jon teaching him how to rub his stomach, pat his head and chew gum, in synchronization with the drum beat of "Jailhouse Rock!" Yes, yessss . . .

"You're getting it."

"No power steering?" he complained loudly. Jason wrestled with the steering wheel. As he crossed two lanes of traffic, he dared the oncoming drivers to hit him. The venomous glare he gave a truck driver made the man's erect middle finger wither into the palm of his hand.

"Clutch. I'm putting it into second. Now! Ooooops." The Studebaker lurched as Jason applied both feet to the pedals. "No brake. Don't let it stall. Gently . . . gently. Ready? Shifting into third. Now!"

Southern Bank was less than five miles from the Seaton mansion; it seemed like five hundred to Jason. By the time he reach their destination, with Faith sweetly murmuring encouragement into his ear, sweat drenched his shirt.

"That wasn't hard, was it?" Faith asked, rewarding him with a quick hug and a kiss on the cheek.

The engine was off, but adrenaline pumped through his veins. He felt the same exhilaration a runner feels after completing a marathon race. Before he walked into the bank he had to calm down. He closed his eyes and inhaled a deep breath through his nostrils. They popped open as thoughts of gardenias, silky legs, and rounded breasts imprinted themselves on his mind. He dropped the keys in her hand, glad to be rid of them.

"It drives like a Sherman tank," he droned blandly, resuming his iron-clad control.

"On the way home, I'll teach you how to shift," she promised.

"Glen should have my car here by then." No way was he going to go through the torture of driving her car with her nudging his arm and leg. As they both got out of the car, he said, "You need to sell this and buy a new car."

"Sell Betsy? Why? Nothing is wrong with her."

"She's a menace on the roads."

Jason buttoned his jacket and automatically reached toward the back seat for his briefcase. It was in his car. He never forgot the smallest detail. How could carrying his briefcase have slipped from his mind?

Irrationally, he shot Faith an accusatory glare. This was her fault. If he hadn't been so preoccupied with her this wouldn't have happened.

Unwilling to let her know he'd turned into an absent-minded idiot, he strode toward the bank entrance, forgetting his manners, too.

Quickly, Faith trailed in his wake. She had to hike her skirt and lengthen her stride, but what she had to ask before they entered the bank was more important to her than proper decorum.

"Jason, I have a favor to ask."

A grim smile curved his mouth as he narrowed his steps. She wanted preferential treatment. He'd been expecting her to ask him to take it easy on her since they'd had that discussion with Walter about how he'd started out in the business.

"I don't want anyone to know who I am," she declared breathlessly.

Jason stopped in his tracks, swiveled at the waist and stared at her.

"You know, that I'm sort of part of the family," she stammered. Her voice lilted upward as though she asked a question instead of making a declaration. "I mean, I'm not a Seaton . . . well, not a blood relative and all . . . and if you introduce me as one of the owners . . . uh, they'd treat me like a boss . . . which I'm not."

She was babbling like a brook after a spring rain, but could not dam the flow of words. His glowering down at her wasn't helping any.

"You want to be treated like someone just hired? No special privileges?"

Her head bobbed; her curls sprung up and down in a bewitching manner. Her eyes were as round as the large buttons down the front of her suit. "I don't want them to think I could get them fired or anything."

"Just plain Faith Jones?"

Jason had all he could do to keep from rubbing his hands together in glee. While masses of women complained about banging their heads on glass ceilings, Faith begged to be relegated to the basement. He didn't have to be concerned with her wanting to share his office, or his power. Her request made him want to jump for joy and click his heels!

Years of training allowed him to contain his elation. He gave her a thoughtful look, as though considering her preposterous suggestion seriously, and hesitated before he said, "If that's what you really want."

"It is."

"In that case, wait here a few minutes before you come inside. I'll tell Luke Cassidy, the head teller, that I've hired a friend of a friend and we'll let him decide where you should begin your training program." Like the moon,

Jason reflected her sunny smile. "I hope you have a good day."

"I will! In a few minutes, I'll go in and ask for Mr. Cassidy."

"Don't mention your degree in math. You'd be over-qualified," he warned.

Again, her hair danced around her smiling face. "I won't." She was hesitant an instant before adding, "I'd better call you Mr. Seaton, hadn't I?"

"The other employees do," Jason agreed.

"And I shouldn't tell anyone I live with you?"

"Definitely not." A stirring in his loins caused by thoughts of her being his mistress had to be squashed. Resuming his walk, over his shoulder, he said, "I'm late."

"Thanks," Faith called. "I'll be the best employee you've ever hired."

And eager to quit, Jason prophesied with a genuine smile. She wouldn't be the first woman Luke had driven crazy with his picky attitude. This was working out better than he'd planned. Walter wouldn't be able to say a word of recrimination against him when Faith decided she hated working for Luke and packed up her belongings.

Just as Luke unlocked the door, Jason felt a sharp pain in his chest. His brilliant smile faded as he attributed his discomfort to Gertrude's fried eggs.

"Good morning, sir," Luke greeted cheerfully.

Jason noted his pointed glance at the clock behind the teller's cages, and the quizzical expression of his face as he glanced at Jason's empty hand. Yes, he was later than usual and his briefcase was missing, but he wasn't going to explain his extraordinary behavior to Luke.

"Morning," he briskly responded. Back in character

and feeling better, he added casually, "I hired a new employee. Her name is Faith something or another. She should arrive shortly."

Luke locked the door and shoved the shiny key into his pocket. "Who'd you fire?"

"Nobody."

Jason heard the loose change jingling in Luke's pocket and suppressed a grin. Did Luke think he'd hired his replacement? The unfamiliar urge to give Luke a reassuring pat on the back made Jason scowl. It was good for an employee to know they were irreplaceable, even if they were.

To keep pace with his boss, Luke had to pick up speed with a skip and a hop. "What do you want me to do with her?"

"Train her to be a summer vacation replacement."

"She's a temporary?"

"That depends on her . . . performance," Jason quickly tacked on. "I expect you to make certain she's diligent. I hired her, but if she doesn't work out, you can fire her."

The way Luke straightened his shoulders and stopped his infernal loping assured Jason that by delegating an ounce of authority, he had a tyrant in the making.

"No special treatment," he added for good measure.

"Yes, sir! You can count on me."

"I knew I could. Now, if you'll excuse me, I have work to do," Jason droned, implying Luke had better things to do than follow him around.

"Yes, sir. I was just on my way to . . ."

"Later."

Jason closed his office door before Luke could rattle off his litany of responsibilities. He sat behind his desk, wanting to spin the chair around in triumph. With Luke as her mentor, Faith wouldn't last a week. Then everything would be back to normal. God bless the status quo!

Outside, Faith said a quick prayer of gratitude. Throughout the night she'd hardly slept a wink because she'd been worried about not fitting in at the bank. It stood to reason that nobody would appreciate someone who'd only been in a financial institution once in their life—being part of management. Jason had been a sweetheart to keep their secret.

He is a sweetheart, she mused. Thoughtful, kind, protective. Although Caroline had drawn her a map of how to get to Southern Bank, Jason must have realized the morning traffic would have scared the be-Jesus out of her and come to her rescue. His male pride wouldn't bend far enough to ask her to ride with him, not after last night. So, he'd come up with a convenient excuse: car trouble.

Faith's stick shift gave her the excuse she needed to sit next to Jason. She grinned, wondering if Jason really didn't know how to work a clutch. For someone who'd been driving a tractor since her legs had grown long enough to reach the pedals, that possibility seemed unfathomable. He'd wanted her near him to quiet her anxieties.

She took great comfort in knowing Jason wanted her with him, closer than propriety allowed. His going along with her idea of letting her be just a new bank employee strengthened her fledgling love for him.

She'd known from first glance that Jason was the right man for her, but was she the right woman for him?

As she stood outside gazing through the bronzed windows, searching for a glimpse of Jason, she compared Jason's actions with Jonathan's definition of the simple, four-letter word.

"Love always protects, always trusts, always hopes, always perseveres."

Jason does protect me, she mused. He trusts me enough to want me at the bank when he could have left me at home. She recalled his smile when he hoped she'd have a good day. The last qualifier, "perseveres," couldn't be put to the test. Only time would reveal Jason's eternal devotion to her.

Faith gloated, "Three out of four ain't bad, Jonathan!"

Confident Jason had begun to share her feelings, she gave the back of her hair a little fluff, tugged at the hem of her jacket, and lifted her chin. She had three weeks until the Fourth of July coming-out party that Caroline and Walter planned. By then, she'd make Jason proud of the woman he loved, or die trying.

And maybe, just maybe, she thought, as she ambled up the sidewalk and pushed against the locked door, Walter will convince Caroline to marry him, and Jason will ask me to marry him. All she had to do was have . . .

"Faith?" Luke Cassidy asked as he unlocked the door.

Eight

"You want that big bag of dimes in these little green tubes," Faith said, carefully repeating Luke's instructions. She pointed to the other white cloth sacks stamped Federal Reserve. "Forty quarters in the orange tubes, fifty dimes in the green tubes, twenty nickels in the grey tubes, and fifty pennies in the purple ones. If any bags are missing coins, I'm to notify you immediately."

"Correct. Adjust the counter on the machine, run the change through it, wrap them, crimp the ends and stack them in the trays neatly."

Faith had noticed how meticulous Luke had been as his thumb had folded the ends and filled the aluminum tray. "With the printing straight up."

"Exactly." Luke moved from the chair in front of the coin counter as he wiped his hands on his handkerchief. "The teller needs to be able to see at a glance which tray holds what coins."

They'd have to be color-blind not to know, Faith thought silently, but she wasn't going to point that detail out to Mr. Cassidy. With a sharp nod, she moved into the chair he'd vacated.

Tall and thin as a rail, with reddish-brown hair and a predominant Adam's apple, the head teller reminded

Faith of a starving mongrel she'd found abandoned by the side of the highway. Whimsically, she'd named the cowering pup Ogre, to give him courage. Ogre had snarled and snapped when she'd tried to help him, but he'd grown up to be a faithful friend.

For a second, she felt homesick. Ogre had a good home with the people down the road where he'd romped and played with their dogs. She'd seen to that, but Lordy, she missed him.

She looked up at the man towering over her.

The name fit her boss.

He should have called cadence as he marched her through the bank, pausing only long enough to make quick introductions. She would have liked to linger long enough to place names with faces, but Mr. Cassidy had hustled her along as though he had an earth-shaking job for her to accomplish, one that only she could do.

"When you've finished with the coins, I'll show you how to strap the bills." Luke folded his hanky at the ironed creases and returned it to his back pocket. "Any questions?"

"No, sir." Faith gave him a cheeky smile, which was not returned. She shoved a green wrapper into the bottom of the machine and flipped on the motor. Her quirky sense of humor would not allow her to let him depart without cracking a smile. Loudly, she announced, "You can't have my first-born."

"I beg your pardon?" Luke pulled down on his earlobe as though by doing so he could block out the noise of rattling coins. "What did you say?"

"I said that you can't have my first-born child. I can magically change silver into rolls of paper, and I can guess your name." She beamed her most beguiling smile up at him. "Sam, short for Samson? As in Samson and Delila?"

Luke raked his fingers through his thinning hair. "Wrong."

"It isn't your hair I was thinking of," Faith quickly said to correct his assumption that she might want to trim his locks. "It's your inner strength. The way you seem to be a pillar of knowledge that everyone here depends on. The whole bank would probably collapse without you."

A ghost of a smile haunted his lips. "My first name is . . ."

"No! Don't tell me. You'll ruin the ending of the story."

Before he nodded, for a fraction of a moment, Faith saw his rust-colored eyes light up. Her suspicion that Mr. Cassidy wasn't a pillar made of stone was confirmed when he gave her a pat on the back and said, "No fair asking the other employees."

"I won't," she promised.

As Mr. Cassidy left the small, windowless room, she raked a pile of silver coins into the counter. Mesmerized by the steady rotation of coins, she began daydreaming, wondering what Jason was doing. The dimes promptly slid through the holder, into her lap, then scattered on the floor. Grateful her boss had left the room, she began picking them up.

Several minutes later, that was how Jason found her, down on her knees in front of the money sacks. He smiled. If Walter had thought of it when he'd brought him to the bank as a child, he'd have had him on his knees worshiping the almighty dollar.

He'd studiously avoided her, not knowing or wanting to know what scut job Luke had given her. He'd still be in his office sorting through loan applications if Phyllis Lawton hadn't stopped by, searching for Luke. She needed a tray of quarters. Luke had disappeared with the new girl and Phyllis said she couldn't find either one of them.

A licentious picture of Luke sexually harassing Faith propelled Jason from behind his desk. He knew it was ridiculous, absolutely asinine, but when he couldn't blink the image from his mind, he decided the only decent thing to do would be to check on Faith's welfare.

"What are you doing?" Jason straightened his face as he leaned against the doorjamb, crossing his ankles.

"I lost two dimes. There is only four-hundred-ninety-nine dollars and eighty cents from that sack. I've counted them twice."

She looked so woebegone Jason was tempted to empty his pockets to make up the shortage. His lips thinned. That thought was foolish; more importantly, it was illegal. Cash was not deposited and withdrawn to make the teller's books balance.

"Sometimes coins stick together."

"I dropped them," she confessed, truly miserable. Observing the tautness of his lips, she knew he was displeased with her. She crawled under the table to search one more time. "They have to be here somewhere. I'll find them if it takes all day!"

With a bird's-eye view, Jason watched gravity take its toll on the V neckline of her prissy suit jacket. Her lacy bra matched the black garter belt. She pivoted on her knees, and continued crawling around the circumference of the table. Her hips swayed. As she stretched, a long expanse of silk-clad calf and thigh caught his eye. The hook came undone of its own accord.

A strong impulse to kiss the vulnerable crease behind her knee sent a shaft of bubbling excitement through him.

"Get up," he ordered, his voice deep and gravelly from his instant arousal.

"Wait a minute." Faith spied a dime caught between the tile and the baseboard. She held up the thin dime as though she'd found the prize egg in an Easter egg hunt. "Yes! One down, one to go!"

His exact thought when her garter came unsnapped, Jason groaned silently. Is she a damned mind reader to boot? Sanely, he realized she wouldn't be sashaying her curvaceous little body on the floor at his feet if she could.

"Get off the floor, Miss Jones." He strode to the table where she worked and made a notation on the Federal Reserve sheet. "You won't be prosecuted for embezzlement if a coin is lost."

He was mad; she couldn't blame him.

"Cassidy should have . . ."

"It wasn't his fault," Faith interrupted, jackknifing gracefully to her feet. Her ankles wobbled, as did her voice. She had no excuse for her carelessness; she'd been daydreaming about Jason when she should have been concentrating on her job. "He showed me how to do it. I didn't insert my finger in the hole the way he did. It's a simple job, once you get the hang of it."

Scowling, Jason watched her demonstrate her proficiency. She emptied the partially filled wrapper into the turnstile, flicked on the motor and seconds later pointed to the counter. "Fifty? There should only be forty-nine. Where did the other dime come from?"

Raising his empty hands, Jason said, "Don't look at me."

"You did put one of your dimes in there, didn't you?" she accused sweetly. "Why didn't I think of that?"

"Because the bank examiners would frown on it? Bankers follow strict rules." Those brown eyes of hers stared at him as though he'd just hung the moon and set the stars. He hadn't done either, or put the damned dime in the tray. "Co-mingling your money with the bank money would get you in big trouble. Understand?"

Deciding there was a proper time to be assertive and a proper time to be submissive, Faith silenced her quest for the truth. He could talk till he was blue in the face and gasping for air, but no matter what Jason said or did, he wouldn't be able to convince her that he hadn't rescued her from having to tell the Ogre she'd lost a dime.

Jason drew a line through the ten cent shortage he'd recorded. "If you're over or under, just put it on the sheet."

"Yes, Mr. Seaton," she replied, respectfully using his last name.

From behind them, Luke Cassidy asked, "Is there a problem, sir? Phyllis said you were looking for me."

"Actually, she was looking for you." Jason stepped back from where Faith worked. "She needs quarters."

"Give her a bag of mine," Faith offered, wanting to be helpful.

"Those aren't counted or wrapped. What if there are quarters missing?"

Her eyes moved from Mr. Cassidy, who appeared thoroughly appalled by her suggestion, to Jason. His face was cold and remote as his eyes watched the Ogre. "Can't she borrow my sheet?"

"No," Jason replied.

"Well, there's more than one way to skin a cat. Have Phyllis give the customer two dimes and a nickel."

Luke rolled his eyes and conferred a did-you-hear-what-she-said look at his boss. Jason shrugged off his silent complaint.

"I'll get Phyllis a tray from my cage." To Faith he directed in a voice that dripped icicles, "Do the quarters next. I'll initial the sheet when you're finished."

After Luke hastily departed, Faith asked, "What's wrong with two dimes and a nickel?"

"Nothing. Phyllis handles the commercial customers. They buy rolls of change from her to use in their cash registers."

That made sense, but it shouldn't have caused the look of abject horror on his face. "Then why'd he look as though I'd poked him in the rump with a cattle prod?"

Jason grinned and ski-sloped his finger down her nose. "I wouldn't mention skinning a cat in front of him. He's an animal protectionist."

"A what?" His smile always left her a little fuzzy around the edges. Her heart pounded in her ears from his slightest touch. "What is an animal perfectionist?"

"Protectionist."

"Okay. Animal protectionist."

"He believes animals have constitutional rights, like people. Walter has had to bail Cassidy out of jail a couple of times for illegally demonstrating against a meat-packing house."

The Ogre love animals? Faith mulled that foreign concept in her mind while Jason strolled toward the door. She didn't want him to leave, not yet. This was how she'd imagined the two of them at the bank. Her asking questions. Him answering them. She didn't expect him to roll up his sleeves and get his hands dirty counting coins, but she would like him to stay a while longer.

"Jason?"

"Yes?"

When he turned around, Faith noticed that his no-nonsense facial mask was back in place. "Thanks."

"For what?"

"Dropping by to see how I'm doing."

Jason felt a twinge of guilt. "Don't give credit where it isn't due."

By Thursday, Jason was sick of watching a steady stream of employees troop down the steps to the cubbyhole Faith occupied. Phyllis Lawton, a queen-sized woman who hated getting off her stool to go to the ladies' room, must have lost ten pounds due to stair-stepping. Faith alternated her gab sessions with the other tellers, Jillian Hopkins and Anita Polk, too. Kristen Riley and Shannon Thompson, who were responsible for new accounts and handling the safety deposit box customers, spent more time in the vault than at their desks. Even Joe Bradbury, the crotchety janitor, started his afternoon shift by mopping the basement level.

Jason wanted to fault their job performance, but damned if several customers hadn't stopped by his office to credit him with the changes in their attitudes. "Snooty," that was

the adjective one loan applicant had used to describe
Southern Bank's employees. He hadn't argued. The middle-aged waitress had made daily deposits into her savings
account at Southern for years, and yet, she'd financed her
car through the dealership where she'd bought it. She readily admitted that the interest rates were too high, but she
was afraid Southern would repossess her vehicle if she
went past the grace period. But recently, she'd noticed a
change. Everyone seemed friendlier, happy to see her.
She'd decided to give Southern her loan business.

After he'd approved her loan, she'd become a walk-
ing/talking goodwill ambassador. Everyone who commented on her sporty convertible received a glowing report
on Southern Bank, which resulted in her listeners showing
up in front of his desk wanting a loan application.

In one week, word-of-mouth advertisement by the
waitress and her customers had outperformed the glitzy
television commercials that Southern paid a fortune to
have aired. Everyone on Grand Avenue suddenly needed
a loan.

It mystified Jason.

And buried him in paperwork.

When he looked up from the credit report he'd been
attempting to evaluate, he saw his assistant, Mary Chambers, tiptoeing from the steps toward her desk. She carried a large cardboard box. Jason could have tolerated
her taking a coffee break, if he hadn't seen a huge smile
on the dragon-slayer's face.

Damn it to hell, he wanted a formidable business-
woman outside his office!

He pushed the intercom button. "Mary, I asked for the
file on Daisy Chain Florist. Where is it?"

"It had been filed downstairs in the archives, Mr. Seaton. It took a while to locate it. I'll bring it right in."

Impatiently, Jason strummed his fingers while he waited. The file should have been on his desk in two seconds flat. What was taking her so long? Through the wall of windows that separated her desk from his, he could see her yo-yoing up and down between her top drawer and the box.

"Mary." He strung her name into three separate vowels. "I need those papers today if that's convenient for you."

"Yes, sir. I'll be right in." Jason wasn't certain, but after she lifted her finger from the call box, he thought he heard, "Hang on to your britches, farm boy. You're breaking wind, not water."

There was only one place Mary could have heard that expression, he fumed. Faith had corrupted his Bostonian secretary with one of his Uncle Jon's favorite expressions.

"Did you say something?" he drilled as Mary entered his office with a file folder under her arm, a cup of coffee in one hand, and a shoe box in the other.

She sheepishly smiled and placed the steaming mug in front of him.

"What is this?"

Jason scowled at the cartoon on the cup, of a man with his feet on his desk, with a stack of papers strewn around him. The caption read, "I must be rich. I owe everybody money." That wasn't funny; it was a banker's nightmare.

"Coffee," Mary replied, "with just a hint of chicory in the blend. Faith brewed it especially for us because she says we've been overworked lately." She put the box beside the cup and lifted the lid. "Dunkers, from the Donut Factory that moved into the vacant store down the street. Phyllis brought them."

Jason refrained from touching the cup or the contents of the box. "The day Walter hired you, you informed him that serving coffee would not be part of your job description," he reminded her.

"That was fifteen years ago. A woman can change her mind, can't she?"

Jason eyed her warily.

"I knew a hot cup of coffee would perk me up. And I could tell you were stressed out, so I brought you one, too. Faith says the whole world would be happier if we all followed the golden rule."

"He who has the gold maketh the rules?" Jason responded drily.

Mary chuckled. Jason glared at her as though she was the original serpent in Faith's favorite book.

"Do unto others . . ."

"Excuse me, but I'm too busy for a philosophical discussion." He picked up the file folder and began leafing through the pages. "Tell Cassidy I want to see him. Immediately, if not sooner."

"You want to personally thank him for helping Faith pick out the plants, don't you?" she hinted broadly.

Jason looked in the direction where Mary pointed. On both sides of the walnut credenza were tall, broad-leaved plants. In the corner to the right of his desk was a ficus tree. He hadn't noticed any of them.

"I suppose Faith had something to say about this?"

Nodding, Mary said, "Aside from their aesthetic value, plants are Mother Nature's best air filters."

"Thank you for the Botany 101 lesson, Miss Chambers." He levered his chair back from his desk and stood. "Don't bother locating Cassidy. I'll find him myself."

Jason stalked from his office straight to the steps. His instincts proved perfectly in tune when he heard laughter floating up from the basement.

"We don't call him that to his face," Kristen injected between fits of giggles. "He wouldn't like that any better than he'd like us calling him Junior."

Luke, who'd been sitting on the corner of the table, rolled to his feet and crossed to the coffee urn where Faith stood. "Or Jason. Heaven forbid we be on a first-name basis around here. It took you ten guesses before you started using my first name."

Both Faith and Luke had their backs to the door. Only Kristen saw Jason. The scowl on his face would curdle buttermilk.

"I guess technically Jason is an s.o.b.," Faith conceded. "But he's a sweet s.o.b." She gave Luke a cup of coffee to take with him, then noticed the horrified, gagging motion Kristen made. Softly, barely above a whisper, she added, "He's standing right behind me, isn't he?"

Luke visibly paled. Kristen sprang to her feet to make her escape, but Jason blocked the door.

"The employees' lounge is upstairs," Jason crooned in a lethal voice. "Is this the annex?"

"Mr. Seaton, Senior, okayed the coffeepot," Luke declared with self-righteous indignation.

Luke's hand shook so hard coffee spilled over the cup's rim, scalding his hand; but Faith was proud of his show of bravery. While she dabbed at his hand, Jason moved into the room and Kristen made a hasty retreat by slipping through the door behind him.

"There's no drinking fountain down here," Faith explained calmly.

"There are two upstairs, located by the exits." His blue eyes appeared hard as flint, shooting sparks at Faith. "Mr. Cassidy, why don't you see if they are in good working order. *Now.*"

"Yes, sir." His face crumpled as he gave Faith a sympathetic look, then pivoted and rushed out of the room. "Right away."

Faith wadded the paper napkin in her hand and tossed it at Jason. "Shame on you!"

"Shame on me?" Jason repeated, somewhat aghast that she dared to reprimand him. He fielded the wad of paper in midair. "You're down here undermining my authority, and it's shame on me?"

"They're scared to death of you."

"That's why you agreed with them when they called me an s.o.b.?"

Faith grinned. She knew she'd made a mistake when the paper pelted off the lapel of her loden green suit. He slowly advanced, like a sleek cat playing with a ball of yarn.

"You are one," she said, not backing up an inch. The toes of his wing-tipped shoes touched the toe of her stiletto heels before he stopped. With the three-inch advantage the heels gave her, she barely had to tilt her head back when she grinned up at him and said, "S.O.B., Son of the Boss."

She thought her explanation would cause his lips to

quirk up at the corners. He wasn't amused; there were no laugh creases beside his eyes.

"The boss has no children."

"Uncle . . ." Her hand flew to her mouth as she realized giving Uncle Walter the title of boss insulted Jason, worse than calling him an s.o.b.!

"Yes?"

"Uncle . . . as in I give up?" she prevaricated, taking a step backward for breathing space.

"You never give up. You're subtle." With each statement he took a step forward. "Plants. Coffee."

"Don't forget the donuts," she said when her shoulders touched the wall.

A shiver of foreboding danced up her spine at the ominous look in his eyes as his fingers threaded through her hair. At the last second, before his lips covered hers, she saw a glint of amusement in his eyes.

It was a brief kiss, hardly more than a peck on the cheek. "What was that for?" she asked cautiously.

Jason saw her lick her lips. A trace of moisture left a slick, inviting trail across her mouth.

"The annex."

Reward or punishment? With his breath fanning her face and his fingertip massaging her scalp, she felt confused and overwhelmed.

"Are you mad?"

"Furious," he admitted, kissing her again, only taking his time about it to make damned sure she understood who was boss around here.

Her fingers stole around his neck, locking her lips to his when he would have ended the kiss.

"I'm moving you upstairs, where I can keep an eye on you."

"I didn't mean to start trouble," she said sincerely.

"I'm beginning to think you can't help it."

"I know," she sighed. Her forehead fell against his shoulder as naturally as summer rains drenched flowers. "Papa Jon called me a trouble magnet. He said I attracted it, like flies to road apples."

"Then I guess I'd better order a gross of fly swatters to keep trouble away from you, huh?"

Faith heard footsteps coming down the flight of stairs.

"Phyllis is coming," she warned, reluctantly squeezing out from between Jason and the wall. For days she'd anxiously listened for Jason's footsteps. Now, when he'd finally come to her, Phyllis intruded with the regimen of exercises Faith had written down to help her improve her health.

A person is supposed to reap what they sow, she complained silently. Must be bad seeds, she decided, pasting a polite smile on her face. Or I need to change my middle name from Persistence to Job!

"Hi, Faith. That's seventy-two steps today." Her hand flew to her ample chest when she saw Jason. "Mr. Seaton, uh, I came down to . . . uh, . . ." She tapped her temple with her finger. "Why did I come down here? I must have had a good reason."

"To get Faith?" Jason supplied briskly, glowering at the flustered woman. "To take her up and start training her on the teller machines?"

"No, Luke didn't mention that to me."

Faith grinned. Jason had rescued Phyllis by promoting her, and Phyllis was still searching for an excuse. She tucked her hand in the crook of the older woman's arm and said, "Isn't it wonderful? Mr. Cassidy taught me enough to work beside you!"

"Wonderful," Phyllis agreed. As they climbed the steps, with Jason following them, she huffed, "A promotion deserves a raise in salary."

"I'm happy just being allowed to work here," Faith replied truthfully. She was part of the family business. Family was more important to her than money.

Phyllis paused on the first landing to catch her breath, which allowed Jason to catch up with them.

"Employees are reviewed every six months for pay raises," he told Faith. "Personnel is Walter's department. I'll mention your change in status to him."

Sticking to her role as a new employee, Faith smiled and said politely, "Thank you, Mr. Seaton. I appreciate everything you've done for me."

It wasn't until after Jason had crossed the lobby to the drinking fountain where Luke stood, that Phyllis said, "To use one of your colloquialisms, don't count your chickens before they hatch. Scrooge Senior hasn't written an evaluation or given a pay raise in months."

"Is that his nickname? Scrooge?"

"It used to be." Phyllis nodded at Anita to press the button which unlocked the door leading to the tellers' stations. She chuckled. "Since he started medical treatment it's changed to Romeo."

Pretending not to know Caroline, but fearing Walter had a bad heart like Jonathan, she asked, "Does he have heart trouble?"

"Nope." Her eyes twinkled as she hoisted her fanny up on her stool. In a hushed voice, she said, "Male menopause. A friend of a friend of mine is his doctor's assistant. She told me . . ."

Faith listened carefully, her eyes growing round while Phyllis explained Walter's testosterone treatment and how it could cause a complete personality change. When she implied that the s.o.b. must have the same deficiency, Faith covered her mouth to stop from giggling out loud.

Jason did not need male hormones. She'd wager a month of her nonexistent salary on that fact!

Nine

Busier than a hungry goat in an aluminum-can factory, Faith mentally tallied the checks listed on the deposit slip for the Daisy Chain Florist. She surreptitiously watched the line in front of her window grow longer and longer. Jillian and Anita's lines were shorter, much shorter, but the wait didn't appear to bother Faith's regular customers. In one short week, she'd developed a rapport the other tellers were beginning to envy.

Faith liked people; in return, they liked her.

"Trade you a long-stemmed red rose for a bundle of twenties," Mr. Boone teased, presenting Faith with his half of the bargain.

Winking at the florist, Faith leaned across the counter. "How about me adding a couple of digits to your deposit? Would that make you happy?"

Phyllis, who stood immediately behind Faith watching to make certain she didn't make any mistakes, cleared her throat loudly.

"Ecstatic!"

He gladly relinquished the bloom and watched Faith add two zeros, *after* the decimal point. The number looked bigger, but the amount remained the same.

"Thank you for the rose." Faith slipped his gift in the

vase containing daisies, eucalyptus, and baby's breath. Each day he'd brought another species along with his daily deposit.

He pointed his deposit receipt at the card she'd made that had his store's name and address in her handwriting. "Business is blooming, thanks to you!"

"It's beginning to sound like the Mutual Admiration Society around here," Phyllis mumbled when the florist stepped aside. "Next."

"Morning, Faith." Ted Ross slid a grey plastic pouch across the marble counter. He continued his sales pitch to the petite woman next in line, a city councilwoman. "I submitted a bid for the bikes and racks."

"It didn't include unicycles or two-seaters," she protested.

"Nobody rides them. I can't rent what nobody rides."

"But the Historic Society's whole theme for the festival is to bring back the atmosphere of the World's Fair that was held in Forest Park at the turn of the century. Tourists will love it."

Ted shook his head and looked at Phyllis. "Would you rent a bicycle built for two?"

"Can't be worse than the exercycle you and Faith talked me into buying. It doesn't go anywhere," Phyllis groaned.

Not wanting to take sides with either customer, Faith smiled and kept counting his deposit.

"It's romantic," the councilwoman said. "Can't you picture Faith perched in front of her sweetheart, riding the bike trails?"

Faith's grin widened. Would Jason let her steer? Not if there were any thorn bushes in the vicinity. She turned the money with the dead presidents' faces in the same direction as she placed it in the cash drawer.

"Thank you for banking at Southern," Faith said politely, handing Mr. Ross his receipt. "Have a nice weekend."

"You take your usual twenty percent service charge?" he joked, putting the receipt in his bag.

"Only at the end of the month," she replied, wrinkling her nose at him.

Phyllis waited until the line had vanished before she put the Next Window sign in front of Faith. "Don't joke with the customers about free samples or service charges," she warned. "Luke would have a stroke and Young Mr. Seaton would fire you. As it is, he watches you like a hawk."

"Does he?" Faith put the arch of her heels on the chair rung, rose, and peeked over the counter. Doing two things at one time, he was speaking on the phone while making notes. "He's busy, as usual."

Day and night, she added silently. They lived in the same house, and yet she rarely saw him. He worked, day and night.

Phyllis smoothed down her dark paisley-print dress and dismounted from the stool. "Nothing goes on in this bank that he doesn't know about, before it happens. He was the first to notice Anita's engagement ring."

Jealousy mixed with her guilt feelings over talking about Jason behind his back. "So you think he wanted to date her?"

"Doubtful. I've never known him to date anyone who works at the bank."

"Ever?"

"Never." Phyllis shook her head emphatically. "Must

be a self-imposed restriction though. Kristen dated the law student who worked here part-time. Young Mr. Seaton didn't object to that."

"I could walk through the lobby naked, pushing a money cart and he wouldn't notice me," she said glumly.

"Uh-oh. Don't tell me you've got a crush on the s.o.b."

"Okay," Faith agreed with a melancholy smile. "I won't tell you."

"Do you?"

Faith nodded silently; Phyllis groaned aloud. "Why would someone like you fall for a guy like him?"

"He is everything a woman could want in a man."

"He's a workaholic," Phyllis disdained.

Faith translated that into, "That's why he's successful."

"He's antisocial."

"His own man."

"He's callous and insensitive."

Anita, who'd been eavesdropping from the station next to theirs, said, "He's a heartless s.o.b."

Faith cocked her head to one side and glanced from one woman to the other. Jason had been nothing other than kind and considerate to her. "Are we talking about the same man? Jason Seaton?"

"I was beginning to wonder myself." Phyllis shook her head in disbelief as she scoffed, "You certainly have a halo impression of your boss."

"Yeah, she does," Anita agreed. "You'd better check to see what's holding his imaginary halo in place. It's horns."

Not the least bit dissuaded from her own conviction, Faith began loading the coin machine. "You have a right to your opinions, but I think Jason is wonderful."

"Who's wonderful?" Luke asked. Silently moving from station to station, he picked up the paperwork to send to the clearing house. He'd only caught the tail end of what Faith had said.

"Everyone," Phyllis answered, unwilling to include Luke in their private conversation. "Faith believes the whole world and everyone in it is wonderful."

Luke grinned, handed Phyllis and Anita an envelope, and proceeded down the line of tellers.

"I think Luke likes you," Anita whispered.

Faith smiled. "I like him, too."

"No, what I mean is, I think he wants to ask you out." Her mouth formed a perfect cupid's bow as she added, "The right woman could work miracles with him."

"Good Lord Almighty," Phyllis gasped, after reading the contents in the envelope. She waved an invitation under her nose as though she were going to faint. "I'm invited to the Seaton mansion for a Fourth of July picnic!"

"Me, too!" Anita squealed.

"I told you Mr. Seaton was a nice man." Gratitude to Jason for proving her claim caused her to rise up and grandly blow a wild kiss in his direction. She had counted on Jason's having his nose buried in his paperwork, but she wasn't that lucky. Faith gritted her teeth behind an engaging smile.

He stared straight at her. His hand moved to the side of his cleanly shaven face as though her lipstick prints were visible.

Holy shit, she thought. *I've done it again!*

Like observers watching a guillotine blade about to drop, everyone, tellers and customers, seemed to catch their breath. A ripple of silence echoed throughout the bank's lobby.

Only Faith saw amusement light his blue eyes; everyone else saw his usual stoic expression.

"You're gonna get fired," Anita warned.

Phyllis tugged on the belt of Faith's shirtwaist dress. "You may be fired already. Did you notice, Anita? She's the only one who didn't get an invitation."

"Uh-oh," Anita groaned, swiveling around on her stool. "He just called Mary into his office and gave her a slip of paper. She's headed this way. I'm taking my coffee break, now." She slid her Next Window sign forward and stepped to the back of her station. "I need my job."

"Me, too," Phyllis said, bending down to where the rolled coins were stored.

"Do you really think he'd fire us?" Faith asked, stunned by their cowardly behavior.

"Yessss," they hissed in unison.

Luke whizzed by, circling his wrist and finger beside his ear in the universal gesture that meant, "You're crazy!"

"A little," Faith acknowledged, feeling slightly giddy as Mary headed across the lobby, straight for her cage.

Jason wouldn't fire her, she reassured herself silently. He couldn't. She was part of the family. Wasn't she?

Beneath her bravado, she inwardly winced. Impetuosity always got her into predicaments. She'd been the one who wanted her identity kept a secret. And she'd blown it. Literally.

"Mr. Seaton asked me to give you this," Mary said with a pitiful look. "I hope it isn't what I think it is."

"He wouldn't fire me for blowing him a kiss," Faith

stated flatly, fervently praying she was right. Her fingers trembled as she unfolded the paper and read it. She grinned at Mary. "You all scared me so bad I nearly peed in my knickers!"

Jaw dropping, Mary shushed Faith.

Feeling exuberant, Faith shrugged one shoulder and teased, "It's just a little love note."

Phyllis missed whacking her head on the corner of the cash drawer, but came close enough to it that she peeled her grey hair forward over her eyes. She ruthlessly shoved it back in place. "A what?"

"Want me to read it to you?" Holding it against her chest so no one could see what he'd written, she said, "Kiss a frog and change it into a . . ."

"Frog!" Mary gasped. "He called himself a frog! I don't believe you."

"Maybe I misread it." She encircled the note with her hand to hide it from prying eyes. "You're right Mary. It says, 'Kiss a prince and he doesn't change into a frog. Eager to be with you tonight.' Signed, 'Your Snuggle Bunny.' "

A blend of Mary's giggle, Phyllis's snort, and Anita's gulp was music to Faith's ears. None of them believed her, which was fine. She balled the note and popped it into her mouth and chewed it like a cow with cud.

"Snuggle Bunny?" Anita repeated drily.

Faith pointed to her mouth and bobbed her head. Her curls silently reiterated her assertion by bouncing vigorously.

"You wouldn't lie to us, would you?" Phyllis asked, wanting to believe those innocent brown eyes of hers, but knowing Jason, she couldn't.

"Me?" Mouth stuffed, her reply was garbled. She'd only stretched the truth a teensy-weensy bit. Okay, she admitted silently, she'd embellished, 'I need a ride home,' with frog, prince and sweetie pie. None of them believed her anyway. No harm done.

"He forgot to give you an invitation so he wrote one and had Mary deliver it. Right?" Anita inquired.

Faith emptied the soggy mass into her hand. No longer decipherable, she dropped the ink-blurred paper into the trash can. With a dramatic flourish, she wiped one finger across her lips as though zipping them together.

"You've got to tell!" Anita wailed.

Phyllis groaned. "She's sweet, but I've seen that stubborn look in her eyes. You might as well take your coffee break, Anita. She isn't going to say another word."

She couldn't say another word. She'd babbled non-stop from the bank's parking lot to the dark interior of the garage. Jason had pulled up the emergency brake, hauled her across the seat, and firmly kissed her.

"One good kiss deserves another," he bantered when he placed her back in her bench seat and opened his door. "Stay put until I open your door for you."

Immobilized by his scorching kiss, she was as limp as Raggedy Anne, with no will of her own.

"Turn," she corrected automatically, though her head spun dizzily as she watched him half-circle the Studebaker. "One good *turn* deserves another."

Jason held out his hand to assist her from the car. Faith took it. She barely had her feet on the ground when he pulled her into his arms.

"Anita and Phyllis thought you were in trouble, didn't they?"

"They thought you'd fire me."

"But you knew I couldn't."

"I'm a good teller."

Jason grinned. "Are you?"

"My cash drawer and ledger book balance daily. My station is neat and tidy. I give quick, efficient service to the customers. That's the job description Luke gave me. He hasn't said so, but I think he's pleased with my work."

"He's going to break his arm patting himself on the back. Fast as you're learning, he should be worrying about his own job."

"You wouldn't replace Luke with me." Luke needed his job. From what he'd told her, a zillion cats and dogs were fed out of his paycheck. In fact, first thing in the morning, he was going to prove it by letting her tag along with him while he made his rounds. "You're just dangling a carrot, like any good executive trying to motivate an employee, right?"

Her concern for Luke caused Jason to tighten his arms around her waist. "And if I am, you should be delighted with the prospects of getting a promotion."

"I wouldn't want his job."

"You don't want a title?"

"Not Head Teller."

A warning signal buzzed in the back of Jason's head. His eyes narrowed, but Faith couldn't see that in the dim lighting.

"What title do you want?" *Mine?*

"One I earn," Faith answered promptly, feeling it would be a disservice to Southern Bank and disloyal to

Luke to put Head Teller at the top of her wish list. "I still have a lot to learn."

Slowly, Jason relaxed his hold on her and his smile returned. Impetuous by nature, she'd have blurted out, 'Your title,' if she'd thought of it. There were some advantages to her not having a filter between her brain and her mouth. Her ambitions did not include upsetting the apple cart, yet.

"Are you a decent cook?" he asked, switching subjects as he guided her from the garage to the back porch.

"I'm not allowed to cook."

She draped her arm across the back of his waist and took a mental snapshot of this moment. The image of them returning from work, his kissing her in the garage, and then companionably walking with her to the back door was one she wanted to remember.

"Gertrude and Glen take a half day off every two weeks. She told me she'd leave a chicken and cheese casserole for me to nuke in her new microwave oven."

More cheese, Faith moaned silently. She'd noticed Mrs. Cavendish wearing the muted eye makeup. Maybe she could make a minor change in their diet before they all sprouted long, hairless tails. She'd been cutting recipes from magazines, but had not had the nerve to put them on her breakfast tray.

"I thought we might fix my favorite dinner," Jason hinted. "Grilled steak, without mushroom gravy. Baked potatoes, without cheese sauce. And a salad?"

"Without grated cheese on top?" Her mouth watered over the simple meal he preferred. "Let's change out of our work clothes, then you light the gas grill while I pop the potatoes into the oven and start preparing the salad."

Not taking a chance on his disagreeing, she beat a path through the kitchen, corridor, and up the steps. Fast as a quick-change artist, clothes flew everywhere until she slipped jean shorts and a red scoop-necked top over her lacy underwear. Feet aching from wearing high heels, she decided to go barefooted.

Standing in front of the mirror, she picked up her brush and gave her tousled hair a lick and a promise. Her cheeks were flushed a rosy pink; her brown eyes bright with anticipation.

For once, she congratulated herself silently, her bizarre behavior had not gotten her up Shit Creek, with a motorboat headed straight at her. Jason wasn't mad because she blew him a kiss. He seemed satisfied with her work. Why, he'd mentioned a promotion.

And he'd kissed her. Twice.

A good omen for the evening, she thought, putting the brush down. With Glen and Gertrude gone and Walter over at Caroline's, they'd have the house to themselves. Humming a bawdy ditty Jonathan had taught her, she dabbed Passion perfume on her pulse points, and . . .

Jason rolled up his cuffs. The kiss Faith had blown him sealed her fate. This afternoon, he'd made a cold, calculated decision: Faith Jones would belong to him. It was his only viable option.

Other men have made similar choices, he rationalized, unable to look at himself in the mirror.

Thanks to Caroline's good breeding and Faith's desire to be accepted, Faith had improved drastically. She still had a few rough edges, mainly those God-awful country phrases, but she'd eventually learn to control her mouth.

After removing his tie and releasing his collar button, he tested his whiskers by rubbing his jaw line. Five o'clock shadow, he assessed with a grimace. Time for a quick shave? He glanced at his Rolex and strode into his bathroom. Before he'd come upstairs he'd started the grill. Steaks would take less time to cook than baked potatoes. He moistened his face, squirted shaving cream in his hand, and applied it.

Aware he was having trouble facing himself because of his decision, he raised his eyes to the mirror.

"You aren't going to do anything morally or ethically wrong," he stated flatly, carefully maneuvering his safety razor across his cheek. "Your intentions are honorable."

They're despicable, his conscience argued. *You're going to seduce Faith.*

"We'll make love . . ."

She'll make love. You'll have sex.

"She'll want to make plans for the future, including marriage."

She'll marry. You'll merge.

"A big wedding should keep Faith, Caroline and Walter busy."

Out of the bank.

"I'll do my part by taking care of business."

The prenuptial agreement.

"And everything will remain unchanged."

Jason raised his chin and swiped the last ridge of white fluff from his throat, nicking himself. Spots of red blood instantly appeared.

"Damn!"

Damnation. You can't marry Faith to get controlling interest.

He dropped the razor in the sink. Carefully peeling one ply of bathroom tissue from the roll, he blanketed the small scratch.

"Faith needs someone to protect her interests, to take care of her," he whispered vehemently. "Who better than me?"

He stared steadily at himself, listening for an argument. His mind could have played devil's advocate and listed Luke or several unmarried customers. It wasn't conceit or arrogance that filled the silence; it was the truth.

For some unknown reason, Faith was attracted to him from their first encounter. He'd be a fool not to capitalize on her attraction. Right now, the men she'd met only saw her as a friendly bank employee. Once the word was out, Jason knew he'd have to buy a baseball bat to ward off her suitors.

Why go through that hassle?

Jason wiped his face with a hand towel. Slowly he unscrewed the cap of his aftershave.

It wasn't as though he found her repugnant. He liked having Faith around Seaton Place. No, he more than liked her. He was genuinely fond of her. She made him feel younger, carefree; something he'd never been.

He splashed the alcohol-based after-shave on his cheeks. Drawing a quick breath, he realized he'd done that often since Faith had come into his life. Her earthy sensuality appealed to him. Nothing artificial or coy about her. Sexually, he had to admit, she had his male hormones exploding like firecrackers.

He grinned. Wide as the ripple on a slop bucket, he thought, quoting Faith's description of Walter when he smiled at Caroline. Smarter than his father when it came to women, Jason opened a drawer in the vanity and extracted a small foil package. Just in case this didn't work out as he planned, he wanted to protect Faith from an unwanted pregnancy. He dropped the packet into his pocket.

$\mathcal{T}en$

Faith balanced the kitchen chair on its two back legs and heaved a sigh of contentment. "That's the best meal I've had in weeks."

"You don't like Gertrude's cooking?" Jason teased, knowing full well she picked at the meals the cook prepared.

"I get a raccoon urge to wash everything before I put it in my mouth," she joked.

His laughter skittered up her spine. She gloried in each chuckle, every laugh. With everyone else gone, they'd had an elbows-on-the-table, kick-off-your-shoes, don't-worry-about-tomorrow dinner.

Jason lowered his forearm and held his hand out for her to take. "You could have some say in what meals are planned."

"Uh-huh." She rejected his idea, but accepted his hand. The front legs of her chair touched the floor as she sandwiched the heel of his hand between her palms. "I'd get tough ol' Frisbee eggs for breakfast and dinner. I'll just scrape off the cheese, thank-you-very-much."

Her finger trailed across the creases that formed a large M, to his life line, following it to the creases around his wrist. The M destined him for money and great wealth. She ignored it.

"You're going to live forever."

"Am I?" He bent forward until their heads nearly touched. "You learned arithmetic and palmistry via the computer?"

"Books." What an opening, Faith mused. She could tell him everything *she* wanted to hear while being allowed to touch him. "Make a fist and I'll tell you how many children you'll have."

Jason complied.

"Oh-ho!" She counted each tiny line out loud. "You're going to be busy."

"Seven!"

"Maybe more. I'd need a magnifying glass to be certain."

He flattened his hand open. "Seven crumb-crunchers? How many wives?"

"One."

"How can you tell when you didn't even look?"

She pointed to the writer's callus on his middle finger.

"One," she reaffirmed. "I noticed it that first day in the library."

Jason chuckled. "Everybody only has one bump there."

"Guess that's God's plan. Two eyes, two ears, one mouth, one wife. Logical, huh?"

"I watched a TV talk show about palm reading. That qualifies me as an expert, doesn't it?" He flipped her hand over. "Ah-ha."

"What do you see?"

"Passion!" He rhythmically prodded the flesh beneath her thumb. "Very passionate."

"Oh, yeah?" Caught in the web of malarkey she'd spun, she hoped this was what he wanted to believe. "What else?"

"From what I see written on your palm, I'm beginning to wonder if it was a talk show I watched." He wrapped her palm around his little finger, brought her knuckles to his mouth and kissed each peak and valley. "Maybe it was a soap opera."

Glad she wasn't precariously tilted back on two chair legs, Faith murmured, "Soap opera?"

"Mmmmm." He'd forgotten that she never watched television. "Racy love stories."

Her eyes drifted shut. He circled the back of her hand against his smoothly shaven cheek. She knew she had a sappy grin on her face, but she didn't care.

Jason had a well-rehearsed line of compliments he'd successfully used to woo other women into his bed. His lips parted, but his glib tongue clove to the roof of his dry mouth. His eyes moved from the shadows caused by her long curly lashes to her cheeks.

"F-f-freckles," he stammered, suddenly tongue-tied.

Wanting him to stop talking and continue kissing her, Faith blurted, "A whole rash of them."

"Not a rash." From the far reaches of his memory he recalled the explanation Uncle Jonathan had given. "Before you were born, God blessed you as a special child by peppering your cheeks."

Faith grinned; her eyes were shiny with tears. "That's what Papa told me when I tried to bleach them with buttermilk."

"He told me the same story about the ones on my shoulders."

"Do you still have them?"

Spontaneously, she rose from her chair and started to unbutton his shirt to see for herself. Letting her have her way with him, he allowed her to push back the fabric.

"You do!" God's stamp of approval, she mused, utterly delighted. His shirt fell back into place. "They're faint, but they're there."

With her standing between his knees with her hands on her shoulders, the most natural thing in the world for him to do was place his hands on her hips. He looked up at her; she felt as though she were on stage, standing in the limelight. She wanted to make a witty quip, something to make him laugh, but her mind went blank.

She watched his lips move, and yet, a comfortable silence hung between them.

He's nervous, she realized suddenly. As nervous as a teller with sticky fingers in a cash drawer. He has a bad case of stage fright, too.

"Jason?"

"Hmmm?"

"Is it true you never go out with any of the women who work at the bank?"

His thumbs tracked down her hip bone and back up again before he drawled, "Have you been listening to gossip?"

"Someone mentioned it in passing."

"Passing through the employee's lounge?"

"Where I heard it doesn't matter. Or who I heard it from, either. Is it true?"

"Yes."

"Why?"

"It would interfere with work."

"How?"

"They'd expect special treatment."

"What kind?"

She earned that certain smile he reserved for her eyes only. "They'd expect me to reach up and grab kisses flung in my direction."

"I expected you to have your nose buried in paperwork. I was as surprised as you were."

"Nothing you do surprises me."

That was as close to a dare as she thought he could get. Her imagination whirled with scandalous notions. As conservative and uptight as Jason was, she knew she could shock his socks off.

Both Anita and Phyllis were horrified by her joking with the customers about giving them money samples or service charging their accounts. He'd be shocked, too.

Brazen as a mother cat parading an unexpected litter of kittens, she asked, "What if I told you I brought bundles of fifty-dollar bills home every night and stashed them in your room?"

"Luke checks your books. I check the computer printouts." With her standing and him sitting, he could easily shock her by drawing her forward until his face nuzzled her breasts. The thought reflexively brought his thighs closer together. "Why my room?"

"It's the last place you'd look for stolen cash." She inched forward. "I'm a computer whiz. I could figure out a way to alter the reports."

Jason chuckled. The sun rays coming through the back window created a golden aura around her head that reminded him of a halo. Angels wouldn't take anything that didn't belong to them.

"Is this a confession?"

"Would you be shocked?"

"Nope."

She reached up and threaded her fingers through her curls, pulling them back from her face. This always helped her think better. Her fingers laced together, forming a thinking cap on her head.

Watching her knit top lovingly cup the underside of her breasts and the hem rise several inches didn't shock Jason, but it did cause his heart to pound faster. His large hands could span her small waist, easily.

Testing his theory, his hands moved against her bare flesh, as she widened her eyes.

"Shocked?" he inquired drily.

"No," she lied bravely.

His thumbs followed the ridges of her ribs until he touched the satin underside of her bra. All the while he watched her eyes growing wider and wider. "Now?"

"I'm the one who is supposed to be shocking you," she answered, her voice breathy.

"You could . . . by finishing what you started." She blinked; the black centers of her brown eyes grew wider when his thumb circled her tumid nipple. "Unbutton the rest of my shirt."

"Shocking people is my way of making them laugh, Jason. M-m-my way of making them h-happy . . ."

He did something so incredibly sexy it had her stammering, gasping for air. Without touching her top, he rose, opened his mouth, and blew his hot breath around her nipple.

"Unbutton my shirt," he urged. "I want to feel you against me."

Faith wanted to touch Jason Seaton more than anything in God's creation, but her habitual routine of doing something outlandish, getting into trouble, and paying a stiff price later, made her reluctant to follow his command.

"Shy?" Jason murmured, his voice vibrating against her. He circled her waist with his arm, which freed his other hand to yank his shirttail from his pants. "Don't be."

Her knees weakened as she watched him push buttons through holes. Unable to stand, with no place to sit, she sank to her knees in front of him.

First her eyes, then her hands moved across the whorls of masculine dark hair that covered his chest. His pectoral muscles grew taut beneath her palms. She circled his flat male nipples with her fingers as lightly as the heat from his mouth had caressed hers.

Her lack of hesitation, coupled with the boldness of her stroking, preening, inquisitive fingers, startled Jason. Like any man, he expected a naive woman with little or no sexual experience to be timorous. He should have known that shyness was never a problem for Faith. He'd underestimated her again.

An irreverent thought crossed her mind, making her smile. When she glanced up and saw one of his dark brows raised, she explained, "The male anatomy is nothing like the two-dimensional computerized renditions."

"Biology 101?"

Faith nodded as she nuzzled her face against him. The masculine aroma she inhaled had an aphrodisiacal effect on her senses. None of the expensive perfumes she'd bought compared to the fragrance of soap, male cologne and Jason's scent.

Curious as a cat with a ball of yarn, and every bit as playful, she pursed her lips and blew an imaginary line from the hollow of his throat to his bellybutton. The low groan she heard and the tremor that visibly passed through him was an accolade to her sensual power.

In one fell swoop, he reached down, shimmied the hem of her top over her head and arms, then tossed it aside.

Modesty urged Faith to cross her arms over her bareness. The hot, appreciative gleam in his eyes commanded her to disregard the impulse. A pinch of hooks and eyes dispensed with the piece of lacy froth concealing her breast. She shrugged her shoulders to be rid of it.

For several seconds, Jason gazed at her.

"Too big?" Faith asked. Without a whit of self-consciousness, she cupped her breasts. The flicker of amusement in his eyes caused her to explain, "The salesladies said I'd be a perfect petite size, if it weren't for them."

"Just the right size for me. C'mere, I'll show you." He nudged aside her hand and replaced them with his own palms. "See?"

His touch felt exquisite. A shallow breath hissed between her lips as he brought her against his torso. As her taut nipples burrowed up from the muscular cuts across his stomach through his mat of chest hair, she became sublimely aware of their differences: his chest was muscular, hard, and furry; hers was plump, soft and sleek, opposites that complemented each other.

Distracted by tactile bliss, she barely noticed he'd moved her to his lap, with her legs straddling him. She felt the hard ridge of his maleness pressed against the seam of her shorts. A sweet ache for the unknown caused her to move slightly against him.

"This chair isn't built for this," Jason crooned close to her ear as he fondled her breast.

She snuggled closer. Her lips nipped the pulsating spot at the base of his throat as she whispered, "We could go upstairs to my room."

"The seducer is seduced," he said, smiling as she placed her feet flat on the linoleum and lifted off him. He kept his hands on her waist to hold her in place while he circled the pert tip of her breast with his tongue. Absolved of the guilt he'd felt earlier, he swirled the dusky pink pearl that beaded beneath his lips, then added, "By a seductress."

Faith arched her back. Her fingers wove through his dark hair until they dug into his scalp. She wanted . . . she didn't know exactly what she wanted, but the craving was intense. The light tug of his lips had the same effect as that of a master puppeteer pulling a string from her breast to the apex of her thighs.

"Yessss," she hissed when he took her into the hot vortex of his mouth and suckled one breast, then the other.

Her knees clenched against the hard wooden seat of the chair as her thighs and buttocks contracted. She heard a snap, felt the teeth of her zipper give, and the elastic of her panties stretch. She would have instinctively crossed her legs had she known that his long fingers were about to nestle in the mound of her femininity. Her eyes squeezed shut as his palm claimed her. One finger gently parted her lips, rubbing the nubbin he found there until she felt an embarrassing hot moistness dampen his hand.

"Jason," she entreated, pushing at his shoulders.

While her mind resisted, her body opened like a flower to him. His finger slipped inside of her. Her resistance withered as the ache exploded. Nothing she'd witnessed at the farm or read in books and magazines prepared her for her first climax.

Only his hand cupping her, his finger impaling her, her arms wrapped around his shoulders, enabled her to remain earthbound.

"What did you say?" Jason asked, believing she must have read his mind.

Her hand made a space between them until she touched the thick bulge in his pants. "I want you inside of me."

"I am." He stretched her to his width. "Sex with a virgin doesn't have to be rough."

Her eyelids seemed to weigh a ton as she opened them to half-mast. She circled his shaft through the fabric. Dissatisfied, she began to unbuckle his belt. He sucked his stomach flat. "I didn't know it would feel like this."

"How?"

"You know." She unbuttoned his waistband, and lowered his zipper. She felt a jolting loss as he removed his hand from her panties. The chair scraped backward. She watched while he raised his hips and peeled his clothes to the edge of the chair where gravity took hold. He provided the same disrobing service for her. She stepping lightly from the puddle of clothing. "You aren't a virgin."

He nudged his knees between hers and coaxed her back on his lap. When she settled on him, hot and moist, he felt as though he'd been swallowed in liquid fire. And yet, he wasn't embedded deep within her as he desperately wanted to be.

"I've never felt anything like this," he admitted freely

with a hoarse groan. He strained to retain control of the impulse to slam into her and rut until he erupted, spewing inside of her. He clenched his back molars. Talk. Count backwards. Talk. Lips closed, he kissed her. "This wasn't what I planned."

Faith's brow puckered as he ended the kiss all too soon. "I ruined your plans? What were they?"

"A leisurely dinner. An after-dinner drink to allay your inhibitions."

Her worried look changed to an impish grin. "Candy's dandy, liquor's quicker?" she asked, quoting Ogden Nash. When he smiled and nodded, she said, "Haven't you noticed I don't have any inhibitions with you."

Her admission caused the impossible to occur in his lower extremities. Jason felt as though he grew an inch, maybe more.

He kissed her longer, harder. His hands trailed down the hollow of her slender back. "I thought I'd swoop you up into my arms and carry you upstairs to my bed."

"You still could."

"My knees are too damned weak," he confessed with a groan. "I'd have to carry you piggyback."

It pleased her to know she wasn't the only one who suffered from a case of weak knees. Right now, she wouldn't be able to stand if her life depended on it. Curiosity gave her the will to move backward on his thighs until she could see him.

"You'll never be able to wear a petite," slipped out of her mouth before she could catch it behind her fingers.

Another inch? As her fingers encircled him, he felt longer and harder than any experienced woman had made him feel. Her hand mimicking the motions he'd made with his tongue on her breasts caused a moan to rumble from deep inside his chest. She slid her fingers down the length of him until the heel of her hand rested in his coarse hair.

"Am I hurting you?" She'd glanced at his face and witnessed his inner torment.

"Only if you stop."

Eleven

"I'm not doing this right!"

"Breathe . . . one . . . two . . . three . . ."

"That's it. Slowly exhale. Again."

Propped with her back against Walter, Caroline listened to him and watched the lamaze instructor, Eileen Jarworski. Natural childbirth, she thought between gasps, was her idea. How come it seemed so damned *unnatural* for her? At any moment she expected to hyperventilate!

"You're daydreaming," Walter scolded.

"I know I look like a balloon." Pant. "Now, I'm beginning to feel like one," she complained, quietly panting. "Anesthesia—wheel me in, knock me out, deliver the baby—is looking better and better."

"It's what I'd do," Walter muttered between counts.

Caroline glanced over her shoulder and scowled at Walter. "Men! The human race would have ended with Adam and Eve if it were up to you all."

"Shush. Count," Walter ordered. "Breathe."

"I want what's best for the baby," she reaffirmed aloud.

"Then you ought to provide it with a daddy!"

"Her," Caroline corrected, avoiding their usual fight. The last couple of weeks, Walter took every opportunity to mention matrimony. "The sonogram reading says it's a girl."

"A baby girl," he repeated with pride. He shifted her to one shoulder while continuing to lightly circle her stomach. "Two. Three. Exhale. I wrote down a list of girls' names." He patted his breast pocket. "I have it here somewhere."

"And they say pregnant women are forgetful because of lack of oxygen going to the brain," she teased. "You gave me the list already. It's in my purse."

"Oh, yeah, in the car on our way over here."

Caroline smiled. Walter enjoyed each phase of her pregnancy—morning sickness, water retention, and now, forgetfulness. While she worked, he spent his days at her condo reading articles and books on pregnancy and childbearing, cleaning, and shopping for groceries. Each night she came home to a nutritious meal and a loving man.

He pampered her. She let him. She refused to take maternity leave; he relished every minute of the unofficial leave he'd taken from the bank.

Her eyes scanned the room, looking at the faces of the younger men and their wives. Some appeared bored, others irritated. None of them compared to Walter.

Curling her hand around his forearm, she rose up to his ear and whispered, "I love you, Walter."

"Then marry me," he said gruffly, his eyes reflecting her love.

"We've been over this."

"We'll go over it again and again, until I get it right," he promised, kissing the top of her head.

Eileen stopped in front of them. "That's what I like

to hear," she enthused. Clapping her hands together, she said, "That's enough for this week, class. Remember. Practice at home. Keep smiling. And I'll look forward to seeing all of you next week!"

Five minutes later, Walter solicitously helped Caroline into his car. Before he started the engine, he checked the air-conditioning vents to make certain they weren't blowing on her stomach or face.

"Walter, the vents haven't changed since I got out of the car. I'm pregnant, not terminally ill." She realized she was being bitchy, but one look at the determination on Walter's face told her that he was going to vigorously push her for a wedding date. "Stop fussing, please."

"July tenth," he stated doggedly, starting the engine and driving out of the Barnes Hospital parking lot. Her condo was within walking distance, but he didn't think it was safe for her to walk after dark. "The Saturday after the Fourth. No big hullabaloo. No engraved invitations. No five-tier cake. We can invite everyone right before the fireworks start."

Caroline stretched her legs to avoid getting a charley horse. Riding in a car caused them. "The purpose of the lawn party is to introduce Faith to our circle of friends. It's her big day."

"She won't mind."

"I would."

"No, you wouldn't. Why won't you let me make the wedding announcement?"

"Walter, I've told you why."

"No, you've given me excuses. You said you wanted a man who'd be there for your baby. Haven't I proved I'll be there for you and our daughter?"

"I don't want to discuss this."

She closed her eyes to shut out his voice. A silent voice from within validated her position. He'd leave her the same way her father left her. Thousands of men walked away from their wives and children, without a backward glance. Sure, for a short while they felt guilty. Like most divorced men, her father had assuaged his guilt with money. Presents. But, he'd denied her what she'd wanted and needed most: his presence.

Caroline frowned as she recalled her mother not taking her to school on the first day of kindergarten because she had a court date. Only five, she'd been confused and angry.

"Mommy," she'd cried, "Don't make me go alone, please. Take me with you."

Her mother had pulled her onto her lap and given her a fierce hug. Was it her tears or her mother's tears she felt on her cheek. Caroline couldn't remember.

But she remembered being scared. Her father had hugged her real hard before he'd left. He'd promised to come see her; that he'd always love her.

She hadn't seen him in months.

One of the neighbors took her to school; her mother went to back to court. Her father's guilt had faded. Happiness with a younger woman squelched it.

Why should he financially strap himself? Her mother was young and attractive. She could get a job or she could find another man to support her. Frankly, he didn't care which. Why should he give his hard-earned money to a woman he no longer wanted? Or support a child who emotionally blackmailed him by bawling crocodile tears each time he saw her.

He'd been fair, hadn't he?

No, Caroline screamed silently.

"Are you tired?" Walter asked, concerned when he saw her wince.

"No. I'm fine." She rubbed her forehead with her fingertips. "A little headache."

Perceptive to her mood swings, he said, "You're shutting me out, aren't you?"

"I'll discuss anything with you . . . other than wedding plans."

Walter turned left into her parking garage. "Did I tell you that you're a damned stubborn woman?"

"Yes." Eyes wide open, she moved her hand to his knee and patted it. "I'm also opinionated, self-centered, proud, self-sufficient . . ."

"I did not say that!"

"No, I did." She smiled. "I know me better than you do. Ten years from now you'll be down on bended knee thanking me for refusing to marry you."

"No. I'll be down on my knees begging you to tell my daughter, Sally, who I am!"

She chuckled over his presumptuousness. "Sally?"

"My favorite aunt's name, God rest her soul."

"I thought your father was an only child," she teased.

"Actually, she was my great-great-aunt, on my father's side of the family—Sally Jane Seaton." He switched off the engine. "I found her name while I was browsing through the family Bible that Faith returned."

"Mmmmm. Last name Seaton? An old-maid aunt? You want to name my child after a woman who never married?"

"Our child," he revised. "You've never married. Why should her marital status bother you?"

Caroline shrugged. "It shouldn't."

"But it does?"

She heard the hope flare in his voice and quickly said, "Nope. Not really. Maybe your Aunt Sally was as independent as I am. Did she have any children?"

"No. Society at the turn of the century frowned upon illegitimate offspring."

Two years ago when her mother had been in the hospital with cancer, she'd told her that every woman needed a child to love. A child's love was the only love a woman could count on.

"That's a shame."

"A good reason to name the babe Sally?"

"I'll think about it," Caroline temporized.

Walter reached across the center console and turned her face toward him. "Some day, Caroline, you'll open your heart to me."

"I do love you," she whispered, kissing his palm. It hurt her to see his eyes light with hope, knowing she'd selfishly used him. "Today. Isn't that enough?"

"Only today? No tomorrows?"

"It's all I can honestly promise."

Taking her hand, he placed it on her rounded stomach. "Don't listen to your mother, Sally. I'll be here tomorrow, and the next day, and the next . . ."

Caroline kissed him to end his promise of eternity. She could live with today. Tonight. Anything beyond that was as chimerical as a fortuneteller's crystal ball. No sane woman would count on her future with any man.

This she believed.

Twelve

Jason came to his senses as she lightly squeezed him. He had to control his desire or he'd disgrace himself. A woman was blessed with instantaneous recovery after a climax; a man was cursed with limpness.

The chair creaking gave him the excuse he badly needed.

"The legs of this chair flattening would spoil both of our plans."

It sounded hollow and garbled to him, but he must have made sense. Faith gracefully stood up and held her hand out to assist him. Fully erect and throbbing, he needed assistance!

"Don't you dare say, Last one upstairs is a rotten egg," he warned, with a grin. "I'm not up to running."

"Is that a pun?" she chided, giggling, and a tad self-conscious as she led him through the kitchen door.

"You're naughty."

He swatted her backside playfully, then reverted to his original plan by swinging her into his arms and carrying her up the steps. Faith looped her arms around his shoulders. In his strong arms she felt light as a feather and deliciously feminine.

As they entered his bedroom, she nibbled his earlobe,

then whispered her secret thoughts aloud, "I love you, Jason."

He dropped her.

Fortunately for her, he stood by the bed when she fell from his arms.

She bounced once and chuckled. "Shocked?"

"You're confusing love with lust," he blurted, without thought. Had he lost his ever-lovin' mind? His scheme depended on her falling head over heels for him. The trust he saw in her brown eyes made him feel like a heel. "What I meant to say is . . ."

"You don't love me," she concluded for him, still smiling up at him. "You want me."

He gestured down the length of his body. His bold erection gave mute testimony. "That's evident."

"Women make love. Men have sex," she responded breezily as though she were quoting from Corinthians. Matter-of-factly, she folded down the coverlet and top sheet. She left room for him when she rolled between the sheets. Feeling adult and sophisticated, she laced her fingers together and stuck them between her head and the pillow. "That's what it says in all the magazine articles."

None too pleased with her source of information, Jason lay down beside her. He raised his arm, tucking her neatly under it, with her head on his chest. His fingers twined a lock of silky hair around them.

"Don't believe everything you read."

"Why not? Don't magazines tell readers how things are? Right down to how to get rid of pimples, warts, and bellybutton fuzz?"

Reluctantly, he smiled. "You believe the advertisements, too?"

The Publishers of Zebra Books Make This Special Offer to Zebra Romance Readers...

AFTER YOU HAVE READ THIS BOOK WE'D LIKE TO SEND YOU 4 MORE FOR *FREE* AN $18.00 VALUE

NO OBLIGATION!

ONLY ZEBRA HISTORICAL ROMANCES "BURN WITH THE FIRE OF HISTORY" (SEE INSIDE FOR MONEY SAVING DETAILS.)

MORE PASSION AND ADVENTURE AWAIT... YOUR TRIP TO A BIG ADVENTUROUS WORLD BEGINS WHEN YOU ACCEPT YOUR FIRST 4 NOVELS ABSOLUTELY *FREE*
(AN $18.00 VALUE)

Accept your Free gift and start to experience more of the passion and adventure you like in a historical romance novel. Each Zebra novel is filled with proud men, spirited women and tempestuous love that you'll remember long after you turn the last page.

Zebra Historical Romances are the finest novels of their kind. They are written by authors who really know how to weave tales of romance and adventure in the historical settings you love. You'll feel like you've actually gone back in time with the thrilling stories that each Zebra novel offers.

GET YOUR FREE GIFT WITH THE START OF YOUR HOME SUBSCRIPTION

Our readers tell us that these books sell out very fast in book stores and often they miss the newest titles. So Zebra has made arrangements for you to receive the four newest novels published each month.

You'll be guaranteed that you'll never miss a title, and home delivery is so convenient. And to show you just how easy it is to get Zebra Historical Romances, we'll send you your first 4 books absolutely FREE! Our gift to you just for trying our home subscription service.

BIG SAVINGS AND CONVENIENT HOME DELIVERY

Each month, you'll receive the four newest titles as soon as they are published. You'll probably receive them even before the bookstores do. What's more, you may preview these exciting novels free for 10 days. If you like them as much as we think you will, just pay the low preferred subscriber's price of $3.75 each. *You'll save $3.00 each month off the publisher's price.* (A postage and handling charge of $1.50 is added to each shipment.) Of course you can return any shipment within 10 days for full credit, no questions asked. There is no minimum number of books you must buy.

4 FREE BOOKS

TO GET YOUR 4 FREE BOOKS WORTH $18.00 — MAIL IN THE FREE BOOK CERTIFICATE T O D A Y

Fill in the Free Book Certificate below, and we'll send your FREE BOOKS to you as soon as we receive it.

If the certificate is missing below, write to: Zebra Home Subscription Service, Inc., P.O. Box 5214, 120 Brighton Road, Clifton, New Jersey 07015-5214.

FREE BOOK CERTIFICATE

4 FREE BOOKS

ZEBRA HOME SUBSCRIPTION SERVICE, INC.

YES! Please start my subscription to Zebra Historical Romances and send me my first 4 books absolutely FREE. I understand that each month I may preview four new Zebra Historical Romances free for 10 days. If I'm not satisfied with them, I may return the four books within 10 days and owe nothing. Otherwise, I will pay the low preferred subscriber's price of just $3.75 each; a total of $15.00, *a savings off the publisher's price of $3.00.* I may return any shipment and I may cancel this subscription at any time. There is no obligation to buy any shipment. (A postage and handling charge of $1.50 is added to each shipment.) Regardless of what I decide, the four free books are mine to keep.

ZB1794

NAME

ADDRESS   APT

CITY   STATE   ZIP

(   )
TELEPHONE

SIGNATURE   (if under 18, parent or guardian must sign)

Terms, offer and prices subject to change without notice. Subscription subject to acceptance by Zebra Books. Zebra Books reserves the right to reject any order or cancel any subscription.

GET
FOUR
FREE
BOOKS
(AN $18.00 VALUE)

AFFIX
STAMP
HERE

ZEBRA HOME SUBSCRIPTION
SERVICE, INC.
120 BRIGHTON ROAD
P.O. Box 5214
CLIFTON, NEW JERSEY 07015-5214

"Sometimes they're the most interesting. Can't you imagine a white tornado whirling through Gertrude's kitchen? Or Glen sprinkling fertilizer on his roses and ten-inch blooms unfolding right in front of his eyes? Or Luke rubbing gook on the thinning spot on his head and bright red hair sprouting from his scalp?"

"You've proven my point." He turned on his side. "Just because you see it in print, that doesn't make it true."

Faith smiled. He'd proven her point. Those articles were as much hogwash as the tornadoes, roses and hair. Men do make love, she mused. Jason couldn't say I-love-you, yet, but the meaning she read into his words banished any doubts she had of his only wanting sex with her.

Immediate physical gratification was only a small part of his desire. He craved more than sex. His actions spoke louder than words.

He loves me, she mused, as much as I love him.

She made no move to stop him when his hand followed the contours of her breast, waist and hip. His lips curved to match her satisfied smile as he kissed her. He teased and tasted, leisurely stroking the velvet softness of her tongue; she massaged it with gentle, suckling sips.

No shy maiden, but a woman who'd recently experienced the first heady feelings of passion, she felt a fiery yearning in her belly that only Jason could assuage. She was impatient for more than his kisses. With a low, intense groan, she wrapped her arms tightly around his back, drawing his upper body across her.

"Don't rush, sweetheart," he whispered, lining her neck with a row of hot moist kisses. "I want this to be so wonderful you'll remember tonight throughout eternity."

Sweetheart. Wonderful. Eternity. Her mind filtered out everything other than the words she wanted to hear. *He loves me. He must. Only a man who truly loves a woman calls her sweetheart and speaks of eternity.*

Her back arched as his line of kisses bent in to a curve around her nipple. Just as she touched the swollen shaft of his manhood, he groaned, then pulled her inside his mouth, causing her to echo his sentiments, almost screaming with the raw pleasure of it. Reflexively, her knees clenched together and her legs drew toward her chest.

She had to stop this torment, this ache deep inside of her that threatened to completely drive her insane.

"Jason?"

He must have heard the urgency in her voice. His dark head rose. The naked desire she saw shining in his blue eyes parched her throat as dry as a creek bed in mid-August. Her lips moved, but she was speechless, unable to communicate how much she wanted him.

The tormented look in her eyes must have spoken volumes. She watched as he unhurriedly retrieved protection from the top drawer of his nightstand. His knowledge of the risks as well as the pleasures, and his willingness to accept responsibility for protecting her vanquished any doubts she had that he loved her.

"Trust me," he whispered, his mouth curving into the special smile she'd come to cherish, then coming down hard against hers. His tongue tangled with hers in an ecstatic dance. Each swirl, each probe, promised her fulfillment.

He moved, his knee wedged between hers, then he shifted until he settled into the cradle of her thighs. At the same time, she felt the heel of his hand slowly, methodically, erotically arousing her.

Her breath caught when he drove into her, swiftly, surely, without hesitation, with a force that scratched a cry from her soul. In a flash of pain, he'd taken her virginity and left an indelible love-print etched on her soul.

For long moments, he held her perfectly still, suspended in time and motion.

"Never like this," she heard wrenched from his heart. He kissed her with such infinite gentleness it brought tears to Faith's eyes. She felt him move within her. "Only pleasure, now," he promised.

The instant of pain was forgotten as he began moving with tormenting slowness. He thrust. Instinctively, she parried by arching, and rotating her hips. Her short fingernails bit into his back and hips, hanging on to him as he steadily increased the tempo of his driving plunges, pushing her higher and higher, closer and closer to her peak. A tingling sensation traveled from her heels up to the calves of both legs, then journeyed like an explosive flash to the nerve endings in her scalp. Her heart beat frantically, as though it would burst. The glorious sensation caused her eyes to clamp shut, her legs to grip his hips, and her buttocks to clench as her mind shattered with his final thrust.

She opened her eyes, wanting to see the same wonder on his face that she felt in her heart. Instead, she saw his dark eyebrows beetled into a straight line. The skin across his high cheekbones stretched tautly. His teeth clenched; his lips grimaced.

He appeared to be in terrible, excruciating pain.

The stark magnitude of his intensity frightened her.

Her hands moved to the solid wall of his chest where she felt his heart pound, hard, fast, and erratically.

And then his eyelids parted; his blues shone with awe and wonderment. Goosebumps sprayed across her chest as his lips curved into that certain smile he only shared with her.

Still within her, he moved to his side and cradled her in his arms. At any moment she expected to hear the words meant only for her.

"Was it good for you?" Jason asked, combing his fingers through her curly hair.

Faith was disappointed, but she hid it behind a broad smile. "Wonderful."

"It's never been like that for me, either," he confessed with a winsome smile. "You're magnificent."

Faith listened to the lovely praise he continued to express, although none of his flattery contained the three words she silently begged to hear. A vague uneasiness nagged at her. She tried to block it out, to push it back into the unconscious level of her thoughts, but it demanded immediate attention.

"Do you love me, Jason?" she blurted.

"You're lovely, the loveliest, sexiest woman in the whole world."

That was not what she wanted to hear. Faith rolled away from him and sat up. She felt naked and vulnerable. Her eyes darted around the bedroom looking for something, *anything,* to cover herself. His room was neat as a pin, nothing out of order.

Frustrated and hurt, she yanked the coverlet off the bed and swung it around her shoulders.

"Second thoughts?" Jason asked drily. He rolled to his

side and reached for her. When she shrugged away from him to the edge of the bed, he added, "Instant regret doesn't become you."

"No regrets," she quipped, struggling to be as nonchalant as he'd been. She'd read somewhere that women reacted differently than men after sex, but she hadn't expected to feel emotionally abandoned.

Jason yawned, both exhausted and exhilarated. "Then why don't you come here and we'll cuddle."

His jaw popping propelled Faith off his bed. The metallic taste in her mouth gave her the excuse she needed to justify a hasty departure. "I'm thirsty."

"There is a glass in the bathroom." He kicked the sheet aside. "I'll get it for you."

She muscled the king-sized spread around her pint-sized frame. "I want something stronger than tap water."

"There's iced tea in the refrigerator downstairs," Jason offered, stifling another yawn behind his hand.

Standing up, she stared at the yards and yards of dark paisley quilt and wondered how she was going to get out of the room with her dignity intact. Emotionally, she felt as though she'd fallen flat on her face. She'd be damned if she'd actually trip!

Pretending she had her courage hat primly on her head, she dropped the coverlet and regally strode across the room. When she reached the door, she glanced over her shoulder for one longing look at Jason. She needed to see him smiling at her, hoping against hope he'd be able to make things right by telling her he loved her.

Jason had curled his arm under the pillow. His eyes were closed. Yes, he smiled, completely satiated from their lovemaking, but she also heard him. His breath gently soughed through his parted lips.

He'd fallen asleep during her grand exit!

No longer concerned with her nudity or being poised, she fled to the sanctity of her own bedroom. Tears slithered down her cheeks unnoticed.

Perplexed, she automatically began making excuses for his crazy behavior while she slipped into her fuzzy terrycloth robe.

Stress. Juggling his responsibilities at work and at home had exhausted him.

Heat. The sun depleted his energy.

Exercise. He must have burned a zillion calories making love . . . no, having sex with her.

Faith dashed the backs of her hands beneath her eyes. Dammit! She wouldn't cry over spilt milk. She should be making excuses for her own behavior, not his!

She racked her brain for reasons to vindicate what she'd done, but came up empty-handed. She loved Jason. Making love with him was as natural to her as dewdrops forming before the sun's rays evaporated the moisture.

It wasn't guilt or shame she felt.

"How do I feel?" she said aloud, trying to get in touch with her true self.

The ache Jason created had gone, replaced by a peculiar mixture of contentment and restlessness. She wanted to take a long, soothing bubble bath——and race around the block at top speed, at the same time. She wanted to climb on the rooftop and shout how much she loved Jason——and simultaneously close her fingers over her mouth to keep it her own private secret.

"Is it possible to feel elated and disappointed . . . both at the same time?" she wondered aloud.

Thoroughly confused, she plopped down on the chaise longue beside the window and stared into the darkness. Is this what love is? Heaven and hell scrambled together?

The two were incompatible, she discounted silently. No such thing as heavenly hellaciousness. And yet, that accurately described how she felt, caught between heaven and hell. Yes, it was heavenly being in love with Jason, but it was hell on earth knowing for certain that he did not love her.

Several hours later, Jason groggily pulled the pillow into his arms and whispered, "Faith." He'd stroked the satin pillowcase before he became fully aware that he'd napped alone.

Grinning sheepishly, he realized that a week of sleepless nights had taken its toll. It would have taken a forklift to prop his eyelids open once his tension had been released.

He rolled on his back and folded his arms behind his head. Next time, he silently vowed, he'd stay awake for pillow talk. Faith would understand, without him making lengthy explanations. She had a knack for only seeing the good in everyone, himself included.

God, he felt good. Ten feet tall, twelve inches long and virile as a ten-balled tomcat.

Jason chuckled, wondering where on earth he'd heard that expression. Probably from Uncle Jon, he decided. Whoever, wherever, it didn't matter. It explicitly described exactly how he felt.

He glanced at the digital clock on his nightstand. After midnight? Suddenly, unexpectedly, the bed seemed wider, lonelier than on any other night. He wanted Faith beside him. Kicking off the sheet and jackknifing up, he realized that was a new and different experience for him. Usually, he liked having his own space, without anyone infringing on it.

After drowsily moving into the bathroom to clean up, he went directly to Faith's room. He knocked quietly and called her name. Again, he glanced at the time. Late, he mused. Too late?

Faith heard his knock. Impulsively, she started to respond, then clamped her front teeth on her bottom lip. He'd been sawing logs for hours. Did he think he could traipse into her room and find her waiting for him with open arms? Her fingers wadded the sheet up under her chin.

Uh-uh, Mr. Seaton. Go back to your lair.

While he'd slept, she'd read two articles on how to catch and hold your man. It wasn't wrong for her to love him, but it was a bad mistake to be straightforward and tell him. According to Dr. What's-her-face, men enjoyed the hunt, the challenge of finding the perfect mate. Deep in her heart, she knew she was perfect for him, but he hadn't come to that realization. And wouldn't if she continued being readily available. She'd been entirely too easy a conquest!

"A man chases a woman until she catches him," was the advice she'd read. That one statement seemed peculiar to her, but after she'd reread it several times it made sense. She'd completely revamped her ideas on how to make Jason realize how much he loved her.

She heard the latch click and pretended to be asleep. Smiling, she felt certain her hypothesis was about to be thoroughly tested.

"Faith, are you asleep?"

"Uh-huh," she mumbled sleepily.

Her toes curled as she heard him approaching her bed. Through a fringe of curly lashes, she watched the moonlight cast lacy shadows across him as he knelt beside her bed. Her scalp tingled as his hand brushed through her hair.

"Move over, sweetheart," he coaxed.

She did what he bade. Perversely, she rolled flat on her tummy, with her arm trailing off the side of the bed and her face turned away from him. She felt him bend her arm and kiss her fingertips.

Be still my heart, she ordered. She wouldn't weaken!

"Did I tell you how beautiful you are?" he crooned, tracking his lips up the vulnerable flesh on the inside of her arm. "How exciting your responsiveness is?"

"No," she whispered, wanting to hear more sweet talk. She'd made up her mind not to be easy quarry, but that didn't mean she wouldn't listen to him speak his piece, she rationalized silently.

"It's never been like that for me," he confessed solemnly. "I've never wanted a woman as much as I want you."

Faith rashly tried to translate that into I-love-you. Uh-uh! Too wordy. She wanted those three simple words. He could blather sweet nothings until the rooster crowed. She would not weaken. His hand stroked her nape, which sent shivers down her spine. His warm breath fanned the curls along her hairline before she felt his lips nibbling down the side of her neck.

Weaken? The temptation to turn toward him, like a flower reaching for the sun's ray, compulsively gripped her. Unless she did something instantly, she'd be pulling him into her bed, devouring him!

Her mind in a sensuous turmoil, Faith did the only thing she could think of while under such a persuasive, erotic assault.

She snored.

Big Z's.

Ones of such magnitude, that Jason immediately stopped kissing her and rocked back on his heels.

She filled the silence with snuffles, snorts and a whistle.

"Night, sweetheart," she heard as she felt him tuck the bedspread around her shoulders. "Sweet dreams."

Certain he'd left the room when she heard the door shut, she rolled to her back and stared up at the ceiling. She'd followed the good doctor's advice. She'd been strong; she hadn't capitulated. She'd led him a merry chase. She'd won!

Faith punched her pillow with both hands. Then, why, dear Lord, do I feel like I lost?

Thirteen

"Let me pull the wagon to the next fence," Faith told Luke. Apparently used to performing the task alone, he was content to have her tag along beside him. She wanted to be useful. "You dish the dog food out."

"It's heavy," he warned as he reluctantly gave her the handle. "Watch it! You have to avoid the broken booze bottles. They're hard on the wheels. These alleys can be damned treacherous."

Faith nodded, wrinkling her nose at the smelly debris littering the narrow passages between the tall, downtown buildings. Caroline had neglected to include the industrial area as part of her tour of St. Louis.

With good reason, she thought silently. Although the sun had been up for over an hour, they skulked through the dark shadows like river rats. When she'd volunteered to help him, Luke had cautioned her. This was no Saturday-morning picnic in the park; this was dangerous business feeding junkyard dogs. They both wore grubby jeans and T-shirts. Knowing how fastidious Luke was at the bank, she was surprised that he owned jeans with holes at the knees or knew his way around this part of town.

Faith grinned. "I can manage a horse-drawn hay wagon

over a dirt road, blindfolded, in the rain," she boasted, slightly exaggerating the truth.

"Right," Luke said skeptically and joked, "For a runt, you're strong."

Faith squealed, "A runt? I'll have you know I bucked bales of hay, with snakes in them, all day and all night, without stopping for a drink of water!"

"You're just a miniature Paul Bunyan," Luke sallied, laughing at her exaggerations.

"Yeah," she agreed, looking up at him, bending one arm to show him her muscle. She heard a crunching noise and veered the back wheels away from the green glass bottle. "Sorry."

"Okay, but be careful you don't dump it. Believe it or not, high-protein dog food is expensive." When he told her how much he spent a week, Faith frowned. "The satisfaction I get makes it worth every penny I spend."

"Could you use some extra money?"

"Is a forty-pound robin fat if he ain't long?" Luke asked, quoting her.

"How much?"

"Well, I don't pay for all of this. A few of the bank's customers make small donations," he admitted. "Anything would be a help though." Coming to an intersection, Luke motioned for her to turn right. "I know you're just starting out, so you don't have much spare cash."

Faith hated to tell an out-and-out lie, but from the half-starved dogs they'd already fed, she knew this was a worthy cause.

"I live with relatives," she lied. "They don't make me pay for rent or food. Would fifty help?"

His eyes lit up. "Fifty a month would be greatly appreciated. I could expand my operations to include several more blocks."

She'd meant a week, but sensing Luke would feel funny if she offered more, Faith didn't increase the donation. Smiling, she wondered how differently he'd treat her if he knew she owned part of the bank. He'd really croak like a bullfrog if he knew what had taken place in Jason's bedroom last night.

He'd never believe me, she thought. He'd think I was exaggerating, again. The idea of the s.o.b. being her snuggle bunny did sound preposterous. Her smile grew. But it was true.

Luke drew her attention from her daydream by grabbing her arm and urgently whispering, "Duck behind the wagon!"

"Why?"

"See that guy in the shack?"

She peered through the ten-foot cyclone fence with barbedwire on top of it. Piles of scrap iron and rusty engines cluttered her view. "Yeah?"

"He's the owner." Crouched behind the yellow plastic garbage cans that held the dog food, Luke backed the wagon behind a dumpster. "The bastard threatened to break every bone in my body last Saturday morning. He claims I'm ruining his watchdogs."

"By feeding them? He should be grateful." She started to rise; Luke jerked her back down. "I was just going to go reason with him."

"You can't reason with animal abusers." Luke checked his watch. "We're a little early. He'll be gone in five minutes or less. I hope the dogs don't smell the food."

"What happens if they do?"

"All hell breaks loose. They'll start barking and we'll have to . . . oh, shit."

Faith peeked around the container. The guy in the shack must have had a twin brother. Less than ten yards from them, the biggest, burliest, meanest-looking Neanderthal God had ever created stalked toward them. Long, kinky black hair, with a full beard and moustache, he looked fierce. He held a ball bat in one hand and slapped it against his other hand.

"Run!" Luke yelled, taking off in the direction they'd come from as fast as his long legs would carry him. "Run!"

Faith was quick; the burly man was quicker.

"Where do you think you're goin', girlie?" he yelled, grabbing her by the scruff of the neck and giving her a sharp shake.

"Let go of me or I'll have to hurt you," Faith screamed with false bravado. She kicked at her captor's shins. Tears came to her eyes as she watched Luke disappear around the corner. "I wasn't doing anything bad."

"Like hell you weren't." He rapped the bat against the wagon as he swung Faith around to confront him. "Me 'n my brother been waitin' for you. Hey, Seth! I got one of 'em. Other one got away!"

She saw Seth give his brother the thumbs up sign and reach for the telephone. "Way to go! Bring 'er on in here, Pete."

"You let go of me, now. My friend's gone to fetch the police," she threatened, flailing her arms.

Pete laughed in her face. Faith nearly gagged. His tobacco- and liquor-coated breath was harsh enough to sandblast graffiti off a brick wall.

"Ya hear that, Seth?" Holding the neck of her shirt with one hand, he wedged the bat between his legs and unlocked the padlock with the other. The chained gate parted with a loud squeak as he forcefully shoved it. "Trespasser says 'er buddy is callin' the cops."

"I wasn't trespassing!" Faith denied loudly.

"Yer on my property without permission. That's trespassing. And I'm here to tell ya that yer goin' to jail. This here's the last time yer gonna be feedin' my dogs."

"Jail?" Faith swallowed, hard. When the door of the shack opened and two shaggy mongrels charged toward her, barking and snapping, she swallowed again, harder. Her mouth felt as though she'd swallowed a bale of cotton. Her sharp elbow gouged Pete in his beer belly as she yelled, "I'm innocent. I didn't do anything wrong!"

Jason poured the coffee dregs from his cup into the sink. The least Faith could have done was leave him a note, he griped silently. Along with giving Gertrude and Glen the day off, he'd also arranged for Phyllis and Anita to open the bank and take care of the drive-up windows.

His eyes narrowed as he glanced at the untouched breakfast tray he'd prepared for Faith. The oatmeal cereal had congealed; the ripe red strawberries had sunk until only the green tops were visible. Gertrude might as well have fixed fried eggs for her.

Where the hell had she gone?

He paced to the back window that overlooked the garage. He'd checked it earlier. The Studebaker was gone. Thinking she might have wanted to surprise him by going to the donut shop, or the grocery store, he'd been waiting for her to pull into the drive.

The phone barely rang before he picked it up. "Seaton Place."

"Mr. Seaton, this is Luke. Faith is in trouble, big trouble."

Between jerky pants, his words spilled from his mouth so fast that Jason had difficulty understanding him. "Slow down, Luke. Take a deep breath and then tell me what happened to Faith?"

"She got caught!"

"Caught? Caught doing what?"

"Feeding the dogs. That bastard down near Broadway grabbed her by the neck. I wanted to go back, but I knew he'd kill me!"

"What dogs? Who's going to kill you? Damn it, man, are you blubbering?"

"No, sir," Luke sniffled. "A little. I had to run six blocks before I found a telephone that worked. I didn't know who to call. She lives with relatives, but directory assistance says there are hundreds of Jones families. And, I don't know their first names or their address. You were the only one I could think of who might help her."

"Tell me where you are." Jason scribbled the address down on a notepad. "I'll be there in less than fifteen minutes. Calm down. You can explain everything when I get there."

"Should I call the police? These are some mean sons-of-bitches!"

Jason paused. "Not yet. Luke, I want you to stay by the phone booth or you won't have to worry about them hurting you. I'll throttle you myself!"

In twelve minutes flat, Jason saw a man dressed like a college kid, with his thin hair standing on end and a wild-eyed expression, waving frantically for him to stop. He had to take a second look before he realized it was Luke.

"Get in," Jason ordered curtly. Concern etched fine lines at the corners of his eyes. People got hurt easily in this part of town. It was no place for Luke, and for damned sure, no place for Faith to be. "Show me where you left her."

"Turn left into the alley and go six blocks." Luke pulled a pristine handkerchief from his back pocket and wiped the perspiration off his brow. "You'll see a metal-recycling place. J and P is the name of it, I think."

Jason floored the gas pedal, which slammed Luke against the passenger door. "Why aren't you with her?"

"I thought she was right behind me. I heard footsteps. They must have been echoes."

Trash sacks and papers flew in the air as he plowed the car through them. He raced down the alley without glancing to the left or right at the cross-streets. The farther he drove the more he wished he had called the police.

"Dammit, I can't believe you brought her down here. I have difficulty believing *you* came down here."

Arms braced against the dashboard, head bobbing with each dip in the alley, he ground out, "Somebody has to take care of them. That's the problem with people today . . . they don't look out for each other or for their pets. I couldn't live with myself if I let them starve."

Jason came to a squealing stop beside the locked gate where Luke had last seen Faith. The scrap-metal yard appeared calm and quiet. Both men got out of the car.

Over the car roof, Jason demanded, "Isn't this it?"

"Yes, sir." He pointed to the spot where he'd left the wagon. "The bastards stole my wagon!"

As Jason jogged to the locked gate, he muttered several foul expletives. "Hey! Anybody in there?"

"This is the place. I swear it is," Luke babbled, running alongside the fence. "What'd they do with Otis and Blackie?"

"Get back in the car," Jason ordered. "Where's your station wagon?"

Luke gave him directions while both of them scanned the area for any trace of Faith. With each passing minute, Jason grew increasingly worried about Faith and hostile toward Luke.

"Take your car, drive back to the phone booth and start calling the nearest hospitals. If you find her, call me on my cellular phone. I'm going down to the police station."

Luke barely had both feet out of Jason's car before it was in forward motion. Distraught, feeling totally powerless, he pounded his against fist the steering wheel in frustration. He should have known she was up to something last night when she'd rolled over and pretended to snore.

She wasn't asleep! She was plotting her next nefarious adventure! Her middle name wasn't Persistence; it was Trouble, with a capital T! Or just plain CRAZY! Jason didn't know which. He only knew he had to find her.

Ten worrisome minutes later, he entered the police station and crossed to the counter. Reading the name plate, he inquired politely, "Sergeant Reeves, has anyone brought Faith Jones in here?"

"She's being booked," the police officer droned in a bored tone, without looking up from his paperwork.

"For what?"

"Assault with intent."

"That's preposterous!" Jason roared. "The woman is barely five-foot-two and weighs a hundred pounds!"

Sergeant Reeves glanced up. His eyes squinted. "Aren't you Jason Seaton, from over at the bank?"

"I am."

Automatically, Jason reached to straighten his tie, but he wasn't wearing one. In a hurry, he'd just thrown on the rumpled clothes that had decorated the kitchen floor. He smoothed his hands down the front of his white shirt, tucking in his shirt under his waistband.

"Couple of years ago, I wanted to finance a car," Reeves said, obviously unimpressed by the man across the counter. He grimaced. "Just as well that you turned me down. My wife would have gotten it. She got everything. Kids, furniture, and the car."

Jason clenched his teeth, wondering if it would be considered bribery if he suggested the officer come in and apply for another loan. Deciding it would, he asked, "Do you know where Faith is?"

"Back there." He hitchhiked his thumb toward a row of doors. "I told you she was being booked."

"For feeding dogs?"

"The charges are assault with intent to do bodily harm," the office responded blandly.

"There's got to be a mistake."

"She caused one helluva ruckus when they brought her in." Reeves smiled and shrugged. "You got a lawyer?"

"Not with me," Jason sarcastically. "Can I see her?"

"No, sir."

"Why not?"

" 'Cause she hasn't been printed, yet." He pointed his thumb toward a room at the back and said, "Soon as you see her come out of there, I guess it would be okay for you to talk to her. You'll have to take a seat and wait, like everybody else."

Jason glanced at the crowded wooden benches that lined the walls. A hodgepodge of men, women and children sat, sprawled and stood on the scarred pieces of furniture. As he scanned their faces, he realized they all, himself included, looked anxious and scared.

Preferring to stand, he leaned against the marred wall. Shoulders slumped, hands thrust in his empty pockets, he wondered if she'd been hurt. She had to be half scared out of her mind. The mere thought of her being locked up behind iron bars made his blood run cold.

Assault with intent, Jason repeated silently, in disbelief. Intent to what? Kill them with kindness? Faith didn't have a mean or malicious bone in her tiny body. And from what Jason had been able to gather from Luke's mumbling, the dogs weighed more than Faith.

"Hey, mister," a dark curly-headed boy said as he skidded across the terrazzo floor, landing beside Jason's polished shoes. He bounced to his feet. "You gotta couple of quarters for the soda-pop machine? I'm thirsty."

"Sorry." Jason wiggled his fingers in his pockets. "I don't have any change."

"A dollar would do." The boy gave him a beguiling grin; his two front teeth were missing. "The man at the desk makes change. I'm really, really thirsty."

Wanting to brood in private, Jason pulled his wallet

from his back pocket. He had an assortment of credit cards and his ATM card, but no cash. "Sorry."

"You ain't got no money?" the kid said loudly. "None?"

Jason grimaced. He could feel every pair of eyes in the waiting area drilling holes in him, including Sergeant Reeves's.

A banker with no money. That had to be one for his record book.

"Do you want a boost up to the drinking fountain?"

"Naw, never mind, mister." He started to run off, but came sliding back. He crooked his finger up at Jason. Jason squatted down to his level. In a hushed voice, the boy warned, "You better be careful. The cops arrested my grandpa for not having no money. Said he was a vinegar ant."

Jason grinned, a first for the day. "Do you mean a vagrant?"

"Yep. That, too. Mama said someday they was gonna lock him up and throw away the key. Don't let 'em getcha."

"I won't," Jason promised, suddenly feeling an affinity for the child. "You sure you don't want a drink of water?"

"Naw. I wanted quarters." He grinned and pointed to the Coke machine. "The machine is empty."

Jason stared after the boy, slowly straightening, aware he'd let a five-year-old con him. He'd let Sergeant Reeves have the upper hand, also. Time to turn things around, he thought, and get control of the situation. He could start by finding the man who filed charges against Faith.

He took a hard look at the men seated in the lobby. From Luke's description, he honed in on the only man who'd "scare his own mother in the dark." Slouched in one corner of the bench, sat a man with his tattooed arms folded across his enormous belly. His coarse, wiry beard rested on his red, sweat-stained muscle shirt. It didn't take a Sherlock Holmes to detect this was the bully who'd sunk low enough to file charges against a woman trying to feed his dogs.

Briskly, Jason strode up to him. "Are you here to press charges against Faith Jones?" he demanded in a clipped tone of voice.

"Yeah," Pete drawled, his posture and voice surly. Slowly, he rose off the bench, jerking up his wide belt that heldup the back of his jeans. "You the wimp that skedaddled out of there?"

"No. I represent Miss Jones."

"Her mouthpiece?" Pete grinned, exposing his yellow, tobacco-stained teeth. "She's gonna need one. She ain't gonna be feedin' nobody's dogs for ten, maybe fifteen years."

Jason neither confirmed or denied the man's assumption that he was an attorney. Thoughts of this guy manhandling Faith made Jason see red. Playing a hunch that any man who'd call a lawyer a mouthpiece had a police record, he said, "You'll need an attorney, too."

"Me? Now wait just a goddamned minute." He bellied up to Jason, fist cocked, one finger raised. Oil stained the creases in his knuckles. Small teeth marks circled the web between his thumb and finger. "That hellcat bit me and took a swipe at me with a iron rod. I don't give a shit that she's a woman. She belongs in the state pen!"

Unintimidated by the man's bullish build or his belligerent voice, Jason said calmly, "There are two sides to every story. I plan on conducting a thorough investigation into you and your company."

"I'm clean," he snarled. "You ain't got shit on me."

Jason shot him a predatory smile, then played another hunch. "No weapons on the premises? No drugs?"

"You can't prove them guns 'er mine!" He took a step to the side, toward the counter. "I'm jest a peaceable fella. I don't cause no trouble and I sure as hell don't want no trouble. I got my rights, too."

"Unregistered weapons?"

"You threatening me?"

"Just getting the facts straight."

"Blackmail?"

"Persuasion," Jason contradicted smoothly. "I'm certain that if you drop your charges against Miss Jones that I'll forget we had this friendly little conversation."

"Friendly, shit! You ain't my friend. And fer sure, she ain't. She stole my guard dogs. I want 'em back, you hear?" He pursed his lips to spit, recalled where he was and swallowed. "Replacing them guard dogs will cost me plenty."

Jason reached into his pocket before he remembered he was penniless. "Where are they?"

"She took 'em."

"The police obviously didn't bring them with her," Jason stated flatly. He pushed his sleeve up to expose his Rolex. With eyes as hard and cold as blue topaz and a voice colder than ice cubes, he ordered, "Go drop the charges."

Over the stench of his tobacco breath, Jason could smell the inner rage boiling inside his adversary. The ex-con wanted to take a swing at him, or at least tell him to go to hell, but he took his frustration out on empty space by punching the air near Jason's head. Wordlessly, he turned and lumbered to the counter. Five seconds later, he wheeled around, flipped Jason off and strode toward the exit.

Assuming the charges had been dropped, Jason silently congratulated himself. His steps came close to being jaunty as he strode toward Officer Reeves. He stopped abruptly when he spotted Faith being led across the back of the room. His narrowed eyes flew wide open.

Dammit, he'd expected her to be teary-eyed, repentant, with her clothes soiled and torn. What he saw was the last thing he'd expected.

Fourteen

"Hi, Jason," called Faith in a chipper voice, as she waved at him from the back of the policemen's office. She took the young female officer that stood beside her by the arm and they both walked to the counter. "I'm so glad you're here. It'll save Sara a trip to the bank. Sara, this is the wonderful man I was telling you about, Mr. Seaton."

Scowling at both women, Jason focused his attention on Faith. Her hair was mussed, as were her clothes, but she appeared uninjured. While relieved, he felt perturbed, too. Faith looked as though she'd gone for a short run in the park, made a new friend, and brought her to meet him!

He eyed the blue uniform and silver badge of the tall woman standing beside Faith. Faith knew no strangers; she had a warm smile and a helping hand for everyone who needed it.

Feeling deflated, he said to Faith, "The charges against you have been dropped."

"They have? I knew Jello Belly couldn't make them stick. Thanks, Jason." Faith grinned at Jason as she nudged Sara. "She was worried."

"You weren't?" Jason asked, his temper beginning to flare.

"A little," she admitted making a wry face. Faith had the ability to minimize as well as exaggerate the truth. She couldn't tell Jason she'd been petrified when those two policemen had handcuffed her and put her in the back of the police car. Jason would be upset if she told the whole truth. "Is Luke okay?"

"Completely unscathed." A twinge of jealousy fueled his animosity. "Are you ready to go?"

"Right after you hear about Sara's terrific idea. You know how the police in Forest Park patrol in cars? Or on horseback? Well, the man who owns the bike shop, who's a customer at the bank, said he wouldn't put unicycles or bicycles built for two at his stand because nobody rented them. Sara suggested . . ." Faith took a deep breath. "You tell him, Sara, it's your idea."

"Several policewomen want to do something special to form a closer bond between the citizens in the community and the officers. I thought if someone approached the bike shop, uh, someone with financial acumen who is well respected in the community . . ."

"Me?" Jason inquired blandly.

Sara nodded. "Faith said you could point out how donating free time on several bikes for a worthy cause would increase his rentals."

"Ted Ross would have to buy them," Faith injected happily. "Jason, that's where you come into the picture. We could offer to loan him the money. Which means more business for the bank! And, the councilwoman, who is a bank customer, too, would be absolutely tickled pink because she's the one who wanted the unicycle and two-seaters in the first place! Neat idea, don't you think so, Jason?"

Jason turned his ears off and heard nothing beyond "we could offer to loan him the money." She was easing into his office, threatening his space, his power. He should have known when she tumbled into his bed last night that she wanted something.

Faith gave Sara a hug at the waist while she waited for Jason to weigh the pros and cons of the proposition. "I think it's a terrific idea. Well? What do you think, Jason? Will you talk to Ted Ross?"

"I'll think about it and call Sara on Monday, during banking hours," Jason replied noncommittally.

Winking at Sara, Faith cupped her hand beside her face and mouthed, "Isn't he wonderful?"

"I appreciate your consideration, Mr. Seaton," Sara said, holding her hand forward. After Jason shook it, she turned to Faith. "Let me get your things. You'll have to sign for them."

"Thanks, Sara." She beamed Jason a megawatt smile. "Can I go on the other side of the counter?"

Sara nodded and motioned for Reeves to push the button to release the door. "I'll be right back."

Faith hurried to Jason and gave him a hero's welcome by flinging her arms around his waist and giving him a bear hug. Then, looking to see that no one was eavesdropping she asked quietly, "Is Luke really okay? He was running so fast, to put it in Papa Jon's words—all I could see was shoe soles, elbows and asshole."

"Your accomplice in crime is fine," he assured her drily. The momentary joy he'd felt while she'd hugged him diminished instantly, replaced by a sharper pang of jealousy.

"Luke didn't do anything wrong, either."

Her defending Luke made the short hairs rise on the back of his neck. "He shouldn't have run off and left you."

"David and Goliath! Poor Luke didn't even have a slingshot!"

"He didn't mind throwing you to the lions. Aren't you just a little peeved at him?"

"Absolutely not. That big bully had threatened to kill Luke. It's a good thing I don't bruise easily or I'd be black and blue from my wrists to my pits. Why, you should see how he treated his very own dogs!"

"I spoke to him." Hearing how the bully had mistreated Faith, Jason had the urge to track him down and beat the hell out of him. Nobody mistreated his woman!

"You did speak to him?" Faith moved backward several steps while glancing anxiously around the waiting room. He'd threatened to shoot her on sight. She didn't want Pete to miss her and hit Jason accidentally.

"He's a real charmer," Jason agreed sarcastically. "I especially liked the teeth prints he's wearing on his right hand."

Faith blushed. "He kicked his dog. I had to make him drop me, so I could get Otis and Blackie away from there."

Groaning silently, Jason closed his eyes and shook his head. Only Faith would be more concerned about two mutts than she was about her own hide.

"He wants his guard dogs."

Faith raised her chin stubbornly. She had plans for Otis and Blackie. "It won't hurt him to want."

"Do you know where they are?"

Sara's calling her name gave Faith the opportunity she needed to temporarily drop the subject. She crossed to where Sara stood with a manila envelope.

"Check to see that everything is there," Sara instructed, smiling at Faith, "then sign on the dotted line."

Shoving her money in her pockets and putting the mustard-seed necklace Papa Jon had given her around her neck, she said, "I'll see you Monday at the bank."

"Mr. Seaton didn't look too thrilled with the idea," Sara commented making a glum face.

"He will." Confiding in a soft voice, she added, "Didn't I tell you he's wonderful? Sometimes it just takes him a while to say and do what's right."

"If you say so," Sara agreed dubiously as she watched Jason scowl at a young boy running and sliding across the floor. "You take care."

After a jaunty wave, Faith spun around toward Jason. "I'm ready."

They were halfway to the door when Jason stopped her. "Do you have any quarters?"

"Yes."

"Can I borrow them?"

Faith dug her hand into her snug jeans. As she dropped two coins in his outstretched palm, she asked "What for?"

"What fer?" he drawled, his blue eyes lit with a secretive gleam. "Cat fur to make kitten britches, Nosy."

It was a familiar saying Papa Jon used when she pestered him for information. Curious, she watched Jason approach the small boy who'd mopped the floor clean with his jeans. The boy's face brightened as Jason took his small hand and let the quarters trickle to his grubby palm. She had no idea what prompted Jason's generosity, but she took it as a good omen.

Outside, she waited for him to open the passenger's door before she smiled up at him and said, "I have to make a stop before we go home. Do you mind?"

"Where?"

Jason had learned to be wary of her angelic smiles. She was up to something. After the debauchery this morning, all he wanted to do was go home, lock Faith safely inside, and take a nap. With her in his arms, he tacked on silently.

"I don't know the name of the place. I'll have to give you directions as we go."

He circled behind the car, trying to figure out what she was up to next. Heaven only knew who else she'd talked to at the police station. He couldn't fault her for being friendly or being good-hearted, but that did not mean he'd rubber-stamp every loan she okayed. While he unlocked his door, he realized he didn't have the capacity to outguess Faith; his imagination was hampered by logic. Faith's imagination knew no boundaries.

He'd started the engine and pulled to the exit of the parking lot when Faith looked both ways and didn't know which way to turn. Her smile sprouted wings when she asked sweetly, "Did Luke show you where the junkyard is?"

"We are not going back there."

"Of course not. Do you think I'm crazy?"

Jason cocked one eyebrow.

"We're going a block past the junkyard. That's as far as I could get before Goliath ran us down with his . . ." Her hands fluttered, searching for the right word. "You know, one of those big trucks that pulls cars around when they're broken down."

"Tow truck? He tried to run over you with a tow truck?" Jason blasted with cold fury.

A picture formed in his mind of Faith sprinting, fast as her short legs would carry her, with that foul-smelling piece of human feces trying to squash her against the bricks. Hell, he could have had a gun in his truck.

Faith watched his face turn a dull red. "Otis. The dog. He nearly ran over him. The dogs were more afraid than I was. We ducked around a corner and ran into a building. I shut them in a room for safe-keeping, then ran back outside and made Pete chase me in the opposite direction."

"You want to go get the dogs?"

"It'll be hot in that room by now."

"You want me to go get the *hot* dogs."

"Please," Faith pleaded. "I know I shouldn't ask, but I'd do the same for you."

"That's a comfort," Jason said drily. "Once we get the hot dogs into my air-conditioned car, where do you plan on taking them." He raised his hand before she could answer. "Stupid question. Right? There is only one place to take them."

"Seaton Place does have a big fenced yard," Faith said, worried by his calm voice. "I'd take care of them."

"Faith, guard dogs are not suitable pets for you. That asshole probably beat them."

"I'm sure he did. All they need is a little tender loving care. You don't want Pete to have them, do you?"

"I don't want *you* to have them," he countered firmly.

She touched his knee when he refused to look at her. "Does that mean you won't take me to get them?"

"Yes."

Faith sighed heavily. "Take me to Seaton Place. I'll go get them by myself. Maybe Luke will help me. Anita mentioned the apartment next to her being vacant. I could rent it, I suppose. Move in there so I can take care of them."

"You'd leave Seaton Place?" *Me?* "For a couple of mangy dogs?"

"What choice do I have? I'm the one who stole and hid them. They're my responsibility. You don't want me to shirk my duty, do you?"

"Yes!"

"Jason!"

"Okay! Okay! We'll go get the damned dogs. But they are your responsibility, Faith Jones, not mine. I will not feed them, wash them, pet them, or have anything to do with them."

Elbow deep in suds, her clothes soaked, Faith said, "Squirt the flea soap on his hindquarters. That's it. Right up above his tail. Those nasty little critters like to hide there, don't they, Blackie?"

"He's growling." Jason hovered over Faith, ready to drop the shampoo and snatch her out of harm's way. "He doesn't like this."

"You're just griping, aren't you, Honeybunch?" she

crooned. She scratched his tummy; his hind leg scratched the air. Thoughtfully perusing him from his bushy tail to his grey eyes. "I think he's part German shepherd, part Labrador, with a little Weimaraner thrown in for good measure."

Blackie wagged his tail and rolled over on his back submissively. Otis, who'd been bathed and deemed part collie, setter and hound dog, presently guarded the porch. He'd permit Faith up the steps, but not Jason.

"Male-bashers," Jason declared, "That's what they are."

"He's a male, too. And he's the one who's scared."

Finished with Blackie's hind end, she began rinsing him with the hose. Instinctively, he wanted to shake the foam off; she held him tightly against her side.

Looking up at Jason, she said, "You have to be nice to Blackie and show him that you won't hurt him. Why don't you give his belly a little pat. It's clean, now."

"And while I'm petting him, he gnaws off my hand. Pass."

"He isn't going to bite you," Faith insisted. "He likes you. Can't you tell?"

Jason squatted beside the mutt and held out his hand for the dog to sniff. "He must want me to brush his teeth. That's why he's baring them at me."

"He's smiling at you."

"Yeah. Right."

She tossed Jason a fluffy towel from the stack he'd put beside her. "Help me dry him, would you?"

"I'd rather dry you," Jason teased, calling her attention to the front of her shirt. The pleasant view of thin cotton fused against her rounded breasts made the price of help-ing her bathe the dogs a fair one. "You're soaked."

"You're dry as a bone." She kinked the hose and pointed the nozzle at him. "We're all wet. That's not fair."

"Don't. You'll ruin my slacks and shoes."

"Take them off, 'cause you're next," she cajoled.

Quick as a wink, Jason made a grab for the hose. Blackie snarled; Otis barked.

Jason froze.

"Hush!" Faith ordered sternly, turning off the nozzle. "You have to be nice to him. He's your new master."

Blackie lolled his long, pink tongue from his mouth and looked up at Jason. He had round, soulful dark eyes, like his mistress. Unable to resist, Jason scratched him behind one ear. Silently, he conceded that since the dogs were bathed they didn't look half bad. The rasp of the dog's tongue on his hand was almost pleasant.

"I wanted a puppy when I was a kid," Jason said, wist-fully.

It was unimaginable for Faith, a country girl, to believe he'd been raised without a pet. "No pets? None?"

"One. A goldfish. I won it at a church carnival."

"Doesn't qualify. You pet a pet. Whoever heard of pet-ting a fish? They have scales where there should be hair."

"I did pet it." He began rubbing Blackie's fur with the towel. "I felt guilty as hell when it died two days after I'd won it. I wanted to bury it in a Ziplock bag, with a ribbon around it."

"And?"

"Walter complied," Jason answered, tongue in cheek. "My father called it a burial at sea when he flushed it down the toilet."

With his head bent over the dog, Faith was unable to see his face. She ran a sympathetic hand over the crown of his dark hair. "Did you get another pet?"

"Nope."

"Why not?"

For several seconds Jason remained silent. "Because when the first one died I wanted to bawl. But I'd been taught better. Seatons don't show emotions." Having thoroughly grounded his lie in a smidgen of truth, the same method Faith used, he added, "Besides, I didn't want to be responsible for stopping up the toilets."

Biting her lip, Faith didn't know whether to laugh or cry. When she caught sight of a tiny smile Jason was trying to suppress, she knew he'd been leading her on, trying to shock her.

"I had a pet pig," she boasted, smiling dreamily as she reached behind her back for the hose nozzle.

"I don't believe that," Jason scoffed. "The first liar never has a chance."

"I did. It would oink as it followed me down the lane, and fetched sticks. It would answer to its name, too."

Finished drying Blackie, he let the dog loose. He chuckled as he watched Blackie put his head in the grass and run like mad to dry his ears.

Maybe there is something to Luke's claim that having a pet relieves stress, he mused. Considering how his morning had started, he felt oddly content. In the corner of his mind was the thought that he'd be content staying in the back yard with Faith for the rest of the day. Maybe longer, he mused.

"What'd you name it? Piggly-wiggly," he teased.

"Swine," Faith said sweetly, poking the nozzle under

his nose. "The same word Webster's dictionary defines as a contemptible or disgusting person. A man who pulls dirty tricks on precious, adorable women is a s-w-i-n-e."

"Precious?" His eyes filled with mirth. "You?"

"You damned betchum!"

His hand inched toward her, ready to grab and turn it on her. Her eyes darted from the garage to the kitchen steps. "You'll never make it."

She let a small amount of water squirt out, like the drinking fountain at work. One short blast and he'd be too busy wiping water out of his eyes to catch up with her.

Before she'd completed calculating her odds of escape, Jason lunged, pushing her back into the bluegrass. "Gotcha!"

Blackie whined; Otis leaped from the porch and started circling them, frantically barking.

Giggling and squirming, she let go of the hose, expecting to drench him.

Jason held up the hose, showing her where he had it doubled. "Call off the dogs, precious," he ordered softly.

"You're supposed to be the boss around here. You call them off!" she goaded.

Ever so slowly, he twisted her hand until the nozzle pointed toward her chest. "I am the boss. A wise executive delegates authority. It's your job to call off the dogs."

"Down, Jason," she squealed, laughing so hard her sides began to hurt. Both dogs continued to yap, but they must have sensed she was not in danger. They began harmlessly chasing each other around the yard. "Down!"

Her eyes widened as she felt him follow her orders by inching the nozzle down the front of her shirt. "Up!"

"You're sounding bossy. Too bossy."

Figuring the best defensive was a strong offense, she latched her arms around his neck. Men loved the hunt; they had to hate it when the quarry hugged them!

"I'm sorry," she apologized with saccharin sweetness. "Please forgive me, O wonderful boss of bosses," she crowed, loudly, clearly, for everyone in Forest Park to hear.

He quieted her the only way he could, with his lips firmly covering her sassy mouth. It's what he should have done when they left the police station, he mused, thoroughly enjoying her hot, sweet moistness as their tongues dueled silently for possession of each other's mouth.

"Did you have a pet?" she whispered, needing to know every detail of his life before she'd bludgeoned her way into it.

"No." He yanked the hose from between them and cast it as far as he could. "No pets."

She held his face between her hands. "Are you sorry we saved Otis and Blackie from a fate worse than death?"

"Being a guard dog is not a fate worse than death, Faith."

"Being unloved is . . . even for a dog."

Fifteen

Rolling her over until she lay sprawled on top of him, he forewarned, "Glen and Gertrude are supposed to be back here around noon."

Faith groaned. "why didn't you give them the whole weekend off?"

"Why would I?" He made a lousy attempt to bat his eyelashes at her.

"Don't give me that innocent look." She moved his hand from her hip and placed it under her breast. "There's one good reason. See if you can find another."

"You're a shameless hussy," he teased, loving her immediate responsiveness to his libidinous thoughts. Her responsiveness never ceased to stun him. Faith was refreshingly honest with her desire. His hand kneaded her until he saw the desire begin to weight her eyelids. "I could phone them."

"You could," she murmured. She stroked the side of his face; it felt like a fine grade of sandpaper. His scent drove her wild; it was so masculine, so earthy.

She heard a high-pitched whine. "Uh-oh. Don't panic, Jason. Otis has decided to check out the strange behavior of his new owners."

He watched Otis coming closer and closer, sniffing

the air, his tail between his legs. "You've got me pinned down. Should I cover my throat?"

"Good boy," Faith sang in a calming voice. Otis stretched out flat on the grass; his front and back legs barely inching toward them. "You want some love, too?"

Jason moved his hand from her breast and gently stroked Otis's head until Otis rolled on his back to have his chest rubbed. "Good dog. You say you want to be friends? Play happy family?"

Happy family, Faith echoed silently, closing her eyes and making believe her miracle had come true. Wasn't this what she prayed for before she came to St. Louis? Well, not exactly, she admitted. She'd hoped Papa Jon's brother would welcome her into his family. But underlying her need to be a family member was the stronger desire to belong, to be loved.

Please make Jason love me as much as I love him.

Was it too much to ask, she wondered, without adding her usual string of rash promises to be good, not to cause trouble, and never to ask for anything again?

This time she wouldn't make promises that she couldn't keep. Despite her good intentions, trouble crossed her path with unpredictable regularity. She tried to do what was right, but somehow nothing worked the way she planned it. In the continual race between her brain and her mouth, her mouth was the odds-on favorite.

"What are you thinking about?" Jason asked having watched myriad expressions flit across her expressive face.

"Having my jaws permanently wired together."

Jason chuckled. "Jealous of me petting Otis? Feel like biting my throat yourself?"

She shook her head in denial. A woman has to have a few secret prayers, she rationalized, lying through a pretty smile as she blurted, "I was wondering if you'd think I was presumptuous if I called Gertrude and Glen."

"I'll phone them, if you can get up without Otis pouncing on top of me."

Careful not to make any sudden moves, she got to her feet. "Do you think you ought to call Walter, too?"

"Walter doesn't work here," Jason joked, following her through the grass and up the steps. On a grimmer note, he added, "Come to think of it, he rarely shows up for work at the bank, either."

"What I meant is, he might come home unexpectedly. I wouldn't want him to find you in a compromising situation."

He held the screen door for her, then closed it behind him before Otis could follow them inside the house. The preposterous notion of her protecting his reputation caused him to pull her into his arms for a quick hug.

"Afraid Walter would load up the double-barreled shotgun and march us down the church aisle?"

Faith grinned. She liked the last part, but rejected the concept of Walter forcing Jason to marry her. "I don't think Walter could force you to do anything you didn't want to do."

"Smart lady," he agreed, picking up the phone. He glanced at the blackboard hung on the wall, called Glen and Gertrude to give them another day off, and then tapped in Caroline's number. "Hello, Walter?"

While Jason spoke to his father, Faith decided to clean up the kitchen. She had plenty of black marks on Gertrude's scorecard without increasing them tenfold by leaving dirty dishes in the sink. Or yesterday's clothes on the counter, she thought, her cheeks turning pink. Jason had neatly folded them, but it would have been embarrassing for her to explain what they were doing in Gertrude's territory to begin with. She took them to the laundry room, where she loaded the washing machine.

"Luke deserves to be a nervous wreck," she heard Jason say grimly as she reentered the kitchen. "He ran off and left Faith hiding behind a container of dog food. I had to make up a cock-and-bull story to make the owner drop charges against her."

"Tell him how you saved Otis and Blackie, too," Faith prodded, eager for Walter to know all of his son's good deeds.

Crossing his lips with his finger, he silenced Faith. His brows knitted together as he listened. He wanted the lines of communication open between them, but he disapproved of Walter's newest scheme to get Caroline to marry him. It violated every principle Walter had preached to him as a youngster and as an adult.

"That's absurd," Jason snapped. "You're making a mistake, a big mistake. She'll only think less of you."

Faith's ears perked up. She? Caroline, she assumed, shamelessly eavesdropping.

"Who's going to take your place? Me? I'm already working twelve-hour days," he burst out furiously.

She watched Jason wrap the coiled telephone cord around his index finger. His fingertip turned blood red, then white. She had difficultly understanding the constant power struggle between Jason and Walter. To her way of thinking, being family and all, they should have been each other's strongest advocates, greatest defenders.

Instead, they were at each other's throat like cats and dogs.

Granted, Walter was terribly preoccupied with Caroline's pregnancy, with fatherhood, and marriage. There were times when she'd felt slighted. She would have liked to spend quality time with Walter. Other than their passing encounters at the bank, she seldom saw him. But he'd always been kind to her. Just yesterday, he had told her he was proud of how quickly she'd grasped the intricacies of the banking business.

"The hell you are," Jason said abruptly. Despite the surface calm of his voice, Faith sensed his inner rage. "I don't give a damn what we agreed would be your responsibility. I'll make that decision."

Her intuitive powers proved accurate when he hung up the phone with such force that the bell inside the base tinkled in protest.

For several seconds she stood holding a plate under the torrent of water gushing from the faucet, while on the receiving end of his thunderous glare. This was the unemotional man the bank employees complained about? He looked as though he wanted to smash china against the walls to relieve his frustration!

"Anything I can do?" she offered.

"You've done enough," *harm,* he completed silently. He considered confiding in Faith. Only a fool would confide in an enemy. Instantly he canceled that notion. "I have computer printouts I need to review. I'll be in the library."

Stunned by his switch from lover to bank executive, Faith dropped the plate into the sink. She strode after him, determined to find the bee Walter had stuck in Jason's bonnet. He swung the kitchen door open; she went through it before it closed.

"Did you and Walter have a disagreement?"

"Did you leave the water running?"

Certain his change in mood had something to do with her, "Did you argue over me? Is Walter mad because of my caper with Luke?"

Abruptly Jason stopped; Faith stepped on both his heels.

"I'm sorry. I didn't mean to walk all over you," she apologized.

Jason grinned, a hard, unamused smile. He couldn't have phrased what she was doing to him with more precision. And if Walter had his way, there would be nothing he could do to prevent her from trampling him under those dainty feet of hers.

He took her by the shoulders and set her against the wall. "This concerns family, Faith. I'd appreciate it if you would stick your nose in someone else's business."

"But . . ." Her arms outstretched in appeal, but she stayed where he'd put her. It hurt to be ostracized from the Seaton family, to be physically and verbally put in her place. She had to change his mind, to change his mood. "But, you called to see if your father is coming home. Is he?"

Jason pushed the library door open, stopped, and turned back toward Faith. "His charade is over. Walter won't be having his suits cleaned in Caroline's closet. He has decided to be a house daddy to prove to Caroline he'll be there for her, day and night."

"Then we will be here alone?" she asked, smiling wistfully at him. "Together?"

The heavy door swung shut. Shards of disappointment stabbed Faith. She comprehended why Walter's moving from Seaton Place would distress Jason. Of all people, she was intimately acquainted with being left behind, alone and lonely. Quite naturally, Jason would feel dejected.

However, she thought in an effort to solve the emotional equation, sadness did not explain how angry he'd been when he'd hung up the telephone.

They must have switched topics, she mused. Something regarding Walter making a decision without consulting Jason. That's when Jason had gone bonkers.

What decision?

And why had Jason taken his anger out on her?

Deep in thought, she trudged back into the kitchen. Why stew over this? she asked herself, turning off the faucet. Whatever decision Walter made must have had something to do with her. That made it her business, didn't it?

She crossed to the phone. While she looked for Caroline's number on the blackboard, a thought entered her mind that justified placing the call: Any blow that struck Jason, hurt her.

She dialed Caroline's number, tapping her toe with impatience while the phone buzzed in her ear.

"Hello?"

"Caroline? This is Faith. Could I speak to Uncle Walter, please?"

"I don't think this is a good time," Caroline replied in a hushed tone. "He's upset with Jason."

Faith could tell that Caroline did not want Walter to hear what she said. "Can you talk?"

"Quietly. Very quietly."

"Well, Jason is upset, too. He won't tell me what the problem is, so I thought I'd ask Walter."

"Typical," Caroline disparaged. "The two of them are feuding so we have to tolerate their foul moods."

Loyal to the core, Faith replied, "Jason isn't taking his bad mood out on me. He's shut himself up in the library."

"Same difference. He's depriving you of his company. It's called passive resistance, Faith. Before my parents divorced, Dad would relentlessly nag at Mother until she'd do something like run up her charge cards just to give him a valid reason to complain. That's when the bickering would start." Caroline sighed heavily. "Who needs this grief?"

Faith didn't respond to her rhetorical question. "I think Jason would feel better if he could share his problems with me."

"That's the prime fallacy underlying every relationship . . . the idea that two people can share problems better than one. Sort of split the problems in half. What women aren't told is that when the male arrives at the threshold of marriage, he has three times as many problems as she had."

Mathematically inclined, Faith mentally figured out the percentages. "Hers aren't split in half? They're multiplied?"

"Correct. Now you can understand why I don't need a husband to solve my *one* problem."

Faith shook her head. There was a flaw in Caroline's arithmetic, but she couldn't put her finger on it. "Do you know what Jason's problem is?"

"As Walter's legal counsel, legally I can't divulge that information. Sorry."

"Walter is doing something legally to Jason?" she quizzed.

"I'm ethically bound by a code that doesn't allow me to reveal private information."

Once again, Faith felt excluded. Caroline wouldn't let her talk to Walter, and even though Caroline was privy to the information, Caroline wasn't going to tell her anything. She was back at square one.

"I guess I'll have to pester Jason until he tells me," Faith said, refusing to give up.

"Don't," Caroline warned. "Let Jason sulk in his cave and lick his wounds. Eventually, being of relatively sound mind, Jason will realize you had nothing to do with Walter's decision."

"Walter's decision has something to do with me?' Getting Caroline to disclose what she knew was tougher than pulling hen's teeth. "It does, doesn't it?"

"Faith, please, stop asking questions I can't answer."

"You've just got to tell me. A simple uh-huh or uh-uh will do." Several seconds of silence gave Faith hope. "Does this legal action have something to do with me?"

"Uh-huh. That's it! Don't try to pry more from me."

Faith's imagination took flight. The only dealings she'd had with the legal system involved testifying when Jonathan had adopted her. "Does Walter want to adopt me, like his brother did?"

"Children get adopted. You're an adult."

Mentally Faith crossed that possibility off her list. "Okay. No adoption. Walter wants . . ."

"Walter wants lunch," Caroline interrupted, chuckling over Faith's effort to pump information from her. "Fighting with Jason makes him hungry."

"The two of you could come here for lunch."

"Thanks, but no thanks. I don't need a ringside seat when World War III erupts. Let the two of them solve their differences. Like I said, I have my own problem with Walter."

"Jason mentioned that Walter is moving in with you."

"That's no problem. We mutually agreed on that."

Perplexed, Faith asked, "If you're going to live together, why won't you marry him?"

"The difference between living and loving together is one letter, *I*. This *I* doesn't need a husband or a father for her child." Caroline sighed. "I've told you how I feel, Faith."

"Papa Jon used to say, 'Why buy the cow when the milk is free?' He was discouraging me from being a woman who lived with a man without benefit of marriage." Her forehead pleated. "Isn't it peculiar that you've switched the meaning to . . why marry Walter when he'll live with you?"

"I don't mean to speak ill of your adopted father, Faith, but he had a few archaic beliefs. Men have always been able to do as they damn well pleased, without worrying about the consequences. Now, women can, too."

"But Caroline, your baby will be   " Faith bit her lip to choke back the offensive word.

"Illegitimate?"

"A bastard child."

"Only men are bastards," Caroline replied blithely. "My baby is a girl."

The semantics bewildered Faith. "But aren't girl babies . . . ?"

"She's a love-child. I do love Walter," she said, testily.

"I just don't need a piece of paper—one that's all too easily set aside—to cause me and my child grief later."

"I think you ought to marry Walter," Faith suggested in a timid voice. She put her heartfelt wish into the advice she gave. "Everybody needs a family. Your baby girl will want one, too."

Exasperation ringing in her voice, Caroline countered cynically, "And I think you need to take a giant leap into the twentieth century. You no longer live on an isolated farm that insulates you from life's harsh realities."

Feeling bruised by Caroline's criticism that followed closely on the heels of Jason's excluding her, tears came to Faith's eyes.

"Walter has lunch fixed. I have to go, Faith. Bye."

Aware Caroline was displeased and wanted to get rid of her, too, she said, "I hope I'll see you soon."

"I'm awfully busy tying up loose ends before I have to go to the hospital, but we'll do lunch together, soon."

"Promise?"

"We'll see," Caroline answered noncommittally. "Bye."

Faith heard the line disconnect and hung up her receiver. The crocodile-sized tear that clung to her dark lashes slid down her cheek. She caught it on her fingertip and stared at the droplet of salt water.

"Seatons don't cry," she whispered, quoting Jason. She wiped it on her jeans and swallowed back her tears of self-pity.

A tidal wave of homesickness washed over her. Caroline was right, she mused, Life was simpler back on the farm where she took care of the animals, tended the garden, and they provided her with the basic necessities.

Without having to ask for it, Papa Jon had given her unconditional love.

Another tear dripped from her chin, proving she didn't belong with the Seatons.

As she stood staring bleary-eyed through the window, Otis and Blackie caught her attention. Neither Jason nor Caroline would talk to her. The dogs couldn't talk, but at least they'd listen.

The two guard dogs froze into a threatening stance when they heard the door creak. Once they saw who it was, they eagerly bounded across low-growing shrubs.

Faith sank down on the back porch steps and gave both of them a hug. After several minutes of being fondled, Otis stretched out at the foot of the steps and Blackie cuddled next to her.

"What do you think, big fella? Do you think we ought to go back to the farm?"

Blackie tilted his head to one side; his black eyes worshiped her.

"It wouldn't take long to round up the animals I loaned to the people who live nearest to the farm. You'd have playmates."

Whining, Blackie put one paw in her lap.

"You'd like that, wouldn't you?" She scratched behind his ears. "That's not to say you'd like everything there. By now the weeds will be knee-high to a giraffe in my garden. I'd have to hoe like crazy to save the crop. If not, as a last resort I could eat canned food from the grocery store."

Blackie barked, once, as though he agreed with her.

"Right now, we'd have the chores done. I'd be fixing dinner . . . we eat dinner at noon and supper at night," she explained. Being city dogs, they'd have to learn country ways. "And after we cleaned up the kitchen, I'd take you down to the pond. Did you know that catfish as big as whales lurk in the murky depths? They're as old as Methuselah and smart as Peter, Paul, and Luke. That's what Papa Jon used to say."

She heard the screen door squeak behind her. Surprised, she swiveled at the waist and saw Jason standing there.

Stoically he said, "I'm hungry. Do you want me to pick up a sandwich for you from the delicatessen?"

Unlike Jason and Walter, who wanted to feed their anger, Faith was queasy at the thought of food. Sitting through a meal with him ignoring her would increase her queasiness to up-chucking nausea. "Thanks for asking, but I'm not hungry."

"You mad at me?"

"No," she replied truthfully. She hugged Blackie; he promptly licked her face. She felt the floorboards give beneath her bottom as Jason moved to sit beside her. They were touching from hip to ankle. A warmth spread through her. "You did hurt my feelings."

"I'm an asshole," he said succinctly.

Faith hated to hear the bank employees make deprecating remarks about Jason. Because she stoutheartedly defended him, they'd stopped. She wouldn't allow Jason to say bad things, either.

"You aren't a butt crack," she said, trying to make him smile by using the slang she'd heard two kids using while at the police station. Amusement lit his eyes as his lips twitched. Encouraged, she added, "Maybe a cheesewad, but definitely not a butt crack."

"Cheesewad?" Jason came close to grinning at her. "What, pray tell, is a cheesewad?"

"I haven't the vaguest idea." She grinned impishly at him. "Remember the little boy you gave the quarters to at the police station? It's what he called his brother."

Jason nodded. After Otis lumbered up to see what was going on, he stroked Otis from head to tail. The tactile feel of the dog's sleek hair gliding beneath his palm doused the remaining embers of fire in Jason's belly.

With good reason, he'd expected Faith's opinion of him to coincide with his own. Because he'd been mad as hell at Walter, he'd treated her shabbily.

It took two Tums and a cool-off period for him to realize he'd undervalued his influence. Sure, his father could make plans for radical changes; but, it took someone who was at the bank daily to carry them out. This was not the first occasion when Walter had come up with a harebrained idea. Rather than having a direct confrontation, Jason had listened impassively, then gone on with business as usual. Walter's latest wild hallucination would meet the same fate.

"Look at your buddy, Blackie. He looks like he's in doggie heaven."

Distracted by his thoughts, Jason hadn't noticed how Otis had sprawled across his knees and had his head cuddled against Jason's chest.

"Must think he's a lap dog," Jason affirmed, scratching the pooch under his chin. Otis licked Jason's ear. "None of that, Otis. We have to establish some ground rules around here."

"I'd like that, too," Faith said, leveling Jason with her

sweetest hundred-kilowatt smile. "Your mood swings change quicker than the traffic signals on Grand Avenue."

"What do you mean?"

"Before you called your father, I got the green light . . . go, go, go! After your call, without a yellow cautionary light, you turned red. I had to slam on my brakes and come to a screeching halt to avoid a major collision."

Amused, Jason smiled at her. "Everyone else accuses me of being too even-tempered."

"Uh-huh. Mad all the time," she jested.

The kernel of truth lodged in her joke stuck in Jason's ear like exploded popcorn. Defensively, he argued, "A Seaton is always cool, calm and collected. Factual. Impartial and objective."

"Yellow light?" Faith giggled, poking him in the ribs with her elbow.

"Green," he countered as he pushed Otis off his lap, grabbed Faith's shoulders and licked her ear playfully. "No yellow light—feel free to pet me, anywhere and everywhere."

She heard Otis growl. "I think he's jealous."

"We'd better go inside?" Jason suggested, giving her a huge smile while he wiggled his eyebrows comically. "I need a nap."

"Before or after?" she teased, caressing the side of his face.

He turned his head and nipped the fleshy pad beneath her thumb. "Neither."

By mutual consent, they happily left Otis and Blackie on the porch to fend for themselves.

"Your room or mine?"

"Are we having sex or making love?" she asked pertly, hoping for the latter.

He embraced her, holding her close to him, feeling his heart ache with his need to completely possess her. He knew what she was fishing for—I love you. Since he did feverishly want her, he could stretch the truth and tell her what she wanted to hear, he rationalized silently.

The hard core of honesty that was his mainstay prevented him from lying to her. To lie now would be an act of cowardice.

"I do care for you," he whispered earnestly against her ear, bravely risking the chance of her rejecting him by not saying what she wanted to hear. "I'm not certain I know how to love. The only person who could have taught me was Jonathan. Do you think he sent you here to teach me?"

Liking the idea of Jonathan blessing their union, Faith nodded. She led him into her room. "He believed in free love given unconditionally."

"And built a barbedwire fence to isolate you." Jason shook his head and began unbuttoning her blue chambray shirt. "It seems paradoxical, but it isn't. I find myself wanting to protect you, and yet, I want what I'm guarding you against."

Faith mimicked the growling noise Otis had made. "I want to protect you, too."

What she bit back was that love always protects, always trusts, always hopes, always perseveres, never fails. It's what Jonathan had taught her from the Bible.

As he untied the knot she'd made to keep her shirttail from getting wet, she reciprocated by unbuttoning his shirt. Magically, what could have been cumbersome seemed like a well-orchestrated dance, with Jason taking the lead. First, their shirts, trousers, and finally their underwear was shed into a puddle of mismatched clothing at their feet.

Seconds later, they lay side by side in her bed. She knew what she wanted. She wanted him to touch her until he drove her insane. And then she wanted him inside of her, driving against her until she felt her world shudder as she reached the pinnacle of her climax.

"Tell me what you want, Jason," she requested unselfishly, her voice husky.

He touched the curls surrounding her face. "I want to touch your hair. Last night I dreamed of winding it around my fingers in golden ringlets." He pulled his gaze from the strands of silk binding him to her.

As his eyes met hers, Faith felt a warmth trickle through her entire body when she saw him smile at her. His tone of voice aroused her. His thumb traced the bow of her lower lip.

"I can taste you—a blend of wild honey and strawberries—sweet and tart." As his thumb followed the curves of her lips, his eyes closed. In his mind he singled out her flavor from the myriad memories she'd imprinted there. "Blindfolded, in a pitch-dark room, I'd be able to identify you by your kiss."

His hand slid down her neck, across her shoulder, to the curve of her breast. "I want to touch them. See how responsive you are?"

It wasn't necessary for her to look; she felt her nipples harden. Dying for him to kiss her, she hooked her leg over his thigh and pulled him closer.

Jason inhaled a long breath as his rigid length pushed

against her softness. "I believed a woman's virginity wasn't important to me."

"Is it?"

Feeling the growing heat and tension between his thighs that placed his self-control in immediate peril, he chuckled to ease the tautness and teased, "Is a forty-pound robin fat if he ain't long?"

He felt her hand encircle him. "That depends on how tall the robin is," was her hoarse reply. He quieted her witty repartee by kissing her with a pent-up emotion building inside of him. Passion made his kiss primitive, rough, urgent.

"You aren't the only one who wants," she whispered between hard, devouring kisses, "or dreams. After you left my room, I wanted to chase after you."

A minor alarm rang in the back of Jason's mind; he ignored it as he fought back his rampaging desire to roll on top of her and plunge himself inside her. Her hand moving across the plains and valleys of his chest made his muscles contract reflexively. And Lord have mercy, what her other hand did brought him to the brink of exploding in her hand.

"Red light," he gasped, in an effort to stop her from disgracing him.

His eyelids popped open when she did the most amazing, sexy thing he'd ever experienced. Her thigh pushed against his hip, rolling him on his back as her hands pushed against his shoulders, and he felt her wet heat as she mounted him. He arched his hips, thrusting upward to aid his penetration of her. Her fingers kneading his chest set the rhythm as she lifted her hips, circling, sinking, grinding against him.

A low groan ripped from his throat when he lost control and exploded inside her. She stiffened; her back arched, and he felt her quicken around him. Her peak shook his entire body, leaving him spent and weak.

A tiny thought crossed his mind as she lay across his chest. Faith had dominated him and though he'd had numerous sexual encounters, he couldn't remember a climax that had spiraled him to a sensual Eden.

One thought led to another as he lay spread-eagled, with her face pressed against his chest. Twice they'd shared the same bed, each with their own separate motives. His desire to control, dominate, and retain power over material possessions motivated him; her love, with a dash of curiosity and lust, had motivated her.

As his breathing returned to normal, he realized they'd both paid a hefty price for sexual gratification. She'd traded her virginity for the love of a man who'd arbitrarily used sex as a means to attain an end result. For a man whose life's cornerstone had fairness, integrity and honor engraved on it, his behavior was despicable.

Needing to right the wrong he'd committed, he propped himself up on the pillows and held her tightly as he said gruffly, "Faith, I think Walter may have come up with a good idea."

"I spoke to Caroline," she divulged, wondering if he'd switched from green light to red light, again. "Are you upset because he isn't going to live here?"

"No. I wasn't surprised or upset by that decision." He felt her finger draw a square box around his flat, round nipple. Was she unconsciously fitting a round object into a square hole? "Do you think they belong together?"

Sensing the importance of their discussion, Faith moved to her side, with one arm over his shoulder and her head held in her hand, while she brushed her fingers across the wrinkles on his forehead. "It doesn't matter what I think, because Caroline and I don't think alike. I'm countrified and she's citified. Our values don't mesh so my opinion is of no value to her."

"It is to me."

Faith smiled, please to know he valued what she thought. "Well, it seems to me that both Caroline and I yearn for the same goals, love and commitment, but Caroline doesn't really believe they are attainable. That's why she's willing to live with Walter but not marry him."

"I wish she'd picked someone other than my father as a sperm donator," Jason said drily. "A man in the middle of his midlife crisis needs . . ." He paused, not knowing what Walter needed.

"Needs to be needed?"

"I need him."

"Do you? Have you told him you need him?"

"He knows. It goes without saying."

"Does it?" Faith knew she was walking where angels fear to tread. "All I've seen are power struggles. He had it. You wanted it. You took it. He made you what you are and you've made him a figurehead—a man in a position of leadership who has no power, no authority and no responsibility."

"He wants to resign at the bank and become a full-time house-hubby," Jason disparaged. "He's made a hundred-and-eighty-degree change and I don't like it."

Glad he hadn't bitten her head off for what she'd said, she dared to ask, "Have you told him?"

"That I resent his going gaga over this unborn child? That the only time he paid attention to me was when I struggled to prove to him that I could be a financial wizard?" Jason scoffed. "I don't think it's what he wants to hear."

"Then you agree with Caroline? Walter won't be a good father for their child."

"No."

Mathematically, she inverted her logic, and asked, "Then you agree with Walter. Caroline should marry him and allow him to father their child?"

Habit decreed he never agree with Walter. Jason stubbornly growled, "No," then grinned, recanting his response.

Pinching his cheek lightly, Faith returned his grin. "I love how you smile at me. It makes me feel . . . extraordinary."

He muffled a joyous chuckle against the crook of her neck. She hadn't solved his problem; she'd allowed him to see it through her eyes. Seeing and doing what's good and what's right made the world appear rosy. He would talk to Walter. Maybe, just maybe, they could call a truce to their silent family feud.

"You are extraordinary," he whispered, meaning it.

Sixteen

Faith stood beside Jason's desk chair in the library. She'd been reading *Body and Soul* while he'd been poring over computer printout sheets he'd brought home from the bank. Although captivated by the spunky female jury consultant and her hero, she felt guilty reading a novel while Jason worked.

"What is it you're looking for?"

"If I knew," Jason replied, stretching his arm out until it encircled her hips, "I wouldn't be down here and neither would you."

She brushed back a lock of hair from his forehead. "The day I arrived you had these same records."

"How do you know that?"

"I corrected a mistake." She pointed to the figures made in red marker. "What intrigues you about them?"

"You solved the mystery of the red mark. I've been casually asking everyone who'd written on the sheets, thinking that would give me a clue as to who is switching small amounts of money from one account to another."

Her hand covered her mouth as she sank to the arm of his chair. She parted her fingers. "An embezzler?"

"Possibly." He followed the service-charge column

from the top of the page to the bottom. "I don't want to accuse anyone of juggling the books, yet."

"Uh, . . . Jason?"

When he looked up and saw misery plainly stamped on her face, his eyes narrowed. "You haven't been messing with the computer, have you?"

"No, but sometimes I joke with the customers and tell them I'll give them free samples."

Making light of her confession, he said, "I wondered why the lines were so long in front of your station."

"And sometimes I kid around and tell them I'm going to deduct a percentage from their deposits." She cringed as she remembered other outrageously incriminating things she'd said. "I told the florist I embezzled more than I earned!"

"No wonder he brings you flowers. Do you think he wants a cut?"

"Jason!" She slapped lightly at his shoulder. "This is serious. If the police question the other tellers, I'd be the most likely suspect."

"Oh, well," Jason sighed. "I guess I should have saved the police a trip to the bank by leaving you at the precinct this morning," he teased, hugging her close to his side. He couldn't seem to get close enough to her, in bed or out of it. That was another extraordinary experience for him.

"Not funny," she groaned, picturing herself in a black-and-white suit, peering out from behind locked bars. "You know I'd go crazy cooped up inside a jail cell."

"You're serious," he stated, somewhat amazed.

Faith unwound his arm from her waist and bounced

to her feet. "Of course I'm serious. I've practically confessed to anyone who'd listen!"

"You're wealthy."

"Everyone thinks I'm the lowest paid employee. I've dodged hundreds of inquisitive questions. Where do you live? I couldn't tell them I lived at Seaton Place. I told them I live with family friends."

She began pacing in front of the desk. Her arms flew every whichaway the more anxious she became.

"That's sort of true."

"What's your phone number? I don't have one. Why not? Because I don't need one or because I can't afford one. Why'd you leave Backwater?" She slapped her forehead. "I can't even remember the excuse I gave."

"Quit worrying, Faith. No one is accusing you of committing a crime, least of all me. I'm not even certain anyone is embezzling funds." He pushed away from his desk. "C'mere, sweetheart. You're getting yourself worked up over nothing."

She brushed off the seat of her white slacks, then rubbed her nose. "I've told so many lies my pants should be on fire and my nose should be as long as a telephone wire!"

"You didn't tell any lies. You don't need a phone and you left Backwater, Missouri to see what life was like in the big city." He folded her into his arms. "That's what you told Anita, who told Phyllis, who passed it on to Luke. I overheard Luke telling the janitor. Some grapevine, hmmm?"

"I've heard you know everything that goes on at the bank." He coaxed a reluctant grin out of her by kissing the corners of her mouth. "They'd shoot Joe for spying if they knew you talked to him. Me, too, if they knew I lived with you.

"Technically, we don't live together," he said.

"We share the same house, eat at the same table, wash our clothes in the same machine, sleep . . ."

"Yes?" Jason hummed, his blue eyes shimmering with laughter. "You were saying?"

"Sleep in the same house," she answered, glibly changing *bed* to *house*. "The circumstantial evidence points to your being my significant other."

He caressed her springy blond curls and gave her one of his breathtaking smiles. "Lovers."

"Significant other. Your suits still hang in your closet."

"I could mingle mine with yours."

"Don't you dare."

"Why not? We aren't wild teenagers. We're both consenting adults." His large hands framed her face. "You don't plan on sleeping alone, do you?"

"Yes. We aren't the only ones who live here. There are other opinions to consider. Mrs. Cavendish would frown on a clandestine relationship. I won't have her accusing me of corrupting you, seducing you into a lifestyle of debauchery."

Jason laughed. "Gertrude doesn't make the rules here."

"She makes the beds."

"I'll tell her to mind her own business."

"Seaton Place is her business."

"End of discussion, Faith." He kissed her to shut her up. When it came to verbal warfare, she had the edge— the sharpest tongue west of the Mississippi.

* * *

Closing her eyes, Faith leaned her head against Jason's shoulder. Frames from *Beauty and the Beast,* and *Jurassic Park* imaged on her eyelids. Humming the theme song of the animated film, Faith truly believed this was one of the happiest days of her life.

"Tired?"

"Exhilarated." She peeked through her lashes to see the expression on his face. That certain smile of his had become perpetual. She couldn't remember seeing him scowl the entire day. "You?"

"Considering you made me sit through a church service, hike through the zoo, and ride bikes to the art museum, I should be asleep at the wheel."

"As long as you're griping, don't forget making you sit through back-to-back movies." She rubbed her face against his sleeve like a contented kitten. "It's been a magical day, one I'll never forget. Thank you, Jason."

He kissed the top of her head, chuckling as her hair tickled his nose. "My pleasure."

It had been a pleasure, he mused silently. The last time he'd been to the zoo his Uncle Jon had held his hand. She'd taken what he'd viewed as mundane for an adult and made it exciting, an adventure. She'd mimicked the monkeys, fed peanuts to the giraffes, and cavorted without inhibition with the children. He made a mental note to make a generous contribution to the zoo and museum funds. Several times she'd glanced up at him with such wonderment shining in her dark gaze that he'd thought tears would come to his eyes. The sheer delight he'd seen on Faith's face as she'd watched the beast dance with Beauty made him want to buy her a VCR so she could watch all the films Jonathan had made her miss.

"Red light," he whispered, tilting her chin up until he could lightly kiss her.

"You purposely slowed down until the green light turned yellow and then red, didn't you?"

"Yeah," he admitted, not the least bit ashamed. "You're the one who devised the game. I'm sticking to the rules you made."

Faith nipped his lower lip. "Turn left on Kingshighway. The lights aren't synchronized."

The light turned green all too soon. A horn blasted. He gave her a quick peck on the tip of her nose and continued down Forest Park Boulevard. He wanted her at home, where he could kiss her leisurely, thoroughly, and eventually lead her up to his bed.

"Do you hear that?" Faith asked, sitting up straight in her seat. "It sounds as though Otis and Blackie are keeping the devil himself from trespassing on your property."

Goosing the gas pedal, Jason careened up the driveway and slammed on the brakes to avoid rear-ending Glen's truck. It was a damned good thing he'd insisted that Faith wear her seat belt or she'd have been propelled through the windshield. "You okay?"

Nimbly Faith unlatched the buckle. She was out the door before Jason heard her reply.

"Miss Faith!" was what she heard as she ran by Glen's truck. "Don't go back there! They'll tear you to pieces!"

Skidding to a stop, Faith circled the front end of the vehicle. "Glen?"

"Ma'am?"

Jason yelled, "Be quiet, Otis. You, too, Blackie!" The vicious barking instantly changed to whines. He lowered his voice and asked Glen, "Why didn't you go in the front door? You have a key."

"And listen to Gertrude moan and groan about the hounds from hell invading her back yard? She called the cops and the Humane Society, but nobody would come so she started bitching—excuse me, Miss Faith—at me to lock them in the garage until morning."

"Does she hate dogs, too?" Faith asked, classifying herself in the same category as the four-legged mongrels.

Cautiously Glen opened his door. "I thought she was starting to like you. She took that low fat cookbook with her this weekend."

The tall man Faith thought of as the gentle giant shook his head when she gestured for him to follow her to the gate. "C'mon. They're more afraid of you than you are of them."

"Mr. Jason . . . ?"

"Faith will protect you. Go ahead. I'll go inside and quiet Gertrude's tizzy."

He waited until he heard the gate creak and Faith crooning sweet talk before he charged up the curved drive. Taking the steps two at a time, he barged through the front door and stormed into the kitchen.

"Don't you let those flea-bitten, no-account dogs in the house," Gertrude mandated.

"Otis and Blackie have both been bathed. What the hell do you think you're doing calling the authorities on my dogs?" he blasted.

Astounded to hear Jason raise his voice, Gertrude backed up against the sink. "Are you yelling at me?"

"Does a horsehair blanket scratch?" he boomed, quoting Faith. He watched her face blanch beneath several coats of war paint. "You're damned right I'm yelling. It's about time someone stood up to you!"

"I'll quit!" Gertrude bluffed. "Nobody yells at me."

"Terrific! You'll probably put the cheese industry out of business, but you do what you think is right." He strode to the back door, opened it and called, "Bring Otis and Blackie inside. Gertrude doesn't want them left outside in the cold, cruel world!"

On a roll, he turned around when he heard Gertrude suck wind. "Right?"

"Whatever you say, Mr. Jason," she answered, humble and sweet as a piece of pecan pie. "I always did think you needed a puppy. I said as much to Mr. Walter, but he wouldn't allow one."

It was Jason's turn for his jaw to drop to his chest. Gertrude had sided with him? Against his father? Knowing how influential the housekeeper was, it was a wonder he hadn't had several litters of dogs.

"Allergies," Gertrude explained. "Mr. Walter claims dog fur makes him sneeze."

"Caroline has poodles."

"That's different." Gertrude wiped her hands on her frilly white apron. "Everything's different since he started testosterone treatment."

This time, Jason felt as though his jaw had come unhinged.

Faith cringed. She'd known since her first day at work that Uncle Walter was under medical treatment. It was no big secret among the bank employees. Phyllis had told everyone—-except Jason. Blackie and Otis followed her heels into the kitchen and sat politely when she stopped beside Jason. Deciding ignorance was the better part of valor, she played dumb. "Walter isn't sick, is he?"

"No," he replied curtly. Unwilling to discuss his father's medical treatment in front of Gertrude and Glen, he gave both dogs' heads a pat, and took Faith by the elbow. "Gertrude, I'd appreciate it if you'd put them in the laundry room. That's where they've been sleeping at night. I'll see both of you in the morning."

"Did I hear her say testosterone treatment?" Faith asked, as she hopped and skipped to keep up with Jason. "I read an article on that."

"Can you believe the servants know more than my father tells me?" Jason roared, kicking the door shut with his foot after she'd entered the library. "I didn't know he'd been to a doctor, much less that he's on medication!"

"It explains his change in temperament," Faith said, flinching as he picked up a crystal ashtray. She could tell by the hard glint in his eyes that he wanted to smash it. This was a golden opportunity to explain to Jason why his father's personality had altered, but for once in her life she kept her impetuous tongue still.

"Male hormones!" Jason eyed the multifaceted crystal, thinking of how his father's personality was similar to the refraction of light in the small cuts. With a flick of his wrist, blues turned to greens and shades of pink. The past year or so Walter had been chimerical, indulging in numerous unrealistic fantasies: marriage, fatherhood, retirement.

Up until two years ago, Jason mused as he returned the ashtray to the table, Walter seldom dated, and dedicated his life to Southern Bank. The only way he would have considered early retirement would have been if he'd looked up and found a tombstone perched on his forehead!

Completely dumbfounded, he shoved his fingers through his hair. "Dammit, he should have consulted with me!"

Why, Faith thought, mentally slipping into Walter's shoes. *So you'd have something new to fight over?*

"It isn't as though he was sick," he thought aloud. Slowly, he regained control of his temper. "Maybe a cold or minor bout with the flu. Nothing that kept him home from work. He's always enjoyed good health. Why would he allow some quack to make a guinea pig out of him?"

After he'd glared at her for several moments, Faith fidgeted with the pleats in the front of her trousers, squeezed her palms together, then volunteered, "The magazine article said testosterone treatment is new. Doesn't that put it beyond the experimental stage?"

"All medicine is experimental," he derided coldly. "That's why doctors are called *practicing* physicians. Any first-grader knows when they get it right, they won't have to practice anymore."

Faith locked her neck muscles to hold her head still. Shaking her head in disagreement would have given him a reason to misdirect his animosity toward her. But, he was wrong to lump the entire medical profession in a flock of ducks, and he was wrong to criticize his father for seeking medical help. Walter was a classic case in support of hormone therapy.

"Do you want to read the article? It might lessen your apprehensions. The scientific results have been dramatic."

"Go get it," he ordered succinctly.

Glad to have an excuse to leave the library before she

began defending Uncle Walter, she scampered from the room. Minutes later, she feverishly searched through the pile of women's magazines beside the bed, while she also considered grabbing her courage hat off the closet shelf.

She could understand why none of the bank's employees wanted to cross Jason. His facial expression looked as though it had been carved from an Antarctic glacier. The icy tone of his voice could freeze popsicles in a record-breaking heat wave. She'd felt less troubled if he had kicked the door shut and roared like a wounded animal.

"Cure for Male Menopause," she read, flipping through the pages to make certain she had the right article. She skimmed the first column. "Yeah, this is it."

She gave her closet a second glance, but decided real courage came from deep within herself. Besides, a straw hat with flowers decorating it wouldn't protect her in a man-made snowstorm.

"Find it?" she heard echoing up the staircase. "What's taking so long?"

"Yes, I found it," Faith answered, her heart clamoring as she glanced at her rumpled bed. Fleetingly, she considered using sex to quick-thaw Jason. She could read the article to him, in bed, then . . .

Hopeless romantic, she silently chastised, piling the sleek covers together. One thing all the experts agreed upon was settling any differences outside the bedroom. Frankly, she thought a rousing pillow fight would alleviate part of Jason's frustrations.

"Faith, are you coming down here? Or do I have to come up there and get the magazine?"

"I'm coming." She picked up the magazine wishing

she hadn't adamantly opposed sleeping with him because Gertrude and Glen were living under the same roof.

Jason needs to be comforted and loved.

Slower than an ant carrying a boulder, she went to the banister and looked down at Jason. "Can't this wait until morning?"

"Procrastination won't make Walter's medication more palatable. While I'm reading the article, you can go over the service-charge figures on the commercial accounts for me."

Faith matched Jason's grimace with one of her own. Her magical day was fizzling to an end. She gave him the magazine and preceded him into the library, where she situated herself behind the desk.

This could be cozy, she mused, using her imagination to put a fresh spin on a unpleasant situation. He'd invited her into his inner sanctum, which was new and different. And, he'd given her an important task—find the bank's imaginary embezzler. Smiling, she decided she could set this up to be similar to the board game called *Clue,* that she'd often played with Papa Jon. The sheaves of data could be the clue cards and the pad of paper her clue sheet. All she had to do to solve the mystery was find obscure information she could link together.

If I were an embezzler with access to the computer, how would I go about bilking the bank out of millions of dollars? She picked a pencil from the central drawer and tapped it against her chin. *I'd change the account number to mine when a customer made a deposit.*

Too simple. The customer would be bouncing rubber checks across the city. He'd complain and the embezzler would be caught.

Taking a hint from what Jason wanted her to check, she skimmed through the names of the commercial accounts. Okay, what if I appropriate monies from inactive accounts, ones never used? She quickly realized that because of the FDIC insurance, few customers allowed the balance to exceed $100,000.00. Nothing unusual there.

Wait a minute, why not pick an account with a multitude of service charges—returned checks, stop payments—a marginal account where the customer doesn't keep track of what funds are going where?

She checked the overdraft sheets. There were several customers who were scraping by monetarily. In fact, a couple of them were her favorite customers. But, only having access to the totals restricted her from gaining the details she needed.

"I need the customers' statements."

She realized she'd spoken aloud when Jason replied, "It's all computerized. Tomorrow ask Mary Chambers for the printouts."

"Are customers charged for printouts when they ask for them?"

"A couple of dollars."

"Hmmmmm." Couple of dollars here and a couple of dollars there could mount up quickly. Again, she discarded the clue. An embezzler would want big bucks, wouldn't they?

"What about returned checks? What's the service charge on them?"

"Twenty dollars." Five twenties make a hundred; a faster means of accumulating cash. But, there remained the problem of overcharging the customer and s/he getting their sticky fingers on the money. "A service-charge scam would only increase the bank's earnings. Would you take a chance on going to jail to fatten the pockets of the bank's stockholders?"

"That's the same conclusion I reached." Jason dropped the magazine on the table. "Two of the majority holders recently became minority stockholders. On paper, their monetary worth is cut in half."

"Who? You and Walter?" Faith chuckled. "Is this a confession or an accusation?"

"Walter's ethics are above reproach," Jason said firmly.

"Well, I guess that leaves me with one burning question— how'd you do it?"

Her joke earned her a dour glare, which she deflected with a cheeky grin.

Rising to his feet he crossed to the window. Softly he said, "Maybe the new majority stockholder wants revenge for having been deprived of wealth during her youth. Could it be she wants more than her adopted father's share?"

"Me?" Faith hiccupped. "You think I stole from the bank?"

"You are a computer whiz, aren't you?"

She would have pitched the sharp pencil at him if he hadn't turned around. The amusement in his eyes warred with his tightlipped expression. "Yes, but there's an easier way to increase my holdings than penny-ante embezzling."

"How?"

She rose from behind the desk, crossed to where he stood and tweaked his earlobe. Sugar wouldn't have melted in her mouth as she replied, "By marrying a minority stockholder."

"Is that a hint?"

"Nope." Her ringlets bounced saucily when she shook her head. "I know you're a confirmed bachelor."

He would have looped his arms around her waist, but she quickly stepped away from him. He matched each backward step she took with one forward. "Walter is the only other stockholder."

"Yes, he is, isn't he?"

Playing along with her shenanigans, he added, "Caroline won't marry him, so Walter is fair game?"

"Nope." Spunky as the monkeys they'd seen earlier in the day, she walked her finger up his zipper. "I'm young, but I hope I don't have to wait until the man I love is on testosterone treatment. But, if I do, it's what I'll do."

Seventeen

On Monday, back at her teller's station, a dreamy smile spread over her face as she licked the end of a money strap and carefully aligned the wrapper over the dead president's face before sealing it closed.

Luke can't gripe about that one, she thought, giving herself a mental pat on the back.

Last night lying alone in her bed, she'd relived the best parts of the weekend until they flowed through her mind as smoothly as a 3-D animated movie. She'd also made several promises she fully intended to keep. Prior to Jason's making love to her, she'd thought of her job at the bank as a way to be near Jason. Now, with Walter talking about retirement, and Jason trusting her to go over the records to ferret out an embezzler, she'd decided to forsake her zany behavior.

Henceforth, she would conduct herself in a judicious manner. Her demeanor would reflect the seriousness of her career goal—for Jason to appoint her as Walter's replacement. The vow she'd made to keep a civil tongue in her mouth would be the hardest to keep. Realistically, she knew the smartest thing she could do would be to super-glue her tongue to her teeth.

Nothing, she swore silently—and nobody—could coerce her into misbehaving.

She tugged the points of her grey pinstriped vest that matched her midcalf-length skirt and suit jacket. Silver haircombs skinned her bouncy curls away from her heartshaped face. A red polka-dotted ascot graced her neck, tucked beneath a cream-colored silk blouse.

Demure and professional, she assessed, except for the slit running from the hem to midthigh. This morning she would have stitched it closed, but needle and thread were nowhere to be found anywhere at Seaton Place. She had to take baby steps to keep the slit from flapping open and drawing attention to her slender legs.

At exactly one minute before eight o'clock, she folded her hands on the marble counter, pasted a welcoming smile on her face, and waited for Jason to open the bank for business. Since he and Walter had closeted themselves behind closed doors in Jason's office, he was yet to see her transformation from rapscallion country girl to sophisticated career woman.

"Guess Mr. Seaton and Snuggle Bunny are too busy arguing to unlock the door," Anita said to Faith, climbing up on her teller's stool. "Where's your cohort in crime?"

In a well-modulated voice, Faith answered, "Phyllis sprained her ankle. She won't be in today or tomorrow. I feel guilty as sin because I'm the one who started Phyllis on her exercise regimen."

"Are you coming down with a cold?"

Frowning, Faith started to shake her head, but stopped because she knew the hair combs would become flying missiles if she did. She cleared her throat, testing it for soreness. "No, I don't think so. Why?"

"You sound different."

Faith beamed, delighted Anita had noticed the change.

"You've lost yer southwest Missouri twang, honey-chile," Anita teased, flashing her a toothy grin.

"Did I sound that awful?"

"Your voice was as melodious as the trill of a mock-ingbird," Anita replied, quoting Faith's description of Jason's voice. "Today you sound like your scarf's choking you."

"I'm trying to speak in a cultured manner," Faith whispered with righteous indignation. "I used to sound like an Ozark Mountain hillbilly."

"That's better than sounding like a stuck-up snob with laryngitis," Anita scolded. "Take a word of friendly advice and be your own sweet self. That's the way we like you."

Maybe imitating Caroline's tone of voice was too drastic a change, Faith admitted silently.

"Good morning, Mr. Boone," Anita greeted.

"Morning, ladies." With his usual dramatic flourish, he produced a vase containing sprigs of honeysuckle, ferns and daisies from behind his back and gallantly presented it to Faith. "How's the prettiest flower at the bank this fine summer's morning?"

"Fine. Thank you for the bouquet." Judging from the thickness of his deposit, he'd had an exceedingly profitable weekend. Her lips parted to tease him about skimming off her usual twenty percent. She pinched a blossom off the honeysuckle vine, placed it between her lips and sucked the nectar with sensuous delight. "Heaven's secret honeypot."

The florist chuckled triumphantly. "I could sell a train-car load of those if you'd stand outside the shop and give a demonstration. City folks are intrigued by simple country pleasures."

Hoping she hadn't made a spectacle of herself, Faith popped the fragile flower in her mouth to dispose of it. While she counted the florist's deposit and tallied his checks, she noticed him opening his bank statement.

"Is there a problem?" she asked. For no explainable reason, her stomach began to flutter as though a hummingbird had been hiding in the petals of the honeysuckle she'd swallowed.

Mr. Boone rubbed his smoothly shaven jaw thoughtfully. "I'm not certain."

After she'd entered his deposit and placed the money in her cash drawer, Faith took the sheet and turned it toward her. It was the monthly statement of his personal accounts. She quickly computed the figures in her head. No errors there.

"Everything appears in order."

"The checkbook balanced. Look at the savings account."

"According to this, you made a small withdrawal from your savings at the first of last month, but brought the balance back to the original amount two weeks later."

"Uh-huh. The balance is right," he agreed readily, "but there's one little bitty problem. I didn't make any ATM withdrawals or deposits."

"Oh?"

He leaned across the counter and whispered, "I figured it out to be exactly five percent."

"Yes, it is."

"Did you have a change of heart?" he whispered between cupped hands.

Slow on the uptake, Faith asked, "I beg your pardon?"

"Did you service charge me, then change your mind and put it back?"

"No! I wouldn't take money from your account," she gasped, horrified that he'd taken her kidding seriously.

Twin flags of embarrassment colored his cheeks. "Gosh, Faith, I'm sorry. My wife must have used her card. I thought she'd lost it."

"Did she report it missing?"

"I told her to, but she said nobody could use it without the secret PIN number."

Faith nodded and felt her combs slip. "I can look the transaction up for you on microfiche."

"I'm certain it's only a silly mixup between me and Opal. No cause for you to worry your pretty head over it." He frowned as he folded the statement and returned it to the deposit pouch.

"Frowns grow wrinkles," Faith blurted before she could bite her tongue.

"Nothing grows without fertilizer," he quipped, his usual good mood restored. "You don't see any Cow Power there, do you?"

Despite her smart mouth's breaking her vow with her first customer of the day, Faith laughed and shook her head. The silver combs came undone. Her riotous blond curls corkscrewed back in place.

"Pitch 'em, Faith. Why try to perfect nature?"

After the early Monday morning rush, Faith straightened her cash drawer while covertly glancing at the other tellers. Mr. Boone's bank statement was of grave concern to her. She suspected Jason was correct in believing someone was filching money; he'd been incorrect in how it was being accomplished.

During the past two weeks, she'd grown to know and like each of the employees. It was hard for her believe that one of them had the motivation to risk imprisonment. From what she'd read in the daily newspaper, criminal behavior was usually linked with drug or alcohol abuse or family problems.

Her eyes focused two work stations down. Jillian Hopkins, she mused, watching the dark-haired, well-dressed teller chatting with an elderly woman procuring traveler's checks. Married to a lawyer/politician, Jillian worked rather than "sit in her empty nest." A seasoned traveler, she'd probably been on more trips to exotic places than her customer.

Anita proclaimed she needed the job, but after chatting with her between customers, Faith suspected Anita dispensed money as a teller because in some peculiar way it satisfied her craving to do charity work. Her husband, an oral surgeon at the medical center, wasn't hurting for coins.

Kristen Riley and Shannon Thompson were both single and living at home. Both sets of their parents were well-to-do customers, with addresses that rivaled Seaton Place. Faith mentally checked them off her list of suspects.

Although Anita had joked about Phyllis being Faith's cohort in crime, the only real sin her best friend at the bank could be convicted of was gluttony. Faith worried her lip as another pang of guilt stabbed her. Phyllis would be here today if it weren't for her. A two-hundred-plus-pound woman had no business on the jogging trails of

Forest Park. With the temperature hovering in the nineties, it was a miracle Phyllis hadn't had a heat stroke.

Her eyes skittered and stopped as she saw Luke Cassidy coming up from the bank vault. Timid and shy as he was at the bank, Luke *would* have a stroke if anyone near him stole a penny and he found out about it. She grinned, remembering how he'd stampeded for cover the moment trouble had started at the junkyard. Luke was the kind of guy who checked the position of the sun so he could avoid stepping on his own shadow.

She watched Luke circle behind the teller's stations until he stopped directly behind her. He glanced from her neat-as-a pin cash drawer to her scrubbed face before he glanced furtively toward Jason's office and said quietly, "You had me worried sick. You could have let me know you were safe."

"I'm sorry, Luke." Bowing her head, she hid her face from his scrutiny. She couldn't tell Luke that once Jason had arrived and they'd picked up the dogs, all thoughts of him had dropped by the wayside. "That was inconsiderate of me."

"Young Mr. Seaton is furious with me." He held up his thumb and forefinger. "I was this close to getting fired. Frankly, I'm surprised he didn't fire you."

"He was upset with me, too." Faith suppressed a grin. *Until later,* she tacked on silently. Memories of their bedroom romps sent a delicious tingle racing up the backs of her legs where he'd kissed them. She was having a devil of a time keeping a straight face. "He's taking care of Otis and Blackie."

Luke rocked back on his heels as though she'd poleaxed him. "I don't believe that any more than I believed he signed that note Snuggle Bunny. Is this another one of your wild stories?"

"He's adopted them." She raised one hand as though taking a solemn oath. "Honest."

"I guess I'll see for myself on Saturday."

"Saturday?"

"At the Fourth of July celebration at Seaton Place."

Good Lord, she'd forgotten all about her big coming-out party! Luke was going to see one heck of a lot more than the two dogs. Everybody at the bank was going to know she was an ersatz member of the Seaton family.

Silently, Faith groaned. She could feel the blood draining from her face.

"Ha! Caught you in a fib, didn't I?"

Anita popped her head over the partition separating the stations and grinned. "Did I miss a good whopper? Did I hear you say Snuggle Bunny?"

"Shhh!" Luke silenced, rising on his toes to peer over Faith's shoulder toward Jason's office. "Mary almost slipped and called Young Mr. Seaton by his nickname. You can bet your bottom dollar that Faith will be fired if he hears it and finds out who started it."

For one single impetuous moment, Faith considered telling them Jason couldn't fire her, that she'd inherited half the bank stock, but good sense prevailed. They'd know, come Saturday, and that was all too soon for comfort. There was a big red imaginary line between management and labor. She had a sneaking suspicion none of them were going to like the way she'd straddled it.

* * *

"She needs to be kept on a leash for her own safety," Walter said, after Jason explained the police-station fiasco.

Jason scowled at his father. He needed to follow his own advice with his own woman. "It isn't as though Faith intentionally sets out to cause a problem," he responded protectively.

Walter glared back. "It seems as though every time she leaves Seaton Place . . ."

"Shit happens," they chorused in mutual agreement for the first time in decades.

Their scowls inverted into smiles. Neither of them used vulgar popular slang often, and yet, those two words described Faith's predicaments perfectly. Jason slid backward, off the edge of his chair where he'd been perched ready for a major battle; Walter settled deeper into the cushions of his chair.

"You don't think much of my moving in with Caroline, do you?" Walter asked, broaching one of several topics Caroline had urged him to discuss with his son.

"I'd prefer she shared your home with you."

"So would I," Walter admitted. "How do you think I felt when you were the last to know she was pregnant? How did you feel?"

"I thought I took her announcement rather well."

"She didn't. Caroline fumed for a week."

"How far along is she?"

Walter beamed with male pride. "Thirty days, maybe less."

"Is it why she wants you to move in with her?"

"Humph! She wants me to continue with the illusion that I reside at Seaton Place."

"Why?"

"Because Caroline says she needs a place she can call her own." His smile sagged. "And, she doesn't want the baby raised in a hostile atmosphere."

"Meaning me?" Jason tilted his chair backward, swinging it to the side until he was almost horizontal with the desk top. He linked his fingers together and propped up his head. "I thought about getting my own place years ago."

"I would have raised holy Cain. I have always felt that until you married, you belonged with me at Seaton Place."

"Ironic, isn't it? You being the one who wants to move out?"

"It's idiotic!"

Jason grinned. His father's change in temperament did have its plus side. Before he'd started treatment, Walter would have gone ballistic if anyone had dared to suggest that anything the President of Southern Bank contemplated doing was absurd. "Do you want me to find another place?"

"We're family. My move is temporary."

"And the early retirement you spoke of yesterday? Is that temporary, too?"

"That's another bone of contention between Caroline and myself. Her father must have been a workaholic. She barely remembers her father's face, and yet she vividly recalls the brawls her parents had and the bitter divorce. Each year her father hauled her mother back into court to reduce his maintenance and child support. She believes that if she marries me, which in her mind is a big if, that I'll revert back to the way I was while you were growing up."

"I survived," Jason replied blandly. He kept a sharp

eye on his father's face to see his reaction. Discomfort, Jason noted, watching the color heighten in his father face. His hands trekked down the sharp pleat of his trousers as though the ridge was a path to sane logic. "Without your guidance, I wouldn't be where I am today."

"I don't know whether I should feel flattered or insulted," Walter admitted with reluctance. When the desk chair squeaked into an upright position, he raised his hand to stop his son from making a cutting remark. "Don't misunderstand me. I am proud of your accomplishments. You're a cool-headed banker. Nothing flighty about you."

"What's Caroline's complaint?"

Walter lifted one shoulder; his eyes roamed around the office as though he'd find a tactful reply written inside a picture frame. "She doesn't speak badly of you. I won't allow it. You *are* my son, after all."

"Yeah, that's true." Jason propped his arms on his desk and bent toward his father. "But then, you can't fault Caroline's mathematics, either. Logically, one and one do make two—she and her baby each being one."

"You're telling me I don't fit into the equation?"

"I don't have to tell you . . . Caroline has. It appears to me that you need to go back to the basic premise and get it straight. Take the offensive. Don't move in with her unless she agrees to a wedding ceremony. Then, and only then, decide where you're going to live and when you'll retire."

Walter pondered Jason's suggestion for several minutes. "The basic premise is Caroline no longer needs me to get what she's wants—a child. She says she loves me, but she doesn't want to complicate raising our child."

"Do you really believe she holds all the aces?"

"Unfortunately, yes," Walter sighed, his face crumpled. "Someday, when you love someone with every fiber of your being, you'll understand how terrifying the thought of losing them is to you. I lost your mother. Look how long it took me to find another woman who's perfect for me."

"How many years did it take Caroline to find the right man to father her child?"

"I never thought of it that way."

"You should. You're acting like a man with bad credit rating who has a multimillion-dollar idea and needs a loan. What do you do if the customer is fearful?"

"Boot him out of here. He'll never make it."

"And if he's confident?"

"Consider his proposal. I might or might not make the loan."

"But you'd be more willing to take the chance, wouldn't you?" Jason asked, getting to his point.

Walter hesitated, then nodded his head.

"Then play the cards you've been dealt. Don't throw in your hand until you've made her show her aces to you. She may be bluffing."

"What if she isn't bluffing?"

"It's better to walk out standing tall than to go with Caroline's shoe print on the backside of your britches."

Walter chuckled. "That sounds like something Faith would say."

"She does have a knack for taking complicated problems and simplifying them until they're either black and white or right or wrong," Jason agreed with a grin.

Laughing, Walter slapped his knee. "Jonathan was like

that. He'd shake me up like a carbonated beverage, then pull the tab and watch me—I'd spew all over everything. Life was a whole lot duller after he left."

"I missed him."

"I know you did, son. I've always been a little jealous of Jonathan's charm. Never more so than when I watched him play with you." Walter got up from his chair and stood by the side of Jason's desk. "Who'd have believed I'd get a second chance at fatherhood at this late stage in my life. This time I'll work at being a good father."

Jason looked up at his father. He'd invariably felt proud of being Walter's son, but at this instant, he was proud of Walter being his father. The difference was subtle, and yet, it was pivotal in their relationship. He could tell by the way his father shifted his weight from foot to foot that Walter wanted to say or do something, but he must have felt extremely awkward.

"Was there something else you wanted to discuss?"

Walter's head bobbed, paused, then shook. He motioned for Jason to stand. "There's something I've been hoarding for years that I want to share with you."

"What?"

"This." Walter pulled Jason into his arms and gave his son a back-thumping hug. "I love you, boy. You got short-changed when it came to having me as a father, but I was blessed by having you as a son."

Eighteen

Faith felt certain she was being called on the carpet for disciplinary action when Luke grimly informed her that she was to report to Mr. Seaton Senior's office, pronto. Luke's I-warned-you look sent her wild imagination out of control as she baby-stepped the length of the bank. She grabbed at the slit in her skirt, wishing she'd had the good sense God gave a goose! Why hadn't she stopped at a store and bought a needle and thread?

Walter had been in Jason's office for ages! What had Jason told him? More importantly, what had Jason *not* told him? She blushed at the possibilities. Would Uncle Walter take one look at her and know she'd lost her virginity? Lost it? She'd given it away with glorious abandonment.

What would she do if her uncle sat her down and began asking personal questions? Crawl under her chair and pray he wouldn't send her back to the farm! She wasn't the least bit ashamed of falling in love with Jason or making love with him, but they weren't topics she wanted to discuss with Papa Jon's brother.

Let it be business, she prayed silently. *He can demote me back to counting money or to washing windows. I'll do anything to stay and be near Jason!*

As she neared the carpeted office area, she decided

business wasn't a safe topic, either. What if one of the customers had filed a complaint? Or worse, what if one of them had shown Walter a monthly statement, like Mr. Boone's, that didn't jive? Any employee at the bank could have pointed their finger at her. Wasn't it her sassy mouth that made embezzler jokes?

She'd told Sara to stop in at the bank this morning. Faith could only hope she wouldn't be stopping in at Sara's place of business—permanently.

"Go right on in, Faith," Mary instructed, shooting her a friendly wink. "Shut the door behind you. Mr. Seaton said he doesn't want his privacy interrupted."

Uh-oh. I'm in deep shit . . . manure . . . fertilizer. She silently upgraded her vocabulary until it reached Walter's standards. She felt a case of terminal hiccups about to attack. Inhaling strongly to steady her nerves, and forcing her lips to curve heavenward, she minced into Walter's office.

"Faith!" Walter stood and gestured toward two upholstered chairs. "Make yourself comfortable. Can Mary get you anything? Coffee? Tea? A soda pop? A donut?"

"No, thank you." Before an execution, she read that criminals were given their choice of meals. No food or drink would pass between her lips. Faith tightened her smile.

Her brown eyes enlarged to the size of pie plates when Walter came from behind his desk and sat in the chair next to her. Reflexively, her hand moved to the slit. One quick prayer had been answered. The slit in her suit skirt wasn't gaping open.

"So, tell me what you have been up to while I've been

at Caroline's?" he asked, noticing she appeared on edge. "Anything exciting?"

Faith swallowed. Her fingers curled tightly together. The blood pounded in her ears louder than the pistons in her Studebaker.

"No, sir," she replied, waiting for a bolt of lightning to strike her. When Walter tilted his head slightly, waiting for her to expound, Faith chose the safest topic she could think of on short notice. "Jason took me to the movies."

"That's nice."

"Fantastic," she blurted. "The movies and Jason."

Walter chuckled at her refreshing enthusiasm. "I imagine I'd feel the same way if he rescued me from jail."

"He told you?"

"Jason and I had a lengthy discussion."

Her fear grew by leaps and bounds. He knew about her being arrested. Jason must have given him a detailed report on the entire weekend! Not wanting Walter to believe that Jonathan had raised her with corrupted morals, she spouted, "I love Jason."

Walter clenched his chair's arms and reared back as though struck by her declaration of love. Certain he'd overreacted and that Faith did not mean what he thought she meant, Walter asked rhetorically, "You mean family love?"

"No! Love-love, like you and Caroline, as in hot for his . . . !" She pinched her mouth shut with her fingers as his eyes grew wider and wider. Walter didn't know! His lengthy discussion with Jason had not included that juicy tidbit of information. Trying to recover to some degree of decorum, she mentally crossed out *body* and substituted, ". . . intellect. His mind. Jason is very, very s-s-s-smart." Only at the last second did she convert *sexy* to *smart*.

"Very," Walter agreed, moving from the chair to gaze through the thick glass partition between the two executive offices. Jason was on the telephone, with his chair turned away from the glass wall. "Does Jason know how you feel?"

Walter's eyebrows raised; Faith ducked her head.

"I told him that I love him."

"And what was his reaction?"

"He hasn't told me that he loves me." She lifted her chin; her troubled brown eyes followed Walter as he returned to the chair he'd previously occupied. "But, deep in my heart, I know he does."

Disconcerted by her forthrightness and naïveté, Walter paused, uncertain as to how he should respond to this startling news. He spread his knees; his elbows dropped to them, and he assumed his thinking position. Thoughtfully, he rubbed his jaw.

It didn't surprise Walter that his son had refrained from telling Faith that he loved her, if he did. Walter himself hadn't heard those special words pass through Jason's lips, either. Well, he amended, not since Jason had entered kindergarten. A few minutes ago, he'd silently begged to hear Jason express his love. Walter thought he'd seen a glistening of moisture in his son's eyes, but he must have been mistaken.

A horrific thought, that of Jason being incapable of love, saddened Walter.

He wondered if Jason had contemplated the advantages of marrying Faith. Recalling the young women he'd arranged to have introduced to Jason, and Jason's icy reaction when the suggestion was made that a marriage of convenience had advantages, Walter seriously doubted his son would callously become involved with Faith because of her inheritance.

It was far more likely that Faith had misinterpreted Jason's courteous, gentlemanly behavior as affection. Much as the idea of the two of them marrying appealed to Walter, as Jason's father and Faith's legal guardian, the only appropriate behavior for him was to gently dissuade her from taking Jason's attention seriously.

"Faith, we want you to be happy here at Seaton Place," he began tentatively. "I'm aware the cultural gap between Backwater, Missouri and St. Louis is . . ."

"Wider than the Red Sea?" Faith supplied when his arms opened wide.

"Exactly. We don't expect miracles from you."

"I can't part the sea, but Papa Jon taught me to bend with the wind, otherwise branches snap. I've tried real hard to sway with the breeze."

Faith uncrossed her ankles from beneath her chair and stuck her high-heeled shoe toward him to demonstrate how she'd traded in her sneakers for fashionable shoes.

What Walter noticed was how she modestly held the flaps of her skirt together. Not that he needed it, but it was further validation of Faith's lack of sophistication. Caroline would have let the weight of the fabric slip to the side, exposing a provocative glimpse of her slender leg. He had few doubts that Caroline had that in mind when she'd offered to help Faith select her new wardrobe.

"Adapting entails more than how you dress. People are different here, don't you think?"

"Different, meaning peculiar or meaning, not like me."

Faith sensed he was trying to tell her something important, but he was going all around the huckleberry bush to get to his point.

"Both," Walter replied, grinning at her. "You and Jason are different."

Faith laughed, beginning to relax. "Thank goodness. You'd be upset if we were the same," she joked.

"I meant, culturally your backgrounds are different. What you might construe as affection, Jason might consider politeness, being a gentleman." Walter took her hand and gave it a fatherly pat. "Faith, what I'm ineptly trying to say is . . . you've had limited contact with men. Don't mistake puppy love for the real thing."

"I haven't. I really and truly love him, Uncle Walter." Her free hand made a cross over her tailored suit's handkerchief pocket. "With all my heart."

He squeezed her ringless hand sympathetically. "I'm certain Jason is fond of you . . ."

"But you don't think he loves me?"

Compassion for the forlorn notes he heard in her voice rendered Walter momentarily speechless. He swallowed over the knot in his throat that prevented him from saying a plain and simple no. "First love is always the toughest. It's a hard lesson to learn that just because you love someone with all your heart doesn't mean they feel the same."

"You don't think he loves me?" Faith asked, her tone shrinking to nothingness.

"No, dear," he acquiesced quietly. Deciding it was far kinder for Faith to hear it from him rather than from Jason, his voice gained emphasis as he came to the point he wanted to make, "I don't think he loves you the way you want to be loved."

Faith inelegantly gnawed the lipstick off her bottom lip. Had her fanciful imagination betrayed her? Had the love she'd thought she'd seen in Jason's eyes merely been a reflection of what she felt? Was Walter right? Had she mistaken good manners for love?

"No, Uncle Walter, you're wrong," she insisted, minimizing her own apprehensions. "No."

Walter knew there was nothing he could do to make her stop loving Jason. After his wife had died, he'd survived by burying himself in work. Time was the only cure for heartache. Time and work.

He stood up and moved behind his desk. "Did Jason mention to you that I'm considering retirement?"

"We'll miss you."

"No, you'll be seeing more of me. As of tonight, my suits will be hanging in my own closet."

"You aren't moving in with Caroline?"

"Do you think I should?"

"I think Caroline should marry you."

"Is that what you told her yesterday?"

Faith nodded; Walter chuckled.

"Now I understand why she was upset when she hung up the telephone."

"I should have kept my big mouth shut. Caroline has been very kind to me."

Walter hesitated, thinking, then a determined smile dawned across his face. "I doubt you said anything I haven't said a million times. She's become deaf to my powers of persuasion, but she listened to you."

"Have you told her you've changed your mind?"

"I will. We're having a late lunch at Al Baker's. Care to join us?"

"No! But I'll watch for an early fireworks display." Seeking an immediate solution to another problem, she asked, "Do you think she might not want to finalize the plans for the Fourth of July celebration at your house?"

"Don't worry, Faith. Caroline had the caterers contact Gertrude. A decorator friend will bring a crew over Friday to string the red-white-and-blue streamers, hang the flags and set up the tent. Pardon the pun, but everyone should get a big bang out of meeting you." He vacillated for a second as to whether or not he should reveal another good piece of news for her. Deciding her career might be her saving grace, he said, "I thought I'd start the holiday off by announcing who my replacement will be Friday afternoon."

Happy for Jason, she flashed Walter her brightest smile. "Jason will be pleased."

"I hope so. He's spoken highly of your progress at the bank. You'll have to work hard, but . . ."

"Whoa, hoss, you just hopped the curb and drove through a plate-glass window!" She popped out of her chair. "Jason is your replacement, isn't he?"

"He'll be President of Southern Bank. You'll be his right hand man, . . . uh, woman," he corrected. He lifted his hand as though it held a champagne glass. "Here's to your being Madam Vice-President."

"I haven't done anything to earn another promotion," Faith wailed, appalled by his intentions. "Everybody will know we're semi-related!"

Walter gestured for Faith to be seated. "I never approved of the employees' *not* knowing your identity. That was Jason's idea."

"Uh-uh," Faith contradicted, slumping back into her chair. "It was mine."

"Whoever. By now you've realized that this is a small, tightly knit business. Sooner or later, the cat would get out of the bag."

"I'd better buy a litter box," Faith groaned. "Sure as dollar bills are green, everyone—Jason included—is going to sssssssh-, uh, defecate," she altered, in deference to Walter's aversion to earthy slang.

"Why don't I go in and tell Jason now?"

"Count to ten, slowly, and give me a head start for the hills," Faith replied drily.

Laughing, Walter said, "He's been your mentor. Jason will be as happy for you as you are for him."

"It's the same power struggle, only with different players. Jason *may* not love me, but he'll hate me if his power is threatened." Faith grimaced. "How would you like to have the majority stockholder as your vice-president?"

"I rather give an embezzler the combination to the vault," Walter admitted with a low groan. "Okay, you win, for now. I'll have to figure out a way for Jason to come up with the idea of appointing you as vice-president."

"And I'll have to figure a way to keep the Fourth of July party from turning into a lynching party."

"Life is never simple, is it?"

Faith closed her eyes and willed a picture of Jonathan's wheat pasture to appear. "It was for me . . . once."

"Don't go getting homesick on me," Walter ordered, reading her mind. "You belong here. You're part of the family."

She'd come to St. Louis wanting to be part of the Seaton family more than anything in the world. She should have rejoiced at hearing what Walter had said. Her prayers had been answered. She could only hope God would understand why she wasn't satisfied, why she wanted more.

She opened her eyes and glanced toward Jason's office. A small smile curved her lips as Jason continued talking on the telephone, but he barely wiggled his fingers at her and smiled. Was the tenderness she saw real or imagined? If only he'd mouth, *I love you, Faith.*

"Do you believe in the power of prayers?" she asked, turning her attention back to Walter.

"Of course."

"Good." She arose from the chair. "I think this is going to take nonstop prayers, from both of us."

None of the tellers spoke to her as she minced behind their stations, and yet, curious eyes followed her every step.

"Are you among the ranks of the unemployed?" Anita asked as she pretended to dust the partition between them.

Faith grinned. "Would you believe I've been offered a promotion?"

"Don't put on a brave front for me, Faith. I'm your friend. There's a cashier position at the hospital. Would you like me to have my husband put in a good word for you?"

"I appreciate your offer, but seriously, I was not fired."

"Given two weeks' notice?"

"No! Mr. Seaton Senior praised my work."

Anita shook her head and tossed her dust rag at Faith.

"You're so windy the weather forecasters are going to name the next hurricane after you."

"Why is it people are eager to hear bad news?" Slightly peeved, she added, "Is good news boring?"

Tilting her head to one side, Anita answered, "In a word, yes. If you don't believe me, watch the news on television or read the paper. Rob, rape and pillage . . . and unemployment figures. You're sure you don't want me to speak to my husband?"

"Did I hear you say you don't speak to your husband?" Jillian asked. Carrying a brown-bag lunch, she'd closed her window and was headed for the employees' lounge.

"No, it isn't what she said—and no, I didn't get fired," Faith replied, to squelch Jillian's next question before she could ask it. To Anita she added, "See how rumors get started."

Jillian peeked inside her bag. "You were in Romeo's office a long time. I heard that he and Caroline are having problems."

"You heard wrong again," Faith said, denying the rumor.

Anita asked, "How do you know?"

"He mentioned that she's made all the arrangements for the Fourth of July blowout." Faith felt it her family duty to correct that misconception.

"Guess you'd better get your hearing aid checked," Anita teased Jillian.

"I'll buy one right after you have your husband put braces on your overbite."

"Ladies," Luke chastised quietly, breaking stride as he hurried to the drive-up windows. "This isn't the time or place to gossip."

"Faith didn't get fired," the squabbling women chorused.

Luke rose on his toes, looked in every direction and whispered to Faith, "We agreed to file a formal protest if he did fire you."

"Yeah, you're cute as a skunk and every inch a stinker," Jillian said to Faith, then, turning to Luke, she tacked on, "but we're partial to wild animals, aren't we Luke?"

Touched by having acquired such loyal friends, Faith gave each of them a quick hug. "You guys are the best."

"And we know it," Anita joked, turning to wait on a customer.

Discomfited by her spontaneous show of affection, Luke brushed his hands down his lapels and straightened the knot in his tie. "Be sure to check the ATM machine, Jillian. It's perpetually low on cash at the end of the month."

"It's so starved for money it's eating the plastic cards," Jillian joshed. "I'll feed it after I've eaten."

Within minutes, word of her employment status must have circulated around the bank. A couple of customers who'd made their deposits while she'd been in Walter's office, stopped by on one pretext or another to make certain she was at her station.

Although she was gratified by their concern, it only made her sense of guilt more intense. None of them were aware of her duplicity. Come Friday afternoon, when Walter made his announcement she'd be part of management, would their attitude toward her change? Would they still unite and support her?

She resumed counting ten-dollar bills that needed to be wrapped for Luke to take them to the vault.

Or would they feel their confidence had been betrayed?

And what about Jason's reaction? Would he believe her when she told him this was his father's idea? Walter had made Jason earn his title. Would Jason feel slighted because the vice-presidency had been handed to her on a silver platter?

There's the rub, she thought dejectedly, licking a money strap. She hadn't earned a promotion. That feat had taken Jason years of hard work and diligence.

She placed the bundle of money in the cash drawer and noticed the slip of paper where she'd jotted down Mr. Boone's personal account number. She couldn't compress time, but catching a thief would be a spectacular accomplishment.

With a grim, determined smile, she locked her cash drawer and pushed the Next Window sign forward. To Anita she said, "I'm going to lunch, then I have some computer work Mr. Seaton requested me to do."

"Okay, Faith. Jillian should be back shortly. I can hold down the fort while you're gone."

Faith folded her only clue and stuck it in her pocket. Determined to validate her worth, to earn the recognition she'd be getting, she strode to the computer room, not giving a rat's ass about the display of leg appearing through the slit in her skirt.

Nineteen

Otis wagged his tail in gratitude when Faith concealed a bite of baked chicken in her napkin and dropped it to him. She thought she'd accomplished the deed undetected until Blackie left his place beside Jason and barked at her.

"You aren't feeding the dogs table scraps, are you?" His tone was stern, but she saw a twinkle in his eyes.

"They're hungry."

"In case you haven't noticed," Jason observed drily, "they're always hungry."

Walter openly took a morsel of meat off his plate and held it directly over Blackie's head. "Sit pretty."

Obediently, the dog rose on his haunches with one front leg pointed at Walter's hand.

"That's a good boy," Walter praised, dropping the meat into Blackie's mouth.

"You two are incorrigible," Jason complained without rancor.

Glen crossed from his post in the butler's pantry. "Finished, Mr. Walter?"

"Not quite." He removed his plate from the table and set it on the carpet for both dogs to lick clean. In no time flat, the china plate gleamed. "Give Gertrude my compliments. Dinner was excellent."

Glen retrieved the gold-rimmed plate and resumed his dignified stance. "We aren't speaking to each other, sir."

Both men at the table followed the path of Glen's eyes, which had honed in on Faith's blond ringlets. With her neck bent, that was all they could see.

"Not culpable!" she muttered, clenching her napkin in her hands.

"No cheese delivered in the grocery order," Glen said sonorously, his lips twitching in an effort to smile.

For several seconds, the dining room was silent. Jason chuckled first, then Walter. By the time Glen joined in, the other two men belly-laughed.

Faith glanced from one end of the table to the other and straight up at Glen before she risked a perky smile. "I did not cancel the order," she claimed ardently over the rowdy male laughter. "I didn't!"

The louder she professed innocence the louder the laughter grew in volume. Otis and Blackie circled the dining table, their barks adding to the pandemonium. Tears rolled down Jason's cheeks; Glen held his sides, and Walter swallowed down the wrong pipe and began coughing between bursts of hysterics.

"What is going on here?" Gertrude demanded, after she'd pushed the kitchen door open and stomped through the butler's pantry. "It sounds like a barrel of hyenas escaped from the zoo!"

Faith lifted her chin. The cook wielded her power with the heavy hand of a meat cleaver, she thought with gleeful admiration. And only Gertrude could make giants in the banking industry cast sheepish glances at each other as they muffled their mouths.

"Nothing," Walter replied, hiding his grin behind his

napkin. "My compliments on dinner. It was . . ." He lost control and another volley of laughter pealed from his mouth.

"Superb!" Jason supplied, lifting his cut crystal wineglass to toast Gertrude. "Utterly superb."

"Would have been better with a sauce," Gertrude grumbled, shooting Glen a dirty look. She sniffed with indignation, then retreated to her kitchen domain.

Recovering from his second bout of laughter, Walter asked Faith, "How'd you do it?"

"I didn't cancel the order," she stated truthfully.

Jason mimicked the sweetness he'd heard so often in her voice right before she zapped him with a zinger. "I saw Jimmy G's manager in your line today. What did you say to him, Snuggle Bunny?"

"I guess my mentioning that I had heart trouble, and cheese had been restricted from my diet might have had something to do with it," she answered lamely, choosing to ignore the pet name. "I sorry, Glen. I didn't mean to get Glen in hot water with Mrs. Cavendish."

"Gertrude looks at me and does a slow simmer," Glen stated matter-of-factly. "It's a relief not to have to listen to her constant bickering."

"And I won't have to eat a bushel of apples a day to counteract the cheese," Walter added wryly.

Jason attached, "Or be called a cheesewad."

"That's fine for you three. I'm the one she'll punish." Remembering how pleased Gertrude had been with the microwave oven, Faith said, "I'll appease her with that newfangled coffee maker she wants. It's a small price to pay for harmony. I'll pick it up on my way to the bank so she'll have it to brew coffee in tomorrow morning."

"You're going back to the bank?" Jason inquired. "At night?"

"I have to." Skittering around the edges of the truth, she explained, "One of the customers is having trouble with his bank statement."

Walter butted in by saying, "That's customer service. Why didn't you give it to Shannon?"

"Or couldn't you have worked on it here?" Jason chimed.

"It has to be checked on the computer terminal. I told him I'd go over it." Wiping her mouth on her napkin, she scooted her chair away from the table. "I'll need a key to get in the bank."

She dropped her napkin and held her palm toward Jason.

"I'll go with you," Jason volunteered. "I have some work I need to catch up on, too."

Gauging from the slumberous look in his eyes, Faith sensed that Snuggle Bunny had things other than work on his mind.

"That's okay, son. I can drop her off on the way over to Caroline's to pick up my things. Faith can give me a buzz when she's finished and I'll bring her home."

Jason shook his head. "I don't like the idea of her being at the bank, at night, alone."

"She's perfectly safe," Walter argued.

"Gentlemen, pleeeeease!" She stuck both hands out in opposite directions. "You're both making a mountain out of a molehill. One of you give me a key."

Walter reached into his trousers. "What do you think, Jason? Should she have a key of her own?"

Pacified by being consulted before Walter gave her the key, Jason said to Faith, "While you're picking up Gertrude's coffeepot, have a copy made. Jason, you'd better call the security people so the alarms won't be set off."

As Glen began clearing the table, he asked, "Dessert? It's apple pie, . . . without cheese topping."

"Sounds heavenly. Any chance of there being any vanilla ice cream in the freezer?"

"Yes, sir, there is."

"None for me, thanks," Jason answered as he got up from the table and fell into step with Faith. He wanted to take her hand, but restrained showing affection in front of Glen and Walter. "See you later, Dad."

Faith grinned over her shoulder at Walter. That was the first time she'd heard Jason call his father anything other than Walter. Son and Dad. They were beginning to sound like a real homey family.

"Before you go, come into the library, Faith. I have a magazine article I want you to read."

"You're reading those 'psychological, mumbo-jumbo' articles in my magazines?" Faith teased lightly.

He followed her into the library and closed the door. "Actually, the article on embezzling is from one of my trade magazines."

The latch had barely caught when he hauled her up against him and thoroughly kissed her. He'd fully intended his kiss to be playful, but the rounded curve of her derrière and the sweet pressure of her breasts against his thin cotton shirt changed his mind. The memory of her sweet taste drove the tip of his tongue inside her.

Faith's head spun dizzily as hot blood rushed to the roots of her blond hair. She sighed when he lightly kissed the corners of her mouth, the sensitive flesh along the curve of her jaw, the pulse rapidly beating at the base of her throat. Lordy, lordy, she thought, the heat her blood generated should make her hair curl tighter than a home permanent.

"I have to go," she whispered, clinging to him.

"You're giving mixed signals—red, green and yellow—all at the same time."

"Must have blown a fuse," she replied, needing to go, but wanting to stay.

"How long will it take you to go over that statement?"

"Hours."

"Walter will be back by then," Jason groaned.

"Gertrude and Glen are here."

"This could become very, very frustrating."

"Very," Faith agreed wholeheartedly.

"I guess the only solution is to come clean." He rocked his forehead against her and her hips against him. "I'll just announce to everyone that we're living, no, *sleeping* together."

Not another announcement, Faith moaned silently. "Walter wouldn't approve."

"How could he not approve? Caroline is pregnant, for Pete's sake. I promise, he doesn't believe we think the Star of David is going to rise in the East when he takes her to the hospital."

Faith nipped his lip as punishment for the sacrilege.

"Ouch."

"Watch your mouth."

"I'm watching yours," he sallied. "Your lips are far more exciting and your teeth are getting increasingly dangerous."

"I mean it, Jason." She pointed to the family Bible, a prominent fixture in the library. "Blasphemy is a sin!"

"I sincerely apologize," he recanted. "I only meant to show you that Walter doesn't have any room to be critical of us."

"I don't want to be the cause of friction erupting between you two."

The friction caused by the hard ridge of male rocking against her stomach caused a dull, sensuous ache between her thighs. His hand moving inside the slit of her skirt and dancing across her buttocks increased her yearning to make love with him.

"Are you telling me no?"

"Yes."

"Was that a yes?"

"No." Faith squirmed from his arms, turned, and stepped away from him. "I love you, Jason. Is sex all you want from me?"

"A slap in the face would have been kinder," Jason said, his tone icy.

"Well?" she demanded. "Is sex what you want?"

Jason relented with a smile guaranteed to remove her hands from her hips and lower the tilt of her defiant chin. She could be a magnificent, blond spitfire when riled.

"You don't know what you want, do you?"

"I want you," he replied softly.

Without love? Without commitment? Forget the happily ever after! Without the others happiness is doomed!

Faith could feel tears clamoring up the back of her throat. She wouldn't disgrace herself by crying! Damn it to Hell, if a Seaton doesn't cry, I won't!

Unable to look at him and control her tears, her eyes hopped, jumped, and skipped around the room before they focused on his desk. "Where's the magazine article?"

"It's there on the desk."

With her vision blurred, Faith marched to the desk. She picked up the only magazine, whirled around, and retraced her steps out of the library.

Jason held on to the back of the chair to prevent himself from stopping Faith.

No grand-exit line, he noted, his heart feeling heavy in his chest.

No teasing remark.

Only silence.

"And the soft, enticing fragrance of White Flowers," he whispered between stiff lips. Absentmindedly, he picked up the crystal piece from the table. He toyed with it, toyed with the idea of hurling it against the door Faith had walked through.

No, he decided, he hadn't completely lost control.

Gently, he returned the fragile decoration to the table, crossed to the telephone and dialed the security service number.

Dry-eyed, Faith unlocked the bank's side entry and flipped on the bank of light switches. During the ten-minute drive, she'd resolutely barred Jason from her thoughts by remembering what Papa Jon used to say about acting foolishly, as she had with Jason. Wisdom comes when a person can separate the wheat from the chaff, the important from the trivial. In her present state of mind, where Jason was concerned, she couldn't separate egg whites.

Jason had her mind warring with her body.

What seemed right was wrong.

What was wrong seemed . . . wonderful!

With logic like that, the best thing she could do was find something else to temporarily occupy her mind. She'd think of Jason tomorrow when the taste of him no longer exploded inside of her.

Inside the computer room, she booted up, pressed in the secret access code. While she waited for a response, she opened her purse and removed the slip of paper with Mr. Boone's account number on it.

As a child, she'd been awestruck when Papa Jon had flipped the red switch; the computer had taken her beyond the scope of the farm into a new, exciting world. Now, as an adult, she respected it for being a complicated piece of machinery, but she considered it only a tool to access knowledge.

"A computer is only as good as the programmer and the operator. Let's see how good you are."

She keyed in the account number. Instantly, Boone's current statement appeared on the screen. She checked June, May, and April, then returned to June. One ATM withdrawal and one ATM deposit, she noted mentally.

She switched to another series of screens that showed all ATM transactions for June. Instinctively, she watched for small withdrawals followed by deposits of the same amount. She scrolled and paused, scrolled and paused, hoping this clue would reveal a pattern.

Four hours later, her back aching and her eyes smarting, Faith turned off the machine. With thousands of accounts, multiplied by thousands of deposits and withdrawals, she finally admitted that she'd be more successful looking for a needle in a haystack.

She'd covered two measly weeks of transactions and

found nothing, zero, zip! Checking her watch, she mentally calculated how long it would take her to do six months of transactions.

"I'd be old and grey, with no teeth and thick glasses, she said, her imagination blowing strong, "before I'd find another account with a similar problem."

There has to be a way, she thought, her fingers rubbing across the fine lines on her forehead. Something simple. Something that would link the Boone accounts with other accounts, which would eventually lead to the embezzler.

Too exhausted to consider coming up with a different angle, she trudged from the room, flipping off lights as she went. With her feedbag-style purse slung over her shoulder, she dug in her right-hand suit pocket for Walter's key. She shifted her purse to her other shoulder and delved into the left pocket. Without the key, not only could she not get in the bank, she couldn't get out.

"Just great," she muttered. She wanted to use Jason's method of venting her spleen by kicking the door.

Uh-uh, an inner voice warned. Security system.

She must have put the damned key in her purse, she decided, fumbling with the brass latch.

"Hey! Lady!"

Startled, Faith's body jerked. Seemingly out of nowhere, a man appeared. Her tired eyes went on alert as they raked over him from the weird skull cap on his head, down his rumpled, baggy green clothes, to the canvas shoes on his feet.

"You work here?" he asked, his hands cupped beside his mouth.

Faith stared at him, neither nodding nor shaking her

head. This was the big city, she reminded herself. A woman alone didn't answer stranger's questions.

She bit her tongue to keep from quipping, "No, I'm a bank robber."

"Can you help me?" He pointed toward Grand Avenue. Close to midnight, the multilaned street was empty. "I ran out of gas and I don't have any cash on me. Since I had my Impact card, I thought I could get money from the machine. It took my card, made a grinding sound, and didn't give me any cash."

He stepped closer to the door, directly under the light. Unshaven, with dark circles under his eyes and lines of aggravation bracketing his mouth, his appearance was of little comfort to Faith. Dark splashes of what looked to Faith like ink stains blotched across the midsection of his wrap-around top.

Ink spots or bloodstains?

Faith took two steps back. Good Lord have mercy, the man is covered with blood! And he's picked me as his next victim!

"Come back tomorrow." She made a shooing motion with her hands. "If you don't leave, I'll have to call my friend Sara at the police department. A dozen squad cars will be here in less than two minutes."

The man rolled his eyes, glanced upward and shook his head as he reached for his wallet. Frustrated that his surgical scrub suit had no pockets, he pointed to the small rectangular badge limply hanging on his top. He brushed at the blood splatters at though he wished he could make them disappear.

"Okay, lady. I know I look like an ax murderer, but . . ." He unpinned his identification badge and held it against the plate glass door. "See? Dr. Michael Pandowitz, Ob Gyn. I had an emergency delivery and didn't have time to fill up the gas tank."

Relief flooded through Faith. Doctors could be trusted. His explanation was plausible.

She scrabbled in the bottom of her purse, hunting for Walter's key "Wait a minute, I seem to have misplaced the key."

"You have got to be kidding me."

"Here it is!" She held up the key before unlocking the door. Stepping outside into the hot, humid night air, she said, "I can't help you with your card, but I do have a ten-dollar bill. Is that enough to get you home?"

Dr. Pandowitz grinned as she handed him the money. Slowly walking with her to her car, he said, "Lady, I think I love you. I'll pay you back first think in the morning."

Chuckling, Faith wondered why a perfect stranger could glibly spout the words she wanted to hear and Jason couldn't. "Do you need a ride to your car? Or to the gas station?"

"No, thanks. I'm just down the street. But I would appreciate your getting my card back for me. I don't know how I'd exist without it since I don't carry a wallet most of the time."

"No wallet? Where do you carry your card?"

"In the glove compartment of my car. Nobody but me knows the PIN number, so I figure I'm safe . . . unless it's held hostage by the ATM machine."

"There's your problem," Faith said, glad to be able to solve somebody's problem if not her own. "In ninety-plus-degree temperature, the heat probably affects the magnetic strip on the back of it. You'll probably have to get a new card."

"Could you take care of that for me? I'm on a tight schedule tomorrow. My PIN number is . . ."

"Don't!" Faith said, covering her ears. "No one is supposed to know the number but you."

Dr. Pandowitz gave a hoot of laughter. "Not even to the gorgeous banker who rescued me?"

"Nobody." Rejuvenated by his flattery, she teased, "I could be a bank robber."

"And I could be a vampire," he bantered. "I do look the part. I introduced myself, but I didn't catch your name."

"Faith Jones."

"Nice to meet you, Faith Jones." He paused while she unlocked her car door. "You aren't just by chance single, are you?"

Faith gave him a second look. Shaven and wearing clean clothes, he'd be an attractive young man. *And he says he loves me,* she mused. But she wasn't tempted in the least.

"I'm in love." She held the slit together as she sat in her car.

"Lucky guy." He started to close her car door. "See you tomorrow. Thanks, again."

"You're welcome."

As she drove off the parking lot, she beeped her horn and waved. *The incident must have pepped up my adrenalin,* she mused, feeling better than when she'd left the computer room.

Mentally making a note to track down the doctor's Impact card caused her to miss a yellow light. She slammed on the brakes as the light turned red.

"That's it!" she shouted. Thinking aloud, she said, "Anyone with a card had access to bank accounts other than their own. They wouldn't have to mess with transferring funds from account to account because . . . they'd step outside the bank, stick the card into the slot, . . . and presto! Instant cash!"

Whoa, girl. No cash unless you know the PIN number.

"Easy. Call and ask. Like the good doctor said. Any customer would trust a bank employee, wouldn't they?"

Certain this brainstorm had potential, she smoothly shifted from third into first gear. Tomorrow, first thing, she'd test out her theory. Then, once she figured out how, she'd find out who.

Twenty

Jason leaned back in his office chair and allowed his eyes to seek and find what his mind had been mulling over throughout the night: Faith Jones. Last night, he and his father had played chess. With their thoughts elsewhere, as Walter listened for the phone to ring and he listened for Faith's return, it was little wonder they both played badly, or that Faith's late arrival irritated him.

By midnight, he'd covered his emotions with a thin coat of ice. She'd come home bright-eyed and bushy-tailed, but he'd been cool. Damn cool, he thought, considering his guts were on fire when she'd told him about helping a man who could have been a rapist or a kidnapper! Or God forbid, a murderer!

Does she have to trust every down-and-out creep in St. Louis? Never mind that the man delivered babies. He could have been a Skid Row bum and Faith still would have given him money.

Jason massaged his stomach; it ached, as did the cross he had to bear below his belt. Gertrude's breakfast of poached eggs, bran cereal with skim milk, and French-roast coffee felt like boulders in his stomach. Nutritionally, he accepted that this food was good for him, but knowing Faith had put the cookbook in Gertrude's hands upset him.

In two short weeks, Faith had turned his household, his bank, and his guts inside out and upside down.

He despised radical changes. Hell, he admitted silently, he even hated minor changes.

As the muscles in his thighs hardened, he begrudgingly conceded that he did not hate the petite, sexy, *brainy* woman who'd made them.

Truth be known, he wanted to cart her sweet little body down to the vault and make mad, passionate love to her. And he could care less who was on top! He wanted to be inside her, where no other man had been, possessing her as no other man could.

Yeah, Stud, with the customers chanting a mating call?

Faith Jones spelled backwards had to be "long line." While Jillian and Anita twiddled their thumbs, Faith waited on the customers.

Isn't that a fine how-do-you-do! Walter ought to cut their salaries for nonperformance of duties. Or fire them. Why have three inside tellers with only one of them busy?

Jason grimaced. He realized he was mentally taking his frustrations out on two innocent women. What could they do? Hogtie customers and drag them over to their teller windows? That's what it would take.

Simply watching Faith smile and greet customers as though they were long-lost friends made his blood boil. Absentmindedly his hand flipped through the ATM reports he'd requested from central banking. He'd much rather be following the womanly curves of Faith's waist and hips or roaming at will through the halo of blond curls on her head.

Jason shifted in his chair uncomfortably, a rush of passion building inside of him. Unwilling to wait until the end of the workday, he quickly scribbled a note and rubber-banded it to a stack of money straps. After leaving the note with Mary, with instructions to deliver it to Faith, he strolled toward the secluded bank vault.

Minutes later, Faith bade the bicycle store owner goodbye and waited for her next customer to empty his deposit pouch. She grinned as Jason's secretary elbowed her way to the counter and delivered a bundle of money wrappers.

What are these for? Faith wondered. Yesterday she'd bundled dollar bills until her fingertips had turned green. Had Jason arranged with Luke to have her count money until the printer's ink turned her hands black?

Busy as she was with the customers, she'd never find out what happened to Dr. Pandowitz's Impact card!

She slipped the note from beneath the rubberband, hesitating before she opened it. Jason hadn't spoken a word to her at the breakfast table. She'd attributed his foul mood to not having a breakfast tray delivered to his door. Good heavens, Gertrude cooked his meals for him. Did the cook have to climb the steps with heavy trays, too?

Faith sighed. She should have consulted him. Seaton Place was his house, operating under his rules. He was within his rights to be upset with her.

"Morning, Faith. Would you mind rushing?" the grocery store's manager asked politely. "My boss is on a rampage. We're running short on quarters."

Caught between doing her job and wondering what Jason's note contained, she dropped the note on the counter and stooped beneath it to get a tray of quarters. With her mind on Jason and not what she was doing, the edge of the aluminum tray caught the lip of the counter. Orange rolls of coins spilled forward out of the tray.

"Grab 'em," she exclaimed.

In her haste, she overbalanced the tray and tilted the remaining rolls in her own direction. In what seemed to Faith like slow motion, the rolls fell off both edges of the counter before she could stop them. Orville Redenbacher's Smart Popcorn would have been put to shame compared to the effect of the rolls bursting open, bouncing, twirling, rolling on edge among the feet of the customers waiting in line.

Squeals of shock and delight bubbled throughout the bank's lobby. Grown men and stylishly dressed women stooped down and crawled across the floor as though the quarters were thousand-dollar bills pitched into a room filled with welfare clients.

On her hands and knees, the city councilwoman began raking the quarters into a large pile as she called to Faith, "Hey! Thanks for the free samples! Got any half dollars you want to throw around? I could use them to balance the city budget!"

Faith's sense of humor kicked into high gear as she shouted, "Check your shoes and the cuffs of your britches. Nobody leaves until every single quarter is accounted for! Hey, you, yeah you!" Giggling, she pointed at Sara, who was dressed in her dark blue police uniform.

"I saw you stuff a handful down your front. Get 'em out of there or I'll have to use your own handcuffs on you!"

Male laughter, interspersed with high-pitched giggles, gave the staid atmosphere of the bank a face-lift. Shouts of "Here's one," "get that one," "there's one rolling under your shoe, you devil," echoed off the marble walls.

Anita and Jillian's heads poked over their counters. A cross between abject dismay and hidden exhilaration was clearly written on their faces as they pointed hither and yon, directing traffic.

"The person who gathers up the most quarters wins a dozen lollipops!" Faith yelled, encouraging the stragglers standing around the edges to get in on the action.

"Faith is giving away candy to the sucker who gives the money back," Mr. Boone joked loudly.

Hoots of laughter increased the festive mood of the customers.

"How many did you drop?" Sara asked, dumping a handful on the counter.

"A hundred dollars' worth, four hundred quarters in all," she replied, "but most of them fell back here. Just pile 'em on the counter and I'll run them through the coin machine later."

"Hey, look there!" a little girl shouted. "Is that a whole roll wedged between those big plants."

A boy who'd been watching while his mother opened a new account charged toward the artificial silk trees.

"Mine!" they each shouted.

"Oooops! No fighting!" Faith yelled. "I'll give both of you a lollipop."

When she saw the look of anticipation on the adults' faces, her outlandish sense of humor expanded to gigantic proportions. "Okay, everybody is a winner," she declared. "You all deserve a reward. Bring your quarters over here, and I'll give the women big hugs and the men great, big smackeroos!"

"Faith!" Luke squeaked from behind her. "You can't kiss all those men."

"Wanna bet? You don't think I'm going to miss an opportunity to show our customers what a friendly bank we are, do you? Besides, honesty is supposed to pay royal dividends!"

An orderly line began to form in front of Faith's station. The grocery store's manager pushed three rolls and a handful of quarters toward her. "Guess I really started something, didn't I?" he asked, his voice filled with glee.

"One of us did," Faith answered dryly, wishing she could lay the blame on him. She reached beneath the counter and very, very carefully placed a full tray of quarters in front of him. "Show me where you want your kiss."

His finger pointed toward his grinning lips, then moved over to his cheek. "I'm married," he explained.

Faith chuckled. "Your wife won't believe this when you tell her anyway," she said before she planted a chaste peck of his cheek. "Sorry for the delay. I hope you don't get in trouble."

She expected a jovial comment back from the grocer. When she saw his eyes round and his finger stabbing the air, pointing behind her, she swiveled around to see what he was pointing at, and felt her heart sink to her toes.

"You're a tad early to be operating a Fourth of July

kissing booth, aren't you?" Jason inquired in a voice as dry as the Arizona desert.

Quick to recover and still on a high, Faith chirped gaily, "Snuggle Bunny, would you mind holding off on firing me? I have a lot of customers who need my undivided attention. You'll have to wait your turn in line."

"Yeah," the councilwoman said with a throaty chuckle. "And no butting in line just because you own the place. You have to find a quarter and wait your turn . . . Snuggle Bunny."

Jason felt his ears light up like twin light bulbs. He'd never live this down. Never! Not if he lived to be a hundred and fifty! He'd go through life nicknamed Snuggle Bunny, thanks to Faith.

"I'd like a lollipop the same color as your boss's face," the councilwoman announced loudly. "Crimson red."

Faith picked up the container of candy she kept beside her coin machine and began digging through it. *This time, I've gone too far. Dad-gum-it, this is Jason's fault to begin with. If he hadn't sent Mary over with that note for me to worry about, I'd have been paying attention to what I was doing.* Instantly flipping the dismal situation over and looking on the bright side, she added silently, *at least I don't have to worry about Walter announcing my promotion!*

"There you go. See you Friday?"

"I wouldn't miss it for all the money in the vault," the woman replied, continuing to chuckle as she stepped from the line.

"I agree with her," Mr. Boone piped up, frowning at Jason, then grinning at Faith as he unloaded his pockets. "Banking used to be dull. I haven't had this much fun in years! Pucker up, Faith. I want a gen-u-ine smackeroo or I keep the loot."

With her mind more on the man in back of her than the one in front of her, Faith stood on tiptoe, leaned over and gave Mr. Boone a swift peck. Before she could drop her heels to the floor, he reached across the counter and firmly gripped her shoulders.

"Like this."

The tips of her toes raised off the floor. She could taste the hint of laughter on Mr. Boone's mouth. Evidently he planned on enjoying her predicament to the fullest.

"All right!" he shouted after he'd set her down. "I'm banking here forever! I think I'm in L-O-V-E!"

Apprehensively, Faith glanced over her shoulder. Jason stoically leaned against the partition, ankles crossed, a bland expression on his face. "He was just kidding around," she muttered in his direction.

"I won't be," Jason threatened sweetly.

She thanked the heavens above that the next three customers were females. As the piles of coins grew bigger, her candy supply dwindled. The two children who had fought over the roll of quarters were next. No way could she lean far enough forward to give them their well-deserved treats.

Giving Jason what she hoped was a sizzling smile, she grabbed the cardboard bucket, and directed her wobbly legs toward the swinging door that led into the lobby.

"You can have the quarters, Lady, but don't slobber on me!" The coins jingled as he dropped them into her palm. "I don't even allow my mother to kiss me!"

Laughing, Faith gave him his choice from the bucket. "Come back in a few years," she teased.

"Boys," the little girl said as she tilted her nose toward the ceiling. "They don't know a good thing when they see it. Can I have a hug, a kiss and a piece of candy?"

"You drive a hard bargain, sweetie," Faith teased, pulling her into her arms and cheerfully complying with the child's demands.

After the miniature fortune hunters ran back to their mothers to show their bounty, Faith ducked her head and marched to the other side of the counter. She noticed Jason had picked up the money she'd spilled on her side and placed it in stacks of ten dollars each.

"Thanks." Not wanting to further embarrass him by giving him a lollapalooza of a kiss, she handed him the near-empty container. "Do you want to fire me publicly, or in the privacy of your office?"

"Read the note," Jason replied, sweet as candied sugarplums.

He strode away from her before she could explain that this situation would never have occurred if it hadn't been for that darned slip of paper. Was he mad? Or did his straight face and calm voice indicate that he'd come to accept her little idiosyncrasies as being perfectly normal.

Faith bowed her head, folded her hands, and mouthed a quick prayer asking for absolution. She took her own sweet time counting and wrapping the coins, hoping that whatever mood Jason was in would alter before he confronted her. As she placed the last roll in the tray, she convinced herself that he wouldn't verbally lambaste her while at the bank.

Here, he never shows emotion, she repeated silently. There were plenty of employees who'd verify that fact.

But, her fingers trembled as she reached for Jason's note. Without haste, she unfolded it and silently read: *Urgent. Come to the cash vault.* She brought the paper closer to her face when she read his signature and title he'd signed underneath it.

He wrote the note before the quarters dropped like a bomb, she recounted, her heart beginning to beat faster.

Impatiently Jason waited for Kathy and a safety-deposit customer to finish chatting and leave the vault area. Eavesdropping, it seemed to him as though each of them had a witty remark to make for every damned quarter that had hit the floor.

He wanted them out of there before Faith came prancing down the steps!

"Compile a list of safety-deposit-box customers and their numbers and get them to my office before you go to lunch," Jason ordered briskly when Kathy finally turned around and noticed him loitering by the gate. "Be certain you include people who no longer have a deposit box."

Kathy glanced at her watch. "Now?"

The elderly woman with Kathy waved her sucker at Jason and excused herself as she passed by Jason.

"There aren't any other customers waiting, are there?"

"No, sir."

"Good." He and Faith would have the vault to themselves. "Don't skip lunch. Before closing will be fine."

"Yes, sir."

Skirting between him and the wall, she came close enough for him to see the faint lines radiating around her eyes. She'd have called him Snuggle Bunny if she'd had the nerve.

Only one woman had that amount of courage. The same woman who had the colossal nerve to make her boss wait on her. She had her share of guts; his share, too.

Originally, when he'd written the note, he'd planned on secluding Faith within the confines of the vault and kissing her until they both were lightheaded. But, thanks to her incredible means of retrieving the quarters she'd dropped, she had received more kisses in ten minutes than he had given her in two weeks.

Unable to watch man after man kiss Faith, he had been reduced to groveling on the floor to gather the rest of the money.

"Snuggle Bunny," he mouthed, chuckling to himself. The nickname she'd given him was far better than s.o.b. Yeah, supposedly the letters stood for son of the boss, but the traditional meaning came closer to the mark.

Particular as Faith was about her work, he figured his note must have caused her uncharacteristic clumsiness. Somehow, the thought of Faith's being shaken up rather than being the person doing the shaking pleased him.

"Mr. Seaton?" Faith called respectfully, stopping near the bottom of the steps. "Are you down there?"

"He isn't. But Snuggle Bunny is," Jason crooned softly.

Faith whispered, "I need to find Mr. Seaton to tell him how the embezzler does his misdeeds."

In four giant steps, Jason stood at the foot of the steps.

His libidinous thoughts were automatically put on hold. "How?"

Not wanting to be overheard, Faith led him into the safety-deposit area in the vault. Since Jason had been trying to track down the embezzler, she felt the only way to sidetrack him from royally chewing her out was to appease his appetite by divulging what information she'd gleaned.

Standing with her shoulder blades touching the cold steel doors of the boxes, she replied, "The ATM cards."

"No way."

"Who are the customers most likely to screw up their checking accounts? And what is usually the culprit?"

"The ATM card," he admitted. "But there are two fallacies to your theory. One, you have to have the card. Two, you have to know the PIN number."

"Have you any idea how many customers must use their Impact cards as identification to cash checks, and forget to get them back? Or how many department stores have Impact machines and the store clerks forget to return them to the customer?" She watched Jason steadily shake his head in denial of her speculation. "When Caroline took me shopping, we had to go back to Nieman's because she left her card there. And what about machines all across the country that have a steady diet of gobbling up silver plastic?"

"It doesn't happen *that* often."

"I believe it does. Computers are programmed to accept only perfect cards. Scratch it, chip off a corner, get it dirty, and the computer signals the machine to snarf it down."

Jason straightened his arm, braced his hand next to

her shoulder. "Let's say your idea is plausible," Jason relented, his voice barely above a whisper.

"Next step. What happened to Dr. Pandowitz's card?"

"Whoever restocked the machine took the card."

"Who? Specifically?"

"It could be any of the tellers. That responsibility rotates among Anita, Jillian, Luke, . . . the drive-up tellers, or you for that matter."

Faith let her inclusion in the crime-ring slide for the moment. "Is there any way to check to see who was responsible for the ATM machine in mid-June, when Mr. Boone's card was used?"

"There's a ledger that's kept in the portable cabinet, next to the cashier's and traveler's checks. Any card received in the mail—which crosses Kathy and Shannon's desks—is entered in it."

"That increases the number of suspects by two." A cold shiver ran down her spine. The closer they came to solving how it was done, the closer they were to discovering who committed the crime. "Then what happens to the card?"

"The customer is notified by phone. If they're local, we put them in the safe. If they are out-of-town cards, the initiatory bank is notified and the card is voided."

"She-He-Sticky-Fingers has the card, and may or may not immediately enter it into the book. Sticky Fingers calls the customer, tells the customer that the bank has the card, and then what do you think Sticky Fingers asks next?

"For the PIN number. But customers are told not to give the number to anyone."

"Ah, but this is a bank employee they see when they make deposits or cash checks or . . ."

"Someone they trust," Jason said thoughtfully. "Which means the only person not suspect is Joe, the janitor."

"Correct."

"We can access the employees' accounts."

Faith moved closer to him. "Would you use someone else's card, get cash, and deposit the money into an account here?"

"Sticky Fingers would be smarter than that. Scratch that idea."

"Where the money went isn't important. Who took it is."

Jason pushed away from the steel wall. A five-fingered vapor print disappeared as the warmth from his hand quickly cooled to the temperature of steel. He shoved his hands in his pocket to stop them from touching Faith.

Turning on his heel, he said, "I'm going to get the ledgerbook."

Faith grabbed his arm. "And tip off the embezzler that you're wise to him? Her? Whoever it is must be paranoid about that ledger. Why don't you wait until after the bank closes?"

"Because the portable cabinet goes into the locked vault. I can't get to it."

"Then let me look. I'm a teller. It wouldn't be suspicious for me to check Dr. Pandowitz's card. I told him I would."

"Scratch that idea, too. I don't want you put at risk," he whispered adamantly.

"What's the embezzler going to do? See me doing my job and be suspicious?" Her fingers tightened on his muscular bicep. "Give me credit for half a brain, would you?"

"I gave you credit for half the bank's stock. The money is in your account. Isn't that enough?"

Baffled by the mercurial change of topics, Faith stared up at him with a dumbfounded expression on her face. "What does my inheritance have to do with the ledger?"

"Power," Jason blurted. "You want to figure out who's taking money because it enhances you and undermines me in the eyes of the employees."

Faith wanted to deny his accusation, but he had hit the nail on the head, partially. She did want to enhance her image. She had seen this as a means of earning her promotion. But, the part concerning undermining him was way off the mark. She never lost an opportunity to praise him!

"Go to hell, you . . . you hairy old fart," she said tersely, tears stinging her eyes. "Find your embezzler and call the cops. I don't want to have anything to do with it or you."

"Fine."

She pushed against his chest to make room to get through the door. "Fine!"

Jason watched her storm out of the vault like a rocket off its launch pad. A slow smile lit his eyes. He'd have said or done anything to eliminate her from danger. She was a damn sight safer being angry with him than she would be if she were faced by a criminal who was about to be exposed.

The guilty person had to be a little insane to think he or she would never be caught.

Twenty-one

"You had a phone call while you were in the vault with S.B.," Anita said, giving her small piece of paper. "Why is Mr. Seaton Senior's lady friend calling you?"

With her mind stuck on Jason, Faith couldn't think of a plausible excuse. "Who knows?"

"Could it have something to do with that long conversation you had with Romeo?" she probed putting pieces together. "Or getting another note from S.B. and running to the vault for a private rendezvous?"

"The two men are related, but not what they wanted to speak to me about," Faith answered evasively. "Trust me. I don't know why Caroline called."

"Something is going on around here." Anita sniffed the air as though she could smell a skunk. "It's not like you to be close-mouthed."

Faith grinned. Following Anita's logic, she replied, "Since you think I'm incapable of keeping my mouth shut, you should feel confident you're up on the latest gossip." She picked up her purse and added, "Would you mind taking care of the customers?"

"Sure. It's good to get reacquainted with my regulars for a change."

Jillian, who'd been listening, asked with false enthusiasm, "Do you mean she's going to let us do some of the work? Oh, thank you, thank you, thank you, Faith. I was afraid Snuggle Bunny had instituted a quota system and I wasn't going to get a paycheck!"

"Your green eyes are showing, Jillian," Anita rebuffed. "Go on, Faith. We'll cover for you."

As Faith strode toward the lounge to use the telephone, she wondered if the green-eyed monster, jealousy, was perched on Jillian's shoulders. What was she supposed to do when the customers lined up in front of her window?

With other important problems crowding her mind, Faith was beginning to feel stressed. She longed for the days when she could take off in the afternoon for a barefooted stroll across the pasture, down to the pond. Staring at her reflection in the water, with sunny blue skies and puffy clouds as a backdrop, invariably brought peace of mind to her. Toss in a boy's choir singing in the background, a few angels' wings, and that was her picture of heaven.

Add a smiling Jason looking over my shoulder and it would be heavenly, she mused, temporarily setting aside their squabble.

Faith entered the lounge. Fortunately the other employees had eaten their lunch. It was too early for afternoon coffee breaks. She pressed the telephone pad with a sequence of numbers.

"Caroline?"

Without preamble or her usual politeness, Caroline said, "I could sue you for alienation of affection, young woman."

Surprised by the verbal attack, Faith stammered, "W-w-what?"

"It's too much of a coincidence for me to believe that one day you tell me to marry Walter and the next day he has a long conversation with you that results in him leaving me. You may be a mathematics whiz, but I can do simple addition!"

"I didn't . . ." *tell him to leave you!*

"Don't deny it. Walter should be here taking care of me and our unborn child, but no, you wanted him at Seaton Place, didn't you?"

"I . . ." *Uncle Walter to be happy. I want you to marry him.*

"Shut up and listen. The last thing I have to say to you, smarty-pants, is that you proved my point. Walter is like all men. When the going gets tough, the tough guy gets going . . . and he leaves his woman way behind him, eating his dust!"

"Walter . . ." *isn't like your father.*

"And since he thinks you are Little Miss Perfect, you can take care of the Fourth of July celebration. I won't be there to watch you gloat!"

"Caroline . . . ?"

Faith jiggled the button to reconnect the line. She'd hung up? Faith redialed the number and heard a monotonous busy signal. Obviously, Caroline had taken the phone off the hook.

Dumbstruck by Caroline's venomous accusations, Faith continued to hold the receiver in her hands. She didn't let me get a word in edgeways, Faith thought, feeling lower than a snake's belly.

Compassionate, she could understand why Caroline was distraught. Only weeks from her due date, she had good cause for her anxiety attacks. This was her first child. She faced the unknown, alone. Not alone, Faith corrected. Walter would be there. Medically, Caroline had the best doctors and medical facilities in the world available to her.

She returned the receiver to the hook, folded her arms on the table, and rested her head on them. Verbal warfare exhausted her; two fights in the last fifteen minutes, had completely drained her energy.

Faith felt too lethargic to throw stones, but she did believe Caroline should have given her a chance to clear up the misunderstanding. Since Caroline was a lawyer, Faith could comprehend why Caroline didn't believe in coincidence. Did she believe a person was innocent until proven guilty? It did seem unfair that Caroline had appointed herself prosecutor, judge and jury.

"Pssssst," Luke hissed from the door. "Are you sleeping?"

"No." With great effort, Faith straightened. She needed to talk to someone, but Luke was the wrong man. He solved animal problems, not people problems. Covering her glumness with a thin layer of wit, she said, "I'm checking my eyelids for holes. You'll be glad to know there aren't any."

"I hope you aren't coming down with a summer cold," he fretted.

"Wanna feel my nose to see if it's cold?"

Luke scrunched up his face. "Not if it's runny."

"I'm fine. A friend of mine has a problem I can't solve."

"Welcome to the big city," Luke said drily. "We all have unsolvable problems."

"You, too?" Faith's shoulders ached as though the

weight of the world was pressing down on them, but she could support a few extra ounces of problems. "I'm a good listener."

"Thanks. You're a nice person." As though embarrassed to be complimenting a woman, he flicked an imaginary piece of lint off his jacket sleeve. "I don't trust many two-legged animals, but I do trust you."

Jason held the sealed envelope he'd found in the ledger book up to the florescent light. Faith's name typed on the front of it prevented him from ripping it open. He'd solved the embezzling matter; he knew how, who, and how much, but not why. Undoubtedly, the handwritten note inside revealed that information.

Anger such as Jason had never experienced coiled deep in his bowels. He'd been a cocky, blind fool. This crime had been going on for over two years!

Jason prided himself on being a good judge of character. Southern Bank relied on his judgments. He could look a loan applicant in the eye and his instincts would unerringly tell him whether or not to make the loan. Discovering that a person he'd trusted implicitly had duped him, struck at the foundation of Jason's confidence.

Hell, he'd have given this person a loan. Only Jason had never been asked. The amounts stolen not only were small, they'd been religiously paid back. Fifty dollars was the amount presently missing.

"A pittance!" Jason growled. "That low-down, lying, deceitful son-of-a-bitch could have emptied the coffers and I wouldn't have been any the wiser! The thief could be halfway to South America! Goddamn, I was a complete idiot!"

Why would a person destroy their career and their reputation for less than one hundred dollars a month? No bank would hire a person with a jail record for embezzlement.

His eyes raised to the empty lobby. The bank had been closed for hours. Dropping the envelope, he pushed back his cuff and glanced at his watch. By now, Walter and Faith had eaten, Glen had cleared the table, and they'd gone in separate directions. Jason had intentionally postponed going home.

Humiliated and enraged, he placed the ledger and the envelope in his briefcase. Procrastination would serve to temper his anger. He'd disclose the facts to Walter and Faith calmly, without rancor.

And then, by God, he'd make arrangements with the chief of Police to lock the embezzler behind closed bars.

Fifteen minutes later, Jason entered Seaton Place. "Where is everybody?" he called.

"We're in here, son," Walter replied from the library. "Join us. I'm just about to . . ."

"Checkmate," Faith crowed. "That's two dollars you owe me."

Walter stared at the chessboard, completely bewildered. "You play an unorthodox game. I should have beaten you."

Faith heard the double snap of Jason's briefcase open before she saw an envelope with her name on it dance across the polished surface of the game table. One glance at him told her to open it, immediately. Perversely she asked, "For me?"

"Open it and read it out loud," Jason commanded,

his tone brooking no refusal. "I found it in the ledger book."

Frowning, she toyed with the glued flap. "You know who it is?"

"The embezzler?" Walter reached for the envelope, but Faith clamped it to her chest. "A confession?"

With slow deliberation, she began peeling up the flap. It reminded her of doing the same thing to the Bible less than a month ago. A sense of foreboding made her hands tremble. Papa Jon had died that day, leaving a will that had irrevocably changed her life. Would the paper inside this envelope do the same?

The sharp edge of the paper sliced into the side of her index finger. She withdrew her finger from the flap. A tiny droplet of blood filled the slim cut. It stung, as only a paper cut can.

Seeing her plight, Walter said, "Here. I'll open it."

"No. Whoever wrote it wanted me to read it first." She gave Jason a steady look as he seated himself beside her. "Silently. You've waited this long. You can wait a few minutes longer."

"Did you bring the ledger home?" Walter asked Jason.

Jason removed it from his briefcase and gave it to his father, without looking away from Faith's expressive face.

She withdrew the page, unfolded it and read:

Puppy Eyes:

    That's what I thought when you looked up at me with those big, trusting black eyes of yours and asked me to share my problems with you. There is no excuse for what I have done, but there are fifty-two pairs of reasons. All of them have eyes like you.

Yes, they have four legs and tails. You were a kindred spirit when you offered to help me feed my stray friends. Remember I told you several of the customers made donations? By now, you've discovered they were unaware of their own generosity. I devised a system that allowed for them to "donate" temporarily. Since you're reading the Impact Lost Card entries, you know exactly how I did it. Presently, the Cassidy Humane Fund owes fifty dollars to the last three entries. It doesn't make me less a thief, but every other penny has been returned. I would have paid them interest, but it would have screwed up the system.

Much as I deplore the idea of disappointing you and the Seatons, of losing my job, of being a criminal, the saddest part is . . . I'd do the same thing again to save those animals.

The Ogre
Luke Cassidy

By the time Faith reached the signature, her eyes had filled with tears. Ogre, her pet's name, the one she'd told Luke about shortly after she'd gotten to know him. One fat tear clung to her lower lashes, then fell, splotching Luke's name.

"Luke wants you to intercede on his behalf, doesn't he?" Jason asked, his face grim.

"No." Faith blinked back the tears. Jason would only consider them a show of weakness. "I'm going to destroy this."

"The hell you are. It's evidence that can be used in court."

Walter interrupted quietly by asking, "What's wrong with the ledger? It looks perfectly normal to me."

"Nothing, unless you check the ledger entries against the monthly bank statement of the card holder," Jason replied. "Luke must have manipulated the date the card came in and the date the customer picked it up. For identification purposes and to gain access, he'd ask the customers for their PIN number."

Faith put a restraining hand on Jason's wrist to get him to be quiet. "The money is back in the customers' accounts. As thorough as Luke is, the customers probably don't even know it was used for a good cause. No harm has been done, only good."

"That's ridiculous!" Jason said, his temper beginning to fray. "The man knows how to siphon funds illegally for his own use. So what if he has a tear-jerking cause. What happens if he decides he wants to finance a gambling trip to Vegas? Or see the world? Time to 'borrow' money again?"

"He won't," Faith promised. She passed Luke's note to Walter. "Jason, he used the money to feed animals. He must have written the note to me because I offered to supplement his food fund."

Walter skimmed the note, pulled his wallet from his back pocket and extracted a fifty-dollar bill. "Have Luke cover his deficit. Tomorrow I'll give him a raise that should cover his expenses."

Appalled, Jason refused to take the currency in Walter's hand. "Are you two crazy! You're going to reward Luke when he used our trust to deceive us!"

"Have a heart!" Faith shouted. "You can't ruin a man's

life because he doesn't want to see animals starve or be mistreated!"

"Watch me," Jason roared, completely losing control of his temper. "First thing tomorrow . . ."

"You'll call Luke into your office," Walter instructed calmly, "tell him you caught him and give him two weeks' vacation to think about his crime."

"Embezzling isn't a pick-your-own-switch punishment," Jason railed.

"Luke made a mistake," Faith argued, her soulful eyes pleading for leniency.

"A two-year mistake? A mistake he said he'd commit again given the opportunity."

"Jason, he won't have to take money if we give it to him."

"Luke Cassidy is a criminal, an embezzler!" Jason declared as he emphasized his edict by slamming the back of his fist against the table. Chess pieces jumped. The king and pawn fell; the queen stood tall. That added to Jason's fury. Faith had her chin lifted in defiance of him. She was standing tall in front of his father, wielding her power, and totally emasculating him. With one last effort to retain his domination, he said, "I won't let you two set yourself up as his accomplices!"

"You'd prosecute us?" Faith ask, her voice raising an octave in incredulous fury. "Your own father? And your . . . me," she transposed rather than let Walter know they had been lovers.

"Yes!" Jason pushed back his chair and strode toward the door. The crystal piece on the end table caught his eyes. Completely out of control, he picked it up and hurled it the length of the room. It made an extremely satisfying sound as it shattered against the paneled wall. "Yes!"

Stunned by his uncharacteristic display of temper, for several seconds after Jason left the room, both Walter and Faith stared at slivers of fragmented crystal. Hundreds of prisms caught and refracted the light from the overhead fixture, which made them sparkle like cut diamonds on a velvet cloth.

"He's right," Faith said softly. She touched her forehead and then her heart. "I know it here, but not here."

Walter stood, stretching his legs as though warding off a leg cramp. "I'm going to go see Caroline and find out what the legal implications are. I don't think we are legally bound to prosecute Luke."

"That's a good idea." Faith opened her mouth to ask Walter to clear up the misunderstanding Caroline had fostered, but decided it could wait. "I know she'll be glad to see you."

Walter gave a harsh chuckle. "Then you're smarter than I am. She left a nasty message on my recorder. What a mess I've made."

"Don't lose faith. It's always darkest before dawn, isn't it?"

Twenty-two

With apprehension in her eyes Faith Jones watched Jason enter his father's office. Luke Cassidy followed him. Four people knew of Luke's crime, and yet, the bank employees and customers were unnaturally quiet as they went about their business. Heartsick, Faith bowed her head and silently begged a higher power for clemency. She feared Luke would be jobless and in jail by noon.

Luke must have accepted his fate. The expression on his face resembled that of a man next in line at the hangman's platform. For a fraction of a second, he'd glanced at her and gifted her with a smile of forgiveness. She'd valiantly tried to bolster Luke's confidence by grinning, but her lips wobbled and her tears threatened to fall as they had throughout the night.

Her eyelids felt heavy, red-rimmed and scratchy. Her brown eyes did not want to watch Jason assume the role of hard-shelled businessmen who considered the corporation more important than the people who performed the daily tasks necessary to keep the business in operation. She couldn't watch.

Not when her impulses charged her to run into the office and throw the weight of fifty percent of Southern Bank's stock on Luke's side of the case. Jason would ignore her pleas. Who owned what, was unimportant in a criminal case. She'd be considered a soft-hearted, soft-headed nuisance.

The cool air pumping from the air-conditioner vent seemed to be directed straight at her spine. Her head jerked up when she heard Walter speak her name and motion for her to join them.

"What is going on around here?" Phyllis demanded from her perch behind Faith. Her right ankle was taped and resting on a small stool. "I'm gone for two days and I come back to a place with the ambiance of a mortuary."

"You'll find out later," Faith answered glumly.

"Did you do something outrageous that got you in trouble?"

Anita answered for Faith. "She can't help herself. You go ahead, Faith. I'll tell Phyllis about the quarters and the kisses while you're gone."

Stepping over Phyllis's leg, Faith tottered on her three-inch-heels to the glass-enclosed office of the president. Her knees and ankles felt weak, unable to support her slight frame.

Inside the glass walls, Jason stood at the window that overlooked the parking lot; Walter sat behind the desk and Luke sat in front of it.

"Don't look so upset, Faith," Luke whispered when she sat in the chair beside him. "I knew the risks and the consequences."

"It was such a piddly amount. Why didn't you borrow it from me?"

"Or me?" Walter interjected. "Or ask for a raise?"

"I was afraid I might lose my job," he answered simply.

"You've been employed here for years. Surely you

have something you could have used as collateral for a loan from Jason," Walter insisted.

"My car, but it's nearly as old and in far worse condition than Faith's Studebaker." Luke shrugged in futility. "I'm at the top of my credit-card limit. The only thing I have of value is my clothes. That's why I have to be so particular about them."

Faith resisted the urge to reach over and give his freckled hand a caring pat. Freckles, she mused dourly, the stamp of a special person. Luke was special. He'd helped her save Otis and Blackie. The tears she did not want Jason or Walter to see were streaming down the back of her throat, making her gulp and choke.

"It's going to be humiliating to have the police take me out in handcuffs, with everyone watching," Luke mused aloud. "That isn't the example I wanted to set, but, I guess it will put the fear of God into the other employees."

He wasn't going to be dragged out in handcuffs, Faith vowed silently.

"I do have one request before I go," Luke said to Walter. "Since my leaving will create a job vacancy, I'd like you to consider Faith as my replacement. She's relatively new and inexperienced, but . . ."

"No!"

"No."

"No."

Faith, Walter and Jason agreed on that issue. The monosyllable shot from each corner of the room like machine-gun fire, as did the glances that followed the word.

Luke slouched further into his chair. "It was only a suggestion."

A fresh well of tears built up behind Faith's eyelids. She plucked Luke's handkerchief from his pocket and blew her nose with a decidedly unladylike honk. "I vote against prosecution."

Jason spun around on his heel. "This isn't a stockholders' meeting."

"I should have some say in the decision-making process," Faith said, wiping her nose.

"A hasty decision is inappropriate," Walter said as he raised his hands in opposite direction to quiet Faith and Jason. He leveled one finger at Luke. "You are officially on vacation. You haven't taken one for two years."

Faith watched Jason's back stiffen while joy began to fill her heart.

"Vacation?" Luke burped.

"Yes, *paid* vacation. Legally, according to Southern Bank's attorney, we do not have to prosecute. Since full restitution has been made," he paused, glaring at his son's back, "which you, Luke will have to enter using your 'system,' I believe there is a slim possibility we can settle this disturbing matter without its going beyond these doors."

Luke bolted upright in his chair. "You aren't going to prosecute?"

"He did not say that," Jason answered in icy tones, without looking at Luke. "You betrayed the trust bestowed on you. You violated the law and . . ."

"That's enough, son," Walter commanded.

A smile wreathed Faith's face until she realized the ramifications behind Walter's edict. Walter had asserted himself, taken back the reins of control. Jason was second in command, a place he abhorred.

Walter continued. "I objected to Faith's replacing you because she'll be filling my shoes."

"She will?" Luke looked thoroughly mystified. "She's to be Mr. Jason's boss?"

"She's my dead brother's adopted daughter—a Seaton, by choice. The big announcement will be made at the Fourth of July celebration at Seaton Place."

Walter smiled at Faith; Luke frowned at her.

"The details have not been worked out, yet," Walter replied. "Getting back to your situation. We have one stipulation that accompanies your mandatory vacation."

Faith had difficulty watching for Jason's reaction and listening to Walter. Her attention was drawn to the man behind the desk when he withdrew the Seaton family Bible from his bottom drawer.

Walter held the Bible toward Luke. "First, I want you to swear that you will never take money that does not belong to you. Second, you will leave without mentioning your embezzlement or how you did it, to anyone."

Luke repeated his solemn vows, then asked, "That's it? I'm free to go? And come back after three weeks?"

"I did consider making you promise to take Otis and Blackie home with you, but we've adopted them, too."

Overjoyed, Faith jumped to her feet and hugged Luke. "Will you be needing help Saturday morning on your feeding route?"

Luke shook off her hug, uncomfortable in the arms of the heiress to part of the Seaton wealth. "No, thanks. Am I excused?"

"You are," Walter replied, dismissing Luke. "Faith, I'd like for you to stay."

Worried that the three of them were going to have a

reenactment of last night's quarrel, and confused by Luke's peculiar reaction to her hug, she sank into the chair.

"I'll talk to you later," Jason said, following Luke out of the office without so much as a backward glance at Faith.

Walter waited for the men to close the door and confided drily, "My son isn't a happy camper."

"Because you discussed my promotion with him?"

"I informed him of my official resignation, effective immediately."

"I wished you'd wait a couple of months . . . years . . . decades?" she implored, postponing the immediate cause of Jason's anger. Not only did Jason not love her, he wouldn't speak to her either. "I'll need your advice. I think my mentor resigned shortly after you did."

Walter smiled. "Jason told me you were the one who cracked Luke's system of embezzlement."

"I wouldn't have if Jason hadn't brought it to my attention."

"You deserve the credit. Take it."

"I don't want him angry with me."

"He'll cool off, given time."

"The Ice Age cometh," Faith said, feeling dejected, but gracefully rising. "My only hope is that this one won't last millions of years."

Faith stepped out of Walter's office and saw Luke going through the front door. Warily, she glanced toward Jason's office and saw his door closed with Mary inside taking dictation.

A blast of frozen glares blasted her from the tellers' stations as she returned to wait on the customers. She passed behind Jillian and Anita without either of them pumping her for information about what had taken place in Walter's office, which Faith found extremely odd. Phyllis was on her feet, waiting on Mr. Ross from the bicycle shop.

"You aren't supposed to be on your feet," Faith protested, sliding in the narrow space beside her. Phyllis blocked her by shifting her ample weight on her bad ankle. "Don't be foolhardy. You're going to hurt yourself."

"I'm capable of doing my job, Miss Jones," Phyllis said as she squeezed Faith backward.

"Hey! Congratulations on the promotion," Mr. Ross greeted Faith. "Sara contacted me about the unicycles. Should I see you about the loan or young Mr. Seaton?"

Faith shivered. Walter had made Luke swear on the family Bible, but he had not included her promotion as one of the items to be kept secret. Suddenly, it dawned on her the reason Luke had refused to let her help him with the dogs. And why none of the women spoke to her.

"Faith? Are you okay?" Mr. Ross asked. "Your face turned white as a sheet!"

"Don't worry about her," Phyllis answered. "She looks fragile, but she's a steel butterfly."

"Mr. Seaton will take care of you," Faith replied, her lips numb from Phyllis's verbal slap.

"Will do. See you at Forest Park on Saturday? I'm letting the police officer have free rides. I guess I should include bank officers, too."

"You'd better be careful," Anita quipped. "She'll run over you and you'll never know it, until it's too late."

Faith looked at the matching smirks on Anita and Phyllis's faces, picked up her purse from the back of the counter, and concentrated on making a regal exit from the bank.

Twenty-three

"Mr. Seaton!" Mary shouted from the bank's interior. "Mr. Seaton. Come quick! She's been taken to the hospital! There's a Mrs. Jarworski on the telephone!"

"Tell her I'm on my way to the hospital." Faster than a sixteen-year-old track star, Walter ran to his Mercedes. No! he screamed silently. It's too soon! Caroline isn't due yet!

During the ten-minute drive to the hospital, Walter blamed everyone for the premature delivery—God, Jason, Faith—but mostly himself. He should have been there for Caroline. It was the only thing she'd asked of him. Be there. Stay with me. Never leave me. And he had been there, until his family had advised him to take a stand, to demand that Caroline marry him.

Where had he been? At the bank. The same place he'd been when Elizabeth gave birth to Jason. He hadn't been with her, either. She'd slipped away in the delivery room without fully knowing how much he loved her or how much he wanted their son.

History wouldn't repeat itself. That horrible experience couldn't happen to the same man twice, could it?

Fear was written in his eyes. His tires squealed as he jumped the curb turning into the Barnes Hospital emergency entrance. Parking next to an ambulance, he turned off the ignition and left the keys in the car.

"Mister! Hey! You can't park there!" came from the driver of the emergency vehicle.

"The keys are in it. It's yours!"

Not a philanthropic gesture, but one coming from a man in dire straits. He had to get to Caroline's side before anything happened to her or his daughter.

"Miss Faith," Glen greeted as he saw her climbing up the stairs. "What are you doing home this time of day?"

"I left a few things in my room that I need," she answered honestly. Caroline had pitched most of the clothes she'd had when she arrived, but there were a few treasures she couldn't leave behind.

"It's close to lunch. Shall I have Gertrude prepare a sandwich for you?"

"No, but thanks."

"I don't blame you. She's fixing grilled cheese." Glen pushed his wire-framed lenses on the bridge of his nose and grimaced. "I think I'll go out myself. The engine in my car is running rough. I'd borrow Gertrude's, but she refuses to speak to me. Mind if I drive yours?"

With her back to Glen, she'd been able to hide her tear-blotched face. Normally, she'd have given him the keys. Not today, she thought. She'd been having a steady stream of bad luck. Unaccustomed to driving her car, Glen would have a wreck and that would be her fault, too.

"Sorry, Glen." She tried miserably to keep her voice from quaking as she added, "I have to leave, immediately."

"I guess one more grilled cheese sandwich won't permanently impair me," Glen grumbled, heading back into the kitchen.

Inside her room, Faith took a last look at the beautifully carved headboard with matching triple dresser and cheval glass mirror. She'd loved being here, and never more so than when Jason had shared her bed.

Don't think about it, she chastised herself when a fresh torrent of tears threatened to spill. He said he doesn't love you. His own father said Jason doesn't love you. You had wonderful, glorious sex with him. That's all it meant to him. You saw the expression on his face. He hates you. They all hate you.

"Time to go home and eat worms," Faith whispered, her sense of humor popping up, trying to save her sanity. "Big ones. Small ones. Little bitty squirmy ones."

The rhyme Papa Jon had taught her as a child caused a tear to leak from the corner of her eye. She'd laughed then. He'd tossed her into the air and she'd felt as though she was flying. Now, without him to catch her, she'd plummet to the ground.

Faith gathered up her meager belongings and stuffed them into a satchel purse. Then she crossed to her closet, stripping off her loden-green suit, kicking off her heels. She'd leave as she'd arrived, with her Sunday-go-to-meeting dress and her courage hat. Nothing else belonged to her. Not really. The expensive clothes Caroline had chosen were bought and paid for with Seaton money.

Looking at herself in the mirror, she placed the flower-bedecked straw bonnet on her head. Then, she wiped the tear tracks off her face with the backs of her hands. "You aren't fit to be a Seaton. Jason is strong, and kind, and honorable. You're the opposite."

She had one last thing she had to do before she left Seaton Place. Hurrying to the nightstand, she sat on the bed as she slid the drawer open and retrieved paper and pen. This might not be legal, but it was something she had to do.

Minutes later, she folded the note and wrote Jason's name on the outside. This being for his eyes only, she picked up her satchel and darted down the hall to his room. Her intentions were pure; she'd stick the note on his mirror and leave. But, the fragrance of his cologne permeated the closed room. His rumpled unmade bed and the dent in his pillow beckoned to her.

I love you, Jason. I've done you wrong, but never, never was I ugly on purpose.

Her hand trailed across her pillow. She picked it up, inhaling his scent, wanting the memory to last her a lifetime.

"You deserve better than me. I ought to have known that, from the first time I saw you. You were so handsome it made my eyes hurt while I had ink smeared on my face. I didn't know better. I'll always be a country girl, Jason. Papa Jon used to say you can't change a sow's ear into a silk purse. I should have remembered that lesson."

She crossed to his mirror and tucked her note in the corner where he wouldn't miss it. Then she moved back to his bed and placed his pillow back where it belonged.

Everything in God's creation has its place, she thought silently, and this isn't mine.

Slowly, she moved to the door. Turning for one last look, she said, "It's all yours, Jason. The house. The bank.

Everything. Your were born to it. The power you wanted has always been yours. I didn't want it or need it. I only wanted to be loved and to be part of the Seaton family."

Firmly pulling her courage hat down to her ears, she sent up a prayer. *God, give me the strength to leave the man I love.*

God must have heard her. She stepped backward, her toes dragging, leaving tracks in the plush carpet. Outside Jason's room, she closed his door carefully, as though she were closing the final chapter in the Seatons' precious family Bible.

As she quietly went down the steps, among her many regrets was not being able to cross her name off the entry page. Generations from now, someone would see Jonathan's entry, with nothing below it and wonder if she'd really existed.

Twenty-four

July 4, 1994
Backwater, Missouri

Lazily, Faith rocked in the cane-backed chair and watched the sun rise over the cluster of cottonwood trees near the pond. Somewhere off in the hills she could hear a mockingbird calling its mate. She hugged her shoulders to ward off the morning breeze that ruffled the American flag she'd hung in its holder.

Stiff and sore from overwork and lack of sleep, she struggled out of the chair and on to her feet as the barnyard rooster began to crow. Another day, she thought, rubbing her eyes, then stretching her arms high over her head.

The days were tolerable. She'd weed and hoe, tend to Daisy Belle and the chickens, then walk and walk, until she reached Papa Jon's tombstone. Along the way, she would collect wildflowers and reverently place them at the grave site.

The first day had been the hardest. She'd had a lot to tell Papa Jon. How could she explain such a proliferation of mistakes? She'd started at the beginning by telling Papa Jon how she'd tried to be glamorous and painted a clown's face for Jason to see. How she'd alienated the cook by wanting to help her in the kitchen, almost getting Miss Cavendish fired. And how she'd denied being Jonathan's adopted daughter by begging Jason not to tell anyone at the bank who she was. She'd tried to help Luke save the dogs and ended up in jail before she unlocked the mystery of who was embezzling money and almost got Luke sent to prison. The women who'd trusted and befriended her, she'd betrayed.

The only thing she hadn't been able to confess to Papa Jon was how she'd fallen in love with Jason and trampled his pride by making him lose control of his temper and by undermining his authority at the bank. Some sins were harder to divulge than others.

When it became too difficult to think about the past, she dutifully recited what she'd accomplished during the daylight hours since she'd returned. She'd torn down the barbed-wire fence. Surprisingly, a few of the neighbors had stopped and chatted a spell with her. When she'd gone into town to stock up the pantry, old Mr. Sheffield had seemed pleased to see her and said she seemed to have grown up in the short weeks she'd been gone.

That had cracked her face into a forlorn smile. She hadn't grown up; she'd grown old and sad and lonely.

It wasn't only the people she missed; she missed living in St. Louis, too. On a clear, sunny day, she could look from her bedroom window and see the arch, the gateway to the west, or she could look out over Forest Park. The views from Seaton Place and the farm were different, and yet, they both had their own special charm.

At the end of each visit to the cemetery, Faith listened closely for a remedy to her problems. But then, like now, only Mother Nature's creatures broke the silence. While he'd been alive Papa Jon had given her the wisdom to make a place for herself with the Seatons. She'd misused it. How could she expect him to help her now that she'd blown it?

Placing her hands at her waist, Faith leaned forward until she relieved the ache in her back. Soon, she prayed, the good Lord would let her get a good night's sleep.

She crossed the wooden porch, went down the creaking steps, and traipsed to the hen house. Mr. Sheffield had asked her if she'd be interested in trading fresh eggs and cream for groceries. While her garden supplied most of her needs, there were basic necessities the farm couldn't produce, such as soap, deodorant, tissue paper . . . and magazines.

From rote memory, she performed her morning tasks. Feed the chickens, gather the eggs, milk Daisy. None of which challenged her mind like tallying up deposits or balancing her ledger. Nor did they give her the pleasure of greeting customers. She'd deliberately put imagination on hold. The chickens couldn't laugh at her windy stories, and Daisy wasn't interested in anything other than chewing her cud.

After a mere three days, peace and solitude had quickly become boredom. Yesterday, without feeling the necessity of wearing her courage hat, she'd broached the subject to Jonathan of selling the farm and moving back to St. Louis, permanently. She did have a college degree in math. Although her experience in banking was limited, she could operate the computerized machines.

As Faith crossed back to the house with those thoughts in mind, she heard a car rumbling up the gravel drive.

Anna Hudson

She wasn't expecting company. The mailman wouldn't be delivering mail on a holiday. She ran to the porch and up the steps, where she had a better view of the lane.

Twin columns of dust flew up behind a late-model pickup truck that she didn't recognize. As it drew closer, she thought she was imagining things when she saw Luke Cassidy's face through the bug-splattered windshield.

Faith didn't know whether to be joyous or scared. The last time Luke had looked at her, he'd wanted to throttle her.

The truck stopped. For several seconds, neither of them said anything. The gust of wind following Luke's truck snapped the American flag to attention.

"Am I welcome?" Luke asked shyly. "I come bearing a gift."

Faith ran down the steps and opened the truck's door. "Of course you're welcome—with or without a gift. What brings you to Backwater?"

"I'm on vacation. Remember?"

As he stepped from the truck, Faith gave him a hug. "You're a sight for sore eyes. Come up on the porch and sit a spell."

"First things first."

He reached over to the floor beneath the passenger's seat. Faith could hear a snuffling, grunting noise, but couldn't imagine what he'd brought her.

"Meet Miss Piggy, a pot-bellied pig," Luke introduced as he proudly held out a squirmy swine with a red neckerchief around its thick neck. "They're the latest rage. Unfortunately, they're also illegal in the city limits. A sweet little lady that lives near Gravois Boulevard called and asked me if I could find him a good home. Naturally, I thought of you."

"He's darling," Faith exclaimed, taking the piglet in her arms. She turned the little animal over and checked it out. "Miss Piggy, huh?"

Luke shrugged. "No accounting for taste. He doesn't seem to mind. He looks pretty good to me."

Luke looked good, too, she mused silently. The lines of tension that had marred his forehead were gone. His eyes seemed brighter and his hands didn't shake when he'd given her Miss Piggy.

Luke held up a bag of pig feed. "He's been fed, but he's thirsty and probably needs to make use of the great out-of-doors."

"Well, Miss Piggy, how'd you like a pail of fresh spring water?" Faith crooned, nuzzling the pig's ear. "Would you like some lemonade, Luke?"

"Freshly squeezed?"

Faith chuckled. It had been so long since she'd laughed, her face muscles felt taut. "Sorry. It's frozen. You'll have to drive farther south than the Ozarks to find lemon trees."

"Frozen is fine." Luke joined her as she mounted the wooden steps. He turned, taking in the view from her front porch. "Anything I can do?"

"Pull up a rocking chair. We'll be out in a minute."

Faith put the pig on the floor and let him investigate while she rushed around the kitchen. She glanced in Papa Jon's shaving mirror that hung near the sink, and she ran into the bedroom to brush her hair.

"Wish I had a place like this," she heard Luke call

from the porch. "Just think of how many animals I could have."

"A truckload full," she teased. "Whose did you . . ." Faith bit her tongue. How insensitive could she be? Don't let him think I'm asking if he stole a truck!

"Borrow?" Luke grinned and opened the screen door. "I borrowed the money—legitimately—from a dealership. Thirty-six months, and it's mine."

"I'm sorry, Luke. I didn't mean to insinuate . . anything."

"Don't be. I went to extremes with my pet project."

Luke scooped the pot-bellied pig up in the nick of time and rushed him outside. Miss Piggy finished his business and was scampering around the yard when Faith headed out to the porch and handed Luke his icy drink. She sat in the rocker next to the one he occupied.

"Since I swore not to discuss this with anyone who wasn't in Mr. Seaton, Senior's office, it feels good to be able to tell you how I feel. I'm relieved. The past few months I'd felt like I'd been flirting with a guillotine. You can't imagine how awful it is to know that at any moment the blade will fall." He took a deep swallow from his glass. "Thanks to you, my worries are behind me."

"I don't think the Seatons will press charges," Faith confided.

"The s.o.b. would. Anita called me yesterday and told me he's more aloof than he's ever been. Won't talk to anyone. Rarely comes out of his office. He's there when they arrive and stays after they leave."

Faith frowned. "Jason is dedicated. He has to shoulder the burden of responsibilities for . . ."

"Stop." Luke covered his ears. "Please. I know you

think he's wonderful, but the rest of the world doesn't. I've been offered a job with the Humane Society, and I'm seriously considering taking it." He rocked forward and stared down the lane. "Does that dust cloud mean you're expecting company and I've intruded?"

"No. I'm not expecting anyone." Faith stood. "That looks like Glen Morrison's truck."

"Who's Glen Morrison? A neighbor?"

"Uh-uh." She crossed to the steps. "The Seatons' butler."

"He's got somebody with him. Looks like a woman."

Faith grabbed hold of the porch railing. "Miss Cavendish? Luke, would you mind fetching them some lemonade. Their throats are probably parched, too."

As she lithely ran down the steps, Luke put his lemonade down, grinned and entered Faith's house.

"Glen! Miss Cavendish! What a wonderful surprise!"

The man she considered the gentle giant wrapped his arms around her, lifted her high, swung her in a wide circle, then returned Faith to the ground. "You look a little peaked. Have you been missing us as much as we've missed you?"

"I've missed both of you," she said, giving Gertrude a quick hug. "Is that a new shade of eye shadow? It makes your eyes look like sapphires!"

"I told you'd she'd be happy to see us," Glen reassured Gertrude.

"Of course!" Faith's empty heart began to fill with gladness. "The rope latch is always out for the two of you."

Gertrude glanced toward the door to see if there was a rope latch instead of a doorknob. Seeing that the house, painted a light grey with white gingerbread trim, wasn't as primitive as she'd believed, she gave Glen a satisfied nod. "Tell her, Glen. This was your brilliant idea."

"We came to apply for a job," Glen said bluntly.

Confused, Faith said, "But you have a job at Seaton Place."

"Not any more," Gertrude countered, dusting her hands together. "Jason decided my cooking wasn't good enough for him. I quit."

"He refused to eat anything with cheese on it," Glen added wryly, trying to keep from smiling. "As for me? I didn't wait to for him to growl at me like a wild dog. I quit."

"Gertrude, you know Jason didn't mean it," Faith placated. "He's must be having a rough time at the bank. Luke says he's working day and night." She leveled Glen to her size by turning to him and saying, "Jason trusts you to take care of Seaton Place for him. You've lived there for years. How can you leave Jason when he regards you all as part of his family?"

"I'm not going back," Gertrude said staunchly.

Glen fervently shook his head. He had to poke his finger on the nose piece of his glasses as they began to slip and slide down his nose. "Me, either."

"We thought . . . uh . . ." Gertrude glanced sheepishly at the ground. "Maybe you needed some help? Living by yourself and all."

"We don't need a salary," Glen said hastily. "Room and board would be fine with us. Right, Gertrude?"

"Right! And we could help buy the food." Gertrude lumbered up the steps with Glen holding her elbow.

"Plain, old-fashioned farm cooking is what I'll be doing. Just like my mama taught me."

Faith's eyes ping-ponged between the butler and the cook, growing wider and wider. Much as she appreciated their generous offer, she couldn't accept. Aside from there only being two bedrooms in the farm house, Jason needed them!

"Why don't we discuss this after you've seen the farm?" Faith suggested gently, not wanting to disappoint them.

"You wouldn't send us back to St. Louis, hat in hand, begging for our jobs, would you?" Glen asked, his voice deep with concern.

Cornered, Faith smiled and replied, "You're always welcome here."

"Smell that fresh air." Gertrude stood on the porch and surveyed the area as though mentally marking her boundaries. "Yes siree, I can hardly wait to see the kitchen."

Luke stepped from inside the house carrying tall glasses of lemonade. "You must be Glen and Mrs. Cavendish. Did you bring Otis and Blackie with you?"

"I couldn't leave the house unprotected," Glen replied, after taking a long swig from his glass.

"Let Seaton Place go to the dogs. That's what I told Glen."

A slight frown blemished Faith's smile.

"Don't worry about Otis and Blackie. I'll check on them when I get back to St. Louis," Luke volunteered. "Why don't you show us around the place? Miss Piggy! Where are you?"

Faith wasn't worried about the dogs or the pot-bellied

pig. Her concern was for Jason. With Luke being an animal protectionist, she could relate to his switching jobs. In fact, it was a relief for Faith to know temptation wouldn't put Luke at risk anymore. But Glen and Gertrude deserting Jason distressed her. Who'd take care of him? Make certain he had meals and clean clothes? Who'd fix Jason's car? Tend to the lawn and flowers?

The thought that no one would be there to care for Jason distressed her mightily.

Gertrude examined the glass and glowered. "Jelly jars. There was a time in my life when I swore I'd never drink from one again."

"You promised you'd stop being critical," Glen reprimanded.

Gertrude huffed, "And you promised to keep your comments to yourself. Did I say anything when you hit every pothole between here and Backwater?"

The bickering brought Faith's attention back to her guests. She nudged her hand into the crook of Gertrude and Glen's arms and led them off the porch. "Why don't I show you the garden? There's a watermelon patch, too."

"Jason likes watermelon," Glen said thoughtfully, his stride lagging behind. "His Uncle Jon taught him how to thump them to see if they're ripe."

"He taught me, too," Faith said as she tugged his arm. "C'mon, Glen. It's easy. I'll show you how."

"It's been forever since I sat on a front porch and spit watermelon seeds," Gertrude said, grinning at Faith. "My grandmother could hit a bull's eye at fifty paces."

"Where's the pond with the catfish you bragged about?" Luke asked. Carrying Miss Piggy in his arms, he caught up with them as they rounded the corner of the house. "Oh, my goodness, do you see what I see?"

Faith followed the direction Luke pointed, which was the opposite of the way the trio had headed.

"I do believe that's Mr. Walter's car," Glen said with delight ringing in his voice.

Gertrude clapped her hands. "And he's brought his new wife and baby!"

"Wife? Baby?" Faith inquired, utterly shocked.

"Oh! That's right!" Gertrude gasped. "You don't know about Mrs. Caroline delivering before her time."

"Must have been a mix-up on the date," Glen said with a hearty chuckle. "I heard one of the nurses say Mr. Walter's baby daughter was gooing and gurgling when Mrs. Caroline said 'I do.' "

"Would you all mind going the rest of the way alone?" Faith asked, running to meet the approaching car. Over her shoulder she yelled, "Just follow the path. It leads down to the pond."

She skirted around the farm house as Walter tenderly helped Caroline and the baby from the car. Tears of joy cascaded down Faith's face. For long seconds before they noticed her, she watched the newest addition to the Seaton family being loved by her father.

That's how it should have been for Jason, she thought silently. Only Jason had been deprived because of his mother's death and his father's grief.

Faith refused to let the intrusion of past sadness mar their visit. Bounding to the side of the car, she beamed them a happy smile.

"Faith, come see my pride and joy," Caroline invited shyly, holding the baby close to her breasts.

"She's beautiful, like her mother." Brushing the blanket back from the child's face, she was greeted with a sleepy yawn and the biggest, bluest eyes—eyes that looked exactly like Jason's. Holding out her finger, Faith felt her heart swell as the baby wrapped her small fingers around Faith's larger one. Awe had difficulty climbing over the lump in Faith's throat as she praised, "So tiny and fragile."

"Do you want to carry her inside the house?" Caroline offered, with a teasing smile at Walter. To Faith she confided, "Walter has the same opinion you have, that she'll break like a china doll."

Walter made a comical face and cradled his daughter in his arms. "Come to Daddy, little princess. Mommy says it's my turn to change your diaper."

"Walter changes diapers?" Faith mouthed at Caroline in disbelief.

With a nod, she boasted, "And bottle-feeds her at midnight."

Walter rolled his eyes heavenward. "You make me sound like a nanny."

"Or a loving father?" Faith rhetorically asked, following in his footsteps as he strode toward the porch with the diaper bag flopping against hip.

Caroline put a restraining hand on Faith's arm. "I owe you an apology."

"It was a little misunderstanding between friends," Faith replied, discounting the importance of Caroline's accusation.

"I'm sorry. The labor pains had started. Walter wasn't there. I was scared and wallowing in self-pity. I took it out on you."

"Apology accepted," Faith said, magnanimously hugging Caroline. A teasing twinkle entered her dark eyes as she asked, "Should I call you Aunt Caroline?"

"Yeah, I like the idea of having you as my niece."

"And Walter as your husband?"

Caroline chuckled. "Most definitely."

"You can come in, ladies. I've finished," Walter called. "Yes, yes little precious one," he crooned when the baby began to fuss. "Mommy has lunch for you. She won't keep you waiting."

Faith held the screen door open and followed Caroline into the living room. "Please, use the maple rocker. Papa Jon made it."

"I wish he was here," Walter said, noticing the other loving touches his brother had left behind.

He opened his arms to receive his hug. Faith moved into his arms and tapped Walter on the pocket of his sports shirt.

"He is. There." She touched the place where her heart beat joyfully. "And here."

"I'd have liked for him to meet Hope."

She turned to Caroline, who'd draped a cloth over her shoulder and had begun nursing the babe. "Hope? Is what you named her?"

"Walter thought it was the perfect name and I agreed." Rocking back and forth, she grinned. "She gave both of us hope. And, it was much better than naming my child after an old-maid great-aunt of his who stubbornly refused to get married."

"She made that up," Walter protested with a chuckle. "She's getting as windy as you are, Faith."

Remembering her manners, Faith said, "Can I get you something to drink? Lemonade? Fresh milk?"

"I'll help you," Walter offered when his wife nodded to the latter.

Lighthearted, Faith said, "I'll have to make more lemonade. I could have made a fortune today if I'd set up a stand along side the highway."

"Speaking of fortunes, Jason showed me the paper where you'd signed over your inheritance to him." He leaned against the counter, watching Faith gracefully move between the icebox and sink pump. "Was that wise?"

"I want Jason to be happy," she replied softly. "He's very, very special to me."

"Special?" Walter snorted with disbelief. "He's a pompous ass, like I used to be."

Faith detected no venom in Walter's tone, only a note of sadness. Unwilling to let Walter berate either of the two men she loved, she asked, "Did you move in with Caroline?"

"That's a sore subject. Jason insists a Seaton child should be raised at Seaton Place. He wants to move out so Caroline will move in. Caroline doesn't want Jason to resent her or the baby, so she wants to wait until Hope is weaned and then start looking for a house in the Forest Park area. What do you think?"

Distracted from her task while devoted her attention to Walter, she poured the frozen chunk of lemonade from its container into the half-filled pitcher. She'd opened her mouth to give her opinion as the sticky, pink liquid splashed across her hands, making a mess.

Faith wiped her hands and shut her mouth. This was

a family matter. She'd only cause trouble if she stirred things up. She'd made enough trouble to last the Seaton family a lifetime.

"It'll all work out for the best," she replied evasively. "Is that Luke, Glen and Miss Cavendish I hear coming up the steps?" Walter moved toward the kitchen door. "I wondered whose trucks those were parked out front. Did you invite them here for the Fourth?"

"No. They dropped by for a visit. Would you mind being the host while I fix a snack for everyone?"

"It'll be my pleasure. I'll deliver Caroline's milk to her and send Gertrude in here. I'm certain she'll want to help."

Faith stirred the lemonade, willing it to melt quickly. For a woman with no appetite who lived alone, she had a well-stocked pantry, but five hungry guests arriving for lunch was a gray horse of a different color.

Gertrude scurrying around in the kitchen increased the problem fourfold. The kitchen at Seaton Place was spacious; hers was tiny in comparison. Faith began to have empathy for how Gertrude had felt when she'd tried to force herself into Gertrude's territory.

"You're a guest, Miss Cavendish. Listen to the fun they're having in there. Why don't you just enjoy yourself with the others?"

"Gertrude," she corrected, rummaging through the pantry. "If I'm going to be working here, you should call me by my first name."

"Today you're my guest. Enjoy yourself."

"I am. Why don't you scoot on back in there with your company?" She spread her hands. "In case you haven't noticed, one of me in your kitchen is like ten people in the living room."

Faith dropped the spoon in the sink, poured a glass of milk, and picked up the pitcher of lemonade. "You win."

"I always do," Gertrude replied glibly. She cocked her head, noticing that the pandemonium had instantly quiet. "I swear I heard them all take a deep breath. You'd better see what Glen did."

Anxious for everyone to enjoy their visit, Faith hurried into the living room. Glen stood at the door with his back to her, and the others were gawking through the windows.

"Lemonade, anyone?" she called happily.

Glen glanced over his shoulder. "You've got more company."

"Oh?" Faith spun around and said, "I'll get another glass."

"Don't bother," Walter huffed angrily as he watched his son climb the porch steps.. "He won't be staying for long."

Faith's heart jumped to her throat. She set the pitcher down before her trembling hand could drop it. "Is it Jason?"

Nodding, Caroline said, "Did you invite him?"

"No, but he's welcome in my home." She nudged between Glen and Walter. "Just like you all are. We're family, remember?"

Jason noticed as Faith sandwiched herself between Glen and Walter. Spellbound, he watched her whisper furiously to one man, turn, and fiercely elbow the other.

Clad in threadbare cut-off jeans and a scoop-necked, flowered shirt, with her hair bubbling around her face, she'd never looked more adorable . . . or thin.

All eyes, he thought guiltily. Larger than the tentative smile she gave him.

"Move back!" she hissed loudly at them. "Or you'll make me have to stomp your toes!"

She'd do it, too, Jason thought, with a smile that reached his eyes. The bully at the junk yard had the teeth marks to prove it.

When the butler and his father didn't budge an inch, Faith popped from between them and came out on the porch. She stood less than ten feet from him. He could see that certain smile of hers and felt his heart flutter.

"Don't you make her cry," Walter warned Jason. "You're on her property now."

Jason narrowed the gap between them by several feet; Faith stood her ground.

"Should I get the shotgun?" Glen roared. "Jonathan always kept a shotgun loaded with rock salt."

"Shhhhhh!" Caroline shushed. "You'll awaken Hope! Don't make her cry!"

Jason's steady gaze remained on Faith. Hope blossomed inside him with each step that brought him closer to her.

"I cried," he admitted hoarsely.

"A Seaton doesn't cry."

He held his hand for her to take. "This one does when the woman he loves leaves him."

"You love me?"

"He loves her!" Glen and Walter chorused before they started hugging and pounding each other on the back.

"Whooooppeee!" Gertrude yelled. To Glen she said, "I told you we wouldn't have to stay here long. I helped raise that boy, and this mamma don't raise no fools!"

Faith closed her eyes, pinched her arm, then opened them again before she placed her hand in his palm. "I thought I'd better check to see if I'm dreaming."

"These past four nights were a living nightmare," he whispered, pulling her roughly against him, inhaling her spring fragrance as he crushed his mouth against her soft lips. "Oh, God, I've been alone and lonely without you."

Faith answered wordlessly with a soul-searing kiss as she wrapped her arms around his shoulders and knotted them behind his neck in a circle of love. She fervently returned the passion and yearning she tasted on his tongue as he wildly flicked it inside of her.

"Rubberneckers," Gertrude scolded. "Get in here and get away from the window. Let the two of them make their peace." She grabbed Glen and Walter by their collars, and yanked them away, then glued her own face to the window.

Not able to quench his thirst for Faith with a hostile audience watching him, he said to her, "Didn't you tell me about a secluded pond where the catfish grow as big as whales?"

Faith turned in his arms. Five smiling faces pyramided behind the screened window, each person's place determined by height. Gertrude had a window of her own.

"I shouldn't leave my company," she replied softly, eager to be alone with him, and yet reluctant to be rude to her guests.

"They're family," he said, kissing her soft curls. "They'll

understand two people in love wanting a few minutes of privacy."

"Go on," Gertrude snuff led loudly. Glen's face appeared beside her as he draped his arm across her shoulder. "Get out of here before we all start bawling. That babe will think she's a sextuplet."

Arms looped behind each other's waists, Jason and Faith started up the path.

"I destroyed the note you left, after I showed it to Walter."

"Why?"

"Because everything I have is yours, free and clear, no strings attached."

"I don't need money or the bank. The day I arrived at Seaton Place, I took one look at you and knew you could fulfill all my dreams and desires." She nudged him in the ribs. "And you saw dollar bills with wings attached zooming into my purse."

"No." Jason mocked himself by scowling at her. "Changes, that's what I saw. Do you know what a rut is?"

Faith shook her head.

"A coffin with the ends kicked out. I don't think I knew how to enjoy life before you barged in and yanked me out of my early grave."

"You love me because I'm a troublemaker?" She grinned up at him. "You should live to a ripe old age. I'm the one they wrote the nursery rhyme about. You know it. There was a little girl who had a little curl right in the middle of her forehead. When she was good, she was very, very good, but when she was bad . . ."

Jason kissed her soundly, and finished, "She was wonderful!"

"Yeah," Faith agreed, think of how she loved being held close to him. "Wonderful."

Still within eyesight of the farm house, Jason ended the sweet pause by tugging her arm. The crest of the hill wasn't far now. Faith looked at Jason and grinned impishly. It was a silent signal, a challenge, one he couldn't ignore.

"A three-second head start," he said drily. "Last one to the pond . . ."

Faith took off, not waiting to hear the penalty for being last. *He loves me,* her heart sang. *Loves, loves, loves ME.* Her song gave wings to her feet and she raced over the hill, laughing with high spirits and exuberance.

As she neared the pond, she felt Jason closing in on her and she slowed her pace, shortening her stride. She wanted him to catch her. To hold her. To make her his own.

But she'd learned patience. They'd be together. If not today. Tomorrow. There were plenty of tomorrows for them as long as he loved her.

"You slowed down on purpose," Jason laughed, grabbing her around the waist and spinning with her in his arms as he traversed the wooden pier that led from the bank.

"Tell me again," she coaxed, planting rows of kisses across his face. "Tell me you love me."

"I love you, Faith Jones," he shouted, listening for it to bounce off the Ozark hills. "I love you!"

"And I love you, Jason Seaton." With her feet on the pier, she led him to where the wooden planks ended. She dropped to her knees. "Look down there and tell me what you see."

He bent over her shoulder and peered into the water's reflection. "I see you."

Faith smiled. She wanted him to perceive the whole picture. "And?"

"Me."

"Look harder."

"And the blue skies overhead."

Faith held up her arms to him. He knelt in front of her, bringing her close to his heart. Slowly, in perfect unison, they lay down beside one another with her head on his shoulder and his arm around her waist.

"This is heavenly," Jason said, utterly content just to be with Faith. He watched her eyes close and a Madonna smile curve her lips as he softly said, "Love is . . ."

Slowly, she brought his fingers to her lips. A man who recognized how close this place was to heaven was a man she could have faith in.

She did have faith in him.

And Him.

Glory be!

Dear Readers,

It has given me great pleasure to share with you Faith's quest for love and happiness. Family is important to her, as it is to me. In today's society where the importance of marriage and family is dwindling, I want to be one small voice in the darkness shouting, "Yes, I know how things are, but let me spin a yarn about how love could be, how it ought to be."

I hope Faith is much like you and me. She yearns for love, commitment and happily-ever-after. She isn't perfect; she makes mistakes; nor does she expect perfection from those she loves. She tries to see good in bad situations. And, she relies on a strong sense of humor to carry her over the rough spots that would make a less-courageous heroine weep and give up.

While you are reading GLORY, I am happily spinning another tale about a lovable Texas misfit who is too tall and too mechanically inclined, but too optimistic to settle for anything other than being all she can and ought to be. Should she be named Ima Optimistic? Sky Scrapper? Or, because she's a Texan, a Southerner through and through, Dixie Mayson?

I'm looking forward, with great anticipation, to your reaction to GLORY. If you would like to receive a free, semiannual newsletter, which will keep you current on my forthcoming books, please write to me in care of Pinnacle Books.

Anna Hudson

Anna Hudson

MAKE THE
ROMANCE CONNECTION

Come talk to your favorite authors and get the inside scoop on everything that's going on in the world of romance publishing, from the only online service that's designed exclusively for the publishing industry.

With Z-Talk Online Information Service, the most innovative and exciting computer bulletin board around, you can:

- ♥ CHAT "LIVE" WITH AUTHORS, FELLOW ROMANCE READERS, AND OTHER MEMBERS OF THE ROMANCE PUBLISHING COMMUNITY.

- ♥ FIND OUT ABOUT UPCOMING TITLES BEFORE THEY'RE RELEASED.

- ♥ DOWNLOAD THOUSANDS OF FILES AND GAMES.

- ♥ READ REVIEWS OF ROMANCE TITLES.

- ♥ HAVE UNLIMITED USE OF E-MAIL.

- ♥ POST MESSAGES ON OUR DOZENS OF TOPIC BOARDS.

All it takes is a computer and a modem to get online with Z-Talk. Set your modem to 8/N/1, and dial 212-545-1120. If you need help, call the System Operator, at 212-889-2299, ext. 260. There's a two week free trial period. After that, annual membership is only $ 60.00.

See you online!

KENSINGTON PUBLISHING CORP.